The GIRLS of PEARL HARBOR

ALSO BY SORAYA M. LANE

The Spitfire Girls
Wives of War
Hearts of Resistance
Voyage of the Heart

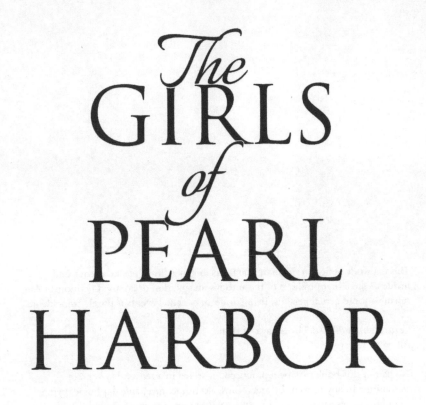

The GIRLS of PEARL HARBOR

SORAYA M. LANE

LAKE UNION
PUBLISHING

Text copyright © 2019 by Soraya M. Lane
All rights reserved.

Published by Lake Union Publishing, Seattle

www.apub.com

Amazon, the Amazon logo, and Lake Union Publishing are trademarks of Amazon.com, Inc., or its affiliates.

ISBN-13: 9781542041904
ISBN-10: 1542041902

Cover design by Lisa Horton

Cover photography by Richard Jenkins Photography

Printed in the United States of America

So much has been written about the plight of men during the Pearl Harbor invasion, but little has been documented about the brave women who served there during the bombing.
This story is for every nurse stationed in Pearl Harbor on December 7, 1941—your bravery, dedication, and genuine courage must never be forgotten.

PROLOGUE

DECEMBER 7, 1941

PEARL HARBOR

'No!' Grace's scream cut through the air, echoing sharply against the drone of aircraft overhead.

'Grace, stop!' April called, her hand slipping from Grace's wrist. *'Grace!'*

The planes were deafening, the roar so low and loud that when Grace looked up, she could see the pilot's face, could see his smile before he unleashed a torrent of bullets raining down around them. They were under attack!

'Grace!' April called again.

But Grace ignored her, her eyes locked on Poppy, so close but so far away, bending down toward a cowering puppy. 'Run!' she screamed to her friend. 'Poppy, *run!*'

Poppy stood still, her eyes filled with horror as she looked up at Grace, her mouth open as if she were about to call back.

Grace started to sprint, desperate to get to Poppy, to do something, *anything*, to save her. What was happening? Who was shooting at them? Why wouldn't Poppy move?

Seconds felt like days as Poppy finally started to run, but then strong arms circled Grace from behind as her scream caught in her throat, holding her back, forcing her to stop.

'Let me go!' Grace yelled, gasping as people started to fall across the field, as the relentless drone continued, ammunition raining from the sky like a ferocious storm lashing the land. 'We need to get to her!'

'No.' The word was whispered, but it was still a command. Teddy had hold of her, Teddy was dragging her back, and no matter how much she clawed at him or struggled, he wasn't letting her go.

Grace could only watch in horror, screaming out to Poppy as one thought echoed over and over through her mind. *Please let Poppy live.*

PART ONE

PART ONE

CHAPTER ONE

PEARL HARBOR, NOVEMBER 1941

GRACE

'You need to stop making eyes at Teddy,' April whispered, nudging her hard in the side. 'It's embarrassing.'

Grace glared at her sister, pulling away from her and crossing her arms tightly over her chest as her cheeks started to burn. 'I'm *not* making eyes at him!' she hissed.

Teddy was her best friend's sweetheart, and whatever she thought about him was never going to come to anything. Period. Besides, Teddy adored Poppy, and her friend adored him right back. It would break Poppy's heart if she knew what Grace felt about her boyfriend.

'I still can't believe we're here,' April said with a smile, linking arms with her again despite Grace's protest. 'Is this paradise or what?'

Grace gave in and leaned against her, forgiving her sister in one big sigh as they strolled along the beach. April had her blonde hair loose over her shoulders, and it was soft against Grace's cheek, her blue eyes so like their mother's when she glanced down at her. 'Definitely paradise,' she agreed, shifting her gaze from her sister and staring out at the turquoise water, the tide gently washing in against the sand. It was her idea of heaven and so far removed from their life in Oregon, with nothing but sand and palm trees as far as the eye could see.

'One of the other girls said that we're in for some football injuries soon,' April said. 'Apparently the boys stationed here all love the start of football season.'

Grace nodded, watching as a horse and rider made their way closer, the girl's feet bare, dark hair streaming out behind her as she rode along the waterline. Grace squinted and held up a hand to shield her eyes from the late-afternoon sun so she could keep watching her. If football injuries were the worst thing they were expecting, then she'd be just fine.

'Do you think we can go horseback riding?' Grace asked.

As a girl she'd always wanted to ride, and seeing the horse crossing the sand was bringing that childhood feeling straight back.

'Wait up!'

Grace turned at Poppy's call, her friend's bright smile infectious as she ran and caught up to them. She looked back at Teddy, strolling away in the distance now, but he still raised his hand to wave at her. Grace quickly turned away, sighing as she watched Poppy blow kisses to him over her shoulder. Her friend's dark hair was glossy under the bright sunlight, her red lips making her look even more striking than usual, and not for the first time she was a little in awe of how beautiful she was.

'Is he heading back to base?' April asked.

'Yes. We'll see him tonight at the party, though.'

Grace grabbed Poppy's hand. 'What party? I thought we had a curfew to keep us all in at night?'

'Apparently there's this big house by the beach, and we're all invited!' Poppy told them. 'The people here love all the nurses and soldiers, so the social life is amazing! We're going to have *so* much fun here.'

'Definitely paradise,' Grace repeated with a smile, shaking her head. 'Didn't I tell you both this would be the perfect place to be posted?'

The three of them walked, laughing, down the beach, in a row with their arms linked. She had no idea how they'd been fortunate enough to have all been sent to Hawaii, but here they were, and she was in heaven. They'd been thick as thieves since childhood, both claiming best-friend status with Poppy, who'd been like the third sister they'd never had. She'd always been the one to smooth things over between her and April, like the middle child stopping the other two from arguing. And now they were all stationed in Pearl Harbor for the foreseeable future, with their gas masks the only hint that things weren't expected to remain peaceful forever.

'How many summer dresses did you pack?' April asked Poppy.

'As many as I could fit in my case!' Poppy replied with a laugh. 'Although the gas mask took up so much space. Honestly, as if we're ever going to need it.'

They walked across the sand as the sun beat down on their bare arms, and Grace turned her face up to the sun. 'What would we be doing if we were still at home?'

'If we weren't on duty and giving soldiers injections in their bottoms to stop them from getting yellow fever?' April said.

'Ohhh, stop!' Grace moaned. 'You know, I never knew men's bottoms could look so . . .'

'Hairy?' Poppy teased.

'Ugh.' Grace flapped her hands and laughed. 'There have definitely been more *unattractive* ones than I expected.'

They all burst out laughing, before Poppy took off running, shoes in her hand, head tipped back as she splashed through the water. Grace ran after her, leaving April behind as she ran as fast as she could, arms pumping to help her catch up to Poppy. Her toes dug into the sand as she caught her, grabbing hold of Poppy's slender wrist as they both collapsed onto the warm sand.

'How did this happen?' Poppy asked. 'How did we get so lucky?'

Grace stretched out, her blonde hair fanning out around her as she watched the clear bright-blue sky above. 'No idea, but I'm so glad we did.'

'Do you think we'll ever see war? My grandfather said no one wants to see our boys sent off,' Poppy said as they all lay, three in a row, arms outstretched. 'He doesn't think it'll ever happen.'

'Let's just hope we get to stay here for at least a year,' April said with a yawn. 'This is the life. Nothing's going to happen to us here—it's the safest place in the world for us to be.'

Grace couldn't imagine war ever coming to Hawaii; from the moment they'd stepped off the boat, it had seemed impossible for anything terrible to ever happen on the picturesque island of Oahu. Until now, home was all she'd known, but this? This was something else.

'Daddy told me that America was pretending the world wasn't at war but that they couldn't stay out of it for much longer,' Grace said, remembering what their father had said the night before they'd shipped out. But when April turned, clearly poised to contradict her, she wished she'd lied and pretended she'd thought it all on her own.

'There's no reason for us to join the war—not yet—whatever Daddy says,' April said, her voice full of authority, as always. 'Besides, we're definitely safe as a church here. I heard it's far too shallow for an aerial torpedo attack, and there's too much fighting in Europe for them to ever bother with this little island.'

'How about we just have fun,' Poppy said, rolling her eyes as if they'd already bored her to tears. 'We can let our leaders in Washington take care of the threat of war while we're here sunning ourselves and enjoying the beach. And how on earth do you know about *aerial torpedo* attacks anyway?'

'Hello, ladies,' said a deep male voice, distracting them all.

Grace tipped back, hand raised to block out the sun, and quickly tugged down her skirt with the other hand when she locked eyes with not one but two navy boys in their starched white uniforms. They looked good, but she still preferred the green uniform with golden wings pinned to the lapel that Teddy and the other flyboys wore.

She rolled over and pushed up to her knees before standing, giving April and then Poppy a hand up. 'Hello, Officers,' she said, smiling at the handsome young men.

'When did you lovely ladies arrive?' one of the men asked.

'Just today,' April said at the same time as Grace opened her mouth to speak. April was always doing that, speaking for her, and it wasn't the first time Grace had to bite her tongue to stop from arguing with her big sister. April was only eighteen months older, but sometimes she made it feel like years. 'Our ship docked this morning.'

Grace fingered the flower lei around her neck as she studied the men, wondering if they tried the friendly welcome routine on every new nurse they met.

'Have y'all been invited to the party tonight?'

'Yes,' she said, before April could answer for them. 'Will we see you there?'

The men nudged each other and smiled. 'You sure will.'

Poppy had lost interest and was taking her sunglasses from her bag, the big white-framed fashion statements pushed high on her nose. Grace waved goodbye at the same time as her sister and turned back to face the water.

'Shall we head back to the hospital, then go explore the island and meet up with the other nurses later?' Grace asked.

'Yes. Then we can all get dinner together before we head out,' April said.

Poppy nodded her agreement, and they all started walking, watching as some aircraft performed training drills in the near distance, darting back and forth. The planes didn't seem real with the towering palm trees as a backdrop, their skinny trunks extending so high in the air, but then nothing about being posted to a tropical island seemed real. When she looked one way, it was sand and water; the other, it was trees and lush green grass, as picture perfect as possible.

'I hope we actually get to save some lives here,' April said.

Grace fought the urge to roll her eyes again. Save lives? She was far more comfortable doing some light nursing duties, meeting handsome officers, and kicking her heels up like a newborn foal every night. April might have grander ambitions, but then her sister's stomach was a lot stronger than hers.

'Anyone up for a swim?' Poppy asked, her perfectly painted eyebrows raised in question.

'You're insane,' April said, hauling Poppy along to stop her from leaping into the water. 'Absolutely not!'

'Tomorrow,' Grace whispered in Poppy's ear. 'We'll leave Miss Prim and Proper behind, and we could ask one of the boys to teach us how to surf!'

She held tight to Poppy's hand as they made their way back toward Tripler General Hospital to get their shift schedules and find out exactly how many hours a day they'd have to make the most of Hawaii. The other nurses would be milling about, and she couldn't wait to see if they were all going to the party, not to mention what their barracks were like and where they'd actually be living for the next year or two. It was going to be the best time of their lives—she just knew it. And maybe she'd finally be able to step out of her big sister's shadow.

———— ✦∾✦ ————

'Let's go, ladies!' Poppy announced, swinging around the room, her pretty skirt flaring out around her. Her hair was pinned up high on her head, her full lips painted red again, cheeks rouged just enough to enhance her high cheekbones.

Grace finished sweeping pink lipstick across her lips, smacking them together as she snapped her compact shut and hoping she looked even half as good as her friend. The little mirror had been almost impossible to do her makeup in, but she was finally done. She touched her hair, the blonde curls just skimming her shoulders, and picked up her purse.

'Ready,' she announced, trading grins with Poppy. There were other nurses busy chatting and getting ready, too, and across the room April was zipping up her dress, her arms twisted at odd angles as she struggled.

Grace crossed over to help, tugging the zipper to the top and gently putting her sister's hair back over her shoulder so it could fall down her back. They were both blonde, almost the same shade as their mother had been, but April's hair was long and wavy, so much easier to curl than Grace's and so impossibly thick. But she knew that to anyone else they looked very much like sisters, their eyes the same deep blue, although April was taller than her and not quite as petite.

'Thank you,' April said as she turned. 'Excited?'

Grace nudged shoulders with her sister. 'Ridiculously!' She'd never lived anywhere but home before, and now here they were, miles from Oregon and about to have the time of their lives. She still felt guilty that they'd left their father behind and worried how he'd be coping on his own, even though he'd happily pushed them out the door and told them to enjoy themselves.

'We might not be so enthusiastic when we have our first shift tomorrow,' April cautioned.

'I've heard it's a cakewalk. It's just cuts and little injuries, nothing difficult,' Poppy said, collecting both their hands as she came between them and dragged them with her toward the door. 'Now come on—Teddy said he'd pick us up in a car to save us walking!'

Grace swallowed away a shiver of nerves, wishing Teddy weren't stationed at the exact same place as they were. He'd been away for months now, and she knew Poppy was insanely excited about being with her man again, but still. It would have been easier without having to see him at every turn so she wouldn't have to worry that someone might figure out how she felt about him. She'd tried to tell herself it was just a crush, but seeing him again made her wonder if she'd ever get over her infatuation with him.

'Teddy!' Poppy called as they stepped out of their quarters, a handful of cars all lined up and waiting nearby.

And there he was. Teddy was leaning against the car, a cigarette dangling from his lips, wearing his olive-green uniform, long legs crossed at the ankles like there was nothing else in the world he had to do but wait for them. His dark-brown hair was pushed off his face and to the side with Brylcreem, making him look even more handsome than usual, especially with his tanned Hawaii skin. He looked up then, his eyes crinkling as he smiled, dropping his cigarette and then crushing it beneath his boot. Poppy leaped down the steps to him, running until her body collided with his, her arms circling his neck as he bent to kiss her. Grace and April stood, side by side, the space where Poppy had been the only thing separating them. They swapped glances before erupting into embarrassed laughter.

'I think they need some privacy,' April muttered. 'I'm blushing just watching them.'

'Come on, ladies,' Teddy called out, one arm still tucking Poppy to his side as he opened the car door for them.

'Thanks,' Grace said as she quickly passed him, climbing in and scooting over to make room for April.

Poppy sat up front beside Teddy, pressed beside him, his arm around her shoulders as they drove. They'd been sweethearts for more than a year now, but Grace could still vividly recall the night they'd met him, at a party, when he'd walked straight over to the three of them, his smile wide. She'd opened her mouth to talk to him, his eyes on her, the anticipation flooding her as this handsome man she'd never seen before stood in front of them; she was excited to tell the others that she had dibs on him. And then Poppy had dazzled him with her larger-than-life smile and batted her lashes, holding out her hand and telling him she was ready to dance. And suddenly the new guy in town was smitten with her best friend and not her.

'All the guys will be so jealous when I arrive with the three most beautiful nurses in the Pacific on my arm,' Teddy teased, glancing back at them.

Grace felt her cheeks heat, but she quickly looked out the window.

'Well, don't go thinking you have the three of us all to yourself,' April teased right back. Her sister might make fun of her crush, but she'd never let on to anyone else, and she always covered for her, although Grace wondered if even April knew how she truly felt about him. 'You're not the only handsome pilot in town, *Theodore*.'

They all laughed, and Grace gave her sister a grateful smile.

'So what do you make of all this peace talk, Teddy?' April asked.

'Let's not ruin a fun night by talking about politics and war,' he said as he drove. 'The Pacific will stay as peaceful as can be—mark my words. Everyone knows we're as safe as could be here.'

Grace looked at April and saw the serious look on her face, the tight set of her jaw giving her away. She didn't know when her sister had become so interested in politics or what was going on, but she seemed all twisted in knots about things today. Did she know more about the threat of war than she'd let on?

'Why are you so concerned about the peace talks anyway?' Grace asked. 'I don't even know what you're talking about. Did you hear about it on the radio?'

'It's nothing,' April said, before frowning and leaning closer. 'Sorry. I didn't mean to ruin the mood—it's just something I overheard the other day about the peace negotiations with the Japanese, and it's made me nervous that there's more going on. I don't know; maybe I'm overthinking things. I just keep worrying that we're not as safe as we think we are.'

'April, just enjoy being here,' Teddy said. 'This island is heaven, and the longer we get to spend here, the better. I want you to forget all about war for tonight, okay?'

Grace watched her sister as she sat back and frowned, clearly still lost in thought. Grace had always been the fun one, the risk-taker, whereas April was more serious and always quick to come to her little sister's rescue. She wished April could loosen up and just relax sometimes like the rest of them could, but she recognized that worried frown. It had started when their mom had died, and it always reminded her just how much had always fallen to her older sister to deal with.

They drove in silence, bumping along, her elbow colliding with April's every so often, until Teddy cheerfully announced they were there.

'Here we go, ladies,' he said. He got out and opened a door for them. 'Don't forget to behave.'

Grace smiled up at him as she got out, before grabbing her sister's hand as they surveyed the beautiful house in front of them, music filtering out and drawing them in, young men in uniform swarming everywhere, and about half as many women in pretty summer frocks filling up the rest of the space. She'd never seen anything like it in her life.

'I feel like I'm finally all grown up,' Grace whispered as they walked up the steps into the house. 'This place is amazing.'

'You *are* all grown up,' April said with a laugh, looking more relaxed again as she slung an arm around Grace's shoulders. 'Now come—let's go find us some handsome men to dance with!'

Grace glanced down at her pretty powder-blue skirt as it twirled out around her and then happily followed her sister, her arm looped around her waist. She could hear Poppy and Teddy behind her, but she didn't turn, happy to leave them to themselves. What she needed was to meet some soldiers, because when she found the right man, she was certain she'd forget all about her crush on Teddy.

'We probably should have brought our gas masks,' April muttered. 'Imagine if something happened so far from our quarters?'

Grace groaned. 'You're such an old lady sometimes. No one's going to tell us off for not having them. Just enjoy the night!'

'Evening, ladies,' a few navy officers said as they passed.

'Evening,' Grace murmured back each time, feeling her cheeks heat up when one of them let out a low wolf whistle.

'Can I get you ladies a drink?' a flyboy asked, his uniform catching Grace's eye.

'Certainly,' April answered for both of them. 'So long as you have a handsome friend?'

'You look after those girls!' Teddy hollered from behind them.

Grace shot him a quick glare, not about to let Teddy get overprotective and tell them who they could and couldn't drink or dance with. He'd chosen Poppy, and as far as she was concerned, that meant he didn't get a say in what she did or didn't do.

'Who owns this house?' Grace asked as they followed the pilot past groups of people, all standing along the walls to make way for dancing.

'Some wealthy family who've told us to enjoy their holiday home!' the flyboy said, passing them each a cup of something alcoholic from the smell of it. Grace took it and held up the paper cup to April's. 'Folks around here love us—they don't seem to mind opening their houses up.'

'To Pearl Harbor, then,' Grace said.

'To Pearl Harbor,' April replied as the pilot clinked both of their cups too hard and made them spill right away. She jumped back, cup extended in front of her to avoid the splash.

'Want to dance?' he asked as another man in uniform appeared nearby.

'Sure,' Grace said as her sister was whisked away by the hand to dance too.

She gulped down her drink to quell her nerves and then set it down, before letting him lead her away from the wall and to the center of the enormous living room. It struck her that she didn't even know his name, but the small band in the corner was playing so loudly now, and she didn't want to lean in any closer to ask him.

Grace placed her hands on his shoulders as he touched her waist, his palms as warm as the balmy air brushing her shoulders. With so many bodies inside it was stifling, and she was already looking forward to finding some cooler air outside as sweat tickled her neck and forehead. She wasn't used to such high temperatures in the fall.

'You know, I think I fell in love with you the moment I set eyes on you back there,' he said into her ear.

Grace tipped her head back and laughed, only to realize when she righted herself that the expression on his face was serious. 'I don't even know your name! You can't be in love with me!'

'Sam Chapman,' he said. 'Saying hello to you was . . .'

'Whoa, stop right there,' she said as his hands moved lower and skimmed her bottom. 'Waaay too low!'

He kept hold of her, smiling away as if he thought she liked having his paws all over her. Grace struggled and yanked at his wrists, trying to force his hands away.

'Hey, back off, flyboy,' a loud female voice commanded. 'Now!'

He jumped back as if he'd been caught red handed by his own mother, looking back sheepishly at Grace. She didn't take her eyes off him, her burning cheeks betraying her as she stared defiantly at him, not about to run away upset. How dare he!

'Go,' the young woman said, appearing from behind the officer. 'And touch a lady like that again, and I'll make sure you regret it.'

A warm palm found its way into Grace's, but this one was welcome, and she held on tight to it. She found herself looking into dark-brown eyes that belonged to a woman easily half a foot taller than her, with a mane of red hair that fell most of the way down her back and over her shoulders.

'You need to be firm with them,' she said. 'They've all been away from their mamas too long, and they've forgotten their manners.'

Grace laughed, grateful for the joke, and squeezed the hand she'd ended up holding.

'Thank you. He was getting . . .'

16

'Frisky?' The redhead laughed. 'Because trust me, I could see that.'

'Grace Bellamy,' Grace said, shaking the hand already in hers.

'Eva Branson,' she said, letting go and touching Grace's shoulder, leaning in as the music became even louder. 'Want to find someone else to dance with?'

Grace shook her head, suddenly not as confident as she'd been earlier. She saw her sister being twirled around and smiled, happy that April was having fun, and then she saw Poppy, folded into Teddy's arms like she was never going to let go of the man. Her heart skipped a beat, imagining what it would be like. Why did Teddy always have to be so perfect?

'Maybe a drink and some fresh air?' Grace suggested instead.

They walked over to get some punch, and then Eva led the way, walking outside and stopping only when they reached the sand.

Grace bent to slip her shoes off, loving the sensation of sand beneath her feet as she wiggled her toes and let it slide across her skin. She'd been so excited about going to a party and meeting boys, but suddenly the best feeling in the world was hearing the music behind her and facing the water twinkling beneath the moonlight. Maybe she wasn't as confident as she liked to think she was, or perhaps it was that the atmosphere was different here, the boys in uniforms more like grown men than the young guys back home she'd flirted with. At home, dances had been strictly supervised, and she would never have talked to men so openly, let alone danced and had a drink with them, but here? It was like a different world from the one she'd grown up in, shielded from anything sinister.

'So how does a girl manage to bark orders at an officer so confidently?' Grace asked, taking a sip of her drink. 'I think I might need to take lessons if I'm going to survive here.'

'Try having two big brothers and an ex–sergeant major for a father.'

Grace felt her eyes widen. 'Ahh, right. Now it makes sense.'

'I learned fast that the only way anyone ever got my brothers and their friends to do anything was by being assertive.' Eva smiled. 'If it doesn't sound like an order, they don't bother listening.'

'Have you just gotten here as well?' Grace asked, intrigued by her new companion. 'I arrived early this morning. My sister's here with me too.'

'Fresh meat,' Eva said with a grin, tipping her head back slightly. 'That's what all those boys in there will be calling you. No wonder he put his hands where they don't belong.'

Grace was starting to realize just how little she knew about dealing with men. Now here she was, with no one but her sister and her own wits to rely on, surrounded by a bunch of men who'd probably had one too many drinks before she'd even arrived. She was going to have to be more careful; not everyone was as polite and friendly as Teddy.

'I've been here a few months already. I'm a Navy Corps nurse stationed on the USS *Solace*.'

'Where is it moored?' Grace asked, staring out at the ocean.

'Over that way in the stream,' Eva said. 'We'll be heading back soon, but we all wanted to come have a couple hours of fun first. It's boring as hell being on that boat all the time with nothing much to do.'

'Please, don't let me stop you. Head back in to dance if you'd like,' Grace said, embarrassed that a stranger had been forced to rescue her and then sit out the party. 'I'll be fine.'

'Don't be sorry; this is nice,' Eva said. And Grace believed her. 'The boat gives me cabin fever, and the heat and music in there are enough to give anyone a pounding headache, so this is perfect. My fiancé wasn't allowed leave tonight, so it's nice to have someone to talk to.'

'He's based here too?' Grace asked.

'Yes. He's air force, but he's being reprimanded for something, and he isn't allowed to leave his barracks. He's pushing the boundaries, and I think he's pushed his luck too far this time.'

Grace smiled over at her new friend, pleased she'd met her. She sat down, her legs curled up beneath her, the sand cool against the tops of her feet. She sipped her drink and glanced at Eva, straightening her shoulders as she noticed the perfect, almost dancer-like way the other woman sat, so elegant and tall.

'So where did you do your training? What made you go into nursing?' Eva asked.

Grace often wondered why she'd decided to train, but she knew why. No matter how often she told people that she'd always wanted to be a nurse and she liked taking care of people, the truth was far removed from her perfect little story. She wasn't lying—she did love people, and she'd always help someone if she could—but nursing wasn't something she loved the idea of, and she doubted it ever would be.

'Promise you won't hate me?' she asked.

Eva frowned. 'Hate you? Why?'

'When I admit that the only reason I'm here is because I didn't want to be left home while my sister and best friend went on the adventure of a lifetime,' she confessed. 'I've never told anyone that before, but the truth is, I'm squeamish around blood. I wasn't about to sit at home, though, and let them do this without me.'

Eva stared at her, her eyes wide, before she erupted into laughter, spilling her drink as she reached for Grace's wrist. Grace knew her cheeks would be bright red, the burn making her entire body flush as she went to stand up.

'Stop! Don't go!' Eva pleaded as she wiped tears from her cheeks. 'I'm sorry, but that's the most ridiculous thing I've ever heard! You can't be a nurse if you're scared of blood—you do realize that, don't you?'

'I didn't say *scared*,' Grace corrected.

'Grace, if you're funny around blood, you need to get out now. What happens if we end up at war? What will you do if you're dealing with amputations and surgeries and—'

'Stop!' Grace begged, her stomach turning just thinking about it all. 'Everyone back home seems so certain we won't join the war, and I'm fine with needles, so I can do the injections when they're needed and bandaging, all that sort of thing. It's just full-on blood that makes me feel sick.'

Eva leaned in closer to her, her smile kind. 'I'm sorry I laughed at you; it wasn't fair, but I'm serious. Maybe you should consider volunteering in another way if you're not sure about nursing? Before it gets worse, I mean.'

Grace shook her head. 'I'm fine. Honestly, I shouldn't have even said anything.'

'I understand why you wanted to stay with your sister, though,' Eva said. 'And it *is* an amazing adventure here. In fact if we don't end up at war, it'll be the adventure of a lifetime. But we need to remember what we're here for if things change. We could be sent anywhere if we enter the war.'

'Grace! We've been looking everywhere for you!'

She turned, looked over her shoulder, and saw her sister standing there with Poppy trailing behind her.

'I was just enjoying the fresh air,' she said, standing and brushing the sand from her skirt. 'April, this is Eva. Eva, this is my big sister, April.'

April came forward and shook hands, her smile wide and her warmth second to none, as always. Sometimes Grace felt it was like introducing people to her mother; April had an elegance and way of putting people at ease that made her seem so much older sometimes.

'You're stationed at Tripler with us?' April asked.

'No, I'm with the navy, on the USS *Solace*,' Eva said. 'It's nice to have my feet on solid ground for the night.'

'Want to join us inside? I met a charming officer who promises me his friends are desperate to meet us. I'm sure they won't mind one more lady to bat their eyes at.'

Eva gave Grace a look, almost as if she was silently asking if it was okay to join them, and Grace smiled and nodded quickly.

'Who's this gorgeous girl?' Poppy asked when she came closer, grabbing Grace's hand and then walking backward to look at Eva.

'This is Eva; she's a navy nurse,' Grace said. 'Eva, meet Poppy.'

'Well, the more the merrier, I say!' Poppy said with a wink. 'Come on, girls—let's dance!'

'You're certain I'm not intruding?' Eva asked.

Poppy tucked her arm into Eva's as Grace watched. 'Of course not. Just promise you'll show us around this gorgeous island the second you have a day off.'

'Done.'

They walked back in together, four of them in a row, and the wolf whistles didn't take long to start.

'I'm off to get more drinks! See you girls soon,' Poppy called out.

Eva took a young man's hand and twirled off onto the dance floor within seconds, and Grace felt a nudge at her elbow and turned.

'Oh, hi, Teddy,' she said.

'You look like you need someone to dance with,' he replied, his grin making her cheeks flush.

April grabbed her other arm then, smiling as she stepped away toward the dance floor.

'Don't go disappearing on me again, Grace. I want to be able to see you at all times, okay?'

Grace nodded, resisting the urge to make a face at her sister for treating her like a child yet again.

Teddy shuffled closer beside her, and she laughed at the expression on his face when she turned, his eyebrows drawn together as he frowned and wagged his finger. 'Don't you move, Grace Bellamy. I want to make sure you're not up to mischief!'

She burst out laughing, play punching Teddy on the arm. 'Stop it! She might hear you, and then you'll wish you hadn't mocked her.'

'She's only looking out for you,' he said. 'But I get it. She's like a mother hen sometimes when it comes to her baby sister.'

'Yeah, and I'm her precious little chick who has no idea how to think for herself.'

Poppy was coming back toward them then, but just as she was about to step away from Teddy to put some distance between them, he grabbed her fingers and gave them a squeeze.

'I dare you to dance all the way over there.' He nodded toward the other side of the room. 'You don't always have to do what she says.'

Poppy passed Teddy a drink and tucked against him, and Grace gave him a quick smile as she accepted an offer to dance from a nice-looking soldier. This time, she ended up in the arms of a well-behaved man who kept one step between them at all times, and she wished her first experience had been so pleasant. She glanced over at Eva and saw her being twirled, her smile wide, and she thought for the hundredth time that day how incredibly lucky they all were. The music became louder, and she laughed as her enthusiastic dance partner spun her around, and she grinned when she passed by Teddy again, who gave a little point to the far side of the room, daring her to defy April.

Teddy might be handsome as sin, but there were plenty of gorgeous men in uniform filling the room. And while it may have broken her heart once that he hadn't chosen her, now she had her pick of eligible young men, and she wasn't going to waste another second wishing she'd been faster to catch Teddy's eye. Even if he was the only person who seemed to see how hard it was for her, struggling to emerge from her sister's shadow. She couldn't help the way she felt, that she'd fallen for the same man as Poppy, but her friend's happiness meant the world to her. She needed to stop mooning over Teddy and just enjoy herself.

CHAPTER TWO

EVA

One thing Eva never tired of was being invited to other ships for dinner, and tonight was no different. It helped to keep her mind off things like the possible approach of war, and her fiancé, who was so close to defying orders and leaving his unit behind to travel to Europe. She shuddered just thinking about the repercussions, not wanting to imagine Charlie joining the war before their country was even involved.

'Welcome!' The captain waved to them as they clambered onto the ship from their smaller rowboat and then held his hand out to assist Eva with her final step. She grasped it gratefully and stood back to let the other nurses pass.

'Come this way!' he announced, gesturing for them to follow, and Eva walked behind him, admiring the big ship and wondering who would have enough money to own something so extravagant.

They were passed drinks, and Eva stifled a laugh as she traded glances with some of the other nurses. They were in civilian clothes, and it was nice to be out of her starched nurse's uniform, even if it was just for a few hours. Although she would have preferred to be on land with the girls she'd met the night before—they'd been a lot of fun, and she'd enjoyed talking with Grace on the beach. All three of the girls had been nice, but there was something about Grace; she was very much the youngest of the group and so innocent, but Eva liked her courage. The poor girl was scared of blood and had been manhandled at her first dance, but she was clearly determined to keep up with the others and not let her sister see her weakness.

'Tell me, what do you think about it all?'

Eva turned and came face-to-face with the ship's captain again, who'd for some reason made a beeline straight for her.

'What do I think about what?' she asked, smiling as he clinked his glass of champagne to hers. She took a small sip, more out of nervousness than a real desire to consume it.

'About this *situation*?' he said, lowering his voice on the last word as if it were a secret. 'Do you think there's going to be a war?'

Eva shook her head. 'I wish I knew, but we don't know any more than you do, I'm afraid.'

'I was certain you'd have heard more of what's going on,' he said, raising a brow.

She had no idea why he thought she'd be in the know, but she had nothing of interest to tell him.

'We're all in limbo, waiting to see what will happen,' she said politely. 'But we couldn't exactly be anywhere more picturesque while we wait, could we?'

He laughed and raised his glass again, before moving on to another group of visitors. Eva moved away from the crowd, then leaned against the rails and stared back at her home away from home for now, the *Solace*. She was a magnificent ship, pure white with a big red cross emblazoned along the side, with a flag flying proudly at the stern. She'd once been a luxury passenger liner, featuring ornate staircases and dark wood paneling, and Eva could only imagine what it would have been like traveling on board on a cruise to Canada or even Cuba for the summer. But now she was a more practical ship, the only hospital ship stationed in Hawaii, and with her interior remodeled to accommodate hospital wards and space for the navy servicemen and nurses. They even had their own mess room of sorts, with comfortable chairs and tables to play cards on.

She gazed out farther, at the water glistening as the sun started to make its departure for the day and at the aircraft in the distance performing a drill in the sky. It was rare for planes to come any closer—they were usually some distance away—which meant that many of her fellow nurses seemed surprised at how many pilots were stationed on the island. But not her. She was reminded of the fact every single time she thought of her Charlie.

It had been only yesterday morning that she'd seen him, staring up into the bluest eyes she'd ever known, eyes she'd been admiring since she was barely fourteen years old. Eyes that she'd never forget even if she didn't see her man for weeks, months, or even years.

'Charlie, you're being unreasonable,' she told him.

Her heart was beating so hard and fast she thought she was going to collapse. There was a roaring sound in her ears, like the ocean, even though they were so far inland, sitting on a grass field beneath coconut trees. It should have been so idyllic, so picturesque, but instead they were arguing over Charlie's role in the war.

'The war is coming, Eva, whether anyone wants to admit it or not. It's only a matter of time before we're all plunged headfirst into the fighting.'

'You're wrong,' she argued. 'What information have you received to make you think that? What do you know that no one else does? Because no one I've spoken to thinks our country is in any rush to join the war.'

He moved away, his hand no longer pressed to hers, his leg no longer brushing her thigh where they sat on the grass. Charlie was in uniform, his tie and jacket looking so at odds with the otherwise relaxed surroundings, and she could tell from the intense look on his face that nothing she said was going to change his mind.

'Charlie, please,' she begged, standing and reaching for his hand. His palm was at his side, hanging, and she put her other arm around him, her cheek to his shoulder, standing behind him. 'I can't lose you.'

'There are other pilots there already, Eva,' he said, his body stiff. 'They fought in the Battle of Britain while I stayed here and waited, dutifully following my orders.'

'I know,' she said, taking a deep breath and blinking away tears. 'But those friends of yours, those other pilots, they can't ever return here, Charlie. You can't just defy our neutrality laws and expect to get away with it.'

They both knew what had been threatened already. Those pilots had been told they could lose their citizenship or be imprisoned if they ever tried to return home. She couldn't have Charlie in that situation!

'Why are you so determined to go? Why isn't it enough that you'll be the first deployed if we join the war?' she asked, holding him, forcing him to relax into her.

Charlie was silent, but eventually he turned in her arms, his eyes softening as he dipped down, his forehead pressed to hers as he stooped lower.

'I want to help them,' he said softly. 'I don't want to leave you—you know that—but they're desperate for more pilots over the pond, and maybe I could help them win this war before America even has to join it.'

Eva stood on tiptoes, gently touching her lips to his. She loved Charlie so much, this gorgeous, courageous pilot of hers, and it broke her heart to think of him being shot down in the sky. She opened her mouth, pausing as she lowered herself to her heels, before saying something she'd never, ever needed to say before this moment. It was her weakness, the one thing that had always been unsaid between them, but if it stopped him leaving and traveling to Europe on some suicide mission, then she wasn't going to stay quiet.

'You've been looking after me my whole life,' she whispered as a single tear slipped down her cheek. 'If I lose you, if you can't ever come home to America, how will I survive going back to my father?'

Charlie was the only one who knew the truth about her daddy. The only one whom she'd ever confided in about how cruel he'd been to her all her life. Her brothers would never have believed her—even as grown young men they idolized their father—and that's why she'd always kept it a secret. Leaving home and marrying Charlie, living with her kind, sweet fiancé, meant more to her than anyone else could ever understand.

'You know I'd never let that happen,' he whispered, cradling her closer, holding her tight. 'I'll never let you go back there.'

'You can't protect me if you're not here, Charlie. Once you're gone, we might never see one another again.'

She blinked away her tears, her cheek to his chest. She wasn't in the habit of guilting other people into doing things for her, and she'd never hold Charlie back from doing anything else, but defying orders to join the war? She just couldn't let him go, not like that.

'Promise me you'll stay?' she asked, tipping back in his arms to study his face.

He stared down at her, his jaw like steel before he finally softened. 'For now,' he murmured back. 'For now, I promise.'

When he kissed her, she wondered if he was lying to her, if he would be gone by morning, but in that moment, all she wanted to believe was that her Charlie would do as he was told and stay on base.

'Eva? Earth to Eva.'

She turned, blinking away the memories and quickly wiping at her damp cheeks. Her fingers brushed her throat, too, as she remembered what it felt like to have her father's hand clenched tight to her skin, choking her, telling her that she'd never amount to anything. When she'd told Charlie he was her lifeline, that he meant more to her than anything else in the world, she hadn't been lying.

'You all right, honey?'

Eva smiled at the two other navy nurses standing behind her, nodding as she stepped back to join them. 'Sorry, I was lost in my own thoughts.'

'It's time for supper. Are you joining us?'

She took a long, slow sip of her drink, followed by a deep breath. Charlie would be fine; he was still there at his base, still safe. She had to believe that he wouldn't go without telling her, that she'd said enough to change his mind.

'Of course,' she said. 'Lead the way.'

Her fellow nurses were a lovely bunch of women, all easygoing and fun to be around, and it was high time she enjoyed herself. Who knew what the future would bring, and so long as she was at sea or in Charlie's arms, she was happy, and she needed to make the most of it.

———— ⚜ ————

Eva made her bed, checking the sheets were tucked in tight and her folds perfect. They weren't held to the same standards as the navy boys, but they still had regular inspections, and she liked to keep her little space in the sleeping quarters perfect. She reached into her case and pushed aside her gas mask, fingering the ugly brown contraption and trying to imagine wearing it. She breathed deep, the ocean air reminding her where she was, how different Hawaii was from her home in Seattle, which would be so much colder right now. Even in the cabin the air smelled and felt different, and she'd finally started to get used to the stickiness of humidity against her skin. It wasn't as hot as it had been when she'd arrived a month earlier, and they'd had sudden bursts of rain that had left the air like pea soup at times, but it was still pleasant.

'Heading ashore in fifteen minutes!' came a call, and Eva quickly gave her long hair a brush, securing a hair tie around her wrist in case she wanted it later. She loved having her hair out when she wasn't on duty, but the dampness of her hair against the back of her neck would probably drive her mad within a few hours.

She checked her lipstick and picked up her bag, smiling at some of the other girls as they ran through their last-minute routines and rushed after her.

'Do you girls have any plans today?' she asked no one in particular.

'My man has the day off, so we're going on a picnic,' one of the girls said.

'Really? You sure he doesn't have a cute friend so we can double up?' another asked with a giggle, joining the conversation.

'How about you, Eva?'

She smiled. 'Well, I'm not seeing my man, that's for sure. He's working today, and I don't think he'll be getting any leave days this week. But I met some great girls at a party the other night, and I think we're going horseback riding today.'

They kept chatting as they left their quarters and made their way to the meeting point, climbing down to the smaller boat that would take them to shore. She still remembered the first time, climbing slowly down on trembling legs and holding tight to the side of the little vessel, but now it didn't faze her.

Once they were ashore, she waved goodbye to the rest of the group and walked quickly toward the beach where she was meeting Grace. They'd organized their day out the night of the party, and she hoped they hadn't changed their minds. But she hadn't been waiting five minutes when a familiar blonde came running toward her, a towel under one arm, the other flapping wildly to get her attention.

'Eva!' Grace called. 'Over here!'

She smiled to herself, wondering how on earth Grace thought she couldn't see her. Eva waved back and put on her sunglasses, before crossing the sand and meeting an out-of-breath Grace where the grass and the beach collided. Grace looked so similar to her sister, with the same shade of blonde hair and beautiful big blue eyes, but whereas April hadn't had a hair out of place the night of the party, her hair twisted up neatly, Grace's was wild and carefree around her shoulders. She was very much the younger of the two and far more energetic compared to her sister's poise. Eva couldn't help but love her all the more.

'Sorry I'm late,' Grace panted, bending over as she caught her breath. 'I ran all the way!'

'It's fine; I was enjoying the sunshine. Where are the others?'

Grace sighed. 'Still getting ready. I told them we had to get up early, but I had to drag them out of bed before I left. They should be meeting us soon.'

Eva smiled and fell into step beside Grace as they wandered along the beach. 'Want to get your feet wet?'

Grace shrugged. 'Sure.'

They padded along the damp sand, the water lapping gently at their toes every few minutes as it washed in and out.

'So how was your first full day?' Eva asked. 'Did you have to deal with any blood?'

She asked it with a straight face, but the moment Grace nudged her in the side, she burst out laughing.

'You're never going to let me live that down, are you?' Grace groaned. 'I should never have admitted it to you!'

'Your secret is my secret,' Eva said, running her fingers across her lips as if she were sealing them shut. 'Now tell me about the hospital, though. What's it like? When's your first proper shift?'

'Tomorrow,' Grace said, and Eva watched as she bent to pick up a shell, rubbing her thumb across the rough edge before throwing it out to sea. 'I'm terrified, to be honest, but according to Poppy it's little more than football injuries and common colds and so forth.'

'She's right. I've had fevers to deal with, some mild injuries and infections, but nothing too taxing.'

She turned and saw April and Poppy coming toward them, pretty sundresses flitting out around them as they walked.

'You know, I'm not sure we're dressed appropriately for horseback riding,' Eva mused. 'Can we even ride in a dress?'

Grace frowned. 'Surely we'll be fine like this?'

'Morning!' Poppy mumbled, twisting her hair up as she walked, hairpins sticking out from her mouth.

'Morning,' Eva replied. 'Sorry you had to get up so early for me on your day off.'

'We can sleep when we're dead. There's far too much to see to waste the day snoozing,' Poppy said, her smile wide as she greeted her. 'You both ready to explore?'

Eva slipped her glasses from the top of her head and put them on, happy to be enjoying a day out with friends. She might not know them well yet, but they seemed like nice girls, and she was grateful to have someone to meet up with. Poppy seemed to be the ringleader, her manner confident and effortless, while Grace was more exuberant Labrador puppy to April's reserved, quiet manner.

'Where do we find our horses?' April asked.

'Down there,' Grace said. 'They should be ready and waiting for us.'

'Eva, didn't you say your fiancé was based here?' Poppy asked. 'You could have asked him to come with us.'

'You're very kind, thank you, but I don't think he's allowed off base for now.' She cleared her throat, wondering how much to tell them about Charlie. 'He's, ah, well, let's just say he's in some hot water right now after an argument with his superiors. Something to do with a handful of pilots who left to fly for the Royal Air Force in Britain, and him insisting that US pilots should be allowed to join without any repercussions. So not only is he in some sort of detention, he's also been grounded for the week.'

Poppy threw an arm around her shoulders as they walked. 'Hey, at least he's courageous. But it's a shame he's been grounded. My Teddy would hate that.'

'Your man is a pilot too?'

'Yes, but unlike your fiancé, mine is happy basking in the sun here, so I doubt he'd ever be gunning to go offshore before he's asked.'

Eva sighed. Why did Charlie have to be so determined to make a difference? All she wanted was him here, safe, away from the fighting, so that she knew he'd be making it home with her when all this was over.

The horses came into sight, and she watched as a man moved around them. They were tied to a large piece of driftwood, quietly standing in the morning sunshine.

Grace was like an overexcited child when they went closer, but Eva quietly made her way to a beautiful chestnut-colored mare, running her fingers through her mane and stroking her neck. It had been a very, very long time since she'd ridden a horse, but it was a happy memory, one of those rare days that her father's smile had lit up his face and made his eyes twinkle.

She blinked the memory away and listened to the man give them a safety talk before helping them up into the saddles.

'Just walk,' he said, pointing as he spoke. 'Head all the way down there—they know the drill.'

Eva imagined they knew the exact path to take, that they took tourists on the same route every day and never deviated from the well-trodden trail, and she settled into the saddle and arranged her dress around her so it didn't flap around and scare the horse.

They fell into formation, the four of them riding abreast but not close enough to touch, and Eva relaxed into the gentle movement of the horse beneath her.

'This was a great suggestion,' Eva said, breaking the silence.

'You can thank Grace for this,' April replied. 'She's been wanting to ride for years, ever since she found photos of our mom all dressed up and riding in some fancy show as a child.'

'Your mother is a horse rider?' Eva asked.

The sadness that clouded April's face made her wish she'd kept her mouth shut.

'She was,' April said softly. 'We lost her when I was fifteen and Grace was thirteen.'

'I'm so sorry,' Eva said. 'Did your father remarry?'

'He didn't need to,' Poppy said, answering for April. 'My mom always says that men remarry so quickly because they can't cope without a woman looking after them, but not Mr. Bellamy. April became the woman of the house, and he never needed anyone else, did he, April?'

Eva studied April, noticing how much older she appeared than her sister even though there was obviously only a year or so between them. Her face was more serious, her mouth in a straight line, eyes cautious as she scanned the beach. Grace, on the other hand, was more child-like about everything, and she could see right away that April was very much the older sibling to a sister who was used to being the baby of the family. As she watched April take some pins from her updo and help Grace secure her hair from her face, it was almost like watching a mother with her daughter.

'Our poor dad did his best, but he more kind of muddled along and hoped we wouldn't get into trouble,' Grace said. 'April was the model child, and she was pretty good at pulling me into line when I acted up.'

April sighed. 'More like I had to grow up and behave like a forty-year-old overnight while you still acted thirteen.'

Eva could imagine the dynamic—it was still obvious now that April shouldered the older-sister burden, just like her older brothers had taken their role of looking out for her so seriously.

Her horse snorted, and she slipped a hand down to stroke her neck, marveling at how hard the muscle was beneath the hair.

'How about you, Eva? Do you have both your parents?' April asked.

'Yes. My mom has recently gone back to teaching, just substituting at the local school when they need someone, and my dad is a retired army sergeant.' She didn't tell them that the reason her poor mother was working had to do with her father drinking away almost all his pension money each week. 'I have two brothers, and I was the baby of the family.'

She missed her brothers; they were trouble, but they were also kind to her, and she loved their Sunday-night dinners, when they always got together. Her father often wasn't there, not if he'd gone out earlier to stare at the bottom of a whiskey bottle somewhere on his own, but that always made it even better. Then it would be just her with her mom and brothers around the table, which was exactly how she liked it.

'Want to try a canter?' Poppy asked. 'Walking is boring. I say we blow out some cobwebs.'

Eva was about to say no, but before she knew it, Poppy had kicked her horse in the side, and they all took off after her. She grabbed a fistful of mane as her body jerked, the wind whipping at her cheeks and picking up her hair as they raced along the waterline. If Grace was the Labrador puppy, then Poppy was the Jack Russell terrier, up to no good and getting everyone in trouble!

'This is the life!' Poppy screamed. 'Faster!'

Her horse was stretching out beneath her now, and Eva marveled at the push and pull of her muscles, the way her long legs seemed to eat up the ground beneath them. She clung tight to the reins, her fingers fisting in the horse's mane, too, to give her a better grip as her knees and thighs clenched tight against the animal's side.

Soon they were slowing, and Eva tried to steady her breathing, taking little gasps of air as her heart beat so loud and fast it almost pounded from her chest.

'Fun?' Poppy asked, her cheeks pink as she slipped from the horse's back.

'More like a death wish,' April muttered.

Eva didn't say a thing, but when Grace grinned at her, she happily smiled back. She'd been terrified, but Poppy was right; it had blown out all the cobwebs, which was exactly what she'd needed. Charlie might be grounded, but it wasn't going to stop her from having a fun day out with friends.

They eventually gave the horses back and walked barefoot down the beach, shoes dangling from their fingers, back the same way they'd come earlier, and Eva smiled as she listened to the three girls chat. It was obvious how close they all were, and it was nice to be part of their little group.

'Why don't we find a nice spot on the beach and sit for a bit?' April suggested. 'We can paddle in the water and sunbathe until we're hungry for lunch.'

Eva nodded. 'Count me in. I have hours until I have to go back.'

'We could always sneak down to see the boys,' Poppy said, sidling up to Eva and giving her a wicked grin.

'No way,' she said. 'If we were caught, my Charlie might end up with another week without leave!'

Poppy sighed. 'Well, if you change your mind, I'm in. Teddy would love a little surprise visit.'

April had found a nice spot up ahead under a cluster of palm trees, and they all sat, leaning against the trunks, their legs stretched out in the sunshine. She stared out at the ocean, loving the twinkling glare it created, watching the waves as they gently lapped in and out.

'What's it like being at sea?' Grace asked. 'Is it nice to be back on land today? I think I'd be sick with all that bobbing around all the time!'

'It's not like that,' she said with a laugh. 'Honestly, the ship's so big and we're anchored so close in, so it doesn't make you seasick. But I do find it weird not being able to walk outside. Wandering the decks isn't quite the same as feeling land beneath your feet.'

'Are you in cabins?' April asked.

'It's a huge ship—honestly, you could get lost in it trying to find your way around,' she told them. 'Our quarters are nice enough—we're in bunks, with about eight of us to a room—and we all get along just fine.'

'Everyone seems so happy to be part of the excitement, don't you think?' Poppy said. 'I've never had so much freedom. I mean, Teddy and I were always with a group or escorted by someone, and now we're here and we can sneak off whenever we're not working!'

'We don't need to hear about what you and Teddy get up to,' April said. 'Perhaps you two *do* need a chaperone!'

Eva noticed the way Grace turned away from the conversation, her arms wrapped around herself as she gazed at the ocean. She shuffled closer, wondering if everything was okay with her.

'Are you missing home? Plenty of the girls get upset at night whenever we're talking about our families,' she said gently.

'Oh, no, it's not that,' Grace said, her smile warm when she glanced sideways. 'I'm fine, just admiring the water. Want to go for a splash?'

Eva stood and held a hand out, tugging Grace up with her. She wasn't going to ask her more—she could sense that her new friend had been deep in thought, but it was up to her if she wanted to share or not. She had her own secrets, her own triggers that pulled her down and made her wish things could be different, but that wasn't something she had any interest in talking to anyone about. Except maybe to Charlie.

'So how long have you been with your man?' Grace asked as they walked down to the water's edge, leaving April and Poppy chatting beneath the tree.

'I'm twenty-two now, and we've been best friends since we were about fourteen, I think,' she confessed. 'We were going to get married before he was posted here, but we decided to wait.'

'I can't believe you've been together so long,' Grace said, walking deeper, her skirt held up high to stop it from getting wet.

'We were friends for a long time; he was so kind to me, and we used to talk for hours. I think I fell in love with him at first sight, but it took him a year to kiss me!' Eva clamped her hand over her mouth. 'Sorry—that was more than you wanted to know.'

Grace laughed. 'No, it's nice. I love hearing stories like that. He must be a nice man.'

'He is. And I like that he's so gentle with me; he's so . . .' She paused, wondering how to explain what she was thinking. *So different from my father;* that was what she wanted to say. 'So caring, I suppose. I know he'd protect me from anything, if that makes sense.'

'It does.' Grace hurried back as a shallow wave rushed in, holding her skirt higher. 'If you meet another one like him, can you introduce me? I need someone like that, someone who can look after me and just be kind, I suppose.'

Eva smiled, studying Grace as she held up her hand, staring out at the ocean again. She seemed to be deep in thought, quieter than she'd been the first time they'd met.

'It must have been so hard for you, losing your mom,' she said.

Grace's eyes were filled with unshed tears when she turned, and Eva reached for her hand, squeezing it tight. She could see clearly now that Grace wasn't just juvenile; she actually wasn't as confident as she tried to portray herself to be around her adventurous friend and grown-up sister.

'I'm sorry; I shouldn't have brought that up.'

'No, it's fine. I've just been thinking about her a lot lately.' Grace sighed and brushed at her cheeks as Poppy and April came running up behind them. 'I suppose I've been wondering whether she'd have let us come here, whether we'd be doing any of this if she'd still been alive.'

Grace's voice had dropped lower as the others approached, and Eva nodded, not saying anything more.

'What are you two gossiping about?' Poppy asked.

'Nothing much,' Eva said. 'I was just telling Grace about a nasty boil I had to lance the other day. I'm lucky I have a strong stomach!'

'Ewww, that sounds revolting. It wasn't on his bottom, was it?' Poppy asked.

Grace gave her a wink, and Eva took it as a thank-you for keeping their conversation quiet. But when she glanced at April, she saw that

Grace's older sister was watching, no doubt aware they'd closed a conversation as soon as she'd come near.

A shimmer of water flicked across Eva's face, and she turned to find Poppy bent over, scooping up water and splashing it at them.

'Poppy!' April scolded.

'What, you don't like this?' Poppy asked, flicking even more water.

April squealed when the water soaked her skirt, but Eva just scooped her own handful of water up, expertly splashing Poppy and then chasing after her. Grace appeared beside her, and they both launched an attack on Poppy, kicking up water and scooping it up until they were all soaked through.

'Enough!' April begged. 'Stop!'

They all stood back, laughing and trying to catch their breath. Eva looked down at her dress, soaked through and clinging to her body, showing every bump and curve.

'Maybe that wasn't such a great idea,' Grace muttered beside her.

She looked at Grace and felt her eyes widen, the outline of her friend's breasts and nipples now visible through her pale-yellow sundress.

'Um, you might need to grab a couple of palm fronds to cover yourself,' Eva warned as April gasped beside her.

'Hey, girls!'

They all squealed and backed into one another, hands over breasts and legs crossed tightly as the navy boys waved at them from farther up the beach. The men were laughing and whistling, and they stood huddled together waiting for them to move on, before bursting into laughter and running out of the water onto the sand.

'You girls are a terrible influence,' Eva murmured, shutting her eyes as she lay on her back to dry out.

'It's Poppy,' April said affectionately. 'It's always Poppy leading us astray.'

Poppy laughed. 'Stop moaning; we were having fun, weren't we? Besides, when else in our lives will we ever have no one caring about where we are or what we're doing? We have to make the most of this!'

'She's right,' said Grace, propped up on one elbow as Eva watched her. 'We're going to look back on this adventure as the best time of our lives. We need to go to every party, stay up late, anything we want to do.'

'I second that,' Eva said. 'I've never felt so free in all my life.' She loved not having to tiptoe around her father, not having to feel like every step, every move she made was being watched and criticized. She was good at her job, she loved nursing, and she wanted to enjoy being posted somewhere so far from home. She'd finally flown the nest, and she was never, ever going back to it.

They all lay side by side in the sun, soaking up the rays, and when Eva felt Grace's fingers brush hers and squeeze for a moment, she did the same back. She'd started the week disappointed that she wouldn't be seeing Charlie on her days off, but Grace and her friends had more than made up for it.

She stared at the sky, squinting hard to keep her eyes open. There was barely a puff of cloud, and the light breeze against her skin was warm, helping to dry her wet clothes as she lay as still as a statue. Hawaii was the closest place to paradise she could imagine, and she wouldn't have wished to be anywhere else in the world.

CHAPTER THREE

POPPY

'Oh lord,' Poppy gasped, elbowing Grace in the side. 'Look at that poor man!'

She tried not to gawp, but there was a man in a full-body cast, with just a big hole cut out in the belly area. Grace started to giggle, but she pushed Poppy away, not wanting to burst into laughter herself. It was awful and somehow funny all at the same time.

'What are you two on about?'

Poppy shrugged. 'Oh, nothing. Just wondering what on earth that soldier did to end up looking like a mummy.'

April didn't crack a smile. In fact, Poppy was certain she heard her make an irritated sound in the back of her throat. 'He was injured during a maneuver, and that's the only way they could cast him properly. Stop staring!'

'Sorry—you're right,' Poppy said, giving Grace a sharp stare until she mumbled 'sorry' as well. She loved both the Bellamy girls, but sometimes they were as different as night and day. April was as passionate about nursing as the rest of them were passionate about going to parties and listening to music, Grace had only come for the adventure, and she'd only signed up to be close to Teddy.

'Anything interesting happening down here?' April asked.

Poppy sighed. 'Nothing much. Although we have been invited to a bedside poker game later tonight if our shift is quiet.'

'Poker?' April asked. 'We're supposed to check supplies and do our rounds if we're quiet.'

'April, you need to stop taking everything so seriously,' Poppy said, taking hold of her friend's arm and pointing around the occupied beds. 'These poor fellas could do with some cheering up, and we're not exactly run ragged. What harm is there in sitting down and playing cards with them if we don't have any nursing to do?'

April raised her eyebrows, but the hint of a smile on her lips told Poppy she'd convinced her.

'I suppose you're right,' April said.

'I'm *always* right. I expected you to know that by now!' Poppy grinned. 'Come on—let's serve dinner, and then we can set up the supply room for the card game.'

Grace had been talking to a young soldier, but she joined them again, her ears clearly pricking up. 'Ohhh, I can't wait! Don over there told me he'd teach me how to play.'

'Hold on—you're moving the patients and setting up in the supply room?' April asked.

'Don't worry your pretty little head, April. We won't get caught, and if we do, I'll figure out a way to talk us out of it,' Poppy told her.

April didn't look convinced, but she went off to check on her patients, and Poppy went with Grace to start on serving dinner. They'd already checked most of their patients and given them their evening medication, but with so few men in the ward, they didn't really have a lot to do.

'She's buttoned up so tight sometimes, isn't she?' Grace said. 'Honestly, half the time I wonder if we're actually related.'

Poppy had heard it all before, and she knew that April was sometimes a little too serious, but she'd also seen firsthand how much her friend did for her little sister. They were so close in age, but what April lacked in letting her hair down, Grace made up for with her childishness sometimes.

'Don't be so hard on her—she's just trying to do her job well,' Poppy said.

Grace's eyebrows shot up. 'You're defending her now? After telling her to lighten up about the card game?'

Poppy bit her tongue, not sure how much to say. She didn't want to annoy Grace, but sometimes she wanted to shake her and tell her to be a little more grateful. 'You know I love to tease her, but Grace, sometimes she has to be your mother, and other times you wonder why she can't be reckless. She's single-handedly run your house for years, and yet you treat her like she's a total pain in the backside.'

She regretted the words the second they left her mouth, seeing the change in Grace's face as her jaw fell open and she stared back at her. 'Why don't you tell me what you really think,' Grace muttered. 'And she *is* a total pain in the backside, for your information.'

Poppy didn't answer; she just slung her arm around her friend's neck and gave her a squeeze. 'Sorry—it's just hard for me being in the middle sometimes. You know I love both of you, right?'

Grace stayed quiet as they went into the kitchen to see how the food was coming along, but Poppy knew she'd probably hurt her feelings. Sometimes she needed to know when to keep her big mouth shut.

'Dinner's almost ready!' the cook called, wiping sweat from her brow with the back of her arm. 'Can one of you girls figure out how to get the fan working again?'

Poppy went over and fiddled with it, flicking the switches and checking it was plugged in properly, but she didn't have any luck. It was stifling in the kitchen, making the humidity in the ward seem like nothing. She flicked it on and off a couple more times, but nothing happened, so she went over and fought with the window for a few seconds to at least let some fresh air in.

'Thanks, doll.'

She laughed. 'No problem, Cookie.'

Poppy went back out and started to fill the glasses of water up beside the patients' beds, saying hello and taking time to smile and pat the hand of each man. She didn't mind nursing—it was nice knowing she was helping, and she was good at making small talk with everyone on the ward.

'It's his fault!' came a yell.

'I'll knock him out for good this time!' came another voice, equally as loud and menacing as the first.

What was going on?

'Help over here, please!' someone else called.

She set down the water jug and hurried over to the entrance into their hospital, finding the corpsmen carrying two men on stretchers. It was obvious they were trying to keep them as far apart as possible, and the yelling continued as she waited for her orders.

'Football injuries?' she asked.

April appeared by her side then, and they exchanged glances as one of the men tried to launch out of his stretcher, blood streaming from his nose.

'These two idiots were spectators, but they've done a number on each other, and they're still going for it,' the driver said. 'We had to restrain one of them in the ambulance.'

Poppy fought the urge to roll her eyes at the injured men, and April took the lead, marching straight over to them. She looked on, not surprised in the least that her friend had stepped into her role so comfortably. She couldn't imagine April doing anything else; she was such a natural at looking after people, and she seemed to thrive on healing injuries and learning about medicine.

'You two want to come into our ward, then button those mouths,' April said, her voice loud and no-nonsense. 'We don't tolerate fighting, and if I have even a hint of that type of behavior in here, then you'll be out there tending to your own injuries. Do I make myself clear?'

There was mumbling from the stretchers, but both men quieted down after their little talking-to.

'Where did you learn to take command like that?' Poppy whispered as she approached one of the stretchers. 'You could have been an army general instead of a nurse!'

April raised her eyebrows, grinning at the compliment, and Poppy was about to introduce herself to her patient when her gaze landed on a familiar pair of dark-brown eyes.

'Teddy?' she gasped. *'Teddy!'*

He groaned and covered his face.

'Theodore Banks, what on earth are you doing *fighting* on the side-lines at a football game!' she demanded.

'Teddy?' April echoed beside her. 'It's *Teddy?*'

'Can you take me to another hospital?' he begged the driver. 'Please, anywhere but here!'

'You're not going anywhere,' Poppy muttered. 'Take him through. And don't even *think* of getting all hot under the collar in our ward.'

She marched after them, trading glances with April as she passed her. When he was in a bed, she glared at him and sat beside him, studying his face. 'You're going to have a black eye, you fool. You'll be lucky if it doesn't close over completely by morning.'

He groaned. 'You wouldn't understand.'

'How men can get so worked up over a game that they attack one another?' she asked, reaching for antiseptic cream and dabbing some on a cloth. 'Because you'd be right about that—I don't understand at all.'

'It was a bit more personal than that,' he said.

She hesitated, her hand hovering over his eye, before pressing the cloth gently to his skin. 'Personal like what?' she asked.

'Well, it started over the game. We disagreed about a call the referee made,' Teddy said, wincing as she pressed harder, 'and then that idiot over there claimed he'd have you in his bed by the end of the month.'

Poppy dropped the cloth, her cheeks burning. 'Why would he say that?'

Teddy's fingers danced against her wrist, and she swallowed, embarrassed as he stared into her eyes. 'He was just trying to get under my skin. You're one of the prettiest girls on the island, and the guys are always hassling me. But no one's stealing my girl from me, Pops. No one.'

She didn't move, unable to resist when he rose up on one elbow and cupped the back of her head. She should have pulled back, but instead she dipped lower and let him press his lips to hers, sighing into his mouth and wishing she had more willpower.

'You're a big idiot, Teddy, but I'm not taking up with any other man.'

He laughed and sat up, looking over at the other bed and making a face at the other guy.

'Teddy! You just did that so he'd see, didn't you?'

He gave her an innocent puppy-dog face, and she swatted at him, pushing him back down.

'Honestly!' She dabbed more antiseptic onto the cloth and pressed it hard to the skin beside his eye this time, taking pleasure in the short gasp that hissed from his lips. How dare he lure her in all sweet as pie, for the benefit of someone watching on! 'You deserve a black eye, Teddy; in fact you're lucky I haven't given you another one. Now let me look at the rest of you. What hurts?'

He held up his right hand, and she started to dab cream into the raw bits on his knuckles, wondering why he was brought in on a stretcher if he just had some superficial wounds to his upper body. But just as she was about to ask him, he bent and lifted his pant leg up, and she realized he was only wearing one boot.

'What happened here?' she asked. But as the words came out, she saw the beginnings of an angry purple bruise spreading around his ankle.

'I was winning the fight until the dirty bastard tripped me up. I went over pretty heavy on it.'

Poppy slapped at him again, this time for swearing, but she touched his ankle carefully, sitting beside the bed and inspecting every inch of his lower leg and foot as well.

'You'd better hope this is just a bad sprain,' she said. 'You're a fool, Teddy. Honestly, I have no idea what I see in you sometimes.'

But as his hands brushed her shoulder and stroked down her hair, she remembered exactly why she loved him so much. The man might be a rogue, but he was one hell of a sweet-talker, and the second his fingertips touched her skin, she melted. Always had, always would.

'I love you, baby,' he whispered.

She stood and folded her arms, trying to look cross with him. 'I love you too,' she whispered, before shaking her head and setting off to find the doctor. The last thing he needed was a broken or fractured ankle. She glanced at Don as she walked down the row of beds, waving to him as she passed.

The only bonus of having Teddy in her ward was that he'd be able to join them for poker night, and she loved the idea of snuggling up beside him and letting her man teach her how to bluff and deal cards with the boys.

—— ❧☙ ——

The next day, Poppy finished her shift and darted into the restroom to check her face, quickly powdering her nose and dabbing on some blush. She carefully applied her lipstick and patted her hair down, wishing she'd had time to go back to her quarters. Teddy was being released, and he had until nightfall to make it back to his base, which meant that for the next two hours, she had him all to herself.

She rushed back out to the ward, looking around but not seeing him. The bed he'd occupied was already made up with fresh sheets, and she couldn't see him standing waiting anywhere.

'Looking for lover boy?' April asked, touching her arm as she passed.

'Maybe.'

'He's just coming out of the kitchen,' her friend said, gesturing over her shoulder. 'I think he's trying to make it up to you.'

Poppy grinned. What on earth was that man of hers up to, and in the kitchen of all places? She hurried over to find him, waving at Don as she passed. He gave her a wink, and she gave him one right back, both keeping a secret about the fun poker night the evening before. He was one hell of a laugh, and she'd noticed him looking at Grace every time he'd dealt a hand. She made a mental note to try to set them up, smiling to herself as she imagined what a cute couple they'd make. A boyfriend was just what Grace needed to give her a confidence boost.

'There's my beautiful girl.'

Poppy stopped in her tracks, eyeing the bag Teddy was carrying and trying not to giggle at his bare feet. His ankle was bandaged for the sprain, and he was using a single crutch, but his grin was as broad as the sun, and he couldn't have been more handsome if he'd tried.

'What's in there?' she asked, planting her hands on her hips and trying to look cross with him. She'd well intended on staying mad with him for days, but every time he smiled at her, she seemed to melt.

'A picnic,' he said, as if it were the most logical thing in the world, to be walking out of a hospital kitchen with a picnic lunch in hand. 'It's my way of saying sorry.'

She shook her head, every last inch of resistance disappearing as she closed the distance between them and scooped her arms around his neck, pressing her lips to his.

'You might be a fool,' she whispered against his mouth. 'But you're *my* fool.'

It took half an hour for them to reach the beach, going slowly for Teddy, and she talked nonstop about their illicit card game the night before and peppered him with questions about the football game he'd been watching and what the other guys were like at his barracks. When they were finally there, she took off her shoes, rolled up her socks, and pushed them into her shoes. The sand was heavenly between her toes, soft and warm, and she lifted her face to the sky, loving the warmth, almost accustomed to the tropical weather on the island now.

'Thank God for the beach. I never thought you were going to stop talking.'

Poppy laughed, punching him in the arm and stealing the bag of food from him, which he'd insisted on carrying the entire way.

'Give me that; I'm starving,' she said, avoiding him when he leaned in and tried to steal a kiss.

'I could be sent off to war any day, Pops. Don't deny me a kiss.' He blinked at her, and she rolled her eyes, sitting down on the sand and looking in the bag.

'Don't give me that,' she said. 'There's no way we're joining this war. We'll be here for months and months, having the time of our lives, and then the war will be over, and we'll go back to our normal boring ones.'

She was surprised by the serious look on his face as he reached for her hand. 'Make no mistake: America will join this war, Poppy. There's no way we can stay out of it forever; it's only a matter of time.'

'But the other night, in the car on the way to the party, you said . . .'

He frowned. 'I know what I said—I didn't want to worry you all— but there's more going on. I have a feeling that we're going to be wading into the conflict faster than we think.'

She bit her tongue, wanting to tell him that she wasn't going to start worrying just because he had *a feeling*, but not wanting to ruin their afternoon.

'Poppy, some of the guys have been talking about how many of us might not make it if we end up in the thick of it.'

'Teddy, stop!' She didn't want to be having this kind of conversation with him.

'No, listen to me, Poppy. I just want you to know that if something did happen to me, if I didn't come back, I'd want you to be happy. I couldn't stand the thought of you wasting years mourning for me when you could meet someone else and have a wonderful life.'

She bit her lip, trying not to cry. 'Teddy, please,' she whispered.

'I won't say it again, but I just want you to know. Okay?'

'Okay,' she repeated, clearing her throat. 'But come on—let's not waste time talking about the war. What did the cook rustle up for you?'

Teddy's devilish grin was firmly back in place as he reached into the bag and pulled out sandwiches, boiled eggs, and even a couple of slices of cheese.

'She seems to like you,' he said, passing her a sandwich. 'The moment I told her who I was taking out for a late lunch, she gave me a wink and set to work.'

Poppy smiled to herself. Giving Cookie the time of day instead of ignoring her like half the other nurses did had certainly paid off.

'Come here,' Teddy said, moving the bag out of the way and opening his arm up so Poppy could scoot over and snuggle up to him.

She sat there, her stomach rumbling as she devoured the sandwich and then happily reached for the cheese, tucked against her man and staring out at the water. Watching the ocean twinkle had become addictive, her favorite thing to do whenever she wasn't working. Her gaze soon landed on a ship anchored not too far out, and she wondered if that was where Eva was stationed.

'What are you thinking about?' Teddy asked, his lips brushing against her hair.

'Another nurse we met,' she said. 'She's a lot of fun, and she's stationed out there on the *Solace*.'

His fingers curled around her shoulder, and she pressed herself even closer to him.

'They've got it good out there,' he said. 'Some of the navy boys have said the nurses have nothing to do, and they often sunbathe on deck with a whole lot of leg on show!'

She pulled back and gave him what she hoped was a withering look. 'They've been spying on them?'

'It's hardly spying if they're doing it in full view, is it?'

Poppy sighed. 'Honestly, you boys are terrible. And those girls aren't sitting around with nothing to do, I'll have you know. Eva said she's been assigned to the ENT ward—that's *ear, nose, and throat*, Teddy—and she's often having to attend to things in there.'

'Well, don't you sound like a real little nurse now,' he teased, grinning at her.

'I'll have you know that I *am* a real nurse, Theodore.'

'Well then, Nurse, can you tend to me? I seem to have something hurting my lips. I think you need to investigate.'

She giggled and decided to play along, pretending to be worried and gasping. 'Oh, sugar, what could that be? Let me see; does this hurt?' she asked, gently pressing her lips to his.

He kissed her back, his mouth barely moving. 'I don't think you have the right spot. Can you try again?'

She moved to her knees and sat in front of him, leaning closer as his hands found her back, stroking down the length of it as she kissed him again. 'This?' she asked.

Teddy chuckled. 'Maybe I need to try them out myself,' he muttered, trailing kisses down her neck and making her heart beat so fast she was certain he'd hear it pounding.

'Mmmm,' she murmured. 'I think you should keep doing that. Nurse's orders.'

Teddy's kisses were heavenly, every touch making her want him all the more. Only weeks earlier, she'd never been alone with him, but here, they had all the freedom in the world. No mother to scold her, no father to warn Teddy about bringing her home late and keeping his hands off her, and no rules other than to complete her shifts and turn up on time.

She let Teddy sweep her into his arms and lay her down on the sand, his hands soft and his lips even softer. Hawaii was heaven, and Teddy being here with her was the icing on the cake.

CHAPTER FOUR

APRIL

April walked through the ward with Grace a few days later, listening to her run through the various patients she'd had come in during the night. They'd had their first separate shift, and April was surprised by how confident her little sister sounded as she talked about her patients, as if she'd known the men for weeks instead of days.

'You're really liking this, aren't you?' she asked.

'I suppose I am,' Grace said, shrugging as if it were no big deal. 'I haven't had to deal with anything gory yet, other than vomit and some broken bones, and they're nice men. I like talking with them while I work.'

April nodded and took the charts from her, scanning the pages before looking back up at her sister. She'd hardly had to do more than take temperatures, give injections, and check bandages, so she wasn't certain that Grace actually knew what she was in for if they did end up nursing soldiers injured in combat, but it was nice to see her so happy and finding her feet. She just needed to remind herself to stop checking up on her; Grace could come to her if she needed anything. 'Any plans for the day?' she asked.

'Sleep,' Grace muttered. 'I'm definitely not made for doing night shifts!'

'Is Poppy back on today?' she asked.

'Yes, she started just before I saw you. She was still full of talk about her romantic afternoon with Teddy, telling me how they kissed until it was almost dark.'

April touched her arm, wanting her to know that she understood. She knew how hard it was on Grace, because she'd been there that night they'd met Teddy. It had been the first time she'd ever seen her sister's eyes grow wide with interest over a man and her cheeks flush red, and she'd known in that moment that she was desperate for Teddy to ask her to dance. And she'd also seen the intense disappointment when Teddy had taken Poppy by the hand and felt her pain when they'd stayed hand in hand until the very last dance of the night. But Poppy was their best friend, and she knew Grace would never step on Poppy's toes or wish her friend's romance to fall apart, no matter how much it hurt her.

'You all right?' April asked.

Grace nodded. 'Of course. I'm just tired. See you after your shift.'

April watched her go and then went to do her own rounds and become more familiar with the new patients who'd come in. There had been some fevers over the past twelve hours, as well as bouts of vomiting from soldiers, and she wanted to make sure they were well hydrated and comfortable.

'Nurse!'

She turned and came face-to-face with a doctor she'd never seen before. His eyes were so dark they were almost black, the same shade as his thick mop of hair, and his smile was bright when he realized he'd caught her attention. She watched as he placed a pencil in the top pocket of his white coat.

'Can I help you?' she asked.

'Yes, I need assistance in surgery, and my usual nurse has already finished her shift,' he said, his eyes seeming to study her face, making her wonder what he was thinking. 'Have you assisted a surgeon before?'

April wanted to say yes, because she was desperate to gain more hands-on experience, but she couldn't lie. 'Unfortunately I haven't, but I'm a quick study, and I would love the opportunity to assist.'

He frowned and turned slightly, looking around the ward and then behind him back down the corridor. Was he looking for another nurse that he recognized? She said a silent prayer, fingers crossed behind her back, that he would take her with him.

'Fine, you'll do,' he said, gesturing for her to follow him. 'Dr. Raymond Grey.'

She grinned and hurried along beside him. 'April Bellamy.'

He started to give her a rundown on the patient, and she couldn't believe her luck. They'd been stationed at Pearl Harbor for less than two weeks, and already she was going to be in surgery!

'The patient broke his leg in a training injury, and the bone has completely penetrated the skin,' he explained. 'I trust you have a strong stomach, Miss Bellamy, because I don't tolerate fainting in my operating room.'

She took a deep breath. 'Please, call me April, and for the record, there is very little that would cause me to faint, sir. I have the strongest stomach of all the girls I know.'

'We'll see,' he said, holding the door open for her and letting her pass through first. 'Scrub those hands clean, and meet me in there. And I like a quiet room when I'm working, so try to listen and anticipate what I need without interrupting me.'

She nodded and watched him walk away, eyes tracking him until he disappeared from view. This might be her one chance to impress a surgeon, and she intended on making the most of it; all she had to do was stay quiet and follow his instructions, and she might just end up on more of his surgeries.

She'd never had the nerve to admit it to anyone other than her sister, but if she ever wanted to be a doctor herself one day, she needed all the experience she could get her hands on. From the day she'd seen her mother die, she'd felt so passionately about healing, about being the one with the power to save others from pain.

A thrill of excitement shuddered through her as she washed her hands, carefully scrubbing beneath her short nails. She wasn't sure if it was the surgery or the doctor she was about to assist that had her all tied in knots, but she suddenly felt as if she were finally taking a step closer to her dream.

April dried her hands and followed after Dr. Grey, hesitating at the door before being waved in by him. She noticed there was no one else other than the anesthetist attending, and she took a deep breath as she surveyed the instruments all laid out on a table.

'Come in, April. Let's test that stomach of yours, shall we?'

She wished she hadn't commented on her extraordinarily strong stomach. What if she wasn't as capable as she liked to think she was?

'Yes, of course,' she said, not letting her nervousness show.

April moved forward as the sheet was lifted to expose the patient's leg. He was already asleep, the anesthetist sitting to one side, and she stared at the flesh ripped apart by the bone that protruded through. She frowned at the sharp edge and wondered how on earth it could be successfully repaired, and as she studied it, she managed to forget all about how horrific it was.

'Is it always possible to splint or repair breaks like this?' she asked. 'It looks so mangled.'

Dr. Grey laughed, and the anesthetist chuckled. She looked up, perplexed and wondering what they were finding so amusing.

'I'm sorry—was that an amateur question?' she asked.

'Not at all,' Dr. Grey said, beckoning for her to stand closer. 'We just had a bet going that you'd either run or faint within, what, twenty seconds of me lifting the sheet?'

The other man nodded. 'My bet was ten.'

She laughed along with them. 'Are new nurses usually so easy to unsettle?'

'You'd be surprised. Scalpel, please, Nurse.'

She stood to his side, passing him the instrument and keeping her eyes trained on his every movement. Before long she settled into an easy rhythm of passing what was needed, leaning over to watch, and even touching the bone to help hold it in place.

'Tell me, what anesthetic do you prefer for surgeries like this?' she asked.

'Well, we prefer ether usually, because of the newly improved techniques with oxygen and vaporizers, but to tell you the truth, if we end up in war, we'll be using intravenous barbiturates, because it's cheap and we don't have to worry about flammability.'

She nodded, watching as Dr. Grey finished the final stitch. He'd done a tidy job, and she wished she'd had the opportunity to try a few stitches of her own under his guidance. Perhaps she could suggest it in the future, under the guise of giving Dr. Grey a well-deserved rest after surgery.

'Now we have to cast him,' Dr. Grey said. 'The bone won't heal unless we can ensure absolute immobility.'

She stood back and waited for instructions as he stretched and yawned, moving his head from side to side as if he had a sore neck.

'Where is it you're from, April?' he asked.

'Oh, I'm from Oregon,' she said. 'So this is a real change in scenery for me, being posted here.'

'I absolutely agree. It's a lovely change.' She noticed his frown as he touched the patient's leg. 'We'll need to cast the entire leg as well as the foot. Have you done this before?'

She shook her head. 'No, sir.'

'You'll learn. So do you have someone waiting for you back in Oregon? A fiancé? Or just a family wishing for your safe return?'

She knew her cheeks had flushed red, but she kept her attention on the plaster cast being prepared, refusing to acknowledge her embarrassment and hoping he didn't notice it either.

'Just my father, actually,' she said. 'My sister is also here nursing, and we lost our mother some years ago.'

'I'm sorry to hear that, but it explains why you're so capable. I'll put money on it that you took over her role in the home—am I right? It's why nothing rattles you, because you've had to develop strong nerves.'

She met his gaze, his dark eyes full of warmth and intelligence as she basked in his praise. She was surprised by how perceptive he was. 'You're right. It's made me get on with things, I suppose. There's never been enough time for me to worry about something that I can just do my best to deal with.'

'What do you say you join my service?' he asked. 'I could do with a capable nurse at my side, especially one who's as quick a study as you.'

She couldn't stop the beaming smile that hit her lips. 'I would like that.'

Dr. Grey asked her to pass him something again, and she quickly fell back into place beside him, listening carefully to what he needed from her. She smiled to herself as she helped with the cast. If only she were brave enough to tell him that one day, she hoped to be a doctor every inch as capable as he was.

—— ❧⟶❧ ——

'How was your shift?' Grace asked, stealing one of April's hairpins before she could stop her. It was Saturday night, and they were all off to a dance at the Hickam Field officers' club, racing to get ready before they had to meet Eva.

She had two pins pressed between her teeth as she carefully did her own do, and Grace was now jostling for space in the tiny mirror.

'Move,' she muttered, with her teeth still clenched. 'You've had hours to get ready!'

'I was napping,' her sister said. 'Any interesting patients? I'm hoping the vomiting stops by tomorrow; I can't stand cleaning out any more buckets.'

April finished her hair and moved back to pull out her compact and do her cheeks and lipstick from the comfort of her bed. It would be easier sitting there than vying with her mirror-hog sister.

'I actually assisted in surgery with Dr. Grey,' she replied. 'No sick buckets for me, just a juicy big broken bone and plenty of blood spurting everywhere.' It was an exaggeration, but she knew it would stop Grace in her tracks.

'Ugh, really? How awful.'

'It was amazing, actually. I'm going to stay on his service, so I'm hoping that there are a few more baseball and football injuries.' The one today had been horrific for the poor young man involved, and she hated that he'd injured himself so badly in a training drill, but she couldn't forget the thrill of the surgery. The feel of the instruments in her hands, the patient lying there, watching the expert push and pull of the needle as Dr. Grey had stitched the flesh back together; she'd loved every second of it.

'Did you say you helped in surgery today?' Poppy asked, dressed to the nines with her hair perfectly curled.

April smiled as she sat on the bed beside her. 'Yes. It was incredible.'

'Wasn't the surgeon on today Dr. Dark Eyes? All the nurses were talking about him yesterday, but I haven't seen him yet.'

She could feel Grace and Poppy watching her, waiting for her reaction. 'I suppose he does have nice dark eyes,' she said carefully. 'And he cuts a handsome figure in his doctor's coat with those broad shoulders. Very easy on the eye.'

'Ohhhh, she likes him! Look at her face!' Poppy teased.

April refused to crack a smile until Grace planted her hands on her hips and glared at her, and then it was impossible to keep a straight face.

'April Bellamy, you've fallen for a doctor and kept it from me!' she exclaimed. 'We're supposed to tell each other everything!'

Why had she even told them about her day? She should have known better.

'Look, he was a very capable surgeon,' she said. 'That's all.'

'A very capable surgeon with lovely dark eyes?' Grace asked, before trading grins with Poppy.

'You two do know I can see you, right?' she huffed, collecting her purse from the bed and hooking it over her arm. 'And for the last time, there is *nothing* going on between me and the doctor!'

'Nothing *yet*,' Grace teased.

'Grace!'

Poppy leaped up and took her arm, tucked in tight as if they were coconspirators while Grace finished getting ready.

'Come on—you can tell me. Is he just gorgeous? I want to know if the rumors are true.'

April bit her bottom lip, trying not to giggle. 'He's divine looking, if you must know. His hair is as dark as his eyes, his skin is all golden, and he's incredible with his hands. So steady in the operating theater.'

As she opened her mouth again, Poppy burst out laughing, screeching to Grace across the room.

'He has the steadiest hands around, Grace! It must be love,' she teased.

April didn't even dignify Poppy's comment with a response. Instead she walked straight from the room, her head held high, not about to let their girlish teasing get under her skin. What was it with those two sometimes? Sometimes they were great company, and other times they were absolute harebrains, like two lovesick, silly schoolgirls.

She smiled to herself as she walked, though, thinking about Dr. Grey. He *was* handsome, and she did like him, but that had nothing to do with anything. What was important was learning from him and being the best assistant she could be during surgery. If he happened to mentor her *and* ask her out on a date, then so be it.

The other two came galloping as loudly as a pair of horses behind her, and she gave them her best withering look.

'Sorry, April,' Poppy said. 'We only tease you because you're so easy to ruffle.'

She supposed she was, but it wasn't exactly the best excuse, and she was ready to change the subject. 'So who's all going tonight?'

Grace gave her a look that she thought might be her saying she was sorry, but she couldn't tell. Even after all these years, her sister wasn't the easiest to read. They were close, and she loved her, but sometimes she was sick and tired of being the older one, the one with the weight of the world on her shoulders. It would be nice for Grace to look after her once in a while, to cook for her or care for her if she was unwell, to worry about their father instead of leaving it all up to her. Or to stick up for her instead of teasing. But when her little sister reached for her hand and squeezed it, she couldn't help but wrap her fingers around Grace's. It didn't matter what she wished for; they were blood, and she'd simply drawn the short straw by being born first.

'Teddy can't come, but it doesn't matter. It'll be nice to just be with you girls, and half the nurses at our hospital are coming.'

April glanced at Grace, wondering if she was pleased or disappointed that Teddy wasn't with them.

'Could you ever have imagined us going out without having to tell anyone where we're off to?' Grace asked as they walked out of the building and crossed the grass. It was slightly crunchy underfoot, not as soft as her yard at home, and peppered with palm trees around the perimeter. 'It's so strange, just being like this, as if we're adults with no one to answer to.'

'Grace, we *are* adults.' April had thought about it often, how different they were treated here, the freedom they had. Although for her, it wasn't as significant, because she'd been the one doing the watching, always careful to know where Grace was and how late she'd be, who was with her, and what was happening. Their father was a lovely, kind man, but he had no idea about raising daughters and how to pick up all the parenting things their mother had done.

'I suppose you're right. Plenty of our friends are already married, aren't they?'

'Yes, but they've gone from their daddies' homes to their husbands',' Poppy said. 'We're as free as a bird here.'

'Teddy might think otherwise.' April smirked.

'Teddy can keep his thoughts to himself,' Poppy said defiantly. 'I love the man, but I'm also loving this. Thank God he didn't ask me to marry him before we left! Imagine if I'd been left behind, with a ring on my finger and nothing to do, while you two were gallivanting over here!'

They all laughed, but April could see that Grace was only going through the motions.

'Have you talked about marriage?' Grace asked. 'With Teddy. I mean, do you think you'll get engaged soon?'

Poppy waved her hand in the air like it was no big deal. 'I suppose so. I mean, not right now, but he's a gorgeous man, and I think . . .'

'Of course you'll get married one day,' April interrupted, beaming at her friend. She didn't want this conversation to go on any longer; Grace didn't need to hear the rest and wish she were the one in Poppy's shoes. 'You make a very handsome couple. Now where was Eva meeting us?'

Just then a woman came into sight, running, her skirt caught up in one hand, her shoes in the other.

'Well, it looks like she wasn't waiting for us,' Grace said, waving at their new friend.

'Sorry! Have you been here long?' Eva was breathless as she slowed, bending forward and laughing. 'I'm so unfit! I haven't ever run that far!'

'We've been here forever,' Grace said, before grinning at Eva's shocked expression. 'Honestly, we haven't—we've just walked out. April just recently finished her shift, and we've been catching up on some sleep.'

'Thank goodness,' Eva said, straightening. 'I went to see Charlie, and we had almost an hour together just outside his base. Then I caught a ride here, but I had to run the last bit down the beach.'

They fell into step, and April looked down the line at the others, admiring how pretty her friends and sister looked. Grace was wearing her favorite summer frock, with cute puff sleeves and a V-neck, covered in flowers and showing off her tiny waist. Poppy was wearing a darker color and a shorter dress, and she had a pretty flower lei around her neck like the ones they'd received the day they'd arrived. Eva was as pretty as a picture, even as she fanned at her face, her skin damp from hurrying down to them, her dark-red hair striking, pinned off her face and falling like a thick curtain down her back and complementing her creamy skin to perfection. April glanced down at her own outfit, the cream dress she'd bought especially to bring away with her. It was snug at the waist, hitting her at midcalf, and she felt feminine and pretty wearing it. She'd left her hair out tonight, curling it in soft waves, and part of her wished that Dr. Grey could see her.

'So tell us, was it nice to see your Charlie?' April asked, realizing no one had even asked her.

'Yes.' Eva didn't hesitate. 'He was very sweet, all apologetic about ever wanting to leave and go join the Eagles in Britain. I think he finally realized how much I needed him, and he promised not to leave me.'

'So he finally came to his senses then about how silly it was?' Poppy asked. 'Sometimes we have to leave them to simmer for a bit, but they always come around eventually. I'm pleased he finally realized how foolish it would be to go all vigilante like that.'

Eva was silent, and April wondered if Poppy and Grace had even noticed how uncomfortable she suddenly looked.

'Is that what you meant, though, Eva?' April asked gently. 'Does he still want to go?'

She nodded, and even in the fading light April could see that her eyes had filled with tears.

'He didn't say, but I know he still wishes he was there. He wouldn't just change his mind like that.'

April waited, not wanting to push. She felt like she'd only scratched the surface of something much deeper. 'It's nice he doesn't want to leave you.'

'It's kind of complicated. My father, well, he's difficult,' Eva said, her voice lower now as if she didn't want the others to hear. 'And Charlie knows what it'll be like for me—if he goes and can't come back, I mean. I'm just so pleased he's not going to keep pushing for it.'

April put her arm around Eva's shoulders. 'You're afraid of going home to your father?'

Eva nodded, but this time the tears fell rapidly down her cheeks before she could blink them away. 'He's not exactly the most pleasant of men, the complete opposite of Charlie. I don't know what I'd do if I lost him.'

April nodded. She understood. Life hadn't been easy for her when she'd lost her mother, but she didn't know what it was to be scared of another human being, and she could tell from the fear on Eva's face that she was very much afraid. She'd seemed so capable and strong, and from Grace's recollections Eva had barked at the soldier who'd gotten all frisky with her sister, but this was a different, very real side to her too.

'Well, at least he can't trouble you here, right? For as long as we're hidden away in paradise here, you've got nothing to worry about.'

Eva brushed her cheeks, and the look of insecurity was gone, her smile fixed again, business as usual.

'What are you two whispering about?' Grace asked, moving closer.

'Absolutely nothing,' April said, linking arms with Eva.

'You were telling her about that gorgeous doctor, weren't you!'

April just laughed. If she had to take the fall and pretend that was what they'd been talking about, then so be it. Eva had opened up to her, and she wasn't the type of person to ever betray anybody's trust.

'Is it far to walk?' Poppy asked.

'About another fifteen minutes or so,' Eva said. 'I heard the party in full swing when I came past before.'

'At least it's safe walking here; we don't have to worry about anything sinister.'

'Yes, Mother,' Grace said. 'No need to worry.'

April bit her tongue. It was just a silly comment, but Grace made them too often for her liking. Perhaps it was about time she stepped back and let her sister find her own way in the world, make her own mistakes and look after herself. Maybe then she'd appreciate her more.

Less than half an hour later, they were standing inside the officers' club, and April couldn't believe how many people could pack into such a small space. Music was blaring from a record player in the corner, and couples were spilling outside onto the patio, in each other's arms or spinning around, dancing like their lives depended upon it. It had the same jovial, fun feeling as the house party they'd been to on their first night, but for some reason she wasn't in the same mood as at the first one.

She usually loved being out, and she was always one of the last to leave, but tonight she had a headache, and her feet were tired from standing all day on her shift. She should have taken a short nap before coming out, but then she'd have missed dinner.

'Want to go outside for a bit?' Eva appeared at her side, holding out a cup of punch. April took it and held it up, clinking it softly to Eva's.

'Cheers,' she said, taking a sip. 'And yes to going outside.'

Grace spotted them and followed, with Poppy close behind her. Poppy usually disappeared the moment they went out, straight into Teddy's arms, but without her man here tonight she was spending the evening with them, like old times.

'Where are you two grandmas off to?' asked Poppy. 'Come inside and dance!'

'We're just going to take a minute outside,' April told her, raising her voice to be heard over the noise.

They navigated past drunken soldiers doing their best to stay upright, and April coughed as she had to squeeze past a couple getting far too frisky by the steps, but within minutes they were back on the beach. Something about the ocean breeze calmed her, and she wished she'd chosen to just sit outside all evening, thinking about her day, relaxing instead of trying to talk over the loud music and shaking her head when she was asked to dance.

'You're not in the mood tonight?' Eva asked as they sat in the sand.

'Sorry—is it that obvious? I didn't mean to be glum.' She sipped her drink, wondering how much alcohol had been poured in. 'I'm just tired, I suppose.'

'You're not glum; you just look lost in thought—that's all.'

They sat in a semicircle, their backs to the house, and the music drifted out on the wind to them, as did the laughter and revelry from inside. She hadn't expected Grace and Poppy to join them, but they'd followed them out and now seemed happy to sit for a moment and chat too.

'Where do you think we'll all be in five years' time?' asked Eva. 'Will we be sick to death of Hawaii and still waiting for war, or will we be back home living our normal lives?'

'You'll be married to your Charlie with a baby on the way.' Poppy laughed. 'And I'll be Mrs. Teddy Banks.'

'I don't think we'd ever be sick of Hawaii,' Grace said. 'I think I could live here forever, actually, even without you all being here. The island life suits me.'

April scoffed. 'Who would look after you here? You'd be miserable if we were all gone.'

'I'd cope just fine,' Grace muttered. 'I don't need you telling me what to do at every turn, April.'

She sucked in a big breath, trying not to take the bait but failing. 'Okay,' she said simply. 'Okay, Grace.'

'Okay what? You won't tell me what to do all the time now? Because I know you think I can't do anything on my own.'

April nodded, knowing the other two were silently listening. 'I'm not your mother, and we're both all grown up now, so I'm well aware you can take care of yourself if you want to. I promise I'll keep my mouth shut and let you live your life.' *Just don't come crying to me over everything; don't expect me to pick up all the pieces and drop everything when something goes wrong.*

'Well, that's decided, then,' Grace replied, sounding baffled.

April sipped her drink and noticed that Grace did the same, shooting her a confused look over the top of her cup. But April ignored it and just smiled. It was dark across the sand, the light filtering from the house casting shadows around them and making it just possible to see.

She wanted to tell Grace that all she'd ever wanted was for someone to take care of *her*, to make sure *she* was all right, to ask her what *she* wanted, but she didn't. It wasn't worth it. She'd learned long ago to accept the hand life had dealt her and to not complain, and she wasn't about to start moaning now. She was used to having these thoughts, so angry sometimes she felt like she was screaming out in her own mind, but she was good at pushing them away and putting them in their little box, never to be shared.

'Back to this five-year plan,' she said, reigniting the conversation since she and Grace had effectively muted it by their bickering. 'How many children do you think you and Teddy will have?'

She heard Grace splutter, choking on her drink, but she didn't look across at her. If Grace wanted to be treated like a grown-up, then she was going to have to deal with Poppy and Teddy.

'I think three—that'd be the perfect number. And a big dog that the children can climb all over.'

They all laughed, although she noticed Grace looked uncomfortable and felt bad for steering the conversation back toward Teddy.

'What about you, April?' Eva asked. 'Are you hoping to meet someone and have children?'

She thought about her answer for a moment, not brave enough to admit that she hoped to be studying to be a doctor within a few years' time. 'I'd really like to keep nursing, to work in a hospital back home, until I'm ready to be a mother.' The truth was she thought more about her career aspirations than motherhood, which she wasn't about to admit to right now.

'Good for you,' Eva said. 'I love nursing, so I'll probably do the same. Charlie and I are in no hurry to have children, not yet anyway.'

They sat, the breeze warm, the ocean's gentle roar almost drowned out by the music drifting from the house. April tipped her head back and gazed up at the bright stars, wondering where she'd be in a year or even a decade. *Would* she have children? Would she ever hear someone call her Doctor Bellamy instead of simply shouting 'Nurse'? The fire inside of her to go to medical school, to fight for her right to join the medical profession, had progressed from a slow simmer to a boil under the surface now, and she only wished she had the nerve to discuss it with someone other than Grace. *If you're up there, Mom, keep us safe. I need you more than I've ever needed you.*

When she sat back up again, Grace was watching her. And she wondered if her sister was thinking about their mom too.

'Did you girls hear that they're looking for nurses to transfer to the maternity ward?' Poppy asked. 'It would be nice delivering babies, don't you think?'

'I heard one of the nurses laughing, saying how lucky we were, being on a holiday-style tour of duty at the taxpayers' expense,' said Grace. 'Honestly, how lucky *are* we? Imagine if we get to vacation here for *two years*. Delivering babies would be fine if it means we get to stay!'

'It's a fun-in-the-sun vacation like no other,' added Eva with a laugh. 'It honestly doesn't get any better than this, and I've been here much longer than you all have. It's paradise every day.'

April stayed quiet, happy to listen to their chatter as she continued to stargaze. It *was* a vacation like no other, but she had this feeling, a whisper against the back of her neck that made the tiny hairs stand on end, that it was all too good to be true.

'Do you want to go swimming tomorrow? I heard that the turtles are incredible, and the snorkeling is the best in the world,' Poppy said. 'You wear this big mask thing that covers your eyes and your nose, and you breathe through a tube. It looks ridiculous, but it's supposed to be amazing.'

'Yes!' Grace enthused. 'Does everyone have Sunday afternoon off?'

'April?' Eva asked.

April looked at her friends, smiling, wondering how long it had taken them to realize she was a million miles away. 'Sounds great. Count me in.'

She was mildly terrified of the ocean, but she wasn't about to say no to snorkeling in such beautiful water. She only wished she could ignore her instincts and just enjoy being posted to paradise, instead of constantly waiting for the other shoe to drop.

'Come on—let's go dance! There's too many gorgeous men in there for you all to be sitting out here,' Poppy announced, leaping to her feet and holding out a hand to first Grace, then April. April turned and offered her hand to Eva, and they all followed Poppy inside. The music changed and April smiled, happily accepting a young officer's hand when he offered it the moment she walked inside.

Poppy was right: it was too good a night to be sitting outside. She happily twirled, seeing Grace dancing nearby. What was it their mother had always said? April smiled as the words filled her head. *Always make hay while the sun is shining, darling.*

'Another dance?' the officer asked when a new song started.

She smiled and clasped his hand. 'Absolutely.'

CHAPTER FIVE

GRACE

Grace stretched and slowly opened her eyes, wishing she could stay snuggled beneath the covers for longer. She smiled to herself as she remembered the night before, dancing and singing until late. Eva had had to leave earlier to get back to her boat, but the rest of them had stayed until the officers' club was closed, then strolled back to their barracks in the dark with only the moon to light the way. April had gotten on her nerves to start with, but in the end they'd all had fun, and she couldn't wait to go snorkeling and see the giant turtles everyone was talking about.

'Do you hear that?'

Grace sat up and glanced across at her sister. Her bed was one over from hers, and she noticed that the bed in between, Poppy's bed, was already empty. In typical Poppy fashion, she'd left it crumpled, which meant either they'd have to make it for her, or she'd be in big trouble if there was an inspection.

'It's like a rumble.'

Grace listened, wondering if she was imagining it, but April was right. There was a distinct drone, a rumble or vibration, that appeared to be coming closer. Her sister had driven her mad the night before, knowing exactly how to rile her by acting as if she was always the selfish, immature one of the two of them, but staring at April's bright-blue eyes, open wide in worry, Grace couldn't hold the grudge for long.

'Quickly, let's get dressed and go see,' Grace said. She jumped out of bed, certain the noise was getting louder. She hastily dressed and noticed some of the other girls were waking too.

The clock on the wall said 7:52 a.m., but she knew why so many of the others were still tucked beneath their covers. Only those with a shift would have risen early, which was why it was so unusual that Poppy was out of bed so early on a Sunday.

April grabbed her hand when the hum of noise became more of a roar, and they both ran for the door.

'Have you seen Poppy?' April asked as they passed another nurse.

'Out there,' the nurse said. 'There's been a little puppy tearing around on the grass, and Poppy's decided to save it.'

Grace grinned. Typical. Poppy loved animals, which meant there was no way she'd let a stray puppy run loose without taking care of it.

'Did you hear that noise, though?' Grace asked.

'Probably just a training exercise,' the other nurse said as she passed.

'They don't ever fly near the hospital,' April muttered. 'We've been here at Tripler for weeks, and when have you ever even noticed that we're close to an airfield?'

Grace shrugged, thinking that April had probably gotten her all worried for nothing. Just because they weren't used to hearing training exercises overhead didn't mean they weren't ever going to do them. They were at a military base, after all.

They walked outside, the bright sunshine making Grace squint. There was Poppy. In her pretty yellow dress, chasing after a scruffy-looking pup that looked to be enjoying the game much more than her friend was. She grinned and closed one eye completely, raising her hand

and looking up, the noise suddenly filling her ears. She opened her mouth, turning to look back the other way, toward the mountain pass between Honolulu and Schofield Barracks, and she grabbed for April's hand just as her sister let out an ear-piercing scream.

Grace's heart started to pound as chills ran through her body, like an electric current hitting her spine and traveling all the way to her toes. She was frozen as she watched in horror, as a plane with a huge red circle came toward her, the face of the pilot so close that she could make out every feature of his face. His eyes met hers, a smile creasing his lips as she stared, as she studied his face and wondered who on earth would be flying so low. He waved, and she slowly raised her hand to wave back. As she looked away, she saw another plane, identical to the first, coming up behind him—she could hear them talking on their radios, they were so close—and then she spun around as she realized that this was no training exercise.

'No!' Grace's scream cut through the air, echoing sharply against the drone of aircraft overhead.

'Grace, stop!' April called, her hand slipping from Grace's wrist. '*Grace!*'

The planes were deafening, the roar so low and loud that when Grace looked up, she could see the second pilot's unfamiliar face, could see him smile at her, too, before he unleashed a torrent of bullets to rain down around them. They were under attack!

'Grace!' her sister called again.

But Grace ignored her, her eyes locked on Poppy, so close but so far away, bending down toward the frightened-looking puppy. 'Run!' she screamed to her friend. 'Poppy, *run!*'

Poppy stood, her eyes filled with horror as she looked up at Grace, her mouth open as if she were about to call back.

Grace started running, desperate to get to Poppy, to do something, *anything*, to save her. What was happening? Who was shooting at them? Why wouldn't Poppy move?

Seconds felt like days as she sprinted, as she watched Poppy's mouth open and then shut, before her friend's body contorted as a bullet hit her and sent her flying backward.

Strong arms circled Grace from behind as her scream caught in her throat, holding her back, forcing her to stop.

'Let me go!' she yelled, gasping as she watched more people fall across the field, as the relentless drone continued, ammunition raining from the sky like a ferocious storm lashing the land. 'We need to get to her!'

'No.' The word was whispered, but it was still a command. Teddy had hold of her, Teddy was dragging her back, and no matter how much she clawed at him or struggled, he wasn't letting her go.

Pain shuddered through her body as tears flooded her cheeks and she gasped out Poppy's name. They couldn't just leave her there! They needed to save her, to check her injuries, to see if she was still . . . Grace swallowed. *Alive or not.*

As Teddy's grip around her waist softened, she turned in his arms, looking up at the pain echoed in his own face, his cheeks as wet as hers.

'Who would do this to us?' she cried.

Teddy gently wiped a thumb across her cheek before pulling her in close.

'The Japanese,' he whispered. 'That's who.'

But why?

Grace froze as the plane circled back, the noise vibrating through every inch of her as Teddy scooped her up and started to run with her in his arms. But it wasn't taking aim at them this time—it was firing at the American flag waving beside the hospital—and it didn't stop until it was torn to shreds.

Her body felt numb as Teddy stumbled, as she wept into his chest, her cries muffled by the constant drone of aircraft, the noise that sent waves of terror vibrating through her, cringing as she braced for them to be gunned down. When Teddy stopped running and set her down, she clung to him, her nails digging into his shirt as her legs shook so hard she wondered if she'd even be able to walk on her own. And then she remembered his injury, his ankle that was probably still bandaged. Was that why he'd been here this morning, or had he sneaked down to see Poppy?

Poppy. They needed to get to Poppy!

'We can't leave her,' Grace mumbled, her teeth chattering as if she were frozen cold, arms wrapped tight around herself. 'Have to go back. Have to get her.'

Sirens wailed, and people yelled; the noise was like a circus, overwhelming and painful all at once. And then she looked up at Teddy and saw tears streaming down his cheeks, streaming into his mouth as he tried to speak, and she knew that he wanted to get back to her as badly as she did.

'We can't,' he croaked. 'She's gone, Grace. I saw it with my own eyes.'

April's hand, familiar and warm, covered her arm then. She looked around, eyes wide, gulping in air as fast as she could, convinced she wasn't getting enough oxygen into her lungs. Grace clenched her teeth to stop them from chattering.

'We need to help,' April said as a man was rushed past them, one of his legs dangling from the knee, blood spurting everywhere.

Teddy, his hand trembling against Grace's shoulder, stared straight into her eyes. 'If she's alive, I'll get her. I promise,' he said, before letting go and running back toward the field, back toward the relentless drone, the loud vibrations of enemy aircraft making the walls of Tripler General shake as if a violent earthquake had struck.

'We need to go. Now,' April said. Grace could hear her, and she could see her mouth moving, but she couldn't seem to answer.

'Grace!' April yelled.

Her sister grabbed hold of her hand and dragged her, and she stumbled forward, trying not to fall, her jaw hanging open as another man was rushed past them, as sirens wailed louder nearby, as she stared at a trail of blood that one nurse slipped on right in front of her. It was like red sauce smeared across the ground, leaving a gruesome trail.

Grace yanked her hand free and doubled over as nausea took hold, vomiting all over the floor, the yellow bile mixing with the blood as she tried not to inhale, terrified of breathing in the acrid smell.

'Grace!'

She ran then, trying to avoid the blood, trying not to think, trying to push away the image of Poppy's body flying backward as bullets had penetrated her slender body, as her smile had turned to a look of horror. How could that pilot have smiled at her, have looked at her like that and waved, and then gunned down her pretty, fun-loving friend as if he were doing target practice?

'Grace!'

She turned, her own name echoing in her ears as she stared at her sister. April's face was tearstained, but she recognized the steely glint in her eye, the determined clench of her jaw. It was the very same look she'd had on her face after they'd buried their mother, the moment they'd walked away from the graveside. She knew that look, and she knew right then that April would know what to do. April would figure this out. April would keep them safe.

'Grace,' April said, squeezing her fingers tight. 'These men need us. We need to save lives today, okay?'

She nodded, still numb. She didn't even *know* how to save a life, did she? 'I can't,' she mumbled. 'I . . . I . . .'

Grace watched as chaos erupted around them and corpsmen filled the room, carrying bodies and calling orders. Where were they even supposed to start? Another wave of nausea rose within her, but she fought it, swallowing it down, trying to stay focused on her sister as other nurses looked to her too. Some were in their dressing gowns still; others had their hair sticking on end as if they'd just woken, perhaps being pulled from bed as news of the attack had hit. Most looked as lost as she felt.

Doctors ran in, their white coats setting them apart from the other men in the hospital.

'Mark them on the forehead with a red *M* when they've had morphine,' April yelled out. 'And a *T* for their tetanus shot. We need to know who's had what. You can do this, Grace—I know you can.'

'What do I use?' she cried.

'Your lipstick! Anything!' April called back.

'I can do that,' Grace managed, fumbling in her pocket for her lipstick. 'I can do that,' she said again, almost to convince herself.

The corpsman closest to her put up his hand. 'Me too; I'll help with that.'

The building rattled, and a large boom sent tremors through Grace's body and fresh tears spilling down her cheeks.

'The rest of you either assist with initial assessments or help to set up theaters. We're equipped to deal with burns and surgeries, but there'll be more than we're prepared for,' called out a dark-haired doctor, possibly the doctor April had assisted the day before. 'Take the dead straight to the morgue; if there's not enough space, put them in the adjoining room. And if any man's too far gone, then he goes there too. We've only got enough space for the living and those who are going to make it.'

Grace looked up, wondering if she'd heard right. They were to take men who weren't even dead yet to the morgue? She swapped glances with her sister, knowing from the pain in her gaze that she'd indeed heard correctly.

A flurry of activity behind her alerted Grace to more patients being brought in, and she scanned them for Poppy, looking for her familiar silhouette, wondering if it could be her. There had to be a chance she was still alive, that she'd survived the attack. But all she saw was blood. There was no time for these men to be tidied up—it was blood and gore like she'd never expected to see in her lifetime, nothing like their training. This was war.

'Nurse!' She spun around and gagged at a man lying with his clothes shredded, bloodied face and closed eyes making it hard to tell if he was even alive or not, but his hand twitched, and she watched as his mouth opened and he cried out, more animal than human.

April was gone now. There was no one to help her, no one to tell her that everything was going to be fine.

She ran to the supplies cupboard and found the vials of morphine and syringes, hands shaking as she carried it all.

'We need more morphine and tetanus shots!' she called to a corpsman, his eyes meeting hers. 'Bring it to me—we need to give it to every patient.'

She ran back to the patient who'd been covered in blood and found three more just like him, lined up and waiting. She almost tripped over a foot sticking out from beneath one of the beds, and when she bent to look, it tucked back under.

'What are you doing?' she asked.

'Making space for those who need it,' a man nursing his arm and dragging an injured leg said. 'Give my bed to someone else.'

She didn't have time to tell him off, because he was right, they did need the space, and she'd already seen plenty of men leave their beds and rip off bandages to get out to fight. She quickly grabbed a cloth, rubbed a space on the first man's forehead, and marked him with an *M* as he writhed in pain, before inserting a needle into his arm and injecting him with morphine. She looked at his wounds and wanted to give him tetanus, too, but she was still waiting on the supplies.

Grace bent low and vomited again, not able to help it, but there was barely anything left in her stomach now, and she hoped she'd be able to get through the rest of whatever she needed to do without fainting. Her hands trembled so badly that she could barely hold the next needle.

But then a hand found hers, a warm, sticky hand that left a print of blood on her skin.

'Sing to me,' the soldier whispered, his cracked, bloody lips barely moving. 'Please, just sing.'

She took a deep breath as his hand slipped away, administering more morphine and trying to think of something, *anything*, to sing. The only thing that came to mind was their national anthem, and she started low, barely able to remember the words, but slowly they came to her, and she stopped stumbling over them, the verses clearer, helping her to concentrate.

The corpsman was back at her side, passing her what she needed, and they started to make progress as eventually every single bed in the ward filled. He took to printing clearly on their foreheads with a pen, sometimes the only part of their bodies that was free of grime and blood when they wiped enough space to write, and she injected pain relief into each body, checked for pulses, administered tetanus shots to those who needed it, and called out to corpsmen and helpers to find out what had already been given to each patient. But as she came back around, almost to where she'd started, still singing, still using her voice to calm her patients and keep herself focused, not letting her mind wander, her voice stuttered and died in her throat. The man who'd asked her to sing, the man who'd touched her arm and left his mark, was dead, his eyes rolled back in his head.

She took a deep breath, wishing for fresh oxygen, wishing she could run to the beach and gulp down the salty air, cleanse her body in the water and wash the day away.

'Incoming!'

The call that more patients were arriving, the shudder of the building again as the terrifying aerial assault continued, jolted her back into action. And as fear threatened to take hold, she held her head high and started to sing again, as much for herself as for the patients crying out in pain around her.

Poppy. Her name echoed through Grace's mind, over and over, but she pushed it away, blinking furiously every time that image came back to her.

'Go away,' she whispered.

'What was that?'

She jumped as a head peeked out from beneath the bed, a patient she'd forgotten about who was lying there to save space.

'Sorry, nothing,' she said. 'Are you still all right under there?'

He nodded, but she saw his grimace as he pulled himself out a little more. 'I'm fine. Just wish I could get out there and help.'

Grace was about to keep walking and tell him to tuck his legs back under, when she realized there was something he could do.

'Would you mind making your way to the office?' she asked. 'I can help you there, and we could put you on the front desk. Then you could try to get on the phone to Hickam and anywhere else you can get through to—you know, to see what's going on.'

He scrambled out, reaching his good arm out to her, as his other was in a cast. 'I'd rather be helpful than stuck in here, that's for sure.'

She remembered when he was upright that he also had an ankle sprain—she'd treated him only a few days earlier—so she waved over the corpsman who'd been assisting her.

'Can you get him to the desk? He's going to help with communications for us.'

The corpsman nodded, and she gave the patient a kiss on the cheek. 'Thank you. And please, if you can, would you try to make contact with the USS *Solace*? I'm desperate to know if my friend Eva Branson is safe.'

Grace turned back and glanced around, the number of patients growing every few minutes, the casualties more horrific with every arrival. But she had to do this; she couldn't give up. And besides, if she wasn't doing initial assessments and injections, she'd have to be working in surgery or with the burn victims, and the thought alone made her stomach turn.

Poppy. Her friend's name, the look on her face, hit her hard again, out of the blue like a fist to the stomach. But she steeled herself as tears trickled down her cheeks. If Poppy were here, she'd be giving her a kick up the backside and telling her to get on with her work, that there were lives to save, and that was exactly what she was going to do. She thought of Teddy and prayed that he was okay, knowing that he'd be doing anything in his power to save Poppy if he could.

As she checked a new patient's pulse, her fingers to his neck, she realized that he was already gone and signaled for him to be taken before moving on to the next man. Only it wasn't a man—it was a woman, a civilian woman who was clutching her baby to her breast. Her lifeless, blood-smeared little baby boy. Grace reached for her, stroking her arm as she gently wiped her forehead clean. The woman was covered in dirt and blood, which made it almost impossible to see what was wrong with her, and then she saw her leg, the bone visible, skin peeled back like a banana. She swallowed down bile and turned to get the morphine at the same moment a radio fuzzed and crackled nearby, before a broadcast played.

She carefully slid the morphine needle into the woman's arm, administering it as quickly as she could, but she doubted her patient even noticed. She was staring at her baby, and Grace didn't know whether to try to pry the infant from her arms or let her hold him, grieve for her child as long as she could. Grace stood and listened, and as she glanced around, she realized the rest of the room had gone still too. Aside from the odd groan from a patient, they were all listening as a voice projected through the room.

'We have witnessed this morning the distant view of a brief, full battle of Pearl Harbor and the severe bombing of Pearl Harbor by enemy planes, undoubtedly Japanese. The city of Honolulu has also been attacked and considerable damage done.' Grace felt as though her body had frozen as the reality of what had happened went through her like a shock wave. The radio crackled and then came back on, the words making it all seem so real. 'It is no joke. It is a real war. The public of Honolulu has been advised to keep in their homes and away from the army and navy. There has been serious fighting going on in the air and in the sea.'

A hand reached for hers, and she looked down to see the woman gripping her, her eyes wide, panic setting in.

'We're at war?' the woman cried. 'Is it true?'

Grace nodded and kept hold of her hand, as much for herself as for her patient. 'Yes,' she said, finding it hard to breathe. 'Yes, I think we are.'

'Help my baby!' the woman cried. 'Please, just make sure he's okay. *Please.*'

Grace bravely nodded and held out her arms, taking the baby and holding him close, her hands shaking as she patted him, knowing she was being watched.

'I'll take him to get help,' she said, smiling and wishing that there was something she could do. But he was ghostly pale, dead probably from the moment he'd been struck. It was incredible that the mother had even made it to the hospital with her leg shredded like that.

Grace forced herself to walk all the way to the other end of the ward before passing him to a corpsman.

'He alive?'

She shook her head. 'Straight to the morgue, please,' she managed, her voice cracking as she choked on her words. Grace dropped a kiss to the baby's little dark head. 'But put him down carefully when you get there, would you? His mother thinks he's still alive, and I want him treated with care.'

The man nodded, his big arms engulfing the child, carrying him as Grace had, as if he were still alive, still a precious little bundle of life. As he disappeared from sight, Grace slowly turned, watching as a stretcher was carried past, yet another body on its way to the morgue, this one covered by a bloodstained sheet. But as she walked past, a flash of yellow caught her eye.

'Stop!' she called, staring, shivers running through her as she stepped closer, hand trembling as she reached to lift the sheet back. That yellow, that shade of color, the pretty cotton fabric, it looked so like . . .

'No!' she screamed, seeing Poppy's dark hair streaked with red, her mouth twisted, blood tracing a line down her chin.

Not Poppy. No. No, no, no!

The room spun as Grace's legs buckled beneath her and she crashed to the hard floor below, her arm the only thing to break her fall as she wailed, as everything turned shades of swirling red and purple before falling black.

'Grace! Grace, what's wrong?'

April was on the floor with her, holding her, stroking her hair.

'What happened to her?' she heard April demanding. 'Why did she fall?'

And then Grace felt her sister stiffen, knew she'd seen what she'd seen too.

'Poppy's dead,' Grace whispered. *'She's dead.'*

'Cover the body, and take her away,' April ordered, sobbing as she bent low and cradled Grace again, as they cried together.

They were at war.

Poppy was dead.

And nothing was ever, ever going to be the same again.

CHAPTER SIX

EVA

'Command battle stations!'

Fear sliced through Eva like a hot knife through butter. It was the vibration that made her look up first, the heavy rattle in the air followed by the sickening noise of something thumping down from above. Over and over again.

She looked in horror at the sky, at the planes flying too low in the distance, raining bullets or bombs or *something* from the sky. Eva couldn't even make it out. Was this a training operation gone wrong? What on earth was happening? Why were those planes flying so low?

Then she looked at sailors nearby, in their dress whites, waiting to go ashore in the liberty boats for a normal day out.

'Command battle stations!'

There went the call again. The sailors all looked at one another; she saw the confusion register, their eyes wide, before they all started moving, some running back down the deck and others commanded to go into the boats still. Where were they going? To shore? Now?

Eva braced herself as a plane whirred closer, and she stared up, watching as the pilot raised one hand in a wave, his smile visible, before flying past and unleashing a torrent of bullets on a nearby ship.

'Take cover!' a sailor screamed as he ran past her. 'Take cover!'

Cover? Where was she supposed to take cover? And who on earth were they taking cover from?

Boom!

The noise was so loud it reverberated through her, a cold chill spreading down her spine as her teeth rattled. She clenched them tight, braced for another explosion, and watched a nearby ship seem to rise up and then smack back down again, red balls of fire shooting upward as things flew overboard and into the water.

She stared, her feet rooted to the spot. They weren't *things*; they were people!

Eva gulped and forced herself to move closer and watch as the plane roared back overhead and sent more bombs into yet another ship while sailors bobbed around in the water like debris, as if a tree had fallen and was broken into limbs in the ocean. Only these limbs belonged to human beings, and the screaming that was echoing off the sea was the men calling in terror as they died.

'We need to help them!' she screamed, her body shaking as she fisted and unfisted her hands, heart beating so fast she wondered if she was having a heart attack. 'We need to help them!'

Were they next? As another plane came, she looked up in horror, running to the railings and staring out, hand clamped across her mouth now as she looked at the shore, at the decimated buildings smoldering, at the carnage she could only glimpse from where she was standing.

And then she looked back, struggling to breathe, gasping as she drank in the sight of her own ship. Surely the giant red cross on each side of their enormous white boat was like a target, marking them to be bombed? How had they not been hit yet?

'What's going on?'

Eva turned at the cry behind her and saw a handful of nurses watching, huddled together. She'd been so paralyzed with her own fear she hadn't thought to run down and alert the other girls.

'I think, I think . . . ,' she stuttered, looking up again, trying to expel the words as she gasped. 'I think we're at war. I think we've been bombed by the Japanese.'

Was that their emblem? The big red sun on the side of each plane? Was that who was bombing their beautiful harbor, killing their men and destroying their buildings and boats by the dozen?

'We can't be at war! Someone would surely have told us!'

Eva just shook her head. 'If this isn't war, then I don't know what it is.'

'What do we do?' asked another nurse, sobbing as she ran forward and grabbed Eva's hand. 'Tell us what to do. How do we get to shore? We need to get to somewhere safe!'

Some of the other nurses were crying hysterically now, and Eva stared back at them as a wave of calm rolled through her, as serene as the overhead scene was violent. She took a deep breath.

'There is nowhere safe,' she said, raising her voice so they could all hear her over the drone of planes and the shouting of men. She turned back to the water and watched as their own sailors dragged people into the small liberty boats. They were going to be bringing them back to the *Solace*, and that meant they were about to be inundated with patients. The reality of what they were about to face sent a quiver through her. 'Those men out there? They need our help. We need to get the ward ready for an influx, and we need the operating theaters prepped too.'

'They're howling in pain,' one of the nurses said, moving close to Eva and leaning out over the railings. 'Do you think it's from being shot?'

Eva looked at the water and saw the curious sight of fire whipping across the water in patches. And then she noticed the bright swirls of oil, and fear clutched at her throat.

'They're burning,' she whispered. 'It's the oil in the water . . . it's . . .' She choked on the words, hating to imagine what they were about to deal with, how horrific the injuries would be.

'Do you think anyone's alive on the island?' the same nurse said. 'Look at the smoke.'

Eva followed her point, refusing to give in to the panic that was bubbling below the surface of her mind, trying to draw her in. She had to stay focused; she had to lead these women right now and try to save as many lives as they could. But knowing that her Charlie was there on land? That his base might have been hit? She gulped. And what of her new friends? Were they among the dead, or were they bravely preparing to save men right now too?

The youngest of the nurses, a young girl named Sally, was crying so hard she started retching, bright-yellow vomit pooling at her feet and running across the deck as she bent over.

'Sally,' Eva said, marching over to her as the ship suddenly jerked. 'Sally, you need to pull it together. We'll need someone to man the phone lines—do you think you can do that? You need to keep trying to make contact with Tripler General Hospital to see what the situation is there, and Schofield or Hickam. Do you hear me?'

Sally looked up and nodded, her eyes swimming with tears.

'This is your job. We're counting on you, but you need to go now.'

Sally nodded furiously, her head bobbing, before she gathered her skirt and ran down the deck just as the first men were being hauled up.

'I could have done the phones,' another nurse offered.

'We need everyone in the ward,' Eva said. 'But Sally would have fainted at her first patient, I think.'

She'd done the right thing in sending her off, but it had also been selfish. She wanted to know what had happened to the people she cared about, and as soon as she got a moment, she'd be calling herself to try to speak to Charlie. She swallowed her emotions as she thought of him, imagined him being gunned down, what that would mean for her if she lived and he didn't. But she needed to ignore the voice in her head. She might not survive the morning; they could all be taken prisoners of war if they *did* live. The only thing she had control over was her ability to care for others and save lives, and that was exactly what she was going to do.

'We need help over here!'

The noise hit her then. It was as if she'd been blocking everything else out, focused only on what she needed to do, on how she could help. Suddenly all she could hear were explosions and the whirring of aircraft, the screaming of men, the yells for help, the smaller boats being hauled in against their ship.

'Bring them straight to the ward!' she called back. 'We're ready for them.'

But as she hurried to the hospital, all set up and waiting for patients that had never come until now, she knew they weren't ready. There was no possible way they could be ready for what was to come. Smoke filled her nostrils then, the dry, suffocating smell of something burning.

Charlie. She shook her head as if it would stop the thoughts, as if she could somehow just shut her brain down. *Charlie, where are you?* Surely she'd know if he was dead? Wouldn't she be able to feel it in her bones? Wouldn't she sense that he was gone?

'Nurse!'

She spun around and saw a man being carried by a sailor. Or at least she guessed it was a man. His hair was gone, replaced with raw, oozing red flesh. His eyes were glued to her as if he was stuck in his body and was begging her with his gaze. The clothes covering what was left of him were wet and torn, and one of his legs appeared to be hanging.

'Get him to the closest bed,' she said, forcing her words out. 'And keep them coming.'

She traded glances with the sailor, saw the pain on his face as tears slipped silently down his cheeks. She bet the young man had never, ever cried like that before, but maybe he didn't even know he was doing it because he was in such a state of shock.

'Great work saving him,' she said, leaning close and patting his shoulder. 'Now go and save some more.'

'They're all like this,' he whispered, his eyes wide as he stared back at her. 'Every single one of them.'

She shuddered and turned, gathering her supplies, grateful that they'd been so methodical with their equipment in the long months of having very little work to do. Until now she'd only had to tend to minor wounds and nurse men through some basic illnesses. But she wasn't like some of the other girls; she had a strong stomach, and she'd survived a childhood that demanded she get on with life. She wasn't allowed to moan or feel sorry for herself; she'd simply had to survive and keep her chin up, to not let anyone see her pain.

'Today is a day for saving lives,' she said loudly. She took a large cotton swab and doused it in alcohol, then placed it against the man's skin so she could prep the site before putting an IV line in.

His scream sliced through the air at the same moment that bile rose in her throat, as the entire length of skin on his forearm peeled away. She stared in horror before buckling over and vomiting, over and over again until there was nothing left in her stomach, then hurriedly grabbed a vial and filled a needle with morphine. She quickly injected it into the man's other arm, before noticing that his eyes were shut, the pain already knocking him out cold.

Eva pressed a careful two fingers to his neck, feeling for his pulse as she stared at his chest. Dread pulsed through her as she realized that he was definitely still alive; she'd almost hoped, with his body ravaged by burns and the suffering ahead of him, that he'd slipped away.

'Help!' a man yelled.

'We've got three boats filled with the injured!' another screamed out.

Eva watched as patient after patient started to fill their beds. How could so many men be missing limbs? How were these men even alive still with burns to so much of their bodies?

If this was war, then she had no idea how they were going to survive it. And as bad as this was, she couldn't decide what would be a worse fate: plunging to her death into the ocean or being taken by the

Japanese. But if there was even a chance of her Charlie being alive still? Tears sprang into her eyes as she moved to the next bed, ready to do her best to save every life she could. Then she would do anything she could to stay alive herself. Charlie needed her, and more than anything in the world, she needed him too.

———— ❧————

Eva looked up when she heard her name being called, using her blood-smudged forearm to wipe the sweat from her face. Every inch of her was wet, the humidity stifling in the cramped hospital quarters, where every bed and other usable surface was now covered with bodies.

Sally appeared at her side, her eyes still swimming with tears, her face so white she looked like a ghost.

'Any word?'

Sally shook her head. 'Nothing.'

'And you've been trying all morning?' Eva glanced up at the clock, wondering how it was almost afternoon already. They'd been working for hours without so much as a ten-minute break, and as she glanced around the room, she knew that it'd be ongoing for hours more to come.

'Sh-should I keep trying?' Sally stuttered.

Eva nodded. 'Yes. But keep the executive officer posted if you make contact, won't you?' She didn't know how or why she'd become a person of authority, but the other girls seemed to want to look to her, for her to take charge in the ward, and their matron had been off duty and on land when the attack had begun. They didn't even know if she was alive or not.

'He's been past three times already. I h-have messages to relay if I get through.'

Eva's patient started to moan again, and she grimaced as she turned back to him, not getting any better at dealing with the horrific burns even after hours of facing them. She wondered, though, if anyone could ever be accustomed to seeing skin peeling from bone, blistered to the point of falling away, or the agony of a man's face as twisted and contorted in pain as those in front of her.

'Help me,' croaked a sailor. 'Please help me.'

Eva took a deep breath, trying not to smell his skin. She moved forward, careful not to touch him, not about to make the same mistake twice and have entire stretches of skin come off at once.

'That's my job,' she said, trying to sound bright. 'First I'm going to take the pain away with morphine, and then . . .'

She stopped talking when his fingers clasped her wrist, holding her tight, before loosening and falling away. Eva stared at his face, at his open eyes, her breath choking in her throat as she tried to speak again.

'Sailor!' she eventually cried, her voice barely a whisper. 'Please wake up. *Please.*'

But as his lifeless eyes stared back at her, his arm fallen limply over the side of the bed, she knew he was gone. She slowly looked in horror around the entire ward, her stomach clenching as she truly saw what was going on around her. The room was filled with the dead and dying. How many would they even be able to save? Shouts echoed around her, nurses whispered as they tried to figure out what to do, and men groaned and cried out for their mothers and wives. And she just stood there, numb, fighting the pull to fall apart, to just collapse to the ground and give up. Were they all going to die anyway?

'Morgue?' someone asked.

She didn't even bother looking up. 'Yes.'

And as he was taken, the sailor with no name, the sailor who'd begged her for help, another man was dropped in his place. She sprang forward, not about to rest on her laurels or fall into numbness when someone needed her. It was when she wasn't needed that she'd slip into a puddle on the floor. She felt like blood had invaded every nook and cranny of the hospital, as if red was now the prevailing color everywhere she looked.

Burns ravaged the man's body, but this one wasn't crying or whimpering. He was just staring at her, and she bent low to whisper to him.

'I'm going to look after you,' she promised. 'First comes pain relief, and then I'll treat your wounds.'

Eva prepared the morphine and slid the needle under his skin, slowly pushing until he'd received it all. She'd given him a lot—she'd had to—and she watched as the relief eventually started, his eyelids fluttering slightly, before she used sulfa powder and mineral oil to treat his burns, methodically working her way over his body, cutting his clothes where she needed to.

And it was then she realized how quiet it had become outside. There were no longer aircrafts buzzing too low or firing at them; the booming quake of American ships firing back had disappeared. She didn't even know how long it had been quiet. It could have been hours, and she wouldn't have even realized.

'Ladies, listen up!' a man yelled.

She finished with the burn she was treating and paused, wiping her brow again as sweat touched her eyelashes, as their executive officer stood to command near the middle of their ward.

'This morning has been a nightmare for us all, but I want to commend you all for what you're doing,' he said, his voice carrying through the big room. 'We don't know what's going to happen next, but we're all still here, kind of like rats in a trap! We're just going to carry on as best we can and pray that the worst of the attack is over.'

Eva blinked as tears slipped through her lashes and onto her cheeks. She took a big shuddering breath and shut her eyes for a moment, wondering for the hundredth time whether she was going to survive the day, whether any of them would.

'I want you all to have a quick break when you can, to catch your breath for ten minutes, and dinner will be served as scheduled.'

The thought of food made her want to vomit, but she knew he was right. Without eating they'd all collapse, and without capable nurses to assist, the injured men had no chance of survival.

'Have the other boats in the harbor been hit?' someone called out.

'I understand that we may be the only vessel that has not been bombed,' the executive officer replied quietly.

'What about on land? What's happened to our boys?' a nurse asked.

'And the nurses stationed at the other hospitals?' Eva called out.

'We've still had no contact at this stage. All lines of communication are currently down; however, we're attempting to turn a radio on in here for you all to listen to.'

He walked away and left them, and Eva turned back to her patient, her hands surprisingly steady despite the tremor within her body.

If Charlie was dead, she'd never forgive herself. She'd been the one to stop him from leaving; it had been *her* begging him to stay.

She smiled down at the sailor, who was still riding the wave of morphine.

She just needed to believe that some nurse with a kind smile was looking after her Charlie if he was injured. She had to believe. She couldn't go back to her father. She just couldn't. Even as she worked to tend to her patient's horrific burns, she couldn't stop thinking about him, about what he'd done to her, what he'd *do* to her again if she had to return.

His fist connected with her stomach, a powerful blow that puffed the air from her lungs and made her double over. She refused to make a noise, because even a tiny yelp of pain would have given him satisfaction, and she would give him none.

A hand slammed into her shoulder then, forcing her back against the wall, her stomach cramping as she was forced to straighten. And then her father's fingers clamped around her throat, like claws, holding her tight as his alcohol-tainted breath filled her nostrils.

'You think you're better than us, with your fancy boyfriend and your fancy new nursing job, don't you?'

Eva stared back at him, struggling for air, trying not to cry even as tears involuntarily leaked from her eyes.

'You leave this house, you'll never come back. You hear me? Don't you ever come crawling back here again.'

She squeezed her eyes shut as his grip tightened, wishing her mother would come for her, wishing her mother would yell at him and tell him to leave the house. But she didn't. Eva knew she'd be cowering in her bedroom, so obedient to a man who'd never treated her right.

He finally let her go, and she slipped to the floor, gasping for breath, her lungs screaming out. But she stayed silent, ready to defy him again if she had to.

Eva was jolted from her thoughts as more yells echoed through the ward and the reality of what she was dealing with hit her full force. She pushed her father from her mind, refusing to think about what might happen if Charlie was gone.

Because without her Charlie, the Japanese may as well just kill her too.

CHAPTER SEVEN

APRIL

April might have always dreamed of being a doctor one day, but until today, she'd barely done more than change dressings and give injections and perform other basic treatments. Assisting Dr. Grey had been the closest she'd been to surgery, but within the past few hours, she'd done more procedures and seen more wounds than any amount of training or textbooks could have prepared her for.

Her latest patient had just been brought in, and she could see from the state of his leg, with flesh and bone protruding and his ankle at a peculiar angle, that he was going to have to be prepared for surgery. She glanced over at the corridor, the one leading to the emergency operating theaters they'd set up, and knew he'd be waiting hours before a surgeon could attend to him.

She touched his hand, hoping her warm pat was reassuring, as she read the smudged *M* and *T* on his forehead. There was no more pain relief she could give him, but judging from the shaking of his body and the bluish tinge to his lips, he was either simply cold or entering into shock. Given his wounds, she was guessing shock.

'I'm going to find you a blanket,' she said, smiling down at him. 'I'll be back in a moment.'

She quickly went to the supplies cupboard where they were kept, but the shelves where they were usually neatly stacked were bare.

'Any blankets?' she called to a corpsman who rushed past her.

'None left here,' he said without stopping.

April glanced back at her patient and decided to run for blankets herself. She had the other patients under her care as stable as she could make them, and others were already lined up in their beds, waiting for surgery. She walked fast, not wanting to trip with so many people everywhere, and pushed through the doors leading past the nurses' mess area and through another set of doors. There were patients there, too, all waiting, all groaning and crying to themselves as if they were trying so hard not to disturb others, but the pain was so intense they couldn't even breathe without a noise coming from their bodies.

'April, is that you?'

The male voice was deep and commanding, and she knew instinctively that it belonged to Dr. Grey before she saw him. She walked into the temporary operating room and found him working alone with a flashlight shining from a shelf where he'd positioned it.

'I need you to help me move this patient,' he said. 'The nurse helping me never came back!'

'Of course,' she replied, hurrying to his side and looking down at the soldier. He was as white as a sheet, and from the flutter of his eyelids, she could see he was drifting in and out of consciousness.

'Where should I stand?' she asked, noticing how extensive his burns were. 'Is it safe to move him?'

Dr. Grey gave her a sharp stare from the head of the bed, and she quickly looked down, wishing she hadn't said anything.

'Please prepare the paper.'

She reached for the oil and slathered it over the fresh paper, ready for the patient. It was what they'd been taught to do for any patient with severe burns, to stop them from sticking painfully to a sheet.

'You take his feet; I'll take his upper body,' Dr. Grey said.

She nodded.

'And thank you,' Grey murmured. 'It's nice to have your assistance again.'

After everything that had happened, all the tragedy, the loss of life, she knew it was stupid to light up over a little comment, but she couldn't help smiling as she reached for the man's feet and counted with the doctor.

'One, two, three!'

No!

April opened her mouth to scream, but no sound came out. She stared at her hand, buckling forward as she dropped what was left of the patient to the paper, before realizing what she still had hold of.

She was holding his ankle in her hand. She was holding half a leg in her bare hand! The man's leg had fallen away at the knee. The rest of the poor man was lying in front of her, and she was holding his burned, bloody leg!

'I . . . I . . . ,' she stuttered, dropping the leg and backing away.

'You weren't to know; it's fine,' Dr. Grey said. 'I may have had to amputate anyway.'

April raised her eyes, looking from Grey to the patient, barely able to make a sound, she was so horrified.

Why had they tried to move him? Why had that happened? Why wasn't Dr. Grey looking as shell shocked as she was? Had he seen this type of thing before?

'April?'

She huddled forward, trying to breathe, trying not to be sick.

'April, we've lost him. We did our best,' Dr. Grey said.

Suddenly she felt a hand on her shoulder, a warm, strong hand that somehow made it easier for her to breathe. April looked up and into dark, warm eyes that were the complete opposite of how she felt inside.

'He's gone, April. He was probably never going to make it.'

She gulped, nodding her head, over and over again. Had she killed him when his leg had come away?

'Don't let this moment stop you. What did you come looking for?'

April exhaled. 'A blanket. *Blankets*. For the patients arriving.'

He extended his hand, and she grasped it, pulling to her feet as he slowly let her go.

'Go get those blankets, and then come back and find me when you're ready to assist again. Send someone else back in the meantime; we need more nurses in surgery.'

She glanced at Dr. Grey one last time before hurrying to get them, taking three just in case. She tried to forget the smell, the feel, the look of the leg in her hand, of the way it had just so casually fallen away from the man's knee like slow-cooked meat from the oven, and ran all the way back to her patient, the one who'd been shivering. The one who was waiting for her. The one she could save.

But he was gone.

And there was already another man in his place.

'Where did he go?' she asked aloud, but of course no one heard her and no one answered. 'Where is he?'

'Water,' croaked the new patient. 'Please. Water.'

She wiped tears from her cheeks and tucked the blanket around him, needing something to do, needing to give the blanket to *someone*.

'Please let this be over,' she whispered. '*Please*.'

She put a straw into the cup of water and gently touched the back of her patient's head to help him rise, terrified skin or bone was going to come away and grimacing as she waited for him to sip.

'Don't let them take me,' he cried. 'If they come for me, kill me first.'

She kept hold of the water, frowning down at him. 'Who's coming for you?'

'The Japs,' he whispered. 'They'll come back for each and every one of us. This isn't over! *They're coming!*'

April set the cup down and stared at her patient as her legs began to shake.

No one was taking her. She'd fight alongside their men if she had to, but no one was ever coming back and taking her prisoner. She knew what kinds of awful things men did to enemy women, and she was never, ever going to let that happen to her.

'You're safe here,' she whispered, not knowing if she was lying or not. 'I'm here to save lives, sir. I promise.'

His smile made her knees knock even harder. She'd already lost more patients than she'd saved today, but as she gritted her teeth and started to assess his wounds, she decided that there was nothing wrong with a little optimism and a dash of a white lie to make someone believe they were going to survive.

—— ⟨🙢🙠⟩ ——

'Grace?' April called, spinning around and looking for her sister. She didn't know what the time was, it had been the longest day she'd ever experienced, and she didn't even know if it was the same day or the next. As the influx of new patients had finally slowed, the corpsmen and some of the less wounded soldiers and navy boys had started to fix big heavy blankets to the windows, which explained why she'd found it so hard to find a blanket for her patient earlier. She pulled at the front of her dress, trying to let in some air against her wet, sticky skin. The humidity was bad enough as it was without the blankets blocking out whatever air was able to circulate naturally. It was like a furnace in the ward now, and she bet the operating theaters would be even worse when they eventually made their way there.

But if it meant their lights couldn't be seen, and the blackout stopped them being hit, then so be it.

'Grace!' she called again, walking around and looking for her sister still. She touched one of the nurses on the arm, apologizing when she saw her jump at the contact. 'Sorry—I was only wondering if you'd seen my sister, Grace? She looks a lot like me, blonde hair in a bun?'

The nurse shook her head, and April thanked her, wondering if she should hold on to her or not. Half the nurses looked like they were about to keel over, either from exhaustion, the heat, or what they'd been through. She grimaced. *More likely a combination of all three.*

'Grace!'

'Under here,' came a muffled call. Only it belonged to a distinctly male voice, not a woman.

April bent when she saw a boot protruding from beneath the bed. 'Who's under there?' she asked.

And then she saw Grace, huddled to the back, and the man whom the boot belonged to lying on his side in the confined space.

'Grace! What are you doing under here?' she asked, shuffling forward on her knees and reaching out a hand to her sister.

'She won't say anything,' the man said. 'She was my nurse until all this happened, and she was fine for a while, but then she just collapsed. I don't know what happened.'

April quickly blinked away tears, as much from exhaustion as emotion. She shouldn't have left her sister after they'd both seen Poppy's body, but she'd stayed with her as long as she could, and if she hadn't gone, how many men wouldn't have received treatment? A group of horrifically burned men had been brought in right after she'd run off to help, meaning to come back at once.

'It's okay; I'll talk to her,' she said. 'And what are you doing under here anyway?'

'I moved to make space for whoever needed the bed more than me. If I could have gone out and fought, I would have.'

April had seen every able-bodied and almost abled man flee from the hospital the second they'd realized they were under attack. One man had even cut off the cast on his arm so he could get out and fight. So she could only imagine how frustrated this patient was not to be able to go.

'Where are you hurt?' she asked. 'Should I try to find somewhere else for you?' His arm was in a sling, and she could see from the grimace when he moved that he wasn't comfortable.

'I'm just fine here. I can tell from the howling that those men in the beds need the comfort more than me.'

'Well, at least tell me if you need some pain relief,' she said. 'And thank you for looking after Grace. She's witnessed some terrible things today.'

She waited for him to say 'haven't we all,' but he didn't, smiling at Grace instead.

'You keep singing when you feel better,' he said to Grace cheerfully. 'Having a little songbird around is enough to keep everyone fighting for their lives.'

'Hang on—weren't you the one who was on the desk, trying to make contact with the other hospitals?' She'd been trying to work out why he looked so familiar.

'Someone else took over, so I came back under here. And that's when I found this one.'

April reached for Grace and helped her out from beneath the bed, wrapping her arms around her like she would a small child and sitting on the floor with her. She'd heard her sister singing earlier, and it had been like listening to their mother, her soft, melodic voice drifting through the ward. It was one of the things she'd noticed the most when she'd died; their house seemed so quiet all the time. There was no humming as their mother went from room to room with freshly folded laundry, or singing as she cooked dinner. The house had seemed empty without her, the only reminder the perfume that still lingered in the air, wafting from her bedroom.

'Grace, I'm going to get you something to eat,' April said. 'You need to keep your strength up.'

Grace's face crumpled as April stared down at her. Her heart broke for her sister, but as she held her, her own tears disappeared. It had been the same way when their mother had passed; April had stepped up to look after her younger sister and care for their dad when he couldn't even get out of bed, and instead of sobbing along with Grace, she'd simply taken over every duty that their mom once had. At first she'd loved it; everyone had told her what a good girl she was, how dependable she was, and she'd liked the attention. It had taken her mind off what had happened and kept her busy. But over time she'd started to resent always having to be the sensible one, always having to run their household and keep up with school and anything else that was going on in their lives that their father should have dealt with. But today she just wanted to hold her sister, and as much as she was missing Poppy, as much as she knew she'd have nightmares about what had happened right in front of them, she needed to care for Grace. And she needed them both to keep putting one foot in front of the other.

'Grace, I need you to listen to me,' she said softly, still holding her sister.

Grace clung to her as she stroked her back.

'Right now, we have men who need us. Without us, they'll die or suffer terribly,' April said. 'What happened to us, *to Poppy*, it's terrible. But we can't give up.'

Grace started to cry again then, softly into April's shoulder, just as the room exploded with noise again. More men were being brought in, more to add to the never-ending stream, and she knew they couldn't just sit there in a puddle on the ground for the rest of the day.

'I want you to go back to doing the injections and checking pain levels,' she instructed. 'That's something you can do. It's something we *need* you to do.'

Grace sat back, and April gently brushed her thumbs across her cheeks.

'I need to hear you say yes, Grace,' April said. 'Tell me you can do it?'

Grace nodded and whispered, 'I can do it.'

April kissed her forehead, then stood, holding out a hand and pulling her sister to her feet. She studied her, watched as she swayed on her feet slightly before meeting her gaze.

'Are they coming for us too?' Grace whispered.

April shuddered. 'Honestly, I don't know. But we're semiprepared now. Our boys will look after us; they won't be surprised again.' Or at least she hoped so.

Her sister looked frozen, the expression on her face never changing.

'You just handle the morphine, okay?' April said. 'Everyone will be grateful if you take care of that, but don't forget to mark them.'

Grace was still standing there, and April gave her a tiny nudge forward.

'Come on.'

She watched her sister walk to a bed, reaching out a hand to steady herself, and then she hurried off to find Dr. Grey again. He'd said to come find him when she was ready to assist him again, and she was. If he needed her, then traumatic or not, she was going to do whatever was asked of her. Too many people had died today already, and she wasn't going to stand by and let her own fear and pain get in the way of saving lives.

The smell of food made her stomach growl as she passed by the cafeteria, but she did her best to ignore it and kept up her brisk pace until she was forced to slow by a backlog of patients waiting for surgery. She went down the line, checking they'd all had some sort of pain relief and had needed blankets, but most men were quietly suffering now, some likely close to death as they were forced to wait.

'Dr. Grey?' she called, before entering the room and finding him bent low, a flashlight balanced nearby for extra light as he operated.

'Dr. Grey, it's April,' she said as she moved closer, exchanging smiles with a nurse positioned to his left. 'Can I help at all?'

'Prepare my next patient,' he said without looking up. 'Oh, and April, thanks for coming back.'

She clenched her hands tight, trying to stop them from shaking as she stood. 'Is it first come, first served, or do you want me to assess those waiting to gauge who's most critical?'

'Just bring in the one closest to the door. Hopefully we'll have another surgeon join us here soon.'

Dr. Grey was working from one of the converted rooms, away from the bulk of the surgeons, who were in the dedicated operating theaters. It wasn't ideal, but it was better than not operating at all.

April turned to leave, but he called to her again.

'April, we're short an anesthetist; would you please run and check what to give our next patient and then administer it when I'm ready?'

Her heart started to thud almost as rapidly as it had when the bombs had fallen. 'You want me to administer the anesthetic?' she asked. 'Just to be clear, sir.'

'Yes,' he said simply. 'If you're not up to the task, then I can ask—'

'No!' she interrupted. 'Of course, I was only making certain I'd heard you correctly.'

April hurried back to the hallway and checked the closest patient. His burns were horrific, although they'd no doubt been cleaned as best they could, but it was his arm that was a mess, one of the goriest sights she'd ever seen.

'We'll be with you soon,' she said, checking his temperature and forcing herself to study his limb. She had a sinking feeling that it would be a straight amputation, and she couldn't stand thinking how many men would wake up after surgery to find they'd lost a body part before nightfall.

She went to find an anesthetist then, confident she could give the man's approximate height and weight. Part of her was thrilled that Dr. Grey had so much confidence in her, but the other part knew that in any other situation, someone like her would never be allowed to administer lethal drugs. She gulped. What if she didn't give enough drugs and had a patient in excruciating pain wake up during surgery to see or feel his arm being sawed off!

She remembered Poppy as she walked, remembered the way her body had contorted, remembered the pallor of her face when they'd brought her body in. April shuddered, trying to focus on putting one foot in front of the other instead, concentrating on the patient she was about to assist with, recalling his basic facts.

But all she could think of was what had happened. *Why?* What was the point of gunning down so many of their men, of taking out their buildings and their ships? Did this mean they'd been plunged into war with the rest of the world?

She didn't need to ask the question to know the answer. America was most definitely at war now; the only uncertainty was what step they'd be forced to take next to keep their country safe.

CHAPTER EIGHT

GRACE

Grace couldn't stop trembling. Her mind was racing faster than her heart—a swirl of thoughts and flashes, images that she wished she could forget. Especially Poppy. *Poppy.* Why had her friend been outside so early? Why had she not come running in when she'd heard the noise? Maybe if she'd moved, if she'd called out to her earlier, if Teddy had let go of her . . . tears welled in her eyes again, emotion choking her throat.

It didn't matter what she thought. Poppy was gone, and no amount of wishing was going to change that.

When she arrived in their mess room, it was already half-full. But instead of the usual chatter—the space always so lively and full of teasing and laughter—there was silence. Except for the odd muffled cry. Grace stood against the wall, leaning hard into it, certain her legs would buckle if she didn't brace herself. How could she keep standing? How could she keep her eyes open?

'Come and have something to eat,' someone said gently to her, taking her arm.

Grace looked at the person and saw it was their matron. She opened her mouth, wanting to say that she was happy to see her, but instead the second she moved, her legs collapsed, and she fell to the ground.

Arms went around her; Grace didn't even know who they belonged to, and she didn't care. All the tears she'd been holding back since April had found her and put her back to work—all the thoughts, the emotions—just bubbled through her, her sobs so loud and guttural they were animallike. As she cried, not even caring, not trying to stop, she heard wails around her, gasps and tears that had no doubt been kept in check just like hers had. But now that they'd been given permission to stop working, to just *be* for a short while, they were all falling apart.

'Grace?'

She heard April's familiar soft voice and looked up, wondering how her sister always managed to find her whenever she needed her. Somehow her big sister was also incredibly capable at holding herself together, and right now she appeared as calm and capable as ever. As if nothing had happened, as if their best friend hadn't just been gunned down.

'Don't you care?' Grace choked out the words as April stared down at her.

'Care? About what?' April asked as she stroked hair from Grace's damp forehead. 'About our patients?'

Grace pulled back, wiping her own forehead. '*Poppy*,' she choked out. 'You're acting like our best friend hasn't just died in front of us; you're not even crying.' She hurled the words at her, regretting them the instant they left her lips as the room fell silent and April stared back at her, stunned as if she'd slapped her across the face. 'How can you just keep acting like normal?' she whispered.

'Grace, of course I care. Poppy was my best friend too,' April said, and Grace saw tears swimming in her sister's gaze then. 'All of us, we've all lost something today, or someone. I'll forgive you since we're all so tired and . . .'

'I just want to see you cry,' Grace said, wiping her cheeks. 'I want to know that you actually feel something. Just for once.'

It was cruel—she knew she was lashing out at her sister—but she couldn't help it. How could anyone hold it together like that? How could April just deal with their mother dying, with Poppy dying, with everything, as if it were nothing?

'Don't you dare,' April said, standing up and glaring down at her. 'All I've ever done is love you and try to shield you from pain. I've taken all that pain in, and I've suffered on my own with no one to hold *me*, so don't you ever say that I don't care.'

Her sister's voice was quiet and rasping, but Grace knew she'd hurt her. She opened her mouth, knowing she needed to say sorry, but the words never came. If Poppy was gone, if it was truly just the two of them, then she needed to grow up and stop being so impulsive. April would be hurting, too, and it wasn't fair to take it out on her.

'There's a broadcast again,' someone said. 'Listen.'

Someone else was passing around hot cups of coffee, and Grace took one, huddling into the corner again and pressing her back against the wall. She hated the way she'd just spoken to April, seeing tears prick in her sister's eyes, seeing the pain on her face. She buried her face in her hand, sobbing again. Why had she been so cruel? April was right. She'd always looked after her—she didn't need to be told that—so why had she lashed out at her? Why did she need to *see* her hurting? Why did it make her feel better to see her pain? She wished for Poppy. Poppy would know how to make things right; she always did. It was always Poppy in the middle, almost as referee, and now she was . . . Grace squeezed her eyes shut even tighter. *Gone.*

'How many men have lost limbs today?' she heard one of the nurses ask.

'I don't know, but I think the burns are almost worse than the limb amputations,' said another.

Grace clasped her cup tight, wishing she could put her hands over her ears. She didn't want to hear it. She couldn't stand to think of all the wounded, of all the lives lost. All she wanted was to see Teddy, to find out what had happened, to find out if he knew anything about Eva and the ships in the harbor.

'It's the president!' someone announced as the radio crackled and a hush fell over the room.

The only movement was from two nurses passing around huge bowls of fried chicken. She saw April glance at her and quickly looked away, taking a piece of chicken even though the smell of it made her feel queasy.

'We are now in this war! We are all in it, all the way! Every single man, woman, and child is a partner in the most tremendous undertaking of our American history. We must share together, the bad news and the good news, the defeats and the victories, the changing fortunes of the war!'

Grace chewed her chicken, forcing it down as she listened to President Roosevelt speak. She glanced at the clock on the wall, wondering how so much time had passed. It had been more than twenty-four hours since the attack, more than a day since Poppy had died, and she hadn't even realized. She shuddered, making herself keep eating, trying to push the haunting images in her mind away again. With the blackout curtains up everywhere and the nurses and doctors all using blue lights to see, it had been impossible to know what time of day or night it was. But it still surprised her how long they'd all been awake, without food or water, and after such a trauma.

She listened to Roosevelt's clear voice as he continued to speak.

'So we are going to win the war, and we are going to win the peace that follows!'

He sounded so self-assured, so confident that they were going to win, when they had barely been in it for a day. But if the Japanese had managed a surprise attack once . . . she shuddered and found it almost impossible to swallow her final mouthful.

'Has there been any news from Hickam?'

Grace's ears pricked at the mention of Hickam, and she shuffled closer to April. Her sister gave her a look that was difficult to interpret, but she didn't move away. April would be as anxious to know that Teddy was safe as she was.

'Nothing from Hickam, but there have been unconfirmed reports that the USS *Solace* has been seen looking unscathed.'

'No, there's been word!' someone called out. Grace watched as a nurse stood and cleared her throat. 'There are reports that many of the men stationed at Hickam Field died in their beds. Many of them were still asleep when it happened.'

A collective gasp echoed through the room, and Grace dug her nails hard into her palms. Teddy might be all right still. He wasn't there when it was hit; he was with them—he'd been with her only . . . she couldn't even remember. Thirty hours ago? She suddenly thought of Eva, remembered her talking about her fiancé. Hadn't he been at Hickam Field? She was certain he was at the same base as Teddy. But she didn't even know if Eva was alive, let alone her Charlie.

'Do we know numbers?' she heard April ask.

'Only that there are many dead, maybe hundreds, and it was worse at sea.'

'Do you think they'll come back for us?' another nurse asked.

Grace bit down hard on her lip. *Would* they come back? Was this just the start of something much, much worse? Their president had sounded so confident in his announcement, but if they hadn't anticipated this attack, would they know about another?

'What if they're waiting for us? If they're planning on coming back to take us all?'

Grace fought the urge to rock backward and forward, her arms clasped so tight around herself now as she imagined them coming for her, the Japanese making a surprise attack in the night and taking each and every one of them.

'They won't,' April said firmly, as if she somehow knew more than all of them. But Grace knew what it was. It was her sister's way. She believed in taking charge, in holding her head high and refusing to give in, refusing to buckle no matter what the stakes. No wonder she'd been so capable throughout all of this. 'If they were going to come back, they would have by now. They might have caught us unawares here, but America is in the war now. There's no way they'll ever get away with anything like that, ever again.'

'I'd go straight to the ocean,' Grace said, surprising herself when her lips moved, the thoughts in her head suddenly shared with the room. 'I'd rather drown in the water than be taken a prisoner of war.'

She could feel April looking at her and knew she wouldn't approve. But she wasn't brave like her sister; she couldn't deal with ever being taken or facing more atrocities.

'I'd run for the caves,' said another nurse. 'The ones we explored when we first arrived. We could hide there!'

April cleared her throat, and the others fell silent. 'I'd fight them to the death if they came for me,' she said, her voice deep, dark, and angry. Grace didn't ever remember her sister sounding so menacing. 'I wouldn't let anyone capture me and take me alive, and I'd rather die fighting for what I believed in.'

And just like that, she'd managed to show them all that suicide or hiding wasn't, or shouldn't be, an option. Her sister was prepared to face the enemy head-on, despite what they'd seen, but Grace was still sure that she'd rather throw herself into the water and face her fate in the ocean.

'Ah, sorry to interrupt, ladies, but I thought you'd all want an update.'

A deep, strong male voice spoke behind them, and Grace turned slowly. *Teddy!* She locked eyes on him and gasped, fresh tears brewing as she saw the man standing there, on both legs. *Alive.*

Grace wanted to run to him, but instead she sat, wrapping her arms tight around herself as she stared at him. He was alive! Teddy had made it!

'The USS *Solace* is the only ship to sustain no damage. Every other vessel in the harbor was either sunk or badly bombed, and Hickam Field took a direct hit by dive-bombers. There are hundreds dead and just as many wounded, and Schofield Barracks, Wheeler Field, Ewa Marine Corps Air Station, they were all hit too.' He took an audibly ragged breath, his eyes bloodshot as he ran a hand through his hair. 'We had the aircraft all packed wingtip to wingtip on the field, and it made them an easy target. They strafed and bombed all our planes.'

They all sat, listening, and Grace finally found her way to her feet and slowly crossed the room as the women around her started to mutter between themselves, some crying, some talking, and some staring blankly as if they were simply in shock still.

'Teddy,' she rasped, shaking her head as she held out her hands to him. 'I can't believe you're here.'

He stepped forward and opened his arms, pulling her against him and holding her tight. She clung to him, inhaling the smell of smoke and war on his shirt as she buried her face into his shoulder.

They didn't say anything; they just stood there, immobile, as nurses came and went, as April touched them and whispered as she passed, as the radio continued to broadcast the news.

When he finally let her go, he stared down at her, and she cried all over again. It was impossible not to.

'I saw her,' she finally blurted, needing to tell him. 'They brought her body in.'

Teddy nodded as a single tear fell down his cheek. Guilt overwhelmed her then; she hated that she was in his arms instead of Poppy, wished she'd never hoped to be with Teddy when her best friend had loved him so much.

'I'm so pleased I didn't lose you too,' he whispered, drawing her close again. 'You're like a little sister to me, Grace. It would have killed me.'

Little sister. The words washed over her. A few days ago, she would have been furious to hear him describe her like that. Right now, though, she was just grateful to be in his arms, to have someone protecting her when the world felt like it had tipped upside down.

But just as she looked up to tell him how sorry she was, as she was about to step back and force herself from his arms, Teddy's eyes flickered, and she felt his body go. He was too heavy for her to do anything other than slightly break his fall as his eyes rolled back and he hit the ground.

'*No!*' she yelled, collapsing beside him and feeling for a pulse. 'No, Teddy. *No!* I can't lose you too.'

———— ❧❦ ————

'Teddy?' Grace whispered, bending over him as she wiped his forehead with a damp cloth.

He'd stirred before and not woken, but this time he opened his eyes, looking alarmed before throwing his arms in the air and trying to leap from the bed.

'What happened? What time is it?'

The room was black from the blankets hanging everywhere, and the patients all looked a strange color from the blue lights they were having to use, so it was impossible for anyone to figure out what time of day it was.

'It's been four hours,' she said to him, gently pushing him back down. 'We're not sure why you collapsed, but the doctor thinks it was probably pure exhaustion. When did you last eat or drink anything?'

'When did anyone last eat?' he muttered, touching his hand to his head as he eased back down. 'My head is pounding.'

She reached for the water and passed it to him, watching as he propped himself up slightly and took a few long sips.

'I need to get back out there. I—'

'You *need* to eat a decent meal,' she interrupted. 'As soon as you've eaten something, I'll let you go. And your head is pounding because you hit it on the way down when you passed out.'

Teddy looked like he was about to argue, but then he nodded and gave her back the water. 'Fine. You're right. But as soon as I've eaten, I'm leaving.'

She wanted to make up an excuse, tell him that there was a medical reason that she couldn't let him go, but there was none. She just selfishly didn't want him to hurt himself, couldn't stand the thought of losing someone else.

'The hospital food isn't great, but we all had some fried chicken earlier. I'm going to try to find you some.' She hesitated, touching his shoulder and then quickly removing her hand, not sure whether it was okay to comfort him like that, even though she'd touched multiple shoulders since the bombing to comfort patients without thinking anything of it. 'Don't leave while I'm gone. I need you to promise me.'

Teddy nodded, and Grace hovered as she saw his hands shaking and wondered if he'd even noticed.

'Teddy?' she asked again.

'I promise. Just don't take too long.'

Grace left him and hurried back to the cafeteria, hoping she hadn't overpromised on the chicken lunch. There was nowhere to get more decent food from, and she wasn't even sure if their cook had survived. She managed to find a couple of pieces of chicken as well as some bread, and she raced back as quickly as she could. There was no sign of April, and she was glad; the last thing she needed was to face her sister and remember how cruel she'd been to her earlier in the mess room. April would forgive her—she always did—but she shouldn't have said such terrible things in the first place.

When she returned, Teddy was helping someone in the next bed over, holding his water for him, and she smiled at how kind he could be after everything he'd been through himself.

'Tell me what it's really like out there,' she asked quietly as he sat back down and she passed him the food.

'You don't want to know.'

She took a deep breath. 'Yes, Teddy, I do.'

Teddy looked unsure, then patted the spot on the bed beside him, and she hesitantly sat down. It felt too intimate, improper for her to have her leg so close to his, watching him eat and talk, but she shook the feeling off. What choice did she have?

'It's grim,' he said, and she could see the pain in his eyes as he looked at her. There was something haunting about the way he stared, something in his gaze that told her he'd witnessed something dreadful. Even more dreadful than what she'd seen, or what they'd seen together. She touched his hand, holding it until it stopped shaking, before nudging the food toward him. 'But we have good men out there, *great* men, and we're not going to let those Japs get away with this.'

'But was it, *is* it, awful out there? What did you see? How many have we lost?'

'Grace, I'm not going to sugarcoat it. It was . . .' She'd never seen Teddy rattled before. He was usually the one laughing or telling stories, the larger-than-life personality who never seemed bothered by anything or anyone. But this had changed him. She could see that. 'It's horrific, but I don't want you thinking about that. You just focus on saving lives in here and staying alive.'

She reached for his hand again and laid her fingers across his, needing to touch him, needing him to know that she was there. 'The day before the bombing, we were all laughing and having the time of our lives. Hours before we were dancing and drinking, thinking we were so lucky to be here.'

'Nothing will ever be the same again, Grace,' he said quietly, setting down the bone from his chicken and sadly shaking his head. 'We're at war now; you could be posted anywhere, and I'll definitely be sent away. I don't think anyone knows what this means for us, but we're fighting for our lives and our country now.'

Grace gulped. 'You actually think we could be sent away?' she asked.

Teddy nodded. 'Yes, I do. We resisted this war for as long as we could, but now that we're in it, there's nowhere we won't be sent. They'll do everything they can to show the world what a mighty force we are.'

She chewed on her lip and withdrew her hand, folding her hands in her lap now as she watched him finish the second piece of chicken. She wished he'd chew slower so she'd have longer with him, just another hour or another night or day to see with her own eyes that he was safe.

'When do you think you'll go?' she finally asked, watching as he stared at his hands before finally looking up.

'This might be the last time I see you, Grace. I need to get back to base before they think I've been added to the list of casualties or deceased.'

The word hung between them, and she suddenly saw Poppy again, saw her body contorting, saw the pain and horror in her gaze.

'I keep seeing her,' Grace whispered, her voice wobbling as she tried to swallow her emotion.

It was Teddy reaching for her hand this time. 'Me too.'

'I keep wondering if I'd just gone out earlier, if I'd shouted sooner, if . . .'

'If I'd come around earlier and stopped her from walking out there in the first place,' Teddy finished for her. 'I'm having the same thoughts, Grace; honestly I am. I keep replaying that morning over and over, wishing I could have done something different, wishing I could have saved her.'

'But you couldn't,' Grace said, squeezing his hand.

'There was nothing either of us could have done,' he said. 'But we can make them pay.'

A shiver ran through Grace as she watched Teddy's face change, his eyes hard, his jaw clenched as he let go of her and stood, clearing his throat and squaring his shoulders.

'Stay safe, Teddy,' she said, not trusting her own legs to hold her. She held her breath as he leaned in and brushed a kiss to her cheek.

'Thanks for looking after me today,' he said, voice barely louder than a whisper as he stepped back.

Grace wrapped her arms tight around herself as she watched Teddy go. She had no idea if she'd ever see him again, if he was walking to his death or not. But there was nothing she could do about it. The only thing she knew was that nothing could ever bring Poppy back; no amount of fighting was going to change what had happened that day.

'Teddy,' she called out. 'If you do go, if I don't get to see you again, will you write to me?'

His eyes filled with tears as he smiled back at her. 'I will.'

'Nurse, is there any more food for us tonight?' a patient asked as Teddy disappeared.

She took a moment to breathe, to steady herself, before finally finding her feet.

'Let me take a look,' she called back, focusing on putting one foot in front of the other.

The only thing she could control right now was how well she cared for these men, and she was going to make sure they were the best-looked-after soldiers in Hawaii.

Poppy was gone. Teddy would be leaving soon. Eva might be dead for all they knew. And April would work until she collapsed.

She'd never felt so alone in all her life.

CHAPTER NINE
EVA

Eva stepped off the small vessel, wobbling as she tried to put one foot in front of the other. It felt like her balance was gone, her entire body quivering as she breathed in the familiar humid air and braced herself for what she was about to see.

The last three days, she'd seen more blood than she'd ever in her life expected to see. More missing limbs than she'd ever thought possible, more broken sailors, more men crying for all they'd lost; they had been the worst days of her life. She took in a big gulp of air. But even after all that, she had a nagging feeling that today was going to be the worst of them all.

She looked around, knowing the other women and men with her were talking, but unable to hear. She didn't want to hear anything; she just wanted to find Charlie, to see him with her own eyes, to hold his hands and hear him whisper to her that everything was going to be all right.

Eva kept walking, used to finding her way to his barracks, but nothing looked the same now. The smoke that she'd seen from the sea had disappeared, no longer smoldering and burning, but the island was decimated. Trees were fallen, their shallow roots sticking up like spooky

Halloween creatures; buildings were blackened and broken; and the once-pristine grass that stretched beyond the beach was littered with debris. It was as if a giant had stomped through, breaking and crushing everything in its way, although this was no fairy-tale giant responsible for the carnage.

'We're at war now,' she whispered to herself as she walked, trying to keep her eyes averted, not ready to see the devastation yet. She'd been through enough, and simply forcing herself to walk as anxiety gripped her was already too much.

After what felt like an eternity, and sticky from the humidity already, she found herself at what was left of Hickam Field. She'd been told the base had been obliterated, and it wasn't an exaggeration. The planes were all in pieces, where before they'd been so immaculately lined up, and the barracks looked as though no one could have survived the hit.

'Ma'am, your name?'

Eva looked up and into the eyes of a soldier, a clipboard in hand as he stared at her.

'Ah, ah . . .' She stumbled over her words. 'Eva. Eva Branson. I'm the fiancée of Charles Alexander.'

He frowned and looked at the list in his hand. 'And you're wanting to find out his whereabouts? I don't have his name on the list.'

Eva gasped. 'The list?' she asked. 'Is that the list of the men who've . . .' She couldn't even bring herself to finish her question. *Who've died.* That's what she'd wanted to ask. If he wasn't on the list, did that mean he *had* survived?

The soldier shook his head. 'I'm just in charge of who's permitted access, ma'am. Have you tried making contact before today?'

'Yes, of course. I'm a nurse on the USS *Solace*; I've been treating the wounded at sea for days, but I've heard no news of my fiancé.'

His smile was friendly. She should have told him from the very beginning that she was a nurse, or even worn her uniform ashore. 'Give me a minute, and I'll try to find out some information for you. He was based here?'

She smiled back. 'Yes. He is. Was, I mean.'

While she waited, Eva looked up, wondering how such a perfect, cloudless blue sky could ever have played host to warplanes. *We're at war.* The words had circled in her mind ever since she'd stepped out of the hospital ward. Exhausted, she'd tried to sleep, her eyes burning from being open too long, but all she'd been able to do was remember the noise, smell the blood, see the burns. Even now she could recall every smell and every vibration.

'Ma'am, someone is coming out to see you,' the soldier said.

Eva noticed that he never met her eye this time. Was she imagining it, or was he trying to avoid her gaze?

'Thank you,' she managed, choking on the words. She cleared her throat as a fresh wave of tears hit. Who was coming out to see her? Why couldn't the soldier with the clipboard tell her himself?

And then she saw a pilot in uniform appear, running his fingers through his hair. His thick brown hair seemed familiar, as did the way he kind of tugged it at the ends, his stubbled cheeks unusual for a man in uniform, although she guessed there had been much more for them to worry about than shaving these past few days.

'Eva,' he said, and the moment he spoke, she knew why he seemed so familiar.

'Teddy?' she asked.

He held out his hand and gently shook hers. His touch felt too soft, too delicate. Or maybe she was overreacting.

'You're Poppy's fiancé, aren't you?' she said, and she could see how uncomfortable he was, shifting from side to side as he nodded.

Eva felt like the world had stopped moving as she watched Teddy look away, his face contorting for a moment before he shut his eyes for a beat. Had she said the wrong thing? Was Poppy not . . .

'I, ah,' he started, clearing his throat before starting over. 'Poppy, well, she didn't survive the bombings,' Teddy said, his voice as rough as gravel. 'She was outside . . . I, we . . .' His breath shuddered, and tears filled her eyes as she thought about beautiful, fun-loving Poppy. 'She was gunned down. There was nothing anyone could have done to save her.'

Eva reached for him, barely able to hold herself together, but Teddy stiffened.

'I'm sorry. I . . .'

Teddy looked into her eyes then, a different kind of sadness passing across his face, a frown bracketing his mouth that had nothing to do with Poppy. This was something different, this was him looking at her differently, this was . . .

'Eva, I want you to know that I understand how you're going to feel, how this is going to rip you into pieces,' Teddy said softly.

'What?' she asked, wondering what he was trying to tell her. 'What will you understand?'

Fear danced across her skin, and she swallowed down a lump in her throat, waiting for Teddy to speak again, but at the same time wanting to run as far away from him as she could.

'Eva, I'm so sorry to be the one to break this to you, but Charlie died in the line of duty the day of the bombings,' Teddy said, his voice so deep and sad as he touched her arm, as if he was worried she'd fall over. 'We didn't know for certain until this morning that he was among the deceased, but we can now confirm that he is no longer with us.'

'No,' Eva said, violently shaking her head. 'No. No, no, no, Charlie is alive. *Do you hear me?* Charlie is alive!'

Teddy held on to her, but she yanked sideways, throwing his hand off as she stared back at him as if it were all his fault. As if Teddy had been the one to do this to her.

'I've been calling—I've been told that there was no news about him, that . . .' She sobbed. 'Let me see him! I need to see my Charlie!'

Teddy stepped closer and tried to comfort her, but she pushed at him, hands to his chest as she tried to force him away. When he reached for her again, she lashed out, thumping the heels of her hands into his chest, fighting him as if he were the enemy. As if he were responsible for everything that had happened.

'No!' she cried as she kept hitting him. '*No!* There must be some mistake!'

Teddy stood there and took it, not moving as she attacked him. It was only when she started to sob, when emotion cut through her and made her legs buckle as she cried, that Teddy moved, catching her in his arms and drawing her against his chest. He held her close, his big warm body cocooning her from the world as she sobbed into him.

'Shhhh,' he whispered, still holding her tight, as if he was scared she might collapse if he let her go.

They stayed like that for what felt like hours, until Eva finally peeled herself away from Teddy, keeping hold of his arm to steady herself. She took a deep, shuddering breath, carefully wiping her cheeks with the back of one hand as they stood together.

'How did this happen to us?' she whispered. 'How did we go from having the time of our lives here to losing everything?'

Emotion lodged in her throat, but she did her best to breathe through it, wanting to talk to Teddy, suddenly needing to stay with him for as long as she could.

'I don't know,' he said. 'I keep reliving that day, I keep remembering what happened, but nothing we did or didn't do . . .' He shook his head. 'Do you want me to take you to Tripler Hospital? Grace and April are both there, and I know they've been anxious to hear from you.'

Grace and April. Thank God they were okay. They must be struggling to cope after losing Poppy, and she bet they'd dealt with as many injured and dying men as she had. She sucked back a breath and clenched her fingers again.

'Is there any chance I can see Charlie?' she asked bravely. 'Is there a morgue?'

Teddy grimaced. 'If it's what you want, I'll find out for you. But it might take some time.'

'I understand.'

'Do you want me to take you to Tripler now?'

Just as Teddy finished speaking, the piercing sound of an air raid siren flooded the air around them.

'Hell,' Teddy swore, grabbing hold of her again and scanning the sky. 'You need to go.'

Terror gripped Eva's body as she looked upward, waiting for the planes, waiting for the menacing rain of bullets to start all over again.

'Do you know how he died?' she asked as Teddy pulled away from her.

'He survived the first wave of bombings and made it to a plane to fight back,' Teddy shouted as he ran backward. 'He died a hero, Eva. An absolute goddamn hero. Now run!'

Eva held up her skirt and looked over her shoulder, not seeing anything as the siren continued to wail, and she ran as fast as her legs could carry her back to the boat. Their ship had been their safe haven throughout it all, the only vessel not to be hit, and she was terrified of not making it back.

But then another thought dawned on her. What if she didn't make it back? What if she walked into the ocean or leaped from the harbor and gulped down water instead of air? What if she could end it all right now?

Her Charlie was gone, and that meant life wouldn't be worth living for her. If she had to go home to her father, if she didn't have Charlie to protect her . . . she stopped running and shut her eyes.

Without Charlie, what was the point?

'Hurry up!' someone yelled and grabbed hold of her arm, fingers digging into her skin. 'Can't you hear the siren?'

Eva forced herself to move then, not wanting to slow anyone else down by dragging her feet.

'Eva, do you want to come closer?'

Eva looked up, numb as she stared back at Grace and April. They were standing with Teddy, holding candles, their cheeks stained with tears as they held hands. She forced herself to walk closer, but her feet wouldn't budge.

'Eva?' It was April this time, walking forward, her hands outstretched as she closed the distance between them.

Grace stayed with Teddy, and Eva could see that she was crying again, her chest visibly heaving as she sobbed, but he hooked an arm around her, and she almost envied her friend being held through her pain. It had been barely a week since her world had crashed down around her, but to her the pain felt as raw and fresh as if it had only just happened.

'Tell me if you want to be alone, but I want you to know that we're here for you.'

She could see April's mouth moving, but it was almost impossible to hear her. There was a sound in her head, a roaring noise like the kind you could hear when you put your ear to a shell, only this was louder. And it hadn't stopped since she'd found out about Charlie.

The first night, when it had started, she'd thought it was from being so tired, that it would be gone by morning, but every day and night since it had been there, and it still hadn't stopped. Although maybe she hadn't slept since then? She could barely remember.

'Eva?'

She let April take her hand, wondering how her friend was holding it together so well. But then she saw a tear slip from her eye, then another and another, until she was steadily shedding tears in her own silent way.

Teddy met her gaze and nodded at her, and Grace grabbed her and held her so tight she couldn't breathe. But Eva stood, lifeless, unable to respond.

Why couldn't *she* cry? What was wrong with her? As soon as she'd gone back to the *Solace*, once her terror that another bombing was imminent after that awful air raid siren had passed, she'd gone cold. Her body was permanently numb, as if she were made of ice, and she'd wanted so desperately to collapse and sob her heart out, but nothing had happened.

Her tears were trapped inside of her, along with the scream she wanted to bellow out at the top of her lungs. Instead it just kept echoing in her head, along with the roaring sound, making her feel like a prisoner in her own body.

'I miss you so much, Poppy,' Grace whispered beside her. 'You were my best friend, the one person in the world who always made me smile.'

Eva looked up as Teddy put an arm back around Grace, drawing her close, and she remembered how warm and safe she'd felt in Teddy's arms herself when he'd broken the news to her about Charlie.

'We thought we were having the adventure of a lifetime here, didn't we, Pops?' April said, blowing her candle out and walking toward the ocean to throw a pretty flower into the water. 'I'll never forget you, my beautiful friend.'

Teddy cleared his throat and stepped forward, shoving his hands into his trouser pockets. 'She would have loved this,' he said.

Grace made a snorting noise. 'She would have hated this! The flowers and candles she would have approved of, but not all the tears and small talk. She would want us to be drinking and raising our glasses to her, or playing music and dancing.'

April laughed, which made Grace and Teddy laugh too. It was so inappropriate it was funny, but Eva couldn't manage to crack a smile as she watched them.

'You're right. She would have told us to smile and have some fun, wouldn't she?'

Eva stared out at the white flower April had thrown. It was bobbing away on the water now, slowly making its way farther out into the ocean. The same ocean that only days earlier had been alive with the horrors of war, with men bobbing around and fighting to stay alive instead of a pretty flower with petals the color of clouds.

'Is there anything you'd like to say?' April asked, interrupting Eva's thoughts with a gentle hand to her shoulder. 'About your Charlie?'

Eva stared at the ocean for a moment, before shutting her eyes, which were burning so intensely it was almost painful to see through them.

'No.'

What was she supposed to say? She'd loved Charlie with all her heart; they'd been best friends before they'd fallen in love, and she'd loved him because he was determined to protect her when no one else even knew how much pain she was in. What she suffered on a daily or weekly basis.

Without him, she would be going home to her father—a man who loved reminding her how useless she was, what a disappointment she was, and what an easy target she was for his fists. A man who'd laughed when Charlie had said he was going to marry her. A man who'd thrown her out and told her never to come back. And if she didn't go home, where would she go?

His cruel words echoed in her head, so hard to ignore as the memories played over and over through her mind.

'You think that a man wants anything more from you than a quick roll in the hay?' He laughed. 'Think again, sweetheart. No one wants you.'

She lifted her gaze, knowing it was going to come with punishment but no longer caring.

'You're wrong.'

He hated the taunt, hated that she'd dared to answer him back. But as he punched her stomach, always in a place where no one could see the bruises, she smiled, because it was so close to being over.

'Eva, I know this is hard for you—we understand—but . . . ,' April said.

She dragged herself from her thoughts, from the memories that kept playing like a film through her mind. 'I should have let him go and join the Eagles,' she heard herself say. Her voice seemed so distant, so much deeper than she expected it to sound, as if she were hearing it for the first time. 'If I'd let him go instead of begging him to stay here, he'd probably still be alive, wouldn't he? So maybe the fact he's dead is my fault.'

April was shaking her head as Grace began to cry softly again, still standing beside Teddy.

'Don't say that, Eva. No one expected this; no one knew this was coming,' she said, reaching for her as she spoke. 'This was not your fault.'

Eva moved sideways just enough that April's hand collided with air instead of her body. She didn't want to be touched or coddled or part of some memorial service. Charlie was gone, and nothing was going to change that.

'Eva, the only ones to blame for this are the Japs,' Teddy said, suddenly in front of her, his big frame blocking the sunlight from her eyes. It was a relief to have shade and not have to squint.

'Charlie couldn't fly for the Eagles without turning his back on his own men and his country; you know that as well as I do, and I think he knew that too. But he was a fighter, and it's why he wasn't content sitting around and waiting,' he said. 'Leaving to fly with them was no more than a pilot's frustration combined with a pipe dream—you hear me? There was no way he was going to Europe without his squadron.'

Eva nodded, more to get Teddy off her case than because she agreed with him. Because he was wrong; Charlie hadn't been dreaming about going—he would have found a way to leave if she hadn't been the persistent ball and chain dragging behind him and forcing him to stay.

'Can you give us a minute?' April asked, stepping between Teddy and Eva.

Teddy nodded and touched Eva's arm as he passed, walking quietly away down the beach with Grace beside him.

'Eva, I think you're in shock,' April said softly, beckoning for her to sit in the soft sand with her. 'It's understandable, given what you've gone through, and so many of our nurses and men are the same right now.'

Eva stared at the water, not able to look at April.

'I want you to know that I'm here for you. Losing Poppy, it's like someone is kicking me in the stomach and winding me at times, and other times I carry on and don't think about her. Then I feel so guilty that I've just gone about my day without acknowledging that she didn't make it, that she's not here with us.'

Eva opened her mouth, but nothing came out. She moistened her lips and tried again, shuddering as she fought to say the words. She wondered if April even knew what a blow to the stomach *actually* felt like.

'He was all I had,' she finally managed. 'It's just, without him, I . . .'

April took her hand and linked their fingers. 'He's not all you have, Eva. You have me and Grace—we're here for you—and you have your family and your work.'

She shook her head, breathing in deep, then letting out a big loud exhale. 'You don't understand.'

April never let go of her hand. 'Try me. You might be surprised.'

Eva wanted to tell her, but she couldn't. She'd never told anyone the whole truth about her father; Charlie was the only one who'd ever known.

'Maybe you should apply for leave? After what you've been through, you should be allowed to go home to your family, for a—'

'No!' she gasped, reeling at the thought of going back.

April looked surprised, her face a question mark of expression, but she recovered and patted her hand in a motherly kind of way. 'All right, maybe not. But time off from work at least, for as long as you need.'

Eva shut her eyes, squeezing them, wondering if tears would stop the burning pain in her eyeballs. But still they didn't come.

'We can sit here all day if you like,' April said, as if she were talking to a child. 'Just you and me, for as long as you need. We don't even have to talk.'

Eva wondered about Grace, whether she'd need her sister and come looking for them, but she didn't ask. All she could think about was the feel of April's warm hand in hers, the breeze lifting her loose hair from the back of her neck, and the roaring that was starting to get louder as she stared at the ocean.

Maybe it was the water calling to her, telling her that her idea about flinging herself into the aqua-blue depths was the right one. Or perhaps it was her body fighting against the pain, refusing to let her collapse into the web of grief that she knew must surely be waiting to catch her.

'Farewell, my friend,' she heard April whisper.

Farewell, Poppy, Eva thought, listening to the words echo in her mind. *Goodbye, Charlie.*

Perhaps the Japanese would bomb them to oblivion and reunite her with Charlie. Maybe their boat would sink, and she'd end up in the ocean anyway. Or maybe this was the world's way of showing her that she didn't deserve happiness. Maybe her father had been right.

Just when she'd found herself, found the one thing she was good at, the one thing that no one could take away from her, the rug had been pulled out from beneath her. If she didn't know better, she'd have thought it was her father playing a cruel trick on her to prove that she'd never, ever be able to escape him.

'We're going to survive this,' April murmured to her. 'No matter what, we're going to get through this.'

Eva lay back on the sand, wondering if April was ever going to let go of her hand.

She had another two hours before she had to go back to her boat, and for now she was just going to lie. Be still. And then she'd go back, start her nighttime nursing shift, and do the one thing she was good at. Because if she had to suffer through all this, she could at least keep nursing the men who needed her. And it was better than sitting in bed and wondering what was wrong with her that she couldn't even shed a tear for the man she loved and the friend she'd lost.

CHAPTER TEN

CHRISTMAS EVE, 1941

APRIL

The thing about Hawaii was that it was never cold. Every day felt like summer; when it was raining, it was still tropical, and the humidity reminded April that she was on an island. *It doesn't even feel like Christmas tomorrow.* It was strange, staring at the clouds as they rolled past overhead and trying to imagine that if they were at home, they'd be following all their usual Christmastime traditions. There would be a tree in the corner of the living room, adorned with pretty decorations their mother had collected when she was first married. April would be in charge of cooking Christmas lunch, as always, and Grace would be sitting on the counter picking at what April was preparing, her legs dangling as she chatted about everything and anything.

She'd often bemoaned having to be the one doing everything at Thanksgiving and Christmas, taking on that role of mother, but now that she wasn't at home, she wished she were there. That things could go back to normal, that Poppy were still with them. If they were at home, Poppy's mother would be waiting to welcome them. They'd arrive at Poppy's on Christmas Eve and be enveloped in warm hugs and kisses;

there would be stockings hanging with gifts, and little homemade gingerbread cookies paired with warm, milky eggnog.

She looked down at the letter clasped tightly between her fingers, blinking away fresh tears as she reread her words. Grace had said she'd write to Poppy's mother, but part of her wondered if her sister would ever get around to it, and she didn't want to keep asking her. Besides, Poppy's mother had been so supportive of them, always helping with her kind words and advice, sharing recipes and being there for her whenever she'd needed someone to lean on.

Dear Deborah,

The grief we've all felt since Poppy's passing has been immense. When I say that she was a light in all our lives, it's no exaggeration. Until that day, we were having the time of our lives. I'm sure she wrote to tell you herself, but the weeks we had here in peace were weeks that I'll never forget. We went horseback riding and on picnics, we walked and explored, and we danced until our feet hurt.

Teddy is understandably devastated, and I hope you know what a kind, loving man he was to Poppy. He never ceased to put a smile on her face, her eyes always lit up when she saw him, and I can't imagine how much he must be missing her.

When I tell you that I understand your loss, you know that I mean it. You were there for me when our mother passed, and without your support I don't know what I would have done. Your house was a second home to us, and Poppy was truly my best friend in the world. When I'm able to return, I want you to know that nothing will change between us. You have lost your daughter, but I will always think of you as my other mother, and I hope that I can help in the same way for you.

With all my love and prayers,

April

There were no words to say how she was truly feeling, the pain inside of her at every turn, but she hoped that the letter would at least give Poppy's mother something to hold on to. She'd lost her only daughter, just as April had lost her only mother, so she knew precisely how that kind of pain could rip a person in half and make it feel impossible to ever move forward.

'April!'

She quickly wiped her eyes and tucked the letter into its envelope. 'I didn't expect to see you out here.'

April smiled when she saw Dr. Grey approaching, finding it impossible not to return his warm greeting.

'I was getting some fresh air,' she said. 'I feel so claustrophobic in there sometimes with all the blackout blankets.'

He grimaced. 'I know the feeling. The humidity and lack of air is unbearable.'

She'd heard they were installing new curtains or blinds that would allow them to at least open the windows a crack, but she didn't bother telling Dr. Grey. She was certain the doctors would be briefed on such matters well before the nurses anyway.

'Do you have plans to celebrate Christmas tomorrow, or do you have a shift?' he asked.

She fell into step beside him when he started walking. 'I'm looking forward to Christmas lunch and some festivities before working in the evening. How about you?'

He met her eyes when he glanced at her, and she quickly looked away. There was something about the doctor that rattled her, the way he smiled at her, his command in the operating theater, the way he seemed so confident whatever he was doing. She couldn't pretend it didn't appeal to her, because it did.

'I'm hoping for a few hours of extra sleep, to tell you the truth,' he said. 'If I'm not called in early, that is. I feel like I never get out of that damn hospital some days.'

April grinned. 'I think we all know that feeling. The last few weeks . . .'

She didn't need to finish her sentence; they all knew what the past weeks had been like, and what they'd endured didn't need to be relived. But the surgeons were always on call, so it was even worse for them than for the nurses sometimes.

They'd reached the hospital doors now, and Dr. Grey stopped, his hand skimming her arm and taking her by surprise. 'Merry Christmas, April,' he said quietly, his gaze warm and steady.

She felt her cheeks flush. 'Merry Christmas,' she replied.

April stood as he turned and disappeared, wondering if he was so friendly with all the nurses. She clutched the envelope and kept walking, needing to mail her letter before it was too late. The sky was slowly getting darker, the sun fading for the day, and she had things to do before nightfall and the early curfew that kept them all inside after dark.

———— ✦ ————

'Can you believe it's Christmas Eve?' April smiled over at her sister as they sipped tea and sat on their beds. The past weeks had been weird and desolate without Poppy. She'd felt closer to Grace than she had in a long while. Her sister had apologized profusely for her outburst the day of the bombing, and even though she would have forgiven her regardless, it was good to see a more thoughtful, grown-up side to Grace.

'I thought we'd be dancing until midnight and having a Christmas like no other this year,' April said. Instead they were still all on edge, waiting for something else to happen, even though the more days that passed with no Japanese soldiers coming running down the beach to capture them or blasting them from overhead, the less likely it was that it would happen. Or so they hoped.

'Eva, what would you be doing if you were home this Christmas?' April asked, wondering if they'd done the right thing inviting their friend over. They weren't technically supposed to have any visitors to their quarters, but given everything that had happened, she was hoping the punishment wouldn't be too severe if they were caught. Eva was another nurse; it wasn't like they'd smuggled someone's sweetheart in.

'I'd be going over to Charlie's,' Eva said, her hands folded in her lap and her gaze fixed past April. 'His family was always very welcoming, and I was there as often as I could be.'

'Just like us with Poppy,' April said, glancing at her sister and pleased to see that she was smiling at the memory. 'And what of your own family? Did you have any special traditions?'

She noticed the way Eva's back straightened and saw her clasp her hands tight.

'I've been told to return home,' Eva said, taking April by surprise.

'Oh. Well, maybe that's for the best. You've been through a lot,' April said. Eva had been so confident and capable, and now she was a shell of her former self.

'You don't want to go?' Grace asked. 'I thought you'd be desperate to get away from here.'

Eva's face contorted in the most painful way, and April quickly shuffled closer to her as Grace did the same on the other side.

'Eva, what is it? What's wrong?'

'I can't go home,' she said, shaking her head and biting down on her lip. 'I don't want to be here, but I can't go home either.'

April exchanged looks with Grace and saw that her sister seemed as confused as she was. 'You can talk to us. If there's something we can do, if there's anything that . . .'

'Charlie was the only one who could help me. When we got married, it was all going to change; I was going to be safe.'

April hugged her and held on to her for a long time, feeling Eva's big shuddering breaths. 'Eva, can you talk to us about it?'

Eva shut her eyes before whispering, 'No.'

Grace was shuffled tight against their grieving friend now, too, and April racked her brain. Eva wasn't exactly the shrinking violet type; before Charlie's death she'd been as determined and forthright as could be, which made April think that whatever was spooking her was no small thing. What had happened to that confident navy nurse?

'Would you rather take time to grieve and recuperate on the island here?' April asked. 'Instead of being sent home, I mean?'

Eva nodded and looked up. 'Yes,' she whispered, her voice quavering.

April thought it through before speaking again. She didn't want to overpromise, but she wasn't going to sit by and do nothing when Eva was clearly so terrified. 'What if we could billet you to a private residence somehow? I'm sure we could find somewhere for you, and then you can take your time before coming back to nursing.'

Eva shook her head, and April noticed that Eva's eyes were swimming with tears. She'd never, ever seen her cry before, even after everything she'd lost.

'But that's it—I can't nurse if I go on leave,' Eva said. 'The *Solace* is leaving for the South Pacific, and if I'm not on it then—'

'Then you can nurse with us,' April said, not pausing to consider whether it was even possible to transfer like that. But the army wasn't exactly overrun with highly trained, capable nurses, so she couldn't see why not. 'I'll do everything I can to help you transfer.'

Eva didn't say anything, but April saw a brightness return to her eyes.

'So she takes the time she needs to recover,' Grace said, 'and then she works with us? You really think you could make that happen?'

April didn't like overpromising, but she could see that Eva was looking hopeful. 'Yes,' she replied. 'You need sleep, Eva. The skin around your eyes is so dark it's almost black. And you need to cry,' she said softly. 'You have so much grieving to do.'

Eva nodded, and April wondered again what had her friend so scared. She would do anything to hightail it home right now, if it weren't for all the patients who needed her, and Eva was acting like home was worse than here.

'Our men need you, Eva. From what I've heard, you're a brilliant, capable nurse, and you held it together and saved so many lives the day of the bombings.' April took her hand and pulled it onto her own leg, searching Eva's eyes. 'When you're ready, you can always talk to us, but for now, we need to help you heal and then find a way to get you nursing again. If you don't want to go home, then I'll do anything I can to stop that from happening. Okay?'

Eva nodded but didn't say anything, squeezing her hand instead.

'Girls! Have you heard the news?'

Another nurse burst into their sleeping quarters, still in her uniform. She must have just finished her shift.

'We're being sent away.'

Fear sliced through April. 'Where are they sending us?' she asked, trying to stop the choke in her voice.

'Somewhere far away, from the sounds of it. They're figuring out who to send in the new year; most will be going to the Pacific, but they said some nurses will be put on boats to Europe and God only knows where else.'

Grace looked like she was about to have a panic attack and Eva was starting to tremble, so April took a big deep breath and squared her shoulders. She wasn't allowed to be afraid or hysterical; she needed to hold it together for the other two.

'I suppose we're to be sent wherever we're most needed,' she said, trying to sound pragmatic. 'Wherever we go, we'll be saving lives. And that's why we chose to become nurses, isn't it?'

Grace snorted with laughter, and April spun around at her sister's inappropriate reaction.

'Grace!' she scolded.

'I'm sorry, but if Poppy was here, she'd have laughed and told you that she only ever signed up for nursing to get a free island vacation!'

April went to reply but couldn't as she burst out laughing herself. They laughed until they cried, sitting on the bed three in a row, until April looked over at Poppy's empty bed and wondered what on earth their friend was thinking if she was looking down on them.

She was as terrified as the next nurse about being sent abroad. Hawaii had seemed exotic yet still close enough to home to be safe, but then look how wrong they'd been about that. She wondered if Dr. Grey would be sent away, too, and then pinched herself for even thinking about him.

'I just about got shot out there coming back from work,' Cassie, a young nurse, said as she stripped down and changed into her night-clothes. 'The soldiers are all so jumpy, and the one on guard told me to put out my cigarette because I was in breach of the curfew and the blackout!'

'Did you put it out?' April asked.

'I don't even smoke! It was the moonlight reflecting off my wrist-watch! Imagine if he'd shot me for that.'

Grace got up then, and April watched as she went over to Poppy's bed and pulled something out from underneath it.

'I think someone would be happy to see us all have a little drink tonight,' Grace said, grinning as she unscrewed the lid of the whiskey bottle and took a swig. 'Merry Christmas, Poppy.'

April watched as Eva took the contraband bottle next and took a long, steady sip before passing it to her.

'Merry Christmas, Poppy,' they both said at the same time.

'And to Teddy,' Grace added.

They all chimed in, repeating Grace's words, and April couldn't help but notice the glimmer of fresh tears in her sister's eyes at the mention of Teddy's name. He'd been gone a week now, and she worried that he hadn't had time to come to terms with losing Poppy before being sent straight into the thick of it. But she'd kept her worries to herself, not wanting to worry Grace.

She took her own sip from the bottle before passing it along. Last Christmas they'd been safely tucked up in their family home in Oregon, tonight they were huddled in their barracks in Hawaii, and next year, well, next year they might be on the other side of the world for all she knew.

She reached for Eva's hand again and sat listening to the other girls talk and catching Grace's eye every now and again. The whiskey had warmed a fiery path inside of her, and she shut her eyes as exhaustion hit her like a brick.

So much for having the vacation of their lives.

Life as they knew it was over. And she knew it would never, ever be the same again.

PART TWO

CHAPTER ELEVEN

MID-1942

GRACE

'Well, this certainly isn't for the fainthearted, is it?' Grace looked over at her sister and burst out laughing. It was either that or cry, but April didn't look impressed.

'So let me get this straight,' April said, her hands on her hips as she glared at the soldier relaying news to them. 'We have *actual* submarines chasing us?' When April's voice ended in a much higher pitch than her usual tone, Grace knew that her sister wasn't coping well with being at sea.

'Yes, ma'am. We're at war, so they are *actual* submarines.' He cleared his throat. 'We actually saw the dark-gray snout of the emerging sub poking out of the water, but they seemed as surprised to see an enemy vessel as we were, because they quickly submerged, and we managed to outrun them.'

April positively glowered at him, but Grace turned away when she heard Eva come up behind her.

'What's going on? What was that big lurch to the side?'

'Oh, that was just an enemy *submarine* chasing us!' April declared as the soldier stared at the ground, no doubt regretting ever relaying the news in the first place.

'Oh.' Eva didn't look as concerned as Grace had expected, yawning and wrapping her arms around herself. 'But we've gotten away from it?'

Grace nodded. 'Yes, we're safe for now, but it means we're going to be sailing to Algeria instead of Morocco.'

'Huh-hmm, ah, ladies,' the soldier said, clearing his throat and looking uncomfortable as he shifted from foot to foot. 'We've actually been avoiding submarine activity for much of the journey. It's why we've zigzagged so often, like a drunken sailor's in charge. But she's a quick ship—that's why we didn't need a convoy—and she's known to have the best luck on the water.'

Grace wished he hadn't told them that. April looked as if she were about to explode, and Eva was sporting the same blank expression she'd worn ever since the day Charlie had died, which was so different from the vibrant, forthright woman she'd been the first night they'd met. Eva just didn't seem to feel anything anymore; her expression rarely changed, and she got on with everything and completed every task, but it was like no one was there when Grace looked into her eyes. Grace knew she was different now, too—after everything they'd all gone through, they all were—but it was as if Eva had numbed herself to everything somehow.

'I'll leave you to it,' the soldier said, backing away. 'We've had a game of craps going for hours, Grace, if you, ah, want to join us?'

Grace shot him a smile as April started pacing, and Eva just stood there as if waiting to be told what to do. A small lurch made her wonder if they were about to get blown apart, but nothing happened, and she let out a breath she hadn't even known she was holding. The attention was nice, though, and she knew they wouldn't even have been notified about the sub if she hadn't known so many of the soldiers so well. She only wished April were enjoying the voyage more.

'Thanks. Maybe we'll see you soon,' she said.

He stepped away, and she smiled back at him, knowing how embarrassed he'd be if he could see how pink his cheeks were.

They'd departed America for Morocco in the converted luxury liner days ago, although at the time they'd been told no details about where they might be going. They'd all speculated about staying in the Pacific with most of the other Pearl Harbor nurses, but with so few nurses with surgical experience, they'd volunteered to go farther abroad. It had been pleasant enough sailing, other than the fact that it had rained for the past two days and they'd been forced to stay cooped up. Nurses weren't allowed on the decks after sundown, which meant they were stuck inside until morning now unless they managed to sneak out.

The ship they were sailing on was enormous, and it was filled to the rafters, with more nurses and soldiers on board than she could ever have imagined. They'd had a number of drills, rain or shine, but Grace wasn't one of the nurses complaining. She was excited about where they might be going and what they might be doing; her father had hugged her goodbye and told her to make the most of everything, to soak up every part of her experience and commit it to memory to share with him, and that's exactly what she was going to do. Not a day went by that she didn't think about Poppy, wishing her friend could have been by her side, but her daddy had been right: she needed to find joy in whatever it was they were doing, and she was determined to find it in Africa. And Poppy's mother had told her the same, writing a short letter to her that Grace had committed to memory, she'd read it so many times.

Live life for her, Grace. Go to all the parties, smile at everyone, find happiness in whatever it is you do and wherever you're sent. And every time you smile, remember that a little bit of Poppy will always be with you. Stay safe and come home to me. You and April are all I have now.

She brushed away a tear and looked skyward, smiling as she wondered if Poppy might be looking down on them. She took a big lungful of air before turning to face the other two, fixing her smile in place.

'Why don't we see if there's something to do?' she said. 'Maybe we could join in with the craps game or start something else or . . .'

April still looked like she was about to start hyperventilating, and Grace stifled a laugh. It wasn't that she was finding her sister's suffering funny, but she'd never had to calm her down before or be the level-headed one. It was as if the tables had turned as April's fear of sailing took hold, and she wanted to help her.

Grace took April's hand. 'You know, it could be fun to play. Take our minds off what could be going on beneath the water,' she said gently. 'They sound like a fun group of guys, but I'm happy to do whatever you feel like doing.'

'Aren't you worried at all?' April asked.

Grace held firm to April's hand on one side and Eva's on the other. 'No. Because when our time is up, our time is up. Right now I'm choosing to trust our captain, so if he says we're safe, then we're safe. He wouldn't have let that soldier tell us if he wasn't confident in our safety, now would he?'

'Fine, let's go for a walk. I need to do something; otherwise I'm going to drive myself crazy with worry,' April said.

'My thoughts exactly,' Grace replied.

Maybe it was losing Poppy and surviving Pearl Harbor, but whatever it was, she wasn't going to waste time crying or hiding from whatever life was throwing at her. She shuddered as she remembered how everything, every nook and cranny and patient, had been covered in blood that day. *That* would make her want to cry and hide, if she had to see that all over again, but everything else she felt that she could face. All she could do now was pull herself up by her bootstraps and get on with life.

'Come on, Eva,' Grace said as she dragged them both toward the mess room, which had once been a no-doubt glorious library. 'How are you feeling today?'

'Um, I'm fine,' she replied. 'There's nothing wrong with me.'

'Well, let's see if a hot cup of coffee and a game of craps perks you up, then.'

She wasn't sure who was rolling their eyes more at her lately, her sister or Eva, but whatever Eva said, there was definitely something wrong with her. They'd all grieved for their losses in their own ways, every single nurse and soldier who'd lived and lost that day, but not Eva. Eva had just seemed to steel herself and keep going, never talking about Charlie, never mentioning what they'd lost. And Grace knew that one day she'd crack; she just wanted to make sure she was there for her when she did.

Two days later, Grace stood at the railings and looked back at the boat, rather than out to sea as she usually did. She couldn't stop thinking how strange it was that their ship had once been a luxury liner reserved only for the very wealthy, because despite the grandeur of her bones, she was very much a workhorse now. The staircases were built from timber that had once upon a time been polished within an inch of its life on a daily basis, and the size of the swimming pool alone, which was now filled with beds, showed how extravagant everything must have been, and Grace wished she could have traveled on her before she was converted. Now, the once two-person rooms were crammed with fourteen nurses each, packed into bunk beds like sardines, with barely space to stretch without connecting with the sagging mattress above, and it was often stifling from so many women breathing the same confined space. But it was almost over now, and suddenly the ship felt safer than the unknown.

She couldn't help but wonder if conditions might be worse wherever it was they were going. She knew nothing about Africa, other than the fact that some of the people there had skin as dark as midnight, and all types of wild, exotic animals lived freely there. But now they were within hours of arrival, and she couldn't ignore the tremors of excitement running through her body as she turned back to face the water and the land they'd been told they would see soon.

'How are you feeling?' April asked, placing a hand on her shoulder as she stood beside her.

Grace looked over at her, smiling at her sister. April looked so young and fresh faced standing there. And she also looked a whole lot more relaxed than she had in days.

'Nervous,' she admitted. 'I'm excited, but my stomach is twisted into knots.'

'I know the feeling. Something about being stuck on this boat has rattled me. I just want to get my feet firmly on the ground again and get back to feeling in control.'

They stood staring out to sea together as the boat moved slowly toward their final destination.

'I think I've felt more comfortable on this boat than I usually feel on land,' Grace admitted, stroking her fingers back and forth across the wooden handrail. 'It sounds stupid, but I feel like, I don't know, the unknown doesn't scare me. I've liked being on here and being part of the anticipation, having so many people around us. It's kind of like when we first arrived in Hawaii, before . . .'

April nodded. 'I know. But *I* can't stand the unknown, I can't plan for it, so I've been a hot mess! All I want is to see a hospital and set it up and get on with our job.'

Grace shuddered at the idea of having to set up the hospital and deal with bloody and dying patients again; she and April were definitely on different sides of the table there. Why was it that her sister was so capable when it came to things like that, and yet they put the fear of

God into her? If they hadn't looked so similar, she would have wondered if they were actually related sometimes.

'Do you think Eva's coping?' April asked, her voice low.

Grace glanced over her shoulder to make sure Eva wasn't nearby. 'I don't know what's going on with her. It's almost like she's, I don't know, going through the motions of everyday things without actually being there.'

'I know,' April said. 'But she lost her fiancé, and we know what it's like to lose someone. Everyone grieves differently, and how long is too long? She's been through a lot.'

Grace watched a ripple in the water, and as her stomach lurched at the thought it was another submarine, a fish slipped through the water and broke the surface.

'I think she's more complex than we realize,' April said. 'There's something going on with her family, or maybe it's just her father, but I think she's genuinely scared. The way she looked at me when we talked about her going home, it was strange. I just can't stop thinking about it.'

'You think he might, I don't know, physically hurt her?' Grace asked. Their father was so kind—aloof and frustrating as anything sometimes, but he'd never raise his voice at them, let alone hurt them.

'I'm not sure. All I know is that she seemed so strong and confident when we first met her, and now I just can't put my finger on it. It was almost like the fear of going home was worse for her than actually losing Charlie, but maybe I have it wrong. I don't know.'

Grace sighed. Her sister was usually right; she always seemed to have the right intuition about what was going on with people and how to help. 'I hope you're wrong.'

April smiled sadly. 'Me too.'

They stood side by side, basking in the warm sun and enjoying the ocean breeze, for almost another hour before they were all called to gather their things and prepare for arrival.

Three hours later, the ship was finally still, and Grace waited patiently with the other nurses to disembark, bumping shoulders with April on one side and Eva on the other.

'I thought Hawaii was hot,' Grace grumbled, blowing damp tendrils of hair from her face. It was impossibly hot, the kind of hot that left skin sticky and foreheads dripping, and it was even worse because they were carrying so much. 'No wonder the people here have such dark skin. Our white skin would probably melt off us if we lived here!'

April laughed, but she didn't get a rise out of Eva. But when she glanced over at the soldiers who'd already disembarked, she gave Eva a little kick to get her attention.

'Would you look at them?' she said. 'I think we're carrying more than they are!'

She watched as Eva followed her gaze. 'Hmm, I think you're right.'

Grace shuffled beneath the weight of her two packs, one on the front, one on the back, filled with her bedroll, uniforms, gas protection suit, cosmetics, and other bits and pieces. That combined with the two army blankets rolled tightly and slung over her shoulder was causing her to buckle beneath the weight and the stifling heat of it all.

As soon as they started moving, she forgot all about what she was carrying, though, her eyes wide as she climbed down over the side of the ship, heart thudding as she tried to balance, terrified of falling into the ominous water lapping below. She gripped tight to the iron ladder and didn't let go until strong hands grabbed her around her middle and hauled her down into the little assault boat. She pushed her helmet up, hating how it kept sliding down low over her eyes, and looked behind her at three medical officers and at least fifteen or more soldiers. Grace managed a small smile and received warm grins in return as she waited for the others to come down the awful little ladder.

Once April, Eva, and two other nurses had safely descended, the boat took them to land, and Grace found her feet were unsteady as she stepped out with the assistance of a soldier and looked around her at the long stretch of beach.

They were finally, after twelve long days, standing on Algerian soil, and she couldn't believe the commotion. There were people with dark skin milling back and forth, interspersed with American soldiers, who stood out with their light-colored hair and skin, and she noticed they were speaking different languages. She was passable at French, which she'd studied for a few years at school, but she certainly couldn't keep up with the rapid pace at which some of the people were speaking.

'This is insane!' Grace hurried to keep up while she gawked around. 'Did you ever think it would be like this?'

'It even smells different,' Eva said, surprising Grace as she touched her arm. 'Look over there at the fish for sale. That poor man is spending all his time waving insects away.'

As Grace was looking, a booming voice carried on the wind to them, and everyone went silent.

'Ladies, listen up! You'll be traveling the rest of the way to Mateur in Tunisia by train. Please walk to the train station in an orderly line, and board when you are called. And try not to keel over in this heat!'

Grace felt her heart start to race again. A train ride? She hadn't even considered that they might have to travel immediately again, but the thought excited her. She wanted to hang out the window and take in every sight, drink in every part of this exciting new country they were in so she could commit it to memory and tell her father when they returned home. Sweat dripped down the back of her neck now, but she'd long forgotten how uncomfortable she was.

'I thought we'd be staying here for a while,' April said. 'Instead they're shoving us straight into a train.'

'Maybe it's safer,' Eva said.

'I think they're sending us even closer to danger, so I don't think we'll be safer,' April answered.

They walked in silence to the train, and Grace grinned when she saw soldiers pass by as another train departed. 'Goodbye!' she called, blowing kisses and waving to the American men on their way. 'Good luck!'

April laughed beside her, and even Eva was smiling as the soldiers called back and returned her kisses, some of them clutching their chests like she was breaking their hearts.

'What?' Grace asked. 'What's so funny?'

'You,' April said. 'Something about you draws the boys in like bees to pollen.'

Grace blushed and felt her cheeks ignite, but she just waved the compliment away. In the past it had been Poppy who'd received the lion's share of the attention. But those boys were off to fight, and all she'd done was give them a little wave. Within minutes they were lined up once again to board, and before she knew it, six of them were crammed in a tiny compartment.

'Do you think they could have split us between two trains instead of this?' she grumbled as they all tried to stow their things. 'We can't even all sleep at the same time in here!'

April looked as unimpressed as she felt. 'I suppose we can take turns on the seats and floor when we want to sleep,' she said. 'Oh, and look! Two of us can definitely fit in the overhead.'

Grace's brows shot up. 'The *overhead*? That's for luggage, you fool.'

April shrugged. 'Come nightfall, I bet we'll all be grateful to lie down on anything instead of stay standing.'

'I'll take the overhead,' Eva said. 'April's right; it's better than nothing.'

Grace shrugged. 'Fine. But we're not staying stuck in here for two days; we need to explore once we're moving.' She wanted to shake Eva. Why would she offer to sleep in the overhead? The Eva who'd given that soldier marching orders the first night they'd met, when he'd had his

148

hands all over Grace, wouldn't have so easily given in to sleeping rough without at least demanding a coin toss to decide the loser.

'What's there to explore?' asked Kelly, one of the nurses who'd ended up in their compartment.

'No idea,' Grace said. 'But I'm not about to get cabin fever and stay stuck in this tiny closet for forty-eight hours with barely enough room to wriggle, let alone breathe.'

Two days later, Grace was about to explode. The train had been moving so slowly she wasn't convinced they'd moved more than a few inches in the past hour, and she was on the verge of hysteria. There was only so long she could take being in such a small space, and her stomach was roaring with hunger. What she wouldn't do for a hot bath or even a warm facecloth to wipe across her forehead and down her neck, or an ice-cold glass of water. Being stuck in their compartment was torturous.

Thump.

'What the heck?' Grace rolled sideways as something large landed on her with a thwack. 'Eva!'

Eva pushed up, groaning as she tried to get off her. 'Ouch.'

'Oh, honey, you poor thing! You fell out of the compartment!' April was suddenly on her feet, hauling Eva up and checking her over.

'What about me? I'm the one who broke her fall and got squashed!' Grace protested.

They all looked at one another and burst out laughing, just as the train groaned and ground to a complete halt.

'You've got to be kidding me,' April muttered under her breath.

Grace walked over to the window and pushed aside the flimsy curtain, taking a peek outside. *Well, isn't that a sight for sore eyes.* Another train was right beside them, and she knew the drill by now. There was only one line, which meant they'd have to wait for this other train to get past. The fact that it was filled with soldiers was the only thing that made it bearable.

'Girls, I think you need to see this,' she said. 'Or should I say see *them*.'

April, Eva, and the other three nurses came up beside her, and they all peered out the window as Grace pushed it open, grinning as she waved and called out. They usually had the windows closed, despite the heat, to keep the insects out, but this was worth letting a mosquito in for.

'Yoo-hoo, boys!' she called as the others giggled beside her.

One of the soldiers suddenly leaped up, and she watched as he nudged his friends in the sides and then jimmied his window open. Next thing they were all hanging out the open side, and more soldiers started to join them.

'Where're you girls heading?' one of them asked.

'Mateur,' Grace called back. 'It's slow going, though.'

'Fancy a ride? You're welcome over here!' another called.

Grace glanced at April and then shrugged, batting her lashes. Meeting men at dances in Hawaii had been exciting but terrifying at the same time, but this was different. There was something fun, something exciting, about being able to flirt from a distance.

'If you have some hot coffee, well then, we might just take you up on that offer.'

April slapped at her shoulder, but Grace just laughed.

'Whaddya say, fellas?'

'Hot coffee, coming right up!' one of them yelled back.

There was no way Grace was going to be able to get on that train even if she tried, but she'd do anything for a coffee, especially a milky, sugary one.

'You got any sugar over there?' she asked in her sweetest voice.

'Like you need sweetening up,' one of the men replied with a laugh.

'What happened to shy Grace?' Eva whispered.

Grace laughed. 'Oh, she's long gone. This Grace is living each day like it's her last.' As the words came out, she wished she could take them back. Why had she said that when Eva had lost her Charlie? When she'd lost Poppy? 'I'm sorry—that was insensitive—I . . .'

Eva's hand was warm on her shoulder. 'It's fine. Actually, it's nice to hear you laugh and have fun.'

Grace looked into her friend's eyes, wishing there was more she could do to help her. 'Really?'

Eva smiled. 'Really. Now quickly, get our cups so we can pass them over to those soldiers before one of these trains starts moving! You've turned into quite the flirt!'

'Boys, start filling these cups, and fill them fast!' she said with a wink and a big smile, leaning forward and laughing as the men ogled her as if they hadn't ever seen a woman before. 'Stop gawking and start pouring!'

CHAPTER TWELVE

APRIL

'So this is it?' April asked, looking first at her sister and then at Eva. They both stared back at her, looking as shocked as she was.

She hadn't expected anything luxurious, but she'd thought basic things like a roof might be guaranteed. It seemed not. The building in front of them looked like it might have been mangled during the war, and she would have thought exactly that if they hadn't just been told it was an unfinished building abandoned for years.

'I was dreading sleeping in tents, but working in this might actually be worse,' Grace muttered beside her.

'Will we even be safe in there?' Eva asked. 'What if there's fighting close by?'

April looked back at the other nurses, who were all in groups and chatting, while their matron stood beside a general, their heads together as they studied something on her clipboard.

'Ladies, listen up!' the general announced.

They all turned, packs at their feet now, and April took the opportunity to pull at her jacket and try to let some air against her skin. She'd never been so hot and uncomfortable in all her life.

'Welcome to the 114th Station Hospital! This is where you will be stationed for the foreseeable future. Sleeping quarters for nurses will be in tents in the adjoining field area up the hill there, with eight women permitted per tent,' he said. 'You will make yourselves comfortable shortly, and then you will be given a tour of the hospital and expected to prepare it immediately for incoming patients.'

April found herself nodding as she listened to him, wondering what it would be like inside. And she also found herself craning her neck to see if she could spot Dr. Grey. They'd been mostly segregated by gender on the ship, other than sneaking out to play cards sometimes with the boys, and she'd only been able to wave to him at mealtimes. She was anxious to talk to him again and ask if she could remain on his service.

She frowned when Grace nudged her in the side. 'Come on—let's go choose a decent tent.'

After what had happened to them in Pearl Harbor, she'd thought nothing would bother her and that she'd just be grateful to be alive, but her heart sank when she saw where they'd be living. It wasn't the sleeping in tents she cared about—they all had blankets and enough clothes to make their beds comfortable—it was the flies filling the air around them. April slapped at her arm and cringed. The mosquitos were going to love her, and she knew she'd have tiny red welts all over her within days.

'Keep walking,' Eva said, prodding her from behind.

April looked back at her but only received a shake of the head in response, and even Grace was following without asking. Eva marched them as far away as possible and then pointed.

'That one will do.'

'*All* this way from the hospital? We're going to have the farthest to walk each day after our shifts!' Grace complained. 'Seriously, we'll be sweaty before we even start working.'

'You see the tent all the way back over there? The one with the makeshift wooden structure next to it?'

April nodded and followed Eva's point.

'So?' Grace asked.

'That's the toilet block,' Eva said. 'Imagine what the flies will be like after a few days or weeks of us all using it. And the smell will be horrible.'

April gestured at the empty tent, grinning at Eva. 'I think you should get first pick. Grace would have had us nestled right up beside the toilets just to make her morning walk shorter.'

Grace rolled her eyes, but they all laughed, and April watched as Eva went to the far corner and set her things down. It had been nice seeing her smile today, almost like having a hint of the old Eva back. After what had happened, April had fought hard to find somewhere for Eva to stay in Hawaii, and a lovely family had welcomed her with open arms for almost a month. Whatever it was stopping her from going home, she'd never truly told her, but she had come back to nursing instead of leaving, so that was something.

'You think the boys will stay on their side?' Grace asked.

April poked her head out of the tent and stared across the field to where the men were stationed, barely able to see them. 'Why, you hoping to find a handsome man knocking at the door tonight?'

Grace laughed. 'More like you hoping to lay eyes on *Dr. Grey* again.'

April bit the inside of her mouth, not about to smile and give her sister even an inkling that she was right. She'd missed seeing him, and she was desperate to work beside him again and see if they couldn't form a formidable team in the field.

'It'd be nice to know where Teddy was sent,' April said, reaching for Grace's hand and giving it a quick squeeze.

She knew Grace was still in love with him and that she'd been eagerly waiting for a letter, but she'd never tease her about it again, not now that Poppy was gone, and she doubted Grace would even look at Teddy that way now no matter how she felt. It just wouldn't be right.

Tears shone in Grace's eyes, but she watched her quickly blink them away. 'You know, when we pulled up beside that train, I was scanning every face looking for him. I just want to know where he is, whether he's still alive.'

'Me too,' April said, setting down her things and unwrapping her bedroll. The ground was rock hard, and she put one of her blankets on top of the canvas and sat down to try it out. 'I think about him a lot, actually.' In her head, she kept seeing him holding Grace, his arms wrapped tight around her as the sky boomed with noise, carrying her as she cried and kicked, screaming out to Poppy. He'd kept her sister safe that day, and for that she would always be in his debt.

'I'm dying to wash my undergarments,' Eva said, her bed looking almost ready, one of her bags propped up to use as a pillow.

'Did I hear you say *wash*?' A familiar dark head poked through the entrance to their tent, and April smiled when she saw it was Cassie. 'Apparently we use our helmets for any washing, so don't get too excited about clean clothes.'

Grace and Eva groaned as April waved her in. 'You looking for somewhere to bunk down still?'

Cassie nodded. 'You girls want me?'

'Make yourself comfortable,' April said. 'How about we go find water and then take a look at the toilet situation.'

Grace shrugged, but Eva finished placing some of her things and then followed her out into the hot, muggy air.

'Is it anything like you thought it would be?' April asked, looking around as nurses milled around everywhere, some still searching for tents and lugging their packs, and others, like them, walking about and taking the chance to explore.

'I honestly don't know what I was expecting,' Eva replied. 'But it's hotter and more—I don't know—raw, I suppose.'

'Isn't it strange that so many of our mothers have never left America, and yet here we are, first in Pearl Harbor, then here, and God only knows where they'll keep sending us?'

So long as they were moving with the American army and not taken prisoners of war, April could handle whatever was thrown their way. She shivered despite the heat at the thought of being captured, and prayed that their boys fought hard enough to stop that from ever happening.

'I'm so pleased you stayed with us,' April said, linking her arm through Eva's as they walked.

Eva's arm was rigid, like she was uncomfortable being touched, but then she softened, and April tugged her a little closer.

'It's better than the alternative,' Eva said. 'Thanks for making me stick with it. If it hadn't been for you, I don't know what would have happened.'

'You would have had to go home,' April said, stating the obvious but wanting Eva to say something, to finally open up to her about why she'd been so scared. Or had she just been grieving and confused?

'Well, that's not an option anymore, so it doesn't matter to me how long this war stretches on for. At least here I'll have food to eat and a roof above my head.'

April stopped walking and looked at Eva. 'What do you mean? And I'd hardly call that tent a decent roof.'

Eva looked down before finally meeting April's gaze. 'My father's cut me off,' she said. 'He's threatened it before, but when I left home to become a nurse, he told me I wasn't welcome back, and he made good on his word. He's told me not to come crawling back expecting him to support me, and I wouldn't go near him even if he would let me. Charlie was my everything; we had a life planned together, and it involved never seeing my father ever again.'

April caught herself before her jaw hung open, clutching tight to Eva's fingers. 'Your own father just cast you aside like that? But what about now that Charlie's gone? Surely your mother wouldn't let him treat you like that!'

Eva shrugged as if it were nothing, but April could see the pain etched in her face, the glint in her eyes that told her how badly her friend needed to cry and let it all out.

She watched as Eva pulled a letter from her breast pocket, unfolding the carefully creased paper and passing it over.

'I don't know why I didn't just throw it out,' Eva muttered. 'But something made me keep it.'

April took it and read the scrawl on the page, hand flying to her mouth as she recognized the cruelty of his words.

> Your mother wanted to send a parcel to you, but
> there will be nothing coming from us, Eva. No words
> of comfort, no parcels, nothing. I told you if you said
> yes to marrying that man and going off nursing that
> you'd be banished from this house and nothing has
> changed. You don't make a fool of me and get away
> with it, so don't come crawling back and expect to be
> welcomed. And don't try to contact your mother, she
> no longer has a daughter and neither do I.

April looked up, carefully folded the letter again, and gulped as she passed it back to Eva. 'I'm so sorry. That's just . . . I don't even know what to say. And your mother won't help? I mean, she wouldn't defy him?'

Eva shook her head. 'My mother's never stood up to him before, so I don't expect it to start now.'

April knew she had to tread carefully. Charlie had been a good man with a strong sense of duty from what she'd gathered, and she knew that his parents had sent parcels to Eva after he'd died, so surely it wasn't Charlie who'd caused the rift?

'Can you ask Charlie's family for help? If you ever need to?' April asked gently. 'Or your brothers?'

Eva shook her head. 'I couldn't. Going to them, it would just be so painful without Charlie. And my brothers will stand by my dad; they'll believe whatever he tells them.'

April took Eva's other hand and held tight to both of them, not blinking as she looked into her friend's eyes. 'Well, whatever happens, you have me, and you have Grace. We will never turn our backs on you, and you will *always* be welcome in our home. I mean it, Eva; I'm not just saying it.'

She hugged Eva and rubbed her back, expecting her to fall apart now that she'd confessed some of her story, but when she finally pulled back, she could see that Eva hadn't cracked even an inch.

'Come on,' she said, linking arms again as they started to walk. 'Let's go see what we're dealing with here.'

'Wait up!' Grace called, running up behind them and catching April's free hand.

'Well, you look excited,' April said, laughing as Grace swung her hand like a little girl.

'I am! It might be stinking hot and the middle of nowhere, but I'm not going to waste a second when we can be exploring!'

April liked her sister's enthusiasm, so she decided not to point out that however exciting it might seem to land somewhere new, they could be posted for months with no running water and more people in one field than should ever be permitted. Not to mention the fact that any day now they could be overrun with patients that would make Pearl Harbor seem like a cakewalk.

'Take cover!'

April dropped the tray she was carrying to the ground with a clatter as she crouched down low, cringing at the unmistakable noise of shells being fired. Since they'd arrived, she'd become used to hearing loud noises without completely losing her composure, but as bullets peppered the roof of the hospital, she tucked low beneath the hospital bed and held on to the legs, bracing herself for the worst.

'What in God's name is going on!' she called out. 'Don't they know we're a hospital?'

Eva crawled up beside her, pushing a flashlight in front of her. 'Apparently they still haven't painted the white cross on top yet.'

April's skin burned as anger pulsed through her. 'You've got to be kidding me.'

She knew from the serious look etched on her friend's face that she wasn't joking.

'Come on,' April said, forcing her trembling legs to work and picking up what she'd dropped. 'If we think this is bad, imagine how our boys are going to feel.'

'If we're hit, we're hit—there's nothing we can do about it, right?' Eva said matter-of-factly. 'Hiding under flimsy beds isn't going to save any of us from a direct hit.'

April didn't know where Grace was, but she was less worried about her sister than she'd ever been. From the moment they'd set sail, her little sister had seemed to come into her own, blossoming as she flirted her way through their days at sea. It might not be the case after some tough days and weeks nursing, but for now she seemed to be coping just fine. Then again they hadn't been fired at before; she could be a basket case by now.

'Don't let them take me,' one of the men wailed. 'Give me a gun— let me protect us.'

April took a deep breath, shutting her eyes as more shells zoomed over them but trying hard not to jump this time. Eva was walking down the row with her, and she gave her a quick smile.

Some of the patients were hysterical at the noise, others were crying or silently rocking back and forth, and as April looked around, she wasn't even sure where to start. Dealing with wounds and breaks, she'd been trained for that, but the psychiatric ward was different. These men weren't right in the head; they'd seen things and done things that had affected them so badly it broke April's heart. And aside from medicating them to induce sleep and reading them stories or feeding them, there was little they could do to make life any easier for them.

'Hold me,' one of the men cried. 'I want my mama. *Mama!*'

She saw Grace then, huddled beside a bed and holding someone in her arms. It was one of the youngest soldiers they were treating, barely nineteen, and she could see that he was half tucked under the bed, half clinging on to Grace. April gave her a little wave and received a smile in reply. Grace might not be great with blood, but she was proving to be excellent when it came to bedside manner and treating their patients with love and compassion.

Another flurry of bullets pinged overhead, and April set down her tray and clenched her fists to stop them from trembling.

'I'm going to go out there and give them a piece of my mind if they don't stop soon!' one of the other nurses yelled.

April cringed. Despite it all, some of the nurses just didn't seem to grasp that they were in a war zone. If they stepped foot outside, they'd surely be dead. *They haven't seen it,* she thought as she reached for the medication to help put her patients to sleep. *They haven't seen their best friend gunned down or seen the anguish and terror of war in their own backyard.* Most of the nurses had come fresh from training in their home cities; there were few of them posted to North Africa who'd been witness to Pearl Harbor.

'Calm down,' she whispered, stroking a man's face, careful to avoid his bandaged eye. 'I'm not going to leave you.'

Stepping foot outside now would be suicide, but come morning when the fighting was over, she'd paint that damn white cross on top of their building herself if she had to.

'Make it stop,' one of the men whimpered. 'Please make it stop.'

April held his hand and waited for the medication to take effect, hoping it made him drowsy and let him drift away soon. Whatever he'd seen, whatever demons were haunting him, she had a feeling they might stay with him for the rest of his life.

'April?'

She fought the urge to duck as another round of shelling echoed out, turning when her name was called. And then her heart raced for an entirely different reason.

'I was told I'd find you here. Can you be spared?' Dr. Grey asked.

April glanced down at her patient, willing him to find sleep and not letting go of his hand. 'Of course, as soon as I'm done here. Where do you need me?'

'Surgery,' he said grimly. 'I've just been called in, and it's going to be a long night.'

She tried not to show how excited she was that he'd singled her out and wrestled with the fact that she was so eager to be back in surgery. Those poor boys with mangled bodies broke her heart as she nursed them through their recovery, but she was fascinated at the idea of being there as Dr. Grey worked his magic.

'I'll let the others know to watch my patients,' she replied. 'Just give me a moment.'

'It's good to see you again, April,' he said as he ran off through the ward. 'Get something to eat from the cafeteria first, though; it's going to be a long night!'

April felt eyes on her and noticed that Eva was watching her. She shrugged and Eva smiled back, and April wished there was more she could do to see her friend's face light up. Maybe next time she'd have to throw herself at Dr. Grey and really give Eva something to smile about.

Less than fifteen minutes later, while quickly gulping down the last of a piece of bread, April found Dr. Grey. He was bent over a patient with another nurse standing beside him, and she hated the tickle of jealousy she felt when the nurse leaned into him.

'Huh-hmm.' She cleared her throat and smiled when he turned to see her.

'Thank you for joining us, April. Eloise, you're excused.'

The other nurse hurried away, and April didn't think she was imagining the frosty look she shot her.

'If you already have assistance, I'm happy to join your next surgery?' she asked, hoping the other nurse heard before she disappeared out the door behind her.

There were three beds in the compact space, but they didn't have too many casualties yet, and she hoped it stayed that way. Grey was working on the far bed, his patient already unconscious, and the anesthetist came back into the room as they were speaking.

'Not at all. Eloise was just assisting me with some preparation.'

April moved closer. 'What are we working on today?'

Dr. Grey glanced at her, and the second she saw his arched brow and surprised expression, she knew she'd pushed too far.

'You,' she stuttered. 'What are *you* working on today?'

He smiled, his eyes crinkling warmly as he turned back to the patient. 'We'll be amputating the leg above the knee,' he said. 'The damage is irreparable, and it's better to do it now before gangrene sets in and we end up taking the whole thing anyway.'

April stared down at the patient, focusing on his leg and the mangled state of his toes.

'Is it so far gone already?' she asked.

Grey looked irritated, and she took a step back, placing her hands on the instruments that were already waiting. She swallowed hard at the sight of the saw and hoped he wasn't going to ask her to help with that part.

'Yes, April, it is. I'm not going to do a minor surgery to remove his toes now, only to have to put him through an amputation in a week or two when someone else realizes the limb can't be saved. We're too busy to be operating on these men twice.'

She nodded. 'Of course. I was only trying to understand. I'm very passionate about nursing.'

His face was hard to read, but she saw him exchange glances with the anesthetist. 'April, your job is to listen to what I need and make sure I get what I ask for, but I appreciate your interest.'

Her face burned as if she'd been slapped. Why hadn't she just kept her mouth shut? But as she prepared to assist the doctor, she couldn't help but look down at the patient's strong, muscular legs and wonder if the right decision had been made. Even if there was a risk of having to amputate later, wasn't it better to do anything possible to save a man's limbs so he could walk again?

'I'm sorry for being so forthright,' she said, apologizing again. The last thing she wanted was to be taken off his service. 'I truly am grateful to be assisting you.'

This time his smile reassured her, and she wondered if perhaps she'd imagined his irritation.

'Of course. I can see that you enjoy the procedures and that you're learning; it's why I like working with you so much.'

April nodded and breathed a quiet sigh of relief.

'Saw,' Dr. Grey said, all business again as he held out his left hand.

April inhaled deeply and reached for the instrument as her heart banged in her chest. 'Saw,' she repeated.

And strong stomach or not, she almost heaved all over the floor when the metal teeth snagged flesh on the operating table in front of her. Tears filled her eyes, and she blinked them away as she listened to Dr. Grey issue instructions, his brow slick with sweat as he carved the bone, back and forth, back and forth.

Perhaps she'd been better soothing men on the psych ward.

It had been a quiet night, and April carefully carried cups of water outside for Grace and Eva, balancing the three between her two hands. She'd put as many lemon cubes in the water as she could find to rid it of the hideous chlorine taste, but she doubted even that would make it bearable.

'Here we go, ladies,' she said.

They'd all worked ten hours straight so far, with another two to go, but all was quiet on the ward. Some days she went to assist Dr. Grey if he requested her or if there wasn't a lot to do, but they hadn't been overrun with injuries so far. And despite the heat and the sticky humidity during the night and her itchy red skin from insects, it hadn't been as bad as she'd expected.

Although she knew that maybe it was simply the calm before the storm.

'Don't you think they're being a bit overcautious on the chlorine?' Grace asked, pulling a face. 'This is revolting.'

'I know,' April replied. 'It's disgusting. I'd rather not drink, but I think we'd expire over here if we didn't.'

Eva was staring at the sky, and as April followed her gaze, she slowly lifted an arm, finger pointing.

'Look.'

There was a noise, something crackling in the air, and as she opened her mouth to ask what it was, the sky lit up in the distance.

'Oh my lord,' she whispered, clasping her cup tightly.

'Should we run?' Grace asked.

Eva's hand fell over her arm, and April glanced sideways. 'No,' Eva said. 'It's miles away. We should watch.'

April was transfixed as the dark night sky was suddenly illuminated by what she could only imagine were their antiaircraft guns shooting at German reconnaissance planes. The bullets seemed never ending, a constant supply of blasts over and over again as they pressed together and watched, sipping their water while planes ducked and dived to escape the torrent.

'It's like the most incredible Fourth of July display I've ever seen,' Grace whispered. 'Is that an awful thing to say?'

April wondered about the pilots, about the young men bravely shooting the enemy down. It brought that day back to her, the sight of the pilots' faces as they smiled before unleashing hell on everyone, how it felt to be caught up in the terror. *Get them,* she thought. *Get every last one of them.*

The sky might have been inky black before, but everything was bright now, the night sky more like a brightly colored child's drawing than the star-filled darkness of only a few minutes earlier. And April couldn't take her eyes off it.

But as she took her final sip of water, her arm circling Eva as she thought about the fiancé her friend had lost, the sky suddenly went silent again. No more colors, no more noise, no more fighting. The odd stray gunfire echoed, and then there was nothing.

They stood, silent, still staring, until Eva stirred beside her, clearing her throat and moving away from April's touch.

'We need to check our patients,' Eva said. 'I'll bet none of them are asleep now.'

April nodded, grabbing her sister's hand as they hurried back into the hospital. She had this awful feeling that the planes could be behind them, that a German pilot could have them in his sights and be stealthily following them, waiting to fire at the hospital and take them all out.

She kept glancing over her shoulder until they were about to walk in the door to their ward, but there was only ever silence.

'Oh heavens,' April whispered as she surveyed the ward. Less than half an hour earlier, all the men had been asleep, and now there were only tangled sheets and bare wire bed bases to greet them.

'What happened in here?' Grace asked. 'What—'

'They're under the beds,' Eva muttered. 'We should never have stayed outside and left them alone.'

While they'd been watching, their poor patients had been terrified, and as April dropped low to the ground and peered under the beds closest to her, she found the men huddled, most of them curled up like little babies. Some had their mattresses tucked over them, ready for the worst.

'Let's start with one each at a time,' she said quietly, glancing at the other two. 'We'll have to medicate them as we go.' These poor battle-fatigued men were still acting as if they were on the front line, trying desperately to protect themselves. While they'd been out watching the spectacular air display, their patients had been hiding, expecting to be killed.

'There you go,' April whispered as she coaxed her first patient out. 'It's all over. You're going to be just fine.'

She wrestled with the first mattress and got it back on the bed, then quickly tucked the sheets in while her soldier-patient dropped to the ground again and curled into a ball, rocking back and forth. It was going to be a long night.

CHAPTER THIRTEEN

Eva

Sweat tickled the back of Eva's neck as she walked, the dry grass beneath her feet crunching as they crossed the field and neared where the planes had been battling the night before. They hadn't had any opportunities to explore until now; setting up and preparing the hospital had taken up any time they had in between shifts, but they'd been given permission to leave camp today, and Grace had been eager to get out and see what Casbah had to offer. Grace was like a child in a candy store for the first time, desperate to see everything and soak in their new surroundings.

Eva could easily have stayed behind and spent longer in bed, not caring how hot their tent was during the middle of the day, but Grace was having none of it, and April wasn't about to leave her behind if Grace was dragging her out.

'Do you think it was near here?' Grace asked.

Eva looked behind them at where the hospital was located and then in front again, trying to picture exactly where the battle had taken place. 'I suppose. We must be close, anyway.'

She thought she could recognize where they were, but then again it had been nighttime, and it could have been miles farther away. And there was a big part of her that didn't want to see the wreckage or think about what had happened to those pilots; she'd rather have walked briskly past any carnage.

'Oh my lord, there it is.'

Eva stopped walking and followed Grace's point, her mouth hanging open, but Grace wasn't going to let them stand around.

'Quickly, come on!'

She half expected a German to leap out and shoot them, wild eyed and ready to kill, even though she knew no one could have survived such a crash. Their own soldiers would have stormed the area and secured it by now; any Germans that had lived through the ordeal would have been brought to their hospital or taken prisoner. This was as safe as anywhere. But it still sent goose bumps coursing across her skin just seeing the plane with the swastika and knowing it had been sent on a reconnaissance mission to see where they were all based and what they were doing. If they'd succeeded in their mission, they could all have been dead within days or hours.

There was another plane farther away, and Eva hoped they weren't going to have to inspect the remains of that one too. She breathed in fast, short pants just thinking about the pilots involved.

'Can't we just keep walking?' she asked.

'No!' Grace insisted almost immediately. 'Can you believe that we're standing beside this? Isn't it huge?'

Eva caught April's eye and gave her a quick smile, hoping to convince her that she was okay, but as her legs began to shake, she quickly bent down before they buckled and gave way.

Was this what Charlie's plane had looked like? Had the front been smashed like this and the wing broken? She shuddered as she saw the dark-red splatter across the glass. That was the pilot's blood. They might be enemies, but he was another human being, and weren't they all just doing what they were being told to do by their own country? Would his wife or sweetheart—his mother, for that matter—hate Americans as much as she hated the Japanese and Germans?

'Eva?' April asked, her hand hovering over her shoulder as she bent low beside her.

'I'm fine,' she managed. 'It's just . . .'

'Come on, Grace. We only have a few hours, and didn't you want to explore the town?'

Grace suddenly turned from the plane and waved them on. 'You're right. Let's go.'

Eva clasped April's hand as they walked away, and she held on tight, needing the contact to keep her going. Some days she felt like she was about to collapse, like she couldn't keep going no matter how hard she tried, but somehow April was always there. It was as if April knew just when she was about to give up. Eva looked over her shoulder one last time, the pain hitting her in the chest, imagining Charlie's final moments, hoping he'd died instantly and hadn't suffered or even known what was happening. It didn't matter what anyone said to her; she doubted she'd ever stop feeling guilty for holding him back instead of letting him go.

'Are you thinking about him?' April whispered as they followed a few steps behind Grace.

She nodded. 'Yeah. I just keep wondering about those final moments, if he knew what was about to happen.'

April gave her a small smile. 'I think about Poppy a lot too. It's almost impossible to block it out sometimes, especially at night.'

'Well, would you look at that,' Grace said, laughing as she nudged them.

Eva smiled as she watched two very young boys walking nearby, wearing only T-shirt-type tops with no underpants on. They stopped to relieve themselves, peeing on the grass in full view.

'I don't think modesty is a concern here,' April said with a giggle. 'I only hope we don't encounter any full-grown men with the same attire!'

They all three linked arms and kept walking, and Eva agreed.

'For sure!' Grace said. 'I wouldn't know where to look!'

'At their eyes, Grace,' April teased. 'You'd be like a man not being able to take his eyes off a woman's chest.'

'Like you wouldn't look!' Grace laughed.

Eva giggled then, too, and the laughter was contagious. When Eva finally straightened and they started to walk again, she felt lighter somehow. It felt good to let it all out, and suddenly the sun was warmer on her shoulders, the air easier to breathe.

'Come on—I want to see what Casbah is all about,' Grace said.

They wandered until they finally reached their destination, finding narrow streets that were so different from where they were based. Lining up single file, they followed Grace, with Eva at the rear, walking down the overcrowded street that seemed to be teeming with people. Sweat clung to the stale air between the buildings, and Eva found herself scanning the dark faces they passed, amazed at how different the people looked, dressed, and even smelled.

'Up there,' Grace called out, looking back over her shoulder as she spoke. 'That's the palace I want to visit!'

Eva was happy to follow along and take in the sights, so if Grace was so determined to visit the palace, then she wasn't going to complain. She wanted to keep busy instead of living in her own thoughts.

She noticed armed guards were posted outside most of the larger buildings, and she wondered who they were protecting or what they were stationed there for.

'Are we supposed to be this far away from our camp?' Eva asked April, shuffling closer to her.

'We weren't told about anywhere being off limits, were we?' April asked.

'No, but I just . . .' She sighed. Maybe she was being overcautious. 'I just wondered about those armed guards, if we're actually safe here or not.'

April's brows pulled close together, and she nodded. 'Hmm, maybe you're right. Grace,' she called.

Grace spun around, wide eyed with excitement. 'It's here. Come on—there aren't even guards. Quickly!'

Eva hesitated, but Grace skipped straight up the steps to the palace, and the last thing she wanted was to be left behind, alone, on the streets.

Her red hair and her friends' blonde locks made them stand out among the sea of women in head scarves, and there were far more men than women filling the town.

'Are you certain we can just walk in?' she asked.

'Well, if we couldn't, wouldn't there be guards stopping us?' Grace asked. 'Come on—I don't want to miss out. I heard some of the soldiers talking about this place and how amazing it is. This is where the bey lives—he's like the mayor of Casbah—and I heard that the bathroom faucets are made of gold.'

'Sounds extravagant.'

Parts of where they were seemed so poor, the homes so basic and the people dressed as if they had no possessions to their names, but this palace was pure opulence. They walked quietly, jaws dropping at the sights: the stuffed animals that looked so real they might spring into life and pounce at any moment, the unusual lights and furniture so unlike anything she'd seen before. Upstairs they silently pushed open the door to the bathroom, and they all stood, stunned.

'This is insane!' Grace whispered.

'Is that *fur* on the toilet seat?' April asked.

Eva stepped past them, laughing to herself as she confirmed that it most definitely *was* fur lined. 'It must be awfully unhygienic,' she whispered. 'And look.'

The bathtub was lined with fur too. It was the oddest bathroom she'd ever seen in her life.

'Do you think they actually bathe in there, or is it just for show?'

April laughed and shook her head. 'Maybe they just lie in there?'

They all pulled faces, the entire room seeming too weird to understand, and quietly went back down the stairs and out the front door the same way they'd come in.

'I have a feeling like we've just walked uninvited through someone's home and we're about to be arrested for it,' April muttered.

'Don't be silly. It wasn't like we forced our way in.'

Outside and back in the narrow street, almost too narrow for them to walk even two abreast, Eva tried to breathe through her mouth so she didn't have to smell the air. It was so hot and humid, so full of people and things, she felt like she was choking.

'Come on—let's go back,' she said, hoping Grace wasn't about to take them anywhere else. 'My stomach is growling.'

April took the lead this time, and Eva happily followed her, smiling back at the curious locals, wondering what they must think of them, scanning their faces as they did hers with open interest. It had been an unusual day, but for the first time she could remember, she didn't have to force her smile, and it felt good.

———— ❧～❧ ————

'Seriously, if they do use that bath, how would they dry it to keep the fur all fluffy?' Grace asked as they crossed back toward the wreckage on their way home.

Eva laughed as she imagined some poor housemaid forced to dry out the fur each day. 'It's ridiculous. I mean, line the floor with fur maybe, but the bath?'

'Oh, and imagine all the pee on the toilet seat! How would you clean it? And imagine how stinky it would get!'

They roared with laughter as they stumbled across the grass, still full of talk about what they'd seen. Grace might have had to drag them out today, but it had been worth every minute.

'Did you hear that?' Eva stopped walking, straining to listen.

'What?' April whispered back.

She waited, ears pricked. 'I don't know—it was like a groan or something.'

There it went again.

'I heard it too,' Grace said, her eyes wide as she took a step sideways and pressed into Eva.

The moan was low and guttural, and fear sliced through Eva as she slowly spun to see where it might be coming from. They were close to the downed planes again, and she had this feeling like they shouldn't be there, like it was a sacred or dangerous place that they should have avoided instead of walking straight into it.

'I think we should go,' she said.

'Are there wild animals around here?' April asked. 'Was there a warning about anything dangerous?'

Grace shook her head as Eva watched her. 'Nothing I heard about. But I still think we should run,' she whispered.

Eva looked at April, but April just stared straight back at her as the low noise met their ears again. This time they all heard it at the same time.

'Run!' Grace yelped.

They bolted, running in the direction of the hospital, but Eva glanced over her shoulder, half expecting a big cat to leap out of the long dry grass to try to catch them, but there was nothing there. Terror gripped her like a hand to her throat, made her think of her father, made fear pulse through every part of her body as she remembered what it was like to fight for her life, to try to stay safe.

Oh lord. 'Stop!' she screamed, tripping as she fell over her own feet in her desperation to halt, wishing her eyes were playing tricks on her.

It wasn't a cat. It wasn't a predator.

Oh hell. Oh lord.

'It's a man,' she gasped, stumbling sideways and dropping to her knees in the dirt, her legs buckling as she struggled not to sob.

A soldier, one of theirs, was dragging his legs behind him, bloodied hands fighting to thump down, one after the other, his face etched with pain as he used only his upper body to move.

He let out a guttural moan before collapsing face-first into the dirt.

'Quickly, help me lift him!' April cried, the first to reach him, her hands under his arms as Eva looked on, frozen.

Grace was there then, too, on his other side.

'Eva! Help us!' April yelled.

She clawed at the dirt to push herself up, forcing one foot in front of the other as she scrambled toward the soldier and then hefted his mangled legs with all her might.

'We need to turn him,' April instructed. 'So he's on his back. Maybe we'll need to drag him if we can't hold his weight.'

Eva nodded, following orders.

'Come on; on the count of three we roll him over,' April said. 'One, two, *three!*'

They flipped him over and then collapsed beside him, all panting as he howled out in pain, regaining consciousness.

'Soldier, what's your name?' she heard April ask as she stared at his face, watching as his cracked, dry lips parted. April bent low to listen, but in the end even Eva heard his whisper.

'Arrr,' he finally croaked. 'Ar-thur.'

'Well, Arthur, we're going to get you to the hospital—aren't we, ladies?' April said.

Eva nodded, over and over again, unable to stop. She anchored her feet and pushed up, taking strength from April as she motioned to both her and Grace.

'Let's try to carry him as best we can. Come on.'

They all groaned as they lifted him up, his weight almost impossible to bear even with three of them trying as hard as they could.

'One foot in front of the other,' she whispered. 'Just one step at a time.'

They all stared at one another, not needing to say anything, determined in silent solidarity to get this broken soldier to safety. How long had he been out there? Had he been part of the battle in the sky they'd watched as if it were a fireworks display? Guilt plagued Eva as they walked, her teeth gritted as she struggled to hold him, her fingers gripping tight into his pants as she fought not to let go. Only hours earlier they'd passed through, and she'd wanted to keep going instead of looking over the wreckage, and while they'd giggled and explored the palace, he'd been moaning in pain, trying to drag himself to safety.

'We're going to save you, Arthur,' she whispered. 'I promise.'

And as Eva stared at his pale skin, dark hair clinging to his forehead, his full lips swollen and burnt, he opened his eyes, and she found herself gazing into the most piercing blue irises she'd ever seen in her life.

'You're safe now,' she whispered, stumbling but never letting go and never looking away. 'You're safe.'

She might not have been able to keep her Charlie safe, but nothing was going to stop her from getting this man to the hospital. Nothing.

'Arthur,' she whispered, shaking his shoulder as gently as she could. There was no response. Eva bent low and stroked his forehead, biting hard on her bottom lip to stop from crying out. 'Please, Arthur. Wake up.'

Eva held his hand and stared at him as if she could will him awake as she waited for April to get help inside the hospital. They'd carried him so far, and he was a big man; her shoulders ached, and the muscles in her arms were burning, but she didn't care. She just needed him to live.

'I don't think he's going to make it,' Grace murmured beside her, on her knees as they both watched him. 'Look at his legs.'

They were mangled—that was for sure—and as Eva looked down at them, her eyes traveling over the peculiar angle of both his lower limbs, all she cared about was whether he'd survive. They had great doctors, surgeons who could surely fix his legs; she just wanted him to breathe. To know that they'd found him in time and given him a chance at life.

'It's my fault,' she whispered. Charlie's death had been her fault, for not letting him go, and now this man was going to die because of her too.

Grace's arm went around her, holding her tight. 'How is this your fault? He was injured in a plane crash!'

'If I hadn't been so desperate to get going instead of looking around, we would have found him earlier. Those couple of hours might have made a difference; he might have lived . . .'

'Stop it! We saved him, Eva. The three of us managed to carry this man all the way back here, so don't you even think like that,' she said as if she were reprimanding a child. Eva had never seen Grace angry before, but she looked furious now. 'It's not your fault this man was injured, and it wasn't your fault that Charlie was either.'

Eva stared back at Grace. 'What?'

Grace's face suddenly collapsed. 'I'm sorry. I should never have said that. I'm just so tired of seeing you with the weight of Charlie's death on your shoulders as if it was your fault he was killed. Because it wasn't.'

Eva opened her mouth and shut it again just as fast. It was easy for Grace to say that.

'Out of the way!'

She looked up and saw Dr. Grey running toward them along with two corpsmen carrying a stretcher. Within seconds they'd hauled him up as the doctor bent over him, stethoscope in hand as he listened to his heart. The frown dragging his mouth down told her it wasn't good, and she clung to Grace as Arthur was hurried away into the hospital. Dr. Grey ran beside the stretcher with April trailing behind. And then they were gone.

'He's going to die,' Eva whispered. 'I just know he's not going to make it.'

Grace kept hold of her hand and dragged her into the hospital alongside her.

'They'll take him straight into surgery, and we can wait for news together,' Grace said, still leading her.

Eva nodded, collapsing to the floor the moment they got close to the operating theater, her back sliding against the cool concrete wall. Her body had started to shake—she knew she was in shock—but it almost felt better than the numbness, the lack of any feeling, that she'd had up until today.

Three hours later, Eva's eyes flew open. She gasped as Grace tugged her to her feet, watching as Dr. Grey walked out behind a stretcher that was heading for recovery. His face was impossible to read, but April was like an open book, her smile telling her the man had made it but the tears glistening in her eyes telling her there was more to the story than simply saving his life, that something had made her friend's heart break despite him surviving. How had she fallen asleep while he was in surgery? She rubbed at her eyes and forced herself up.

'Any word on who he is?' Grey asked. He stopped by them, yawning and pulling his surgical cap off. He looked weary as he stared down at them.

'We haven't heard anything,' Grace said for them both.

Suddenly there was a commotion as two air force pilots strode into the hospital, the medals on the jacket of the older man making it clear he was someone distinguished within their military.

'Are you the doctor who performed surgery on Captain Arthur Jones?' he asked.

Dr. Grey stepped forward. 'I did just perform lifesaving surgery on a pilot found and brought in by three of my nurses. Someone can take you to see him for a formal identification if you would like?'

'Arthur is one of the best pilots we have, Doctor. Thank you for your service.'

Dr. Grey's face clouded over, and Eva looked between him and the pilots, wondering what he was thinking. He'd just said he'd saved his life, hadn't he?

'I'll take you, sir,' Eva blurted, her voice sounding stronger, more resilient, than she'd expected.

'Thank you.'

Eva didn't look back at Grace or April. She walked through the corridor, listening to the loud, heavy-booted footsteps of the men echoing behind her. The recovery ward where they watched their high-risk patients after surgery wasn't full, and she could see Arthur's dark head of hair, knew exactly what bed he was in as she moved toward him.

'You said he's one of our best pilots?' she asked.

'Yes, ma'am, he's our most highly decorated pilot. He temporarily left our service to fly for the Eagles—successfully, I might add—and then he returned to our service to take over command of a squadron. He's the best we have.'

Eva blinked away tears. They shuddered within her, threatening but not falling, as she watched Arthur's face, wondering when those brilliant-blue eyes would open and focus on her again. This man had done what her Charlie couldn't. He'd followed his beliefs, listened to his gut, and instead of being shunned by their armed forces for defying orders as they'd threatened, he'd been welcomed back with open arms.

She took the final step toward his bed, the pilots right behind her. 'We found him out in the . . .'

No. No, no, no!

She slammed her fist to her mouth, silencing her cry as she stared at the bed. At the empty space where one of his legs should have been. At the puckered blanket tucked around one leg, at the sight of half a lower body in the bed. Arthur had been tall and strong—he'd been a big, heavy man—and now one of his legs had been discarded as if it had never existed in the first place.

'Aww, hell, Art,' the younger pilot muttered, his hand flying to cover his mouth as he started to swear.

'Was,' the pilot in charge muttered.

'What?' Eva asked, the word choking in her throat. *What did he say?*

'He *was* our finest pilot. He won't be flying a goddamn plane ever again now, will he?'

Eva shuddered, listening to the men walk away as she stared at Arthur, slowly lowering herself onto the stool next to his bed to wait. She wasn't going to let him find out on his own; she'd wait all night if she had to.

CHAPTER FOURTEEN

GRACE

'Thank you,' Grace said, opening her eyes and wishing they were still shut. The light felt like bright pricks of fire slicing right through her.

'What for?' Eva mumbled, her head buried beneath the covers.

'For making us pick this tent. I couldn't have dealt with it.'

It had been the most horrific few days, with nurses dropping like flies as dysentery swept through their camp. The nurses with the tents closest to the toilets had been hit first, and then it had rapidly spread until almost everyone was vomiting and running to the toilets all hours of the day and night. The doctor in charge had dosed their drinking water with excessive amounts of chlorine to keep them from getting sick, but he'd never thought to treat the latrine water, and the flies had been having a field day going back and forth. She shuddered and buried herself under her covers. She knew he'd never make that mistake again, and she doubted any of the nurses would ever sleep so close to the latrines again either.

'I still can't believe we all managed to avoid it,' April said, yawning as she spoke. 'Come on, sleepyheads—let's go.'

They were short on nurses with so many being sick, and the three of them had been working much longer shifts to make up for it. But they had the following day off, and she couldn't wait to get back out and explore again. The nursing hadn't been terrible, she'd managed to deal with everything that had been put in front of her so far, and even the blood wasn't making her as queasy as it once had.

'So what do you think of a picnic tomorrow?' Grace asked as she stretched. She finally forced herself out of bed, smiling to herself as she heard the crinkle of paper beneath her pillow. 'Maybe we could try to find some food to pack and go to the ocean?'

April nodded and got out of bed, but Eva stayed quiet as she rose and started to dress. Grace stuck her hand under the pillow, wanting to feel the letter from Teddy just to remind herself that it was real.

'Eva?'

'Yes, I suppose I'll come,' she said.

Grace finished putting on her uniform, sliding the folded letter into her breast pocket as she watched Eva for a moment. She didn't know what to do with Eva; just when she'd finally started to catch glimpses of her old friend again, along had come Arthur, and it seemed to have retriggered all of Eva's feelings of guilt.

'How was Arthur when you left the hospital last night? I heard you come in late,' Grace said, studying her face as she spoke.

'Not much of a change,' Eva said. 'I sat with him after my shift finished, but he was still unconscious.'

'I'm sure when he does open his eyes he'll be mighty happy to see your pretty face,' Grace teased. 'You're being very sweet staying with him so much. I'll bet he can hear you reading to him.'

It had been almost a week since they'd rescued Arthur, and Eva seemed to have made it her personal mission to care for him. Grace guessed that there was something about the man that reminded her of Charlie, but she hadn't wanted to ask. If Eva was ready to open up, she'd talk. And it was admirable that she wanted to be there for the poor man; she was just worried that it was going to stop Eva from moving on from the past and starting to find herself again.

'Come on. Let's go to the latrine, then head for breakfast.'

'What's in your pocket?' Eva asked. 'A letter from home?'

Grace grinned, unable to hide her happiness. She'd kept it secret the day before, reading it over and over, but she couldn't hide it from Eva or April any longer. 'It's from Teddy. He finally wrote to me.'

April was suddenly frozen, her eyes on Grace. 'What did he say? Where is he?'

'Close to here, I think, but he couldn't say,' Grace said with a sigh. 'I'm just so happy he's safe. I've been so worried about him.' Of course the letter was dated a month earlier, and a whisper went through her, a silent knife of fear, that he could already be injured or worse by now.

She knew the letter by heart, but she didn't want to share it all with Eva or even her sister. 'He said he's doing fine, missing Poppy but doing fine. He's hoping to see us one day if our schedules permit and if he has leave.'

April made a murmuring sound, and Eva just nodded before going back to getting ready. So Grace stood waiting, imagining where Teddy might have been when he'd written to her.

Dear Grace,

I can't believe it's been months since I last saw you, but thank you for your letters. They're the only thing that manage to make me smile these days. The days feel like weeks here, the heat so desperate that I feel like I can't breathe sometimes, and the nightmares so bad it makes sleep almost impossible. I hoped you wouldn't be sent here, it's the worst posting of all. Can you imagine Poppy's face? She would have screamed after one night with mosquitos in her tent! I hope you're made of stronger stuff, but after everything we went through, I think we can all cope with anything that comes our way.

I hope our paths cross again soon. I miss Poppy, but I miss spending time with all of you too. If I have any leave and I'm close to your hospital, I promise I'll come calling. All I want is to see your smiling face, and have someone to talk to about what happened to us that day.

With love, Teddy

'Grace? Are you ready?'

She nodded and touched her pocket, needing to feel the letter there, and followed the others. They left the tent, which looked more like a washhouse than sleeping quarters with all their laundry hanging about the place, joining the other nurses as they all made the pilgrimage to breakfast. They'd fast learned not to hang their washing outside—it went missing every time they did—and they were already making do with only a few pairs of panties and other garments they needed. Grace put her hand into her skirt pocket and touched the square of toilet paper she had there, still horrified at how unsanitary everything seemed. She cringed at the thought of getting her period again—it was horrible trying to deal with it with so few supplies—and quickly went about her business, thankful there was no line this time.

The chow line was a different thing altogether, though. There were hundreds of them needing to be fed each day, which meant that the wait was always terrible. And when they eventually got to the front of the line, she knew what would greet her: a pile of everything all mixed together. The night before, she'd managed to consume beef, mashed potatoes, gravy, and apple pie all in one mouthful, and it had almost turned her stomach. But food was food, and she was doing her best to be grateful for whatever they were given.

'You know, the locals would be disgusted with the way we use both hands for eating,' Grace said, receiving stares from April and Eva. Even the nurses ahead of her turned around to listen.

'And why is that, wise sister?' April asked.

'Because they eat with one hand and wipe their'—she lowered her voice—'*backsides* with the other. We might have to start doing the same thing if they keep rationing our toilet paper so vigilantly!'

They all burst out laughing and shuffled forward a few steps.

'Seriously, how did you know that?' April asked.

'Oh, one of the nurses told me she'd been invited with a few others to go to a local house for dinner.'

'Well, aren't you full of information today. Are you sure Teddy didn't tell you that in his letter?'

Her cheeks ignited. 'No, he didn't, actually. He didn't say much at all.'

'I'm only teasing,' April said. 'I'm pleased he wrote to you, but you don't have to share it with me.'

They kept chatting and eventually made their way to the front, holding out their plates for food and filling their metal cups with something resembling tea. Only it didn't matter what they drank or how many lemon drops they used—it still tasted like chlorine.

'I think being over here suits you,' April said, surprising her as they sat down. 'The rest of us moan about the heat and suffer through the conditions, but you seem to thrive on it.'

Grace laughed. 'I wouldn't say I'm thriving, but I do like it. I like nursing more than I thought I would too. It's kind of incredible.'

'If you call living in a tent under a burning ball of sun and surrounded by buzzing flies incredible.'

'I don't think Arthur will know his leg has been amputated,' Eva suddenly said, her food falling back off her spoon and into her bowl as she talked. 'I had this other patient—the doctors called him a basket because he didn't have any arms or legs after his surgery—and he didn't even know. He asked one of the other nurses out on a date, and he was laughing and joking around, and someone had to tell him. I suppose Arthur's lucky only to have lost one, but he might not think so.'

'April, you were there; why did Dr. Grey have to amputate his leg? Was there no way he could have saved it? It seems so many men are losing limbs.'

April grimaced. 'It was horrible. They thought his heart was going to give out; he'd lost so much blood, and they had to deal with a general surgery to repair damaged organs on top of everything else,' she said. 'It went on for a long time, and when Dr. Grey finally moved on to his legs, he said it was too late. It was his opinion that the tissue was so damaged, and it would only become infected if he tried to save his right leg, so the decision was made to—'

'Wasn't it worth trying, though? Unless there was no other option, why would he take his leg off? I'd rather have the chance to save my leg if I had a choice, even if I had terrible odds!'

April's face flushed a deep red. 'What are you saying? That Dr. Grey didn't know what he was doing, or that he didn't have the best interests of the patient in mind? I'll have you know that he was going to amputate both legs but decided to just do the one at the last minute.'

Grace could see she'd hit a nerve. She knew that her sister liked the doctor, but she hadn't expected her to take her questions so personally when all she was trying to do was show Eva that there hadn't been another option. 'I'm not saying anything of the sort. I just wanted to understand what had happened. I thought it might help Eva or, you know, the poor man when he finds out what happened.'

'Well, Dr. Grey saved his life—that's all he needs to know.'

Grace put her spoon down and leaned over the table to touch Eva's arm. She could feel April glaring at her, but she wasn't going to argue with her sister, not now. She hadn't meant to upset her, and she wasn't used to her being so sensitive. 'It doesn't have to be you,' she said gently. 'You don't have to tell him. He's not your problem, Eva. Let the doctor tell him or another nurse. Heck, *I'll* tell him if it stops you from worrying. This isn't your burden.'

'No, it has to be me,' Eva said, shaking her head. 'I'll tell him.'

Grace carefully took Eva's spoon from her hand and lowered it into the bowl, lifting it and waiting for Eva to open her mouth so she could feed her.

'What you need,' she said, 'is to eat your breakfast. Then we'll go do our shift. And then tomorrow we're going to have a great day out, and you're going to forget about everything for a few hours, okay?'

Eva closed her mouth and swallowed the spoonful. 'Okay.'

'He's not Charlie, Eva. I know you care for him, but . . .'

'I know,' Eva whispered. 'I know he's not Charlie, but I still need to be there.'

Grace had no idea when she'd become the grown-up, but some-how she'd become the one looking after Eva and dealing with whatever was thrown at them. And it wasn't like she'd forgotten that less than a year earlier, she'd felt as if she'd met the strongest, most capable young woman in Eva that she'd ever encountered. Not to mention that April had always been the one to look out for everyone, but now she seemed so busy with her extra surgical duties that Grace was starting to worry about how much she'd taken on. It was so different from when they were in Pearl Harbor, their roles all reversed almost.

But so much had happened since then. Enough for a lifetime, and yet only months had passed. She sighed and swatted a bug on her arm before going back to eating her bowlful of mush.

Tomorrow. She needed to get Eva through today, and tomorrow she'd find a way to put a smile on all their faces. Or at least she hoped so.

———— ❧ ————

'Before you tell me that this is the worst picnic in the world, I have a plan,' Grace said as they headed out for the morning.

They'd originally planned on sleeping late if they could and then going out around lunchtime, but the sun was still blistering in the afternoons, and they'd decided to leave earlier. She plucked a little package from her pocket and held it out, waving it toward April.

'Somehow we missed out on getting our official guidebooks when we disembarked,' Grace said, passing it to April. 'It clearly states in there that bargaining is more than acceptable, and it just so happens that I have some cigarettes in my pocket to trade with.'

'Grace, it clearly says that bargaining is acceptable, but in the context of not paying the asking price from a street vendor,' April said. 'You're talking about *bartering*.'

April laughed, and Grace watched as Eva moved closer, reading over April's shoulder.

'It also says that you should never offer the locals alcoholic drinks,' Eva said. 'Do you think cigarettes are permitted?'

'I'm not offering them a bottle of whiskey, for goodness' sake; I'm offering cigarettes and some US dollars. I've heard they have amazing food, and I'm sick of our camp chow and cans of mush.'

Eva let out an audible sigh. 'Me too.'

'So what do you say? Shall we find us some locals to barter with?'

'Ohhh, it's full of interesting notes. Listen to this,' April said. '"Men walking together holding hands are not to be regarded as deviants, and no one should ever touch a local man, as they do not like being touched by strangers." And you're right about not eating with your left hand; it's considered *very* unclean because they eat with their fingers here.'

'I think maybe the guidelines were more for the soldiers than us. It also makes it very clear that United States men should never go near a veiled woman.'

'Why?' Eva asked.

'They're the respectable women; the *prostitutes* are the ones without their heads covered.'

April made a snorting sound that made them all laugh. 'Not exactly a concern for us, is it, ladies? Unless of course we get mistaken for one.'

'It must be awfully hot, don't you think, for all those women wearing the veils and long, ankle-length dresses,' Eva said.

'Maybe it helps to keep them cool—I don't know,' Grace replied. 'I'd love to understand more about their culture. Everything about them is so different; there's nothing similar to what I've ever seen at home.'

Suddenly there was a chorus of calls and shouts from farther down toward the town, and a crowd of children ran at them, waving and grinning from ear to ear.

'Incoming,' April muttered. 'I think we're about to be mobbed!'

They'd seen children crowded around the American trucks before, flapping their little hands and hoping for a treat of some sort to be dropped into their palms, but they'd walked about the other day without being disturbed.

'Chocolad!' the first little boy yelled. '*Chocolad!* Please!'

'Hello!' a pretty girl said, coming closer and stroking Grace's arm. 'Smoke?'

Grace smiled down at her, staring into beautiful dark eyes that were blinking back up at her.

'Aren't you sweet. And you speak English! Maybe I have something for you.'

'No,' Eva said sternly, her hand closing over Grace's pocket.

When she looked down, she saw the child's hand was caught, and she realized what she'd been about to do. The girl was a thief!

'Well, aren't you full of surprises. You don't need to steal,' Grace told her, waving her finger at her and shaking her head. 'No stealing. I would have given you something.'

'Chewn gum! Chewn gum!' the other children shouted, holding out grubby little hands for treats.

'Here you go,' Grace said, giving some gum from her pocket to the girl.

She was expecting a smile, maybe even a thank-you, but the second she gave her the gum, the girl snatched it, poked her tongue out, and started yelling something that Grace couldn't understand. Was she cursing at her? After she'd been so generous?

Most of the others ran off when they realized there was little being offered, but the boy who'd originally approached couldn't take his eyes off Eva.

'It's your hair,' Grace murmured. 'He's never seen hair the color of flames before, I bet.'

Eva stepped closer to him and bent, dropping to her knees. The boy hesitated, then moved forward and carefully touched Eva's hair before throwing his arms around her and giving her a quick hug.

'Pretty,' he said, his cheeks flushing.

'Where have your friends gone?' Grace asked.

The boy shrugged, but he stood to attention as Eva placed something in his hand and then closed his palm around whatever the gift was.

'Here, have some cigarettes too,' Grace said, handing them over.

The boy grinned and gave them a wave, before darting off, running fast in the direction his friends had gone.

'I think he's in love with you,' Grace teased.

'If a little boy wants to be in love with me, then I'm okay with that,' Eva said, shrugging, and Grace couldn't help but smile. They'd tried so many things to draw Eva out of her shell these past few months, and then a little boy full of innocence had stroked her hair and touched her face, and suddenly there was a lightness about her again. Maybe for only a short while, but it was there. She only hoped that being around Arthur and seeing him suffer wouldn't send her straight back into sadness again.

'What is the little ponytail for?' April asked. 'All the younger boys seem to have shaved heads with little ponytails at the back.'

'It's in case they die,' Eva said quietly, taking Grace by surprise. 'Arabic boys are circumcised when they turn thirteen—it's a religious thing—and the pigtail is to signify to the angel of death that they're little boys who haven't yet turned thirteen. The angel lifts them by their pigtail to take them to heaven.'

'It's so unusual; how different their customs are,' said Grace.

'Different is always hard to understand, though, isn't it?' April replied, still staring after the children, fascinated by the myth behind their hairstyles. 'I like that it's so different here—it makes you realize that we're all fighting for the same thing, even though we're so far removed from one another.'

'Going back to the topic of being in love,' Grace said, changing the subject as they continued to walk. 'How's your love life going, April? Has the dashing Dr. Grey asked you out on a date yet?'

'Grace! Nothing is going on between me and Dr. Grey.'

'Nothing *yet*,' Grace said smugly, loving how quickly her sister had become defensive. 'There's nothing to be embarrassed about; he's a gorgeous surgeon who happens to like having you on his service with him. You'd have to be a nun not to be attracted to him, and he clearly likes you right back. You should, I don't know, try to get trapped in a supply room with him or something.'

'Stop!' April begged. 'Please, stop. Yes, he's handsome, *yes*, I like him, but nothing has happened. If he asked me out, I'd say yes, but he hasn't even hinted that he's interested, so can we please just leave it?'

Grace shrugged. 'Fine, but are we going to buy food, or are we just going to go for a swim?'

'Food,' Eva chirped. 'I think we should go straight down there and get something to eat, then swim.'

They walked casually into the Arab quarter of town, elbowing their way past more people than Grace had ever seen in one space, the narrow streets and alleys packed with bodies and hungry-looking dogs with their ribs poking out. There were even donkeys tethered to doors, their eyes shut and their lower lips drooping as they waited for someone to return for them.

There was everything presented for sale, from rugs and handbags to shoes and copperware, and smoke billowed out into the alleyways, filling the air with smells that merged with the thick sweat emanating from the men shouting and laughing loudly at one another.

Grace's heart beat fast as she looked around, amazed all over again at how a regular girl from Oregon had somehow ended up on the other side of the world, in a place so different she couldn't have even imagined it in her wildest dreams.

'Here,' April suddenly said. 'Let's stop here.'

A street vendor was cooking what looked like vegetables and rice with some sort of meat, and Grace decided not to ask what it was. Perhaps she'd rather not know and just enjoy the taste of something other than army rations.

'You,' someone said to them from behind.

Grace turned. 'Are you talking to us?' she asked politely.

'You, you give my boy cigarettes and candy,' the man said.

Grace glanced at Eva, not about to point the finger and tell him exactly which of them had given out the treats to the little boy earlier.

April was the one who nodded. 'We did. Yes.'

His smile took Grace by surprise. 'You must come to our home for dinner. Tonight. We cook you a feast.'

Grace tried not to laugh, looking first at Eva, then her sister. She'd thought they were about to be told off, and instead they were being asked for dinner!

'I told you the other nurses had been asked to have dinner with a family,' Grace whispered.

'Well,' April started.

'We'd love to,' Grace said, ignoring her sister and speaking loudly. 'Thank you. It's an honor to be asked.'

'You go over there,' he said, pointing back toward the way they'd come. 'I'll meet you, walk you to our house.'

Grace made arrangements with him, but she noticed Eva moving closer, smiling at the man.

'Your son, he is very polite,' Eva said, stepping toward him. She saw her reach her hands out and then quickly drop them and wrap them around herself. 'You should be proud of him.'

The man nodded an acknowledgement before walking off. They all looked at one another and laughed.

'Well, we wanted different food. Now we have it!' Grace said with a grin.

April smiled. 'We'll need to bring a gift for them, to say thank you. It must be a big deal for them to offer strangers food when they don't have a lot.'

'Do we need to cover our heads in his home like the women here do, out of respect?' Eva asked.

'I think we should just wear our uniforms,' April said. 'They know why we're here, that we're nurses, and I think that shows respect, don't you?'

They took their food and walked away, heading for the beach to see if they could swim. It was an hour before they got there, and Grace looked out at the ocean and felt like she'd been transported back to Hawaii. She shut her eyes, inhaling the familiar smell of the sea and imagining the water washing against her feet. She could see Poppy running, splashing through ankle-deep water, chasing after her as April watched.

'Hello, ladies.'

Grace opened her eyes and blinked away tears as she braved a smile and turned. She quickly wiped under her eyes when she saw the soldiers sitting farther down on the sand.

'Hi,' she called back. 'Have you tested the water?'

The four men laughed, and they all stood, pants rolled up past their ankles, bare feet lost in the sand.

'It's mighty good in there,' one of them said, his British accent making Grace grin.

'You're a long way from home, soldier,' she said.

'Not as far as you, love,' another said, making all the boys laugh.

Eva had sat down on the beach, looking out to sea, but April was still standing, one hand raised to block out the sun.

'You look familiar, actually,' April said. 'I don't know why, but—'

'The train!' Grace interrupted. 'You passed me coffee through the window of the train when we were stopped!'

The fair-haired one of the four laughed and came closer, holding out his hand.

'You've got me. You know, you owe me for that. I got in big trouble for giving away our coffee rations!'

Grace smiled. 'Really? And what exactly can I repay you with, soldier?'

The men on either side nudged him in the ribs, and she held his gaze, trying not to look away, enjoying their banter.

'Well, how about we go out for dinner one night?' he said, his cheeks turning a dark shade of red.

Grace glanced at her sister, who was looking like a mother about to drag her infant away from danger. She chose to ignore her.

'Why not? I'd love to go out with you.'

He grinned and stepped forward, his blue-green eyes full of sincerity. 'I'm Peter, by the way.'

She took the hand he held out and smiled as he gently shook it. 'Grace.'

'Well, Grace, how about you meet me on Saturday night? It'll be my last night of leave.'

She nodded. 'Where?'

'There's a place we all go, a place on the edge of the Arab quarter with a green sign out in front. There's plenty of British and US soldiers there every night.'

'I guess I'll see you then.'

When he let go of her hand, the other men grabbed at him, and Peter took off as they chased, darting through the ocean and sending water flying. Grace watched him for a while, then turned back to April.

'What?' she asked.

Her sister looked unhappy. 'It doesn't feel right, Grace. You don't even know the man.'

'He's a soldier; we're all fighting on the same side,' she said, shrugging. 'What's to know? And I'm not exactly going somewhere isolated with him—there'll be plenty of people around.'

'I just feel nervous about it; that's all.'

Grace met April's gaze and bumped shoulders with her, standing close as they both looked out at the water.

'Remember how you said you weren't going to mother me?' Grace asked gently.

April sighed. Loudly. 'I know. But I can't help worrying about you.'

'I promise I won't intervene if the doctor asks you out.'

'Grace!' April glowered at her. 'Can you please stop with the doctor talk?'

Her flushed cheeks were a giveaway; Grace knew how much her sister liked the man. 'Fine. I just wish Poppy were here with us. She'd be teasing you mercilessly, and she'd be the first to encourage my date with the gorgeous soldier.'

April groaned. 'She would have. It'd be me against two of you if she was here.'

'She'd be setting me up on dates at every opportunity. Did you know she tried to set me up with one of her patients just before the bombing? The one we played cards with?'

April laughed. 'No, I didn't. Typical, though; Poppy was always trying to matchmake everyone.'

Talking about Poppy made Grace think of Teddy. They'd been so happy together; Poppy was always hanging on to his arm and gazing up at him, and Teddy was smitten with her right back. She hated that she'd been so in love with him herself, her infatuation with him never disappearing no matter how much she'd tried, and now that Poppy was gone, even thinking about it made her feel guilty. And ever since his letter, those old feelings had flared up again. If they'd ever gone. She needed this, a night out with a gorgeous foreign soldier, because being there for Teddy was one thing; falling still more for him was something else altogether.

'Are you two done squabbling?' Eva asked.

Grace turned and saw Eva by the water, waiting for them.

'For now,' she replied, winking at April, who only groaned at her in response.

———— ᘒᓀᕉᓇᘓ ————

Less than four hours later, Grace was smoothing out wrinkles in her uniform in their tent as the other two waited for her. She hastily applied some lipstick and opened her bag to find some chewing gum to give the family they were visiting.

'What are you two taking?' she asked.

April held up gum as well, and Eva produced some chocolate from her pocket. 'I figured they'd like some American things. This will be enough, won't it?'

Grace shrugged. 'I hope so. Let's go.'

They walked back down the hill toward town again, the heat still stifling despite it being early evening, and Grace swatted at bugs that continued to land on her skin. She loved the thrill of being stationed overseas, but the flies and biting bugs she could do without.

'There he is,' April said, gesturing toward a man waiting for them. He nodded and beckoned for them to follow him, and they walked behind him to a modest house that seemed more like a hut to Grace. She plucked at her jacket and wondered why they'd decided to wear their hot class A uniforms. Most of them lamented frequently about the suitability of their clothes; the thick, buttoned-up jackets were hardly appropriate for somewhere as hot and dry as a desert!

'Come in,' the man said. 'Come in and sit.'

They walked in, past a cat with some young kittens lounging by the front door, with April in the lead. They all stopped the moment they were inside, greeted by the woman of the house waiting for them, her hands clasped together as she smiled and nodded, and the little boy, along with two older sisters, standing beside their mother.

'Thank you,' Grace said, 'for having us in your home. Thank you.'

April and Eva echoed her thanks, and they were ushered to the table, where there was only enough room for the adults.

'My daughter,' the woman said, pointing to her eldest. 'She was sick, and one of your doctors, he helped her.'

Grace beamed at the woman, wondering who it might have been. 'We have good doctors. I'm happy he helped you.'

'And our son, he said you were very kind.'

This time it was Eva smiling as the young boy came forward. She bent to talk to him as Grace stepped forward and took her place at the table.

'This doctor, what was his name?' she asked.

'Evans,' the man said, nodding. 'Dr. Evans. Good man.'

'I don't know him personally, but I'm sure he's a very good doctor.'

'We have food now,' the woman said, moving toward the little kitchen.

The house was so humble, smaller and more basic than anything an American would expect to live in, but it was impeccably clean. Grace thought back to their first impressions of North Africa and its people; they'd all been horrified at how primitive their lives were. Locals seemed to relieve themselves wherever they wanted to, with no hygiene to speak of, but she could see now how much pride this woman had in her home to keep it so orderly.

'Can I help?' April asked.

'No!' the woman said. 'I have daughters; we cook for you.'

Soon they were being presented with a dish put in the center of the table, some type of vegetable, and Grace reached for the food first as the man beckoned her to do so. The others followed suit, and she was surprised at the flavor, wondering what spices might have been used.

'Many plates,' the woman said. 'You try everything.'

Grace wasn't sure what she meant until the woman reappeared with another dish, and after that another. There was rice and more vegetables, things that brought Grace's taste buds to life, and she could barely remember ever being so well fed.

'This is our last dish,' the woman announced. 'Please enjoy.'

Grace was baffled at the plate that was presented. It was a small creature, cooked whole with its head intact, and she studied the little cat-like ears and wondered what on earth it was. Whatever it was, though, it smelled delicious, and she glanced at her friends to ask what they thought it might be. But irritation rose within her as she saw Eva's worried expression.

Grace smiled for her hosts before glaring at Eva. 'Stop looking like you've sucked a lemon,' she whispered under her breath.

'But it's a whole animal,' Eva whispered back.

'It's no different from eating meat at home; it's just a different way of presenting it.'

She looked over at April, pleased that at least her sister didn't seem concerned by the plate on the table.

The knife was passed to Grace, but she shook her head. 'Please, cut for me,' she said, making the motions of cutting. 'I'm not sure where to start.'

The woman laughed at her and patted the bottom of the animal. 'This part is best.'

'The bottom? Is it nice and juicy?' April caught Grace's eye, and she erupted into giggling, the entire table suddenly laughing as Grace's cheeks flushed and she laughed along with the others.

'Some *bottom* for me, then,' she said, rolling her eyes at her sister and trying not to laugh again.

The woman nodded, her face eager as she leaned forward and sliced the meat while Grace held out her plate. She kicked Eva until she lifted her plate, but when she noticed that Eva had tears in her eyes, she reached for her hand under the table and gave it a little squeeze.

'It's okay,' she whispered. 'Just be gracious and eat a little. Just think of it as beef or something.'

Once they all had some meat, their host family waited for them to begin, and Grace smiled as she took her first mouthful, surprised at how tasty it was. It might look peculiar, but she wasn't complaining.

When the night was over and they'd thanked their hosts and said goodbye, the three of them retraced their steps, not speaking until they were far, far away. Grace couldn't stop thinking about the family, about what they'd sacrificed to have enough food to share with them. It had been a lovely night.

'What was that animal?' Eva whispered. 'I just couldn't eat it with its eyes watching me.'

Grace cleared her throat. 'Eva, come on. Whatever it was, they shared what little they had with us. And it was actually delicious.'

April nudged her with her shoulder. 'I thought so too.'

'Give me roast beef, peas, and apple pie all in the same bowl again any day,' Eva whispered. 'Seeing an animal on a plate with its head intact is too much for me. My hands are still shaking. But you're right: it was so generous of them to share it with us.'

And as rain suddenly started falling, pelting the ground around them, they all huddled together and quietly made the long walk back to camp. Grace thought of Teddy, wondered where he might be and whether he'd have shelter. Whatever it was they'd eaten tonight, she bet any of the soldiers out there fighting would have given just about anything to be eating it. And she'd happily go back for seconds if she ever had the chance, even just to be with a family for a night. For some reason, even though it was so different, it still reminded her of home.

CHAPTER FIFTEEN
EVA

Eva stared down at Arthur's face, so peaceful in slumber, yet so pained when he was awake. She resisted the urge to reach out and stroke his skin, wanting to comfort him even though he'd made it so clear that he didn't want any contact. Not from her or anyone. But it was only early days, and she had time on her side, as well as patience.

Whenever she sat with him, she relived the moment over and over again—the way his face had crumpled, his guttural moan as she'd told him what had happened. When she'd sat and waited for him to come out of surgery, she'd expected the horror of finding him to be the thing that weighed on her mind, but it was the very raw moment at his hospital bed that still plagued her.

'Arthur,' she said as she took his hand, shuffling closer and smiling down at him, hoping he could tell how much she cared.

He looked up, smiling back at her, clearly trying to push himself up but groaning from the effort.

'How long have I been out of it?' he asked, motioning for the water. 'I'm so thirsty.'

His voice was thick and raspy, as if he had gravel in his throat.

'A week,' she said. 'Your injuries were severe, and your surgery took hours.'

Eva held the cup for him, keeping the straw still and watching as he greedily drained the water. His side profile was so handsome, his jaw strong even beneath the stubble, his eyes bright despite how sick he'd been. She imagined he would have carried more weight usually, but for now his cheekbones were prominent.

'Arthur, I've been with you since you arrived. I, well . . .' Her voice trailed off, and she set the water back down, reaching for his hand again.

'What's wrong? Did something go wrong in surgery?' he asked, confusion echoing across his face.

Eva took a big breath and squeezed his fingers. 'Your surgeries were all successful, and you're expected to make a full recovery. No one expected you to survive, but you've shown true strength in your recovery.'

'When can I get back to my unit, then? I'll go stir crazy waiting in here; I need to get back into the sky.'

She blinked away a tear and then another, trying desperately to stop them from falling. But she was no good at hiding her feelings, and the look on Arthur's face mirrored her own, his smile falling as a mask of horror was cast across his features.

'Arthur, I'm so sorry to tell you that one of your legs had to be amputated.'

He thrust upward, hurling his body up as he stared down at his lower half. His bellow echoed through the hospital, a bloodcurdling yell that sent waves of pain ripping through her body.

Arthur's eyes met hers, no longer bright and blue but instead like tumultuous ocean water, swimming with shock, pain, and horror all blended into one.

'I know this is hard to come to terms with, and you'll first experience sadness and then anger. It's all normal, it's—'

But he never let her finish.

'Leave me!' he screamed. 'Leave me the fuck alone!'

As her thoughts drifted back to the present, she noticed Arthur stir, and she shuffled her chair back a little. He hadn't spoken to her since that day, and she was never sure how angry he'd be, although every day seemed to get worse with him rather than better.

The moment his eyes opened, she smiled and reached for his water. Every day she hoped that her smile and presence would help, that she could show him that every day became a little easier to deal with, but she wasn't convinced that it was working.

'Good morning, Arthur,' she said brightly.

He just stared at her before rolling slightly and shutting his eyes again.

'Arthur, would you like water or—'

'Leave me.'

Eva sat silently for a moment, trying to choose the right words. She couldn't imagine what he was going through, the devastation he must feel at what had been taken from him, but she could never seem to say the right thing to convey how she felt.

'Arthur, if there's anything you need, I want you to know that I'm here for you,' she said quietly. 'I can't imagine what you're going through, but you're not alone in this, okay?'

He kept his eyes shut, still with his back turned, and Eva heard the matron calling names. They were supposed to have a meeting before her shift started, and she was running late from sitting with Arthur for so long.

Reluctantly she rose, setting his water back down and patting his shoulder, before heading toward the mess room. There were other nurses already filling the room, and she stood just inside the door, finding her way to April.

Her friend turned, smiling and making space for her.

'How's Arthur this morning? Any change?'

She shook her head. 'None. I think he's withdrawing even further.'

April put an arm around her. 'I know we've all said it before, but he's just another patient, Eva. We all get attached to some of the men, but the way you're . . .' April's voice trailed off.

'The way I'm what?' Eva whispered, head bent as the matron started to address the room.

'It's almost like you think he's connected to Charlie. We just don't want you pinning too much hope on him, and the way he's treating you is appalling.'

'*We?*' she hissed. 'So you and Grace are talking about me?'

April sighed. 'We're just worried about you—that's all.'

Eva took a step away from April, fuming as she listened to the matron talk about supply shortages and changing rosters. She knew Arthur wasn't Charlie—of course she did—and what was wrong with trying to help a man she felt a connection to? April reached for her hand, and Eva let her, not wanting to cause a rift. April had been unfailingly kind to her, a loyal friend, and as much as she didn't like hearing what she'd just said, she'd rather have a friend who told her the truth than one who told her only what she wanted to hear.

If Eva had thought Arthur was difficult before, she'd come to have a new appreciation of just how difficult nursing him could be. She stood by his bed, smile fixed, ready to pepper him with care and kindness.

'Leave me!' he barked, glaring at her with such hatred in his gaze that she almost turned and walked back the way she'd come. But if she did that, she'd be neglecting her nursing duties, and the one thing she'd never be was negligent when it came to her work. And she also wasn't the type to give up on someone.

'Arthur, I know this is difficult, but I can make this fast if you'll only let me—'

'What part of *leave me* are you not understanding.'

He was sitting with his arms folded, his head turned away from her to show her a profile that would have been devastatingly handsome had his lips not been pulled down into a scowl. Or his brow furrowed with anger, causing his eyebrows to knit tightly together.

He didn't look at her again, so Eva moved quietly around him, filling his water cup and taking a deep breath before reaching for his bedsheet to take a look at his leg.

'I'm just going to check your dressing to make sure it's clean,' she said.

The sheet was pulled up quicker than she could look. 'There's no damn leg to look at, is there? So why don't you go help someone who wants it.'

Eva nodded, turning away and swallowing down the words she wanted to say to him. What was wrong with him? Wasn't he happy to be alive? She wanted to curse him and cry out that he was so fortunate to have made it, that her Charlie would have done anything to still be alive, that *she'd* have sacrificed anything to have him here. But she didn't. Instead she walked away and decided to come back to him after she'd seen her other patients.

'It's all right, love,' a British soldier said as she passed his bed. 'He doesn't mean to take it out on you.'

Eva stopped and refilled the soldier's water cup. 'I just have to figure out a way to help him—that's all. I'm sure he'll come around eventually.'

Trouble was, her belief that she could get through to him was fading, even if she didn't want to admit it yet. She'd expected Arthur to be grateful that she'd saved his life and stuck around to help him, but instead he seemed to hate her.

'Just give him time. He'll appreciate you soon enough.'

Eva smiled and gave the soldier a pat on the arm before continuing on, checking dressings and trying to take temperatures despite the mercury being so hot it was useless, until she ended up beside Grace.

'How is he today?' Grace asked. 'Still grumpy as a bear with a thorn?'

Eva groaned. 'Worse, if that's even possible. I know it's a lot for him to take in, what's happened and all, but he's so ungrateful.'

Grace gave her a quick hug. 'Then tell him that. There's nothing that says we can't be honest with our patients. Show him that spitfire of a woman I met in Pearl Harbor. You remember the one who barked orders as if she were a sergeant?'

Eva laughed. 'Have you and your sister been talking again? Because I'm not under any delusions that he's Charlie, not after the way he's treated me.'

'Then tell him the truth. It's about time he heard it instead of you pussyfooting around him.'

She took a deep, shaky breath. Her old confident self seemed hard to remember now; it was as if the bombings had stripped her of everything that used to make her feel alive. When Charlie had died, a piece of her had died too. 'Promise you'll come pick me up off the floor if it doesn't work?'

Grace grinned. 'Oh, it'll work. Trust me.'

Eva turned and straightened her shoulders, staring at Arthur's bed. 'You'd better be right,' she muttered.

She marched back over to Arthur, smiling to herself as she approached him. He could be rude to her all he liked, and it wasn't her problem if he was ungrateful for his life being saved. She was going to smile and chat with him and thoroughly ignore his behavior until he started showing her the respect she deserved.

'How are you doing now, Arthur?' she asked. 'It's time for me to check your dressings and take your temperature.'

He didn't even look at her. 'I thought I'd already told you to go away?'

She kept smiling. It actually made her feel better just keeping her smile intact, grinning away like a Cheshire cat.

'Arthur, I'm sure you can understand that I have a job to do. So I'm going to go ahead and do it, and you can either talk to me and enjoy the company, or you can sit there all full of misery, but either way I'm doing my job. Are we clear?'

He turned then, and she nearly lost her nerve. His sharp blue eyes met hers, and just when she thought he was going to smile back, just when she thought that gaze was going to soften, he slapped her hand away without saying a word.

Eva ignored him, swallowing down her anger as she reached for him again. This time when he slapped, he connected with her metal tray of equipment, including the bowl of saline water that she had in case his wound needed to be cleaned.

The liquid dripped down her front. It wasn't the wet patch she cared about—it wasn't large and would dry soon enough; not to mention it was better than blood splatter, which she'd become all too used to—it was the way he just turned and stared the other way as if he'd done nothing. Without saying a word. She'd seen this behavior before, knew exactly what a bully looked like, because she'd grown up with one as a father, and she wasn't ever going to let anyone treat her like that again, no matter what the excuse.

Fire rose within her as she breathed, feeling her nostrils flare as she waited for him to apologize. Eventually she bent and retrieved her things before straightening and considering the man lying on the bed before her. What was wrong with him? How could he be so rude, so nasty, when he'd managed to survive an accident that should have killed him!

'You owe me an apology,' she said quietly, gritting her teeth as she waited.

Arthur didn't say a word.

'It's my duty to nurse you to the best of my abilities, and I don't appreciate you making my job so difficult,' she continued, grabbing the sheet this time and pulling it back so hard he didn't have a chance to stop her. Holding the sheet out of reach of a man not used to balancing with one leg was cruel, but so was he.

'Get away from me!' he yelled.

Eva's heart beat fast and loud as the ward seemed to fall silent behind her. She had the distinct feeling that she was being watched, that all eyes were on her, including Arthur's.

She took a step closer to him, refusing to break his steely gaze. When they'd rescued him, carrying him desperately to the hospital, she'd stared into those eyes and thought they reminded her of the ocean. Now, they were so cold they reminded her of ice.

'You let me do my job as quickly as I can, I leave you alone,' she said. 'We don't have to talk, we don't have to have any other contact, but you need to let me check your wound.'

Arthur looked like he was going to explode, and she had no doubt that if he'd been able to walk, he would have swung his legs down and marched off, never to be seen again. But that was the problem—he couldn't walk away no matter how desperately he wanted to, and her heart broke to see such a strong, capable man struggling.

He never replied, but he did finally look away, and she tentatively touched the bandage around his stump, methodically checking the color of his wound and making sure there was no gangrene or other infection setting in. Arthur had had general surgery as well, to repair damaged internal organs, and she carefully raised his shirt to check that was healing. He grunted when she touched him, and she hesitated before stepping back and letting out a breath she hadn't even known she was holding.

'Thank you, Arthur,' she said, pulling up the sheet and tucking him back in. 'I'll come by soon with your lunch and to see if you require any morphine.'

'I'm not hungry,' he muttered.

She paused, wondering if she'd already pushed him far enough or whether she needed to be assertive again. Eva studied his face, the strong angle of his jaw, the broad shoulders that were impossible not to notice even as he sat slumped in his bed.

'You should eat,' she said gently, reaching to touch his arm and then thinking better of it when he flinched before she'd even made contact. 'I'm not going to force you, but it's a waste of good food, and you're only going to make yourself sick if you don't.' She watched him, wishing there were a way she could get through to him. 'I'm sorry, Arthur. I'm so sorry for what happened to you, but it doesn't have to define the rest of your life, not if you let me help you.'

She turned to leave him, waiting for a beat, almost expecting him to say thank you or apologize—something, *anything*. But he didn't.

Eva walked away and saw Grace with a patient, but her friend paused to give her a quick thumbs-up as she passed.

'I think he's warming to you,' Grace whispered.

'Warming? He's as cold as the South Pole!' Eva muttered.

But when she caught Grace's eye, she couldn't help but laugh. And if she hadn't laughed, she'd have cried.

───── ⟋ ✦ ⟍ ─────

'Excuse me—that nurse over there said you'd know where to find a pilot by the name of Arthur?'

Eva looked up at the deep male voice, almost dropping her pen when she found two airmen dressed in uniform standing in front of her.

'Sorry—I didn't even hear you approaching. Come this way,' she said politely, beckoning for them to follow. 'You're colleagues of Arthur's?'

They both nodded.

'Yes, ma'am,' the same man said. 'We thought he was dead. Everyone did.'

Eva sighed. 'I certainly didn't think he was going to make it when we found him. He was already half-dead then.'

'You were the one who found him?' the other man asked.

Eva slowly nodded as she watched the surprise show on their faces. 'Yes. I was with two friends, other nurses, and we struggled back with him.'

'He must be so grateful,' he said.

Eva laughed and pointed toward Arthur, who they'd moved to the far end of the ward now so he could stare at the blacked-out window. 'You'd think so, wouldn't you?'

They both looked confused, and she waved them on, eager to watch Arthur's response to his visitors.

'You'll see soon enough.'

They took off their hats and walked toward him, and Eva pretended to be busy checking something so she could watch. Sure enough, just as she'd expected, they both took a huge step back as Arthur first ignored them and then turned nasty; he yelled at them to leave him the hell alone and folded his arms again, slumped forward and staring at the window.

They were walking back out again within five minutes, heads hanging. She was starting to think she'd done well suffering through his behavior for so long when no one else could handle him for more than a few minutes.

'I'm guessing he hasn't always been like that?' Eva asked when the two men stopped beside her.

They both looked bewildered, the confusion etched on their faces. One of the men ran his fingers through his hair, tears shining in his eyes.

'That's not Arthur,' he said, shaking his head. 'Did he have a head injury? Did something happen to his brain?'

'Arthur was the best,' the other said. 'He was clever and quick witted, never missed a chance to give someone a ribbing, but when it came to flying, he was single minded.'

'Losing a leg has affected him terribly,' Eva explained in a low voice. 'Most men are grateful to live at all, but Arthur's been difficult since the moment he woke up. I think he wishes he was dead.' Her tongue struggled around the word, hating the sound of it as it passed her lips. *Dead.* She'd seen enough death to last her a lifetime, and yet Arthur seemed to resent that he hadn't died like all the other poor men who'd probably have done anything for a chance at going home, able bodied or not.

'We'll come back on our next day of leave. I hope he gets, well, easier.'

Eva nodded and watched them leave. She hoped so too. Nursing him was taking up all her energy, and she alternated between feeling sorry for him and wanting to beat him around the head and scream at him.

She cleared her throat when she approached his bed, although she was certain he knew exactly what was happening around him despite pretending otherwise.

'Your friends were worried about you,' she said, checking his water and then picking up his chart to read for something to do. 'They told me that you weren't usually so uncommunicative.'

Arthur still didn't move. Or speak.

'Would you like me or one of the corpsmen to help you move?' she asked. 'I don't want you getting bedsores from sitting in the same position.'

That made him turn. His head slowly moved, and she shivered when his cold eyes locked on hers.

'Bedsores?' he asked. 'I couldn't give a damn about *bedsores*; I'm a little more worried about the fact I'm missing my fucking leg!'

Tears sprang into Eva's eyes as he swore at her, his anger palpable as he glared, the pulse frantically beating at his neck and the bulge on his forehead impossible to miss. Her father had been cruel and physically nasty to her, but she'd never had a man swear directly at her like that before.

Refusing to give in to her fear, she stood her ground, biting her tongue, wishing she could scream and yell at him.

'Did you hear me?' he asked, his tone low.

'Loud and clear,' she whispered, struggling to find her voice. 'But if you think that you can swear and yell at me to make me go away, then you're sorely mistaken, because I'm tougher than that.'

He continued to stare at her when she expected him to look away, but she almost felt as if April and Grace were right behind her, giving her strength and telling her to stand up for herself.

'The way I see it, you've pushed away everyone who cares about you and every nurse who tries to come near you. But I'm tougher than them,' she said, then cleared her throat as she stepped closer, not afraid of his gaze now as she set her hands on the edge of the bed. 'I know how to deal with a bully, because I've had to live with one my entire life, so that's enough. Do you hear me?'

'Leave me,' he muttered. 'Just leave me the hell alone.'

A tear slid down her cheek, followed by another and another. All this time she'd waited to shed tears over Charlie, to sob her heart out, and they'd stayed locked inside of her. And now here she was, standing before a man who seemed to hate everything about her, and her emotions were no longer being held prisoner. 'No.'

Arthur didn't say another word; he just turned and stared, like he always did. Only this time he let her check him without complaint, as stiff as cardboard, but without trying to throw her hand away.

Small steps, she told herself as she fought another wave of tears. *Just small steps.*

As soon as she was finished with Arthur, she went to find Grace, and they made their way out of the hospital, heading for the short walk up the hill to where their camp was. They were late, so they'd end up at the back of the line for dinner, but she was starving, and it was better than being in the hospital with Arthur.

'Where's April?' she asked.

Grace looked tired as she yawned and wrapped her arms around herself. 'In surgery with Dr. Grey, last I heard. She loves surgery as much as I hate the thought of it.'

Eva nodded. It still amused her when she thought of how much Grace despised the sight of blood. 'Maybe I should offer up my services. I'd rather be in surgery than taking care of Arthur.'

'No better?'

Eva sighed. 'He's at least letting me do my job now, but he's awful. I've never had such an obnoxious patient.'

They shuffled forward a few steps as they joined the chow line.

'Were those two airmen friends of his earlier? I sent them down to you.'

'Yes. And Arthur sent them packing within minutes of arriving. He just erupted like a volcano and had them running for the hills.'

'Why don't you offer to take him outside for fresh air? Or get someone to talk to him about getting mobile once he's healed?' Grace asked.

Eva took another few steps forward. 'Honestly, I think he might be better on the psychiatric ward.'

She loved the idea of taking him outside for air or doing anything to make him happy; it was why she'd sat with him from the day they'd rescued him, to help him and care for him. But the more she offered, the kinder she was, the more he seemed to push back.

'Have you told him that it was you who saved him?' Grace asked, leaning into her.

'No.' She'd wanted to, when he'd first come around, but the words had never come, and then he was so angry that she hadn't bothered.

'I would. Give him something to be grateful for.'

Eva wished she were right, but she feared that if he knew she'd saved him, then he might hate her even more than he already did.

'Morning, Arthur!' Eva said, breezing past him and reaching for his chart. 'It's a beautiful day today, and I thought you might like some fresh air.'

He didn't reply.

'Arthur? I thought you might like—'

'You thought wrong,' he muttered. 'Just get this over with.'

She hesitated, staring at him and hating the way he wouldn't look at her. Did he dislike her that much, or was it that he was embarrassed? She wasn't so sure anymore.

'It's important that you breathe in some fresh air and have the sun on your skin,' she said, deciding to keep her smile fixed and continue on as if he hadn't refuted her. She was going to take it as a good sign that he was letting her go about her nursing duties instead of fighting her now.

'Is that doctor's orders or just some fancy idea you've had to get me out of this bed?'

She froze and looked up, expecting to see a smile to go with that little bout of sarcasm, but the second she met his gaze, she saw that he wasn't trying to be funny.

Eva checked his dressing and took his temperature before setting her things down and sitting on the edge of his bed. The hospital beds were narrow, but with his leg not taking up the space on one side, she could fit beside him.

'I'm not sure if anyone's told you, Arthur,' she said softly, wishing she could take his hand but knowing that he'd refuse the contact, 'or even if you remember that day you were rescued, but it was me.'

He folded his arms, always in the same position with his shoulders slumped and his arms crossed, his lips permanently pulled into a frown.

'I was walking that day, the day you were found. I heard a noise and found you, and I helped to carry you back here,' she said. 'You were in such bad shape, but you looked at me; I held your hand and you told me your name, and I stayed with you until you were rushed into surgery.'

His eyes were dark and stormy now as he slowly turned his head. 'You?' he asked.

'Me,' she whispered. 'And I sat with you when I was off duty, all those days until you finally woke up. I was here with you.'

He looked away again, and she wanted to scream at him to look at her, to be grateful, to not give up on living. The words choked her, the anger pulsating as she tried to breathe and couldn't. She folded her hands so he wouldn't see them shaking, staring down at them, and his words took her by surprise when he finally spoke.

'Why?'

'Why what?' she asked.

'Why did you save me? Why didn't you just leave me to die?'

Eva studied him. She wanted to tell him about Charlie—she wanted to tell him so many things to make him appreciate his life—but she couldn't. 'Because I saw a man in pain who needed help, and the second I looked into your eyes and saw your injuries, I knew I had to get you back here. You're one of the lucky ones, Arthur. You get to live. You get to go home.'

It was the first time he'd maintained eye contact with her, the first time he hadn't turned away in a huff and refused to engage with her.

'Well, you should have left me,' he muttered. 'I'd rather be dead than a cripple.'

'You'd rather be dead?' she echoed.

He didn't reply.

Eva looked at the pillow propped up behind him, wondering for a split second if she could grab it and smother him, bury that angry, ungrateful face of his and suffocate the life from him. But she didn't. Instead she took a deep breath and stood, her hand resting where moments before she'd been sitting.

'Fine, then,' she said, glaring at him as she thought of Charlie, as she imagined what he would have given to survive, what *she* would have given for him to survive. 'You want me to leave? I'll leave.'

'Go,' he said, defying her, his stare arrogant, as if he was daring her to actually walk away from him.

She stood there, watching him, waiting for him to change his mind.

'Go!' he suddenly shouted, his voice reverberating through her, hitting her hard like a punch to her body.

She sucked in a breath through clenched teeth as tears pooled in her eyes, but she refused to give in to him. Her father had treated her like this and gotten away with it all her life, but this man couldn't hurt her with his fists. He couldn't even get out of his bed.

'I'll go,' she whispered, leaning closer to him so he could hear every word. 'But I'm the only person you've got on your side now, and one day I might just leave you here and not come back.'

She watched him, saw recognition flicker across his face, before turning and leaving him, her words weighing heavily. She'd been cruel, but Arthur had been just as cruel to her, and unlike him, she was only trying to be helpful.

CHAPTER SIXTEEN

GRACE

'Are you certain you don't want me to come with you?'

Grace rolled her eyes at her sister and glanced at her over her shoulder. 'For the last time, why can't you just tell me I look great and leave it at that.'

April sighed. 'You do look great. Fantastic, even. But you don't even know this soldier, and—'

'I'll be fine. Honestly, I'm walking there with other nurses, and it'll be busy there. There's nothing to worry about; you just don't like that you're not the one in charge of what I'm doing.'

April had come to stand behind her, and Grace stayed still as she stroked a hand down her hair, watching her in the little handheld mirror she was holding.

'I do worry about you. I can't help it,' April said.

'I know, but you don't have to. Can't you see how much I'm loving being here? I'm fine.' Grace turned and kissed her sister's cheek.

'You look so much like Mom with your hair up like that. I remember sitting and watching her get ready to go out, and honestly I can see her in you so clearly right now.'

Grace opened her arms and held April, hugging her tight and trying not to cry. 'And here I was always thinking you were the one who looked like Mom.'

April finally let her go and stepped back, reaching up to wipe under her eye. 'Now look, I'm going to make you smudge your makeup.'

'So I can go?' Grace asked.

April smiled and squeezed her hand. 'Of course you can. Have fun.'

Grace grinned and waved to Eva, who was getting dressed for her night shift after sleeping most of the afternoon. Part of her wished Eva and April were coming with her, but the other part was feeling exhilarated that they weren't. She didn't want April watching over her shoulder—she wanted to laugh and flirt and have fun with Peter without worrying about anyone else. Being away from home, it suited her. She'd never felt so alive, and she couldn't get enough of the rush she felt at going exploring, the excitement every time she set foot outside of their quarters and got to see more of the world.

'You coming?' A few nurses were already waiting at the edge of camp for her, and she ran to catch up with them.

'Sure am!'

They all walked together, and Grace soaked it all up, listening to the other nurses talk about the soldiers they were excited about seeing and giggling about kisses and someone getting pregnant. She was so swept up in listening that the walk passed quickly, and soon they were outside a noisy venue, where she could see plenty of soldiers and airmen inside.

'I'm keeping my eye out for Australian soldiers,' one nurse whispered to her, squeezing her arm on the way past. 'You've never seen such gorgeous men in all your life!'

Grace laughed and followed her in, looking through the smoky haze for her date but not making him out in the sea of uniforms. Music blared from a record player somewhere, and women's laughter echoed against the deep baritones of the men talking. It was so . . . she smiled to herself. It was so grown up; that's what it was. She felt like she'd finally come into her own. She had a job she was good at now, she was loving the independence of being away from home, and she was out on her own, about to meet one of the most handsome soldiers she'd ever laid eyes upon.

'Grace?'

She turned, her heart racing when she found Teddy standing behind her, a drink in one hand and a cigarette hanging from his lips.

'Teddy!' she squealed, throwing her arms around him as he dropped his cigarette and did the same to her, holding her in a one-armed hug.

'It's so great to see you. How long have you been here?' she asked, stepping back and studying his face.

'Long enough,' he muttered. 'But you, look at you.' He grinned and shook his head. 'It's so good to see you.'

Suddenly Grace felt embarrassed being the center of attention. Letter writing had been one thing, but seeing him standing there, looking up at him as he watched her? It brought everything back.

'You promised to spend some of your leave with us,' she said, regretting how desperate she sounded the moment her words came out. 'I've been so worried about you.'

'I'm sorry; it's been a rough few months,' he said, running a hand through his hair.

She noticed how tired his eyes looked, his face pale and gaunt where before it had been full. 'It doesn't matter; it's just good to see you now.'

'Are you here with April?' he asked, looking around. 'Come and sit—let's get a drink.'

'I'm actually, ah, meeting—'

'Grace!' An arm snaked around her waist, and she saw Teddy's eyes narrow as he stared at the man beside her.

'Hi, Peter,' she said, taking a step sideways and gesturing toward Teddy. 'Ah, Teddy, this is Peter. Peter, this is Teddy, an old friend from home.'

'Great to meet you,' Peter said, sticking his hand out and shaking Teddy's. 'Sorry to interrupt, but I've been looking forward to seeing this young lady all week. Come on!'

Peter grabbed her hand and tugged her along with him as the band erupted into a new song.

'Sorry,' she called as she watched Teddy's face. 'I'll come back; we'll talk later.' He nodded, his eyes never leaving hers until she finally looked away.

'You look beautiful tonight,' Peter said, spinning her and then pulling her back in so she landed against his chest before he swung her back out again.

Grace shut her eyes, feeling the music and letting it wash over her. Seeing Teddy had rattled her, but nothing was going to ruin this night. Teddy was a friend. He'd already told her she was like a little sister to him; she couldn't let herself get lost in the fantasy of Teddy again.

When she looked up, Peter was smiling, his eyes bright as he twirled her again. She was on a date with a handsome soldier; Teddy wasn't hers, and he never would be, so whatever feelings she might have had for him? She smiled up at Peter as he laughed and spun her again. They had to disappear.

'Want to get a drink?' he asked when the song ended.

He proffered his elbow, and she slid her hand through, holding on to him as they made their way through the crowd. 'I thought you were never going to ask.'

She saw Teddy, still watching them, and gave him a little wave as they walked away. Peter's friends were up ahead—she recognized them from the beach and the train ride—and they all called out to her and whistled. There were other nurses nearby, too, but she happily sat sandwiched between Peter and his friend, a drink in hand as she listened to them talk and laugh. She could make her way over to Teddy later.

Grace took a little sip and fought a cough, not used to such strong alcohol. She didn't even know what it was, but she was determined to like it.

'Cheers!' Peter said, clinking his glass to hers.

'Cheers,' she said back, sipping again and feeling the warmth of the alcohol surge through her, finding it easier to swallow the second time and then the third.

Her back was turned to Teddy, and she was grateful. As happy as she'd been to see him, she didn't want to be reminded of the past. Not tonight.

———— ⌘ ————

'So how many men have you saved?' Peter asked later as he passed her another drink. 'I bet they can't believe their luck when they look up into your pretty eyes.'

Grace laughed and took a sip, feeling light headed after the first one. She hadn't realized how much the alcohol would affect her, but when she'd stood earlier, the room had spun a little.

'I've spent a lot of time in the psych ward, as well as in the main ward,' she said with a little shrug. 'I just do whatever I need to do, wherever I'm needed.'

His thigh brushed hers, and she felt a warm tingle through her body, liking the contact. Peter had been charming all night, alternating between taking her out on the dance floor and finding a seat for them to sit and talk. She glanced back toward the table where drinks were being served, where she'd last seen Teddy, but he wasn't there.

'You must miss home,' she said. 'What's it like in England?'

'London is great. Well, it was before the war anyway. Maybe you could come one day, once all this is over?'

Grace tried to hide her smile behind her drink. 'I'd like that.'

Peter leaned forward and touched her face, his fingers stroking gently down her cheek. 'I wasn't kidding about how beautiful you were earlier. I don't think I've ever seen anyone so pretty.'

'Stop!' She giggled and took another sip of drink but regretted it when Peter stood and grabbed her hand, hauling her to her feet.

'Come on—let's go outside. Get some fresh air?'

Grace nodded. 'Sure.' She left her drink, legs wobbly as she followed him, clasping his elbow and leaning in against him. He smelled of aftershave, which filled her nostrils as they walked, and she loved the feel of his big strong arm beneath her fingers. She'd wanted to feel grown up, to be in charge for once, and she'd never been so pleased she'd ignored her sister's advice.

'You like being in this shithole of a place?' Peter asked, slurring as he kept hold of her, tucking her tight against his body now.

Grace tried to pull back a little, stumbling as she tried to keep up with him. It was suffocating being so close against him, even if she did like the feeling that he was protecting her.

'It's not so bad. I like it here.'

'You do?' He laughed. 'They joke that this place is like being sent to the asshole of the world. You're not supposed to like it.'

She bristled, wondering how he could make such snide remarks. Where had the charming man she'd been with earlier disappeared to? 'Maybe it's different for us, because we're not fighting. It's hot and sticky—I'll give you that—but it's a whole new world to explore here, and the people are lovel—'

Peter didn't give her a chance to finish. He stopped walking, his breathing heavy, the stale smell of too much alcohol and lingering cigarettes on his breath as his mouth collided with hers. She'd been mid-word, trying to talk to him, and suddenly his lips were hard against hers, his fingers digging into her waist as he held her.

'Stop!' she managed, fighting to move back from him. 'Peter! You're hurting me.'

He looked down at her, and she anxiously smiled up, wondering why he'd gotten so carried away. She knew she'd drunk too much, and maybe he'd done the same, but he'd acted like he was used to drinking alcohol.

'You're so pretty,' he muttered, grinning at her as he reached to pull her closer again. 'It's nice to have something pretty to look at for once.'

The tiny hairs on Grace's arms were suddenly alert as goose bumps spread like wildfire across her skin. The man who had seemed so exciting, so handsome, was suddenly making her feel afraid. Only minutes earlier she'd felt so grown up and in charge of her destiny, and now the only thing she felt was helpless. She glanced around, realizing how alone they were.

His eyes had been kind earlier, his gaze happy and dancing. But now she feared there was only one thing he wanted from her, and it wasn't something she wanted to give.

'I don't feel so well,' she lied, doing her best to give him a small smile. 'Maybe we could go back inside?'

Grace glanced over her shoulder. The music was blaring from inside—so even if she tried to scream, no one would hear her.

'Let's stay here a bit longer,' he said, his fingers digging into her skin again as he forced her closer, making her hips touch his.

Bile rose in her throat as he tried to press his lips to hers again.

'No,' she whispered. 'Please, no. Let me go back inside.' She hated the whimper in her tone and the shake in her legs, but Peter was a big, tall, strong man, and she knew there was no use in fighting him.

He laughed. 'Come on—let's have some fun. You were happy being with me before. I just want a little kiss, and I bought you those drinks, didn't I?'

Grace turned her face. 'You weren't like this before. I want you to stop!'

He grabbed a handful of her hair and forced her face to turn back, his smile cruel. 'I'll stop when I'm ready. You have no idea what it's like being here, what I've been through. I just need some lovin'.'

He forced his mouth on hers again as tears started to fall, as she gasped and fought against him, her hands pounding at his chest to get him to stop.

'I do!' she sobbed. 'I save men every day! I know what you go through—I do, I do!'

'Shhh,' he muttered, his eyes dark now as he ripped at her jacket, sending the buttons flying as she struggled against him.

This is not happening to me. This is not happening! Grace cried out as he tried to stick his hand down her shirt and touch her breasts, slapping at his hands and kicking out, fighting with everything she had.

'Stop!' she screamed. 'Stop it!'

Peter's hold on her was painful, and he turned her around, one arm choking her as he pinned her against him, his hot, sticky breath against her cheek as he ripped at her skirt, tearing it as he yanked it up.

'Please. *No*,' she sobbed as the distinctive jingle of his belt being undone echoed, as he fumbled with his trousers, telling her exactly what was about to happen.

'Help!' she sobbed as his grip on her tightened, as his arm choked the sound from her and he pressed into her from behind.

His arm loosened enough for her to breathe, but only for the split second it took him to grab her hair, his fistful almost pulling it from the roots as he bent her over.

'Get your hands off her!'

The yell came at the same moment as her hair was released and she tumbled forward, her face smashing into the dust as she hit the ground. Her hands almost broke her fall, one palm colliding with a rock.

A grunt behind her sent her scrambling, tripping over her own feet as she tried to escape, half crawling, half walking from her attacker.

But she needn't have worried. As she attempted to cover herself with her torn clothes, Peter lay on the ground while a familiar figure punched him over and over again, his fists slamming into Peter's face.

She cried when she realized there was nothing she could do to preserve her modesty, her skirt pulled back into place but with a big rip, her stockings torn, and her shirt gaping open along with her jacket.

Grace was numb as she stood, her eyes glued to the scene in front of her, feeling as if she were floating above it all watching from somewhere else. She should have cried at Teddy to stop, or maybe she should have run, but she didn't. She couldn't.

And then it was over.

'Grace?' Teddy called, stumbling toward her, away from Peter's unmoving body.

There was a cut above his eye, and his hands, open and hanging at his sides, were dripping with blood that she wasn't even sure was his own. Grace sobbed and wrapped her arms tight around herself, not wanting Teddy to see her like this. She shut her eyes, not even wanting to look at him.

'Grace?' he whispered, and when she was brave enough to open her eyes, she found him standing in front of her.

Only his eyes were nothing like Peter's. Teddy's were soft and warm; Teddy's were filled with worry as he lifted his arms and slowly enveloped her, drawing her against him.

She collapsed into Teddy, his arms the only thing stopping her from slipping to the ground, clinging to him as guttural noises escaped her lips. Teddy didn't say anything, didn't move; he just held her as she cried her eyes out, terrified of what could have happened.

A few seconds later and she would have been raped. Her virginity stolen from her without a second thought by her attacker. A few minutes later? Would he have found her covered in blood in the dirt? Would Peter have kept on attacking her or left her for dead? Discarded her like rubbish and not bothered to look back? Or would he have helped her up and pretended like nothing had happened?

She shuddered deeper into Teddy.

'I'm going to take you back,' he whispered, his lips against her hair as she refused to let go. 'We need to get out of here.'

She peeked past Teddy, her cheek to his shoulder, and saw Peter twitching, his arms moving as he moaned. More tears slid down her cheeks.

'I . . . I . . . ,' she stammered. 'I can't.'

She wanted to run, but her legs were like lead, so heavy she couldn't seem to move, her knees knocking.

'Here,' he said, unbuttoning his jacket. He quickly took it off and wrapped it around her. She clung to the front of it and tried to button it, but her fingers fumbled, and he took over, gently moving her hands away and doing up each button for her.

She wanted to say thank you, but the words never came.

'Come here,' Teddy muttered, pulling her closer and bending slightly. 'I'm going to pick you up, okay? Don't be scared.'

She nodded and let him scoop her up as if she were a child. This would be the second time he'd carried her to safety, the second time he'd put her before everything else to save her.

'I'm not going to hurt you,' he said. 'I promise I won't hurt you.'

She wanted to tell him that she knew that—that the only man she was scared of was lying on the ground behind him—but she didn't. Instead she tucked her face into his chest and cried as he strode away from what had started out as the best night of her life and ended as one of her worst.

— ⚜ —

'Grace,' Teddy whispered.

She blinked, her eyes sticky from all the tears, realizing she'd been asleep.

'Grace,' he whispered again. 'I need you to tell me which one is your tent.'

She cleared her throat, the words like glue as she peered around her, clinging to Teddy's shirt. She was disorientated as she looked around in the dark, the moon the only light. Grace saw the toilet block then and lifted one hand to point.

'There,' she croaked. 'Last tent, down the end.'

Teddy started walking again, and she shut her eyes, feeling every movement of his body. Her eyes flew open then as she saw Peter's face, as she felt the painful grip of his fingers into her skin, his hot breath as he tried to push inside of her.

'Stop,' she whispered.

Teddy kept walking, his arms tightening around her. Had she been muttering in her sleep? Did he know that she didn't mean for him to stop walking?

After another few minutes, the heavy thump of his boots on the dry, packed earth stopped, and she inhaled, her nose congested from all the crying. Teddy gently set her down, his hand lingering on her arm as if he wasn't sure she'd be able to stand on her own.

'I don't know what to say,' she said, eyes downcast, not wanting to look at him now that the enormity of what had happened, what he'd seen, hit her. She was drowning in the embarrassment, mortified at what had happened.

'Look at me,' he said, taking a step closer. He hooked his thumb beneath her chin to force her to raise her eyes.

Grace stared into his warm brown eyes. She saw pain shining there, but she also saw compassion.

'You don't have to say anything, Grace. We don't ever have to speak of this again.'

She nodded, and his hand fell away. But when she didn't move, he stepped past her.

'Knock, knock,' he called out, waiting before opening the tent and holding the canvas back for her.

'April's working tonight,' she managed. 'The others are working, too, or still out for the night.'

Teddy poked his head in, appearing to look around, and when he saw that the beds were all empty, he took her hand and walked in with her.

'Which one is yours?' he asked.

Grace pointed and shuffled forward, taking off his big, heavy, warm jacket and passing it to him. She held one hand over her chest to pull the fabric of her own uniform together.

'Thank you.' Her voice was still so husky she could barely get the words out. Her throat felt like sandpaper, as rough as if she'd swallowed a handful of sand.

'Can I, ah, get anything for you?'

Grace shook her head. 'No.'

They stood awkwardly, and she wondered what she'd do with her uniform. Could she even sew it properly, or was she going to need a new one? What would she tell anyone who asked what had happened? Her lower lip started to tremble again.

'I'm going to go now,' Teddy said. 'Or I can wait if you'd rather—'

Teddy seemed to sense her fear and reached for her. He lowered her until she was sitting on the bed before sitting down beside her and opening his arm up. She hesitated, drawn to him like a moth to light, but knowing she shouldn't go to him so willingly. In the end, he made the decision for her, his fingers closing around her shoulder as he gently pulled her into him.

'I'm sorry I never wrote to you again,' he whispered.

Grace tucked even closer to him, feeling the safest she'd ever felt in all her life against his firm chest.

'I started writing, but I never knew what to say,' he said. 'And instead of coming to find you, I convinced myself that you were better off not seeing a broken, exhausted reminder of your past.'

She pushed back and looked up at him, his face only half-visible in the almost darkness.

'Why would you think that?'

He let out a deep sigh. 'I don't think you want to hear me talk about war and the man I've become.'

Grace reluctantly moved away from Teddy and folded her legs underneath herself, facing him now. 'Try me. You don't have to protect me from what you've been through, Teddy. I want to hear.'

The words hung between them, but he was too kind to remind her that he'd already had to protect her tonight. A moan seemed to gurgle through his throat as he wrestled with the words.

'I don't even know where to start.'

Grace reached for his hand, holding his palm in hers. 'I see men every day who've lost everything. They come in filthy and hungry, broken in their bodies and sometimes their minds too,' she confessed. 'I'm already seeing the reality of war, Teddy, so you don't have to shield me. It's already all around me.'

He bowed his head, but she never let go of his hand. 'They never tell you what it's like to take a life,' he quietly said. 'What it's like to shoot at targets that are actual human beings or buildings and places with people inside.'

Tears slipped down her cheeks as she heard the pain in his words.

'I keep thinking about those pilots who surprised us at Pearl Harbor, how they were so close they could see their targets, and yet they had no qualms about shooting us unawares when we weren't even at war yet.'

'I think about that day a lot still,' she said. 'I think we probably always will.'

Teddy was silent before finally speaking again. 'I think about it every time I fly.'

They sat together, silent for a long time, before she eventually found the nerve to shuffle closer to him again, her head to his chest as his arms circled her. She could have stayed like that all night, listening to the gentle huff of air as he breathed, his steady heartbeat managing to calm her as if nothing terrible had even happened to her.

'Argghh!'

The sharp scream echoed through the tent, and Grace balked at the noise. Teddy leaped up, ducking as something was swung at his head.

'Eva!' Grace gasped. 'Stop! It's Teddy.'

'Teddy?' Eva exclaimed. 'What are you doing in here?'

Tears started to fall in big plops then, streaming down her cheeks as Grace stood and stared at Teddy standing motionless before her and Eva, who was holding the bag she'd used as a weapon. Everything that had happened that night came flooding back to her, making her want to flee back to Teddy's side and stay there until the war, until everything, was over.

'Go before you're caught, Teddy,' Eva said. She dropped her bag and rushed forward, enveloping Grace in one big hug as soon as she saw her standing there. 'Whatever has gone on here . . .'

Eva's voice trailed off as she seemed to take in the scene, as she looked, horrified, between Grace's torn clothes and tear-streaked face and Teddy standing with his jacket in hand.

'He saved me,' Grace whispered. 'Teddy brought me home, he saved me, he—'

'Shhh,' Eva whispered, holding her close. 'Thank you, Teddy. You can go.'

'Don't tell anyone. Promise me you won't tell April,' Grace sobbed. 'I don't want her knowing—you have to promise me, both of you!'

She looked at Eva first, who grudgingly nodded, and then at Teddy. He crossed the space inside the tent and spoke into her ear.

'He won't ever touch you again, Grace,' Teddy murmured. 'You don't want to tell anyone, that's your business, not mine.' His lips brushed her cheek, and she fought the urge to grab hold of him and never let go. 'Don't let one creep ruin your time here, Grace. You have every right to go out and have fun on your nights off—you did nothing wrong.' He paused. 'And thank you for listening. You're stronger than you realize.'

Teddy held her gaze, watching her as if he didn't want to leave her until Eva cleared her throat, and suddenly he turned and slipped out, disappearing into the night.

Eva didn't say a word as she found her nightgown and placed it on her bed, helping Grace to remove her coat and shirt, until she was standing in her undergarments, shivering despite the warm air.

But Eva's hand stopped when she saw her bare skin, and Grace stood, letting her friend look at her.

'How bad are the bruises?' she asked, not wanting to look at her marked skin.

Eva didn't say anything as she reached for the nightgown and helped her into it, as she might have assisted a small child.

'Who did this to you, Grace? We should be reporting him. Are you sure it wasn't Teddy, because you can tell me.'

'No! Teddy would never hurt me.' She shook her head. 'But I don't want anyone to know; I don't ever want to talk about it again.'

Eva stood, and Grace watched as she poured some water into a bowl and collected a piece of fabric.

'Let me check you over, wipe your skin,' she said softly. 'Do you need me to check down there?' she whispered. 'Did he . . .'

Grace's lower lip wobbled as she shook her head and whispered, 'No.'

'You know you can tell me, if he did hurt you down there. I can nurse you, and we don't need to talk to anyone about it.'

She shook her head again. 'Teddy got me just as he was . . . when he was about to, he was . . .' She stumbled on her words as it all came back to her: the smell, the fear, the pain.

'Shhh, you're okay. No one's going to hurt you now.'

She let Eva coax her down onto the bed, her hands gentle as she traced over her skin and wiped her forehead.

'As soon as you're asleep, I'm going to mend your clothes,' Eva said. 'The others won't be back for a few more hours, and I'll have everything all as good as new by then.'

Grace listened with her eyes shut, clasping Eva's left hand as she wiped her face with her right.

'Thank you,' she whispered.

Eva kissed her cheek and tucked the blankets up over her. 'You've nothing to thank me for. But I do think you should tell your sister.'

Grace gulped. 'No. She'd be so disappointed in me; she told me not to go, she told me I wasn't safe, and I rolled my eyes at her and told her to stop telling me what to do.'

Eva shifted beside her and made another lamp flicker to life as she collected up all her clothes.

'I can't stop thinking if Teddy hadn't found me, if Teddy hadn't been there—'

'But he was,' Eva interrupted. 'Did I ever tell you that it was Teddy who told me about my Charlie? That it was Teddy who held me in his arms after I yelled and punched at him for telling me the news?'

Grace snuggled deeper into her bed. 'You never told me that.'

'Well, he did,' Eva said, threading her needle. 'He's a good man, Grace. The world could do with more like him.'

Grace squeezed her eyes shut. Teddy *was* a good man, and she would never forget what he'd done for her.

And Eva. She was the kind of friend who'd never let her down, no matter what.

April was a good sister, too, the kind of sister who'd risk her own life to save hers. But that's why she couldn't ever let her find out, because she'd never forgive herself for letting it happen. And nothing about this was April's fault.

It was all on her. She'd been the stupid one. And she'd almost paid the ultimate price.

'Tell me about Arthur,' she whispered, wanting to listen to Eva speak rather than be left alone with her thoughts.

Eva laughed, just a gentle noise as she leaned in toward her. 'Arthur is awful,' she said. 'But if I don't laugh about the man, I'll only start to cry.'

CHAPTER SEVENTEEN

APRIL

'Grace?' April asked, touching her sister's shoulder and shaking her gently to wake her. 'Grace, are you feeling all right?'

April watched as her sister's eyes finally opened, but unlike their usual sharp, vivid blue rimmed with white, they were shot with red.

'What on earth did you do last night? You look terrible!'

Grace didn't move, and April sighed. 'Come on—you have a shift to get to. If you don't get up, you'll miss out on breakfast.'

'Take it easy on her; she had a late night,' Eva called out from the other side of the tent.

The other nurses they shared with had already gone down for breakfast, and April wanted to get moving so they didn't end up at the end of the line.

'Since when do you think it's okay to sleep half the morning away?' April asked. 'I thought you'd be the first to tell sleepyhead here off for being tardy just because she had a night out.'

She looked between them, wondering what on earth was going on.

'Is there something I don't know about?' April asked, perplexed.

'I saw Teddy last night,' Grace muttered. 'We talked for hours, and it got so late that he had to walk me home in the dark.'

April's eyebrows shot up. 'Teddy? How was he?'

She watched as Grace pushed the blankets back, not used to seeing her sister move so slowly. Grace was usually first up, as bright and bubbly as could be when the rest of them were aching to be back in bed again.

'He was good. He has a few days' leave, I think, and we just talked.'

'Did he ply you with alcohol, or was that your own doing?' April asked, picking up Grace's jacket and sniffing it. 'Ugh, this stinks.'

Grace snatched it off her. 'I'll air it out for a minute while I wash up and get dressed.'

Her little sister filled her helmet with water from a large jug April had prepared that morning, splashing her face and under her arms. April watched for a moment before turning away and going outside, lifting her face to the sun and feeling the now-familiar warmth spread across her skin. The mornings were always pleasant, before the depth of the heat swept through every room in the hospital and left them all sweaty and desperately craving cooler weather.

'I'm ready,' Grace mumbled from behind. Eva was standing with her, and April studied them both, certain there was something more going on than just her sister seeing Teddy.

'Nothing happened between you and Teddy, did it?' she asked.

'I would never do that to Poppy,' Grace answered quietly. 'You know that.'

April nodded. 'Of course. You just seem a bit under the weather today, and it got me wondering if you were regretting something—that's all.'

'Only the number of drinks I had and the lack of sleep I got,' Grace said, seeming more like her usual self. 'Next time I have an afternoon and night off, I'm going to spend it sleeping.'

'Good idea. I think when we finally get home, we could all sleep for a week without waking.'

They all walked down to the breakfast line, and April braced herself for whatever goop they'd be eating. She was craving home cooking almost more than sleep right now.

'How's everything going with Arthur?' she asked Eva.

'Ugh, that man is infuriating. I'm in charge of his physical therapy at the moment, and I can't even convince him to get out of the bed, let alone actually do any of the exercises. I've gone from being so compassionate to just wanting to shake him.'

April smiled over at Eva. Arthur might be driving her friend crazy, but something about him had almost brought her old friend back; she wasn't as withdrawn or quiet as she'd been when they'd arrived. She'd been so worried about Arthur reminding Eva of Charlie, but it didn't seem to be the case anymore.

After they'd finally eaten and slugged down a cup of lukewarm liquid that was supposed to resemble coffee, April made her way through the wards, checking on her patients as she passed on her way to find Dr. Grey.

'Good morning!' she said as she bustled into the surgical ward where he was working.

'Morning, April,' he said, without looking up. 'It's been a busy morning. We've already had one surgery this morning, and I'm going to be going all day from the look of it.'

She nodded. 'What can I do?'

When he finally looked up, she couldn't stop the warmth that spread up her body and flushed hot into her cheeks. His gaze was long and steady, his hazel-brown eyes appraising as he studied her.

'I'd like you by my side today,' he said. 'Prepare the patient while I get ready.'

He passed her, almost too close, their shoulders an inch from brushing.

'Your hair suits you like that, April,' he murmured, and she instinctively raised her hand and brushed her hair, pleased she'd played around with the style while she'd waited for Grace to wake up. Her pulse was racing as she realized just how hard she'd started to fall for the doctor and how capable she now felt after all the responsibility he'd given her.

April bent over the patient and reassured him, taking his blood pressure and temperature and getting him ready for the anesthetist to put him under. The poor soldier had a tourniquet around his leg above the knee, and he was bleeding heavily from his arm and leg too.

While she waited for Dr. Grey to return, April murmured to him and bathed his face, cleaning him up and smiling down at him, hoping that at the very least she might be distracting him a little from his pain.

Within minutes he was out cold on the table, and she stood beside Dr. Grey and watched him work, cringing as he took the leg off with a saw—the most gruesome thing of all to be witness to—and although she tried hard, she had to look away. The smell of flesh and bone being hacked at and the noise of the bone splintering away sent ripples through her, and she knew she'd never become used to the sound of a limb being discarded and thrown into a container to be disposed of.

If she'd been braver, she'd have asked the doctor how he'd decided to remove this particular limb, what had made him choose that option over any other alternatives, but she was always too shy to bring it up again. *I don't want to offend him by questioning his medical skills.* She smiled as she passed him an instrument. She knew that was the reason, and the last thing she wanted was to be asked to leave his service when there was so much for her to learn in the operating theater. *Just do it. Don't just stand by.* Eva's questioning of his practices and the way she'd so gallantly defended him were playing on her mind too. She knew he was an excellent doctor, but she wanted to understand him and the choices he made instead of just blithely accepting them. He certainly seemed to remove a lot of limbs.

'Dr. Grey, may I ask a question?'

He barely paused, reaching out his hand as she passed him the scalpel. 'Of course.'

'I'm very interested in medicine, and I wondered if you could explain how you make your decisions? Are you working instinctively in here, or are you following specific guidelines about when or when not to amputate, for instance?'

'And you're back to questioning me again.' He laughed and glanced at her. 'You're very inquisitive for a woman, aren't you?'

She swallowed, not sure whether he was praising or criticizing her. He didn't answer her question, but he seemed relaxed about what he was doing, so she decided to confide in him. They got along well working side by side, and she was tired of hiding her ambition. Why wouldn't he be supportive of her desire to work in the medical profession one day?

'The reason I'm so inquisitive,' she said in a quiet voice, 'is because I would like to study to become a doctor once the war is over.'

He was silent, finishing the stitch he'd moved on to, before straightening his back and holding the needle in the air. He was smiling, but it wasn't directed at her.

'Did you hear that?' he called out to no one in particular, but she realized his words were meant for the anesthetist who was tending to another patient nearby. 'My nurse here wants to be a doctor one day. *A doctor!*'

She gulped, hand shaking as she took the needle from Dr. Grey. But when she saw that he thought it was a joke, both men laughing at her statement, she bravely cleared her throat.

'I've always dreamed of being a doctor, and working here with you has only made me want it more,' she said. 'You've been an inspiration to me, Dr. Grey.'

Another nurse joined them, a patient with her that she'd prepared for surgery, and April's cheeks burned as she realized it wasn't just Dr. Grey who'd know her ambitions now. Soon everyone would know.

'April, I'd caution you against dreaming,' he said, and she couldn't help but notice the cool edge to his tone. 'You need to remember your place as a nurse.'

She nodded. 'Yes, of course. I was only—'

'And as a woman,' he added, before smiling and gesturing to the other nurse.

'I'm sorry; I should have kept my thoughts to myself,' she muttered, feeling a fool.

'You're an excellent nurse; I just don't want you getting carried away.' Dr. Grey was smiling again as if they'd been talking of something as trivial as the weather or what she might wear out to dinner. 'But I'll forget you ever mentioned it. Thank you, April—please get the patient to recovery, and then come back to assist me again. I have two more to operate on with extensive internal injuries, so it's going to be a long afternoon.'

'Yes, of course, Dr. Grey.'

She assisted the corpsman to move the patient and walked slowly from the room. All these years she'd never admitted her dreams to anyone, and now she'd been made to look the fool. *Why did I tell him? Was I trying to impress him?* April shuddered. Nothing was going to stop her from becoming a doctor one day, but from now on she was keeping her mouth shut.

'You look like you've seen a ghost.'

April looked up as she almost collided with Eva. 'Sorry. I was a million miles away,' she replied.

'I know the feeling,' Eva muttered. 'You have time for a coffee? I don't know how I'm going to keep my eyes open for another four hours until the end of my shift.'

'Let me finish up here, and I'll join you. I have to go straight back into surgery with Dr. Grey, but I could do with a coffee first.'

April settled her patient into his bed, blanket tucked around him and his chart updated at the end of his bed. Then she did a quick walk-through of the ward, pleased most of her patients were asleep, before she found Eva again.

'How's your day been?' she asked.

Eva sighed. 'Same as usual. I deal with Arthur as best I can, but it's almost a relief when I'm called away.'

'He's no better?'

'No.' Eva shook her head as she poured them both a coffee.

The coffee tasted terrible. 'You know, the only thing this drink has going for it is that it's hot.'

They both sipped and sat back, and April studied Eva. She'd been so withdrawn ever since the bombing, but she was starting to see glimpses of her again, and it was nice. Now that Eva was holding her ground with Arthur, he actually seemed to be good for her.

'Is it hard for you? With Arthur being a pilot, I mean?'

Eva didn't look up right away, but when she did, April saw tears glistening in her eyes. It surprised her; she'd never, ever seen Eva cry before, and she certainly hadn't expected it then.

'Yes, it is. Sometimes I just want to shake him,' Eva said. 'He's so infuriating, and I want to scream at him, but when I feel like that, I bite my tongue and walk away until I feel I can deal with him again. I can't imagine what he's going through inside.'

April set her coffee cup down and reached for her hand. 'I should have known how hard it would be for you. I'm sorry.'

Eva gave her fingers a quick squeeze before withdrawing her hand. 'Tell me about you. Are you still enjoying working with Dr. Grey? Grace is convinced you're having some secret love affair.'

April laughed. 'Oh, I wish we were having some clandestine affair! The most exciting exchange we've had is side by side, scalpel in hand, unfortunately.'

'I've seen the way he looks at you,' Eva said. 'All jokes aside, I think your sister's right about him being interested.'

It was on the tip of April's tongue to tell her about her dream of becoming a doctor, but she didn't, not wanting to recount what had happened when she'd told the doctor. She also wasn't ready to be rebuffed twice in one day, even though she was almost certain Eva would encourage her.

'I promise I'll keep you posted if anything happens between us,' she said with a wink.

They sat a minute longer, drinking their coffees, before April reluctantly stood. She took Eva's cup to rinse them both out.

'Do you think everything was all right with Grace this morning? She seemed—I don't know—not herself, I guess.'

She was certain she saw Eva hesitate. 'I think seeing Teddy rattled her; that's all. And she probably had too much to drink.'

'Hmm, maybe.' April stretched out her neck and sighed. 'She always was sweet on Teddy, but after Poppy, after everything we all went through, I don't know. I suppose I thought those feelings would have disappeared.'

'Would it be so bad if she and Teddy got together after the war?' Eva asked. 'After all we've all been through, it wouldn't be the worst thing in the world to see them together, if it made them both happy.'

April's brows shot up. 'Has she said something to you?'

'No. But you'd have to be blind not to see that there's something between them, something they're both trying far too hard to pretend doesn't exist.'

April watched Eva go and thought about what she'd said. Perhaps she was right; maybe it wouldn't be the worst thing. She just couldn't stand to see her sister get hurt, and as great as Teddy was, she had a feeling it would be her sister who'd end up with the broken heart. April picked up her pace and hurried back to Dr. Grey, not wanting to give him any excuses to be angry with her. Again.

———— ⌘ ————

'Morning, April.'

April smiled as Dr. Grey approached, falling into step beside her. She hadn't seen him since their day of back-to-back surgeries two days ago; she'd been resting in the tent most of yesterday, but she was still on a high from their work together.

'Good morning,' she replied.

'I'm liking this cooler weather. The heat these past couple of months has been stifling.'

'Not to mention the ants. They've been eating me alive.'

Dr. Grey held her gaze then, and she laughed. Right now he looked like he could eat *her* alive. Maybe the girls were right—maybe he did like her—but after he'd made it clear that he didn't approve of her doctor aspirations, she'd wondered if he'd even want to work with her again. They stopped at the door, and she waited, unsure of what to do. He reached out and touched a tendril of hair that was caressing her face, tucking it back behind her ear with the softest of touches.

'You brighten up my day in there,' he murmured.

She leaned into his touch just a little, her cheek against his fingers, and he moved closer, his lips finally brushing against her cheek where the hair had been.

'I'll see you in there.'

Dr. Grey opened the door for her, and she quickly walked through, hoping no one had seen. As she glanced back one last time at him, he winked, and she could have fallen to the ground.

'Nurse, do you have a moment?'

She pushed away thoughts of the barely there kiss and followed the young doctor who'd called out to her. He'd only just joined them, and she hadn't met him properly yet.

'I'm told this patient is under your care,' he said, and April rushed to his side when she recognized the young soldier. He'd needed extensive surgery, but he'd been fine during his recovery so far.

'Yes, his name's Patrick Hunt. He had a long surgery two days ago, but he pulled through with flying colors.'

The doctor frowned and moved around to the other side of the bed, looking up at her as he listened through his stethoscope. 'There's something wrong. He's been in chronic pain this morning, and he's developed a fever. I can't pinpoint what's going on with him.'

April reached for the patient's hand and shut her eyes, thinking back, trying to recall the exact moments throughout the surgery. It had been the one where she'd assisted on stitching, side by side with Dr. Grey, the same day she'd confessed her doctor aspirations. The day she'd been so exhilarated by only moments earlier. She remembered this particular patient, because it was after her coffee with Eva, and she'd assisted him with two more surgeries, both general surgeries to repair internal bleeding and organ damage. With this patient and the following one, he'd asked her to help with stitching once he was ready to close, because his hands had been cramping and he hadn't wanted to be compromised for the next surgery.

'Can you recall anything? If he doesn't get any better, we'll have to open him up again.'

'We did multiple surgeries the day before yesterday together, Dr. Grey and I. You should probably ask him—he's just arrived—but it all seemed to go according to plan from what I could tell. This was one of the ones we did later in the day, before my shift ended.'

'Dr. Evans,' he said, moving back around to her side of the patient's bed. 'I should have introduced myself before.'

'April Bellamy,' she said, surprised when he took the time to shake her hand. Most of the doctors couldn't care less what their nurses' names were or about making introductions.

'Come and find me personally if his condition changes.'

She was about to speak when an urgent call rang through the ward, and just like every other time, the hairs on April's arm stood on end as corpsmen came running with stretchers.

'Incoming!' someone yelled, and the deep male voice jolted April into action. She dropped her coat onto her patient's bed and ran beside Evans.

'I need morphine, now!' he yelled. 'Get these men out of pain, and start assessing their wounds!'

She snatched the morphine vials as he assessed the first patient, and other doctors and nurses flocked around the others.

'Start with morphine, and ask any lucid patients whether they've had tetanus shots,' he said as he fought to stop the first soldier's arm from losing so much blood. She watched as it pooled on the floor before he stemmed it with a tourniquet. 'And let's save lives today, April. We've already lost enough men and enough limbs to this goddamn war. It's time we started figuring out how to save every body part and their lives along with them.'

April stole a quick glance at this new doctor, at the determination etched on his face as he ran beside the stretcher on its way to surgery. And just like that, a flicker of doubt punched through her. Had too many men lost limbs under Dr. Grey's care? Had Grace been right to question that the other day? She shrugged the thought away and focused on the next patient. A few minutes earlier, she'd been filled with excitement about her almost kiss with Dr. Grey, but now all those doubts were creeping back from the day before, and she had no idea what she was supposed to make of it all.

Six hours later, April was exhausted. The time had passed by in a blur, and they'd saved more lives than they'd lost, but it still hurt knowing how many hadn't made it. She looked around the ward and slowly made her way toward Patrick's bed, hurrying the last few steps when she saw that he was far worse than he'd been that morning. His pallor was gray, and he had an obvious fever.

Grace came past then, quietly standing beside her.

'He looks dreadful,' Grace said.

'I know. Something's gone wrong, but I just don't know what,' she said with a sigh, dipping a cloth in cool water to cleanse his forehead. 'Would you mind finding Dr. Evans for me?'

'The new doctor?' Grace asked. 'I met him a couple of days ago. He's full of as much energy and enthusiasm as all the other doctors combined. Is he the one the locals said had helped them?'

April nodded. 'I wondered why his name sounded so familiar; you're right.'

Grace hurried off, and Dr. Evans was by her side within a few minutes, but from the look on his face, she knew it wasn't good.

'We need to open him up, figure out what's wrong. April, can you assist?'

'Of course. Should I find Dr. Grey?'

'Nurse!' he said, beckoning to Grace. 'Find Dr. Grey; tell him we're opening up a patient of his and that I need to consult with him.'

Grace ran off again, and with the help of a corpsman they moved the patient and hurried him into surgery. Within half an hour, Dr. Evans was slicing through his skin, cutting past the stitches in the man's abdomen she'd helped with only two days prior.

'This is unusual,' he said as he reached his hand out and April placed an instrument in his palm. 'I can't see any bleeding or ruptures'—he paused and bent lower—'no cause for infection—'

She leaned closer as he went silent; then she gasped as he reached into the patient and pulled out a wad of fabric bandage and a metal clamp. He raised it and looked at her before depositing it into a metal bowl.

'We're losing him!' April cried as blood poured out of him and his pulse vanished; she met the doctor's horrified gaze.

He frantically started closing, and she held the soldier's hand, shaking as she prayed that he'd make it.

'What the hell is going on in here?'

Dr. Evans didn't look up, but Dr. Grey marched in, a cloth lifted to cover his mouth as he fixed his stare on her.

'We tried to alert you immediately, but there was no time. He had an infection and . . .' She shook her head, and Dr. Evans threw his instruments down with a sudden bang, ripping his mask off and looking like he was about to punch Grey.

'You're the doctor who did this?' he said, seething.

Grey folded his arms across his chest, brows raised. 'Did what? Saved that man's life before you managed to kill him on the table?'

Dr. Evans pointed to the bowl on the table beside the patient as April watched, silent tears sliding down her cheeks as she let her hand rest on the patient, knowing he was gone but hating that his last moments were filled with such rage.

'There's only one doctor who killed that patient, and it's you,' Evans shouted. 'I found a goddamn *instrument* inside of him!'

Dr. Grey moved silently toward the dish before speaking again, his eyes flickering to hers, holding her gaze as if to silence her. 'You want someone to blame, how about Little Miss Doctor over there?' he said, gesturing at her as if she were nobody important. 'This was all her.'

April's jaw dropped.

'You're going to blame the nurse?' Evans spluttered.

'Hasn't she told you that she wants to be a doctor? I humored her little confession and let her take a look at my handiwork,' Grey said with a nonchalant shrug. 'Silly girl must have dropped it in there. She shouldn't be allowed near a patient again.'

'No!' April gasped. 'You're lying! You know I didn't have anything to do with this!'

Grey shook his head and gave her what she imagined was supposed to be a sympathetic look. 'Dr. Evans,' he said quietly, 'I haven't wanted to embarrass April, but I've noticed she has quite the crush on me, and well, I should have mentioned it earlier, but I'm wondering if this might have affected her work?'

What? She gasped, staring between the two men.

'I mean, I'm a married man, and it's highly inappropriate, but I was hoping it was harmless.'

'*Married?*' she whispered. 'But it was you, it was you who led me on, you kissed me, you . . .'

'Please don't embarrass yourself any more than you already have,' he said, frowning at Dr. Evans past her head.

April was shaking, staring at Dr. Evans, desperate to explain it all to him, hating the lies he'd heard. He might not believe her, but she needed to try.

'It's not true,' she pleaded. 'None of this is true, and I'm sure I didn't do anything wrong! You have to believe me, Dr. Evans.'

'April, that's enough. Please,' Grey said, shaking his head. 'Don't you remember that I went to the bathroom and left you to watch the patient? What on earth did you do while I was gone, try to play doctor?'

'I didn't,' she sobbed. 'Dr. Grey, you know that's not true!' She racked her brain. He *had* stepped out to relieve himself—she remembered that—but wasn't it after the surgery was completed? She tried to recall it, wishing her memory weren't so fuzzy.

Evans moved in front of the door, and she clenched her fists, waiting for the worst to happen. Was he going to side with Grey too? But instead he seemed to block the door.

'Get out of my way,' Dr. Grey demanded.

'You try to pin this on her, and you'll have me to answer to,' Dr. Evans said. 'We're all fatigued and doing the best we damn well can, but we don't blame our nurses for our mistakes. We're surgeons, and this is on you. No matter what the personal circumstances, no nurse can be blamed for a surgical error, and she certainly never should have been left alone with a patient open on the table!'

'Look, the nurse did it. You know and I know it,' Grey said. 'Try pinning this on me, and I'll make sure neither of you ever work in medicine again. Do I make myself clear?' Dr. Grey stormed out, slamming his shoulder into the other doctor as he passed, and the second he was gone, April thought she was going to collapse. Suddenly there wasn't enough oxygen in the air, her breath coming in short, sharp gasps.

'Is it true?' Dr. Evans asked in a low voice. 'Any of it?'

'No! I was just assisting at his side, like I was with you today. I didn't do anything wrong, I *couldn't* do anything wrong,' she stuttered, trying to remember, reaching desperately for the memory. 'I mean, I can't have, can I?' Could it have been her fault? *Had* she done something wrong?

'I meant about you wanting to be a doctor?'

April slowly breathed deep and nodded, not about to lie. 'Yes, it's true.'

He shook his head, and she waited for him to ridicule her just as Dr. Grey had. But he didn't.

'You'd make a better doctor than him—that's for sure.'

'You don't think it's a stupid idea? That a woman might want to become a doctor?' she asked.

Dr. Evans laughed. 'What's stupid about it? The fact a woman *could* be a doctor or that you want to be one?'

April was baffled. 'Both, I suppose.'

'You want to train to be a doctor, that's your decision. I've grown up with three sisters, and I know full well what women are capable of and just how determined women can be when they set their mind to something.'

April couldn't believe how supportive he was being. 'Well, that went down better with you than with Dr. Grey.'

Evans scribbled something on the patient's notes as two corpsmen came in to move the body.

'What did he say?' he asked, without looking up. 'When you told him, I mean?'

'Something about women needing to know their place,' she muttered.

'He's going to come after you, April. I hope you're prepared for it.'

April shivered as she watched Dr. Evans leave the room and then turned and surveyed the blood on the floor and the instruments still covered in fluid and blood on the table. Someone would be taking the fall for this, and she had a feeling it would be her.

'April, you look like you've seen a ghost! What's wrong?' Grace asked as she made her way into the tent and collapsed on her bed later that night. Even with all the bedding and clothes beneath it to try to make it comfortable, it was impossible to mask the stony, hard ground beneath.

Eva and Grace were both sitting up now, both awake, their faces bathed in a combination of light and shadows from the gaslight burning between them.

'I think I'm about to lose my job,' she said, her voice devoid of emotion as she stared at the ceiling of the tent.

'What are you talking about?' Grace asked. 'What happened?'

'Dr. Grey kissed me this morning,' she confessed. 'Only on the cheek, but he also told me how pretty I looked, or that I lit up the ward or something.'

'And you're going to lose your job because he kissed you?' Eva asked.

'No,' she said, pulling up her blanket over her uniform. 'I'm going to lose my job because he's married and something happened during a surgery that he's trying to blame on me.' She wished she could remember, but all the surgeries had seemed to blur in her mind.

'He's married!' Grace choked out. 'He was so—I don't know—flirty with you all the time. How is that your fault?'

'And what can he possibly blame on a nurse?'

April filled them both in, telling them exactly what had happened and why she thought she was going to be sent home.

'It's not over until it's over,' Eva said firmly. 'If Dr. Evans sticks up for you and tells the truth, then—'

'Nurse April Bellamy!' came a brisk call. 'Please step outside your tent.'

April froze.

'Get up,' whispered Eva. 'Maybe it's good news.'

April slowly pushed the blanket back and rose, her feet heavy as she trod toward the tent opening, holding the gaslight as she emerged outside.

'Yes,' she said, surprised to see their head nurse, Matron Johnson, waiting for her, with a doctor by her side.

'Nurse Bellamy, we've had a serious complaint made about you by one of our most senior doctors,' she said. 'We're placing you on leave pending an investigation into the allegations.'

'*On leave?*' she asked. 'I'm one of your hardest-working nurses! I love what I do. What use is there having me sitting in a tent when I could be helping?'

The older woman's face didn't change. 'I'm sorry, but our decision is final.'

She stood outside the tent in the dark, watching the old matron go. She dropped to her knees then, sobbing as she fell forward into the dirt. Because just like that, all her dreams of ever being a doctor were gone. She'd never get into medical school as a failed nurse. *Never.*

CHAPTER EIGHTEEN
GRACE

'Come on—it'll do you both good to go for a swim,' Eva said. She opened the tent up to air it out before hanging her spare clothes up to dry from a piece of string as they looked on.

'I'd rather sleep,' Grace mumbled, but she finished getting dressed anyway. She'd woken from a dream about Poppy, chasing her friend on the beach and splashing in the water, and she'd rather have fallen straight back into it than gotten up. Some days she missed her so much; she'd give anything to hear Poppy laugh or just sit and talk with her. But April needed to get out and do something to take her mind off the suspension, and she wasn't going to be lazy when her sister needed her. April was always there for her, she'd looked after her for years, and hurting or not, she was going to help her.

'I might just stay,' April said. 'You both have fun, though.'

'April Bellamy! Get your shoes and your sun hat; we're going out whether you like it or not,' Eva declared.

Grace gave a little salute. 'Yes, ma'am.' She received a glare from Eva in return, and she liked it. Eva had really started to emerge from under the dark cloud she'd been trapped in, and it was nice to see the old her again.

'Come on; let's go. I don't want to waste a second of today in this god-awful tent.'

Grace put her hat on as Eva grabbed her arm. 'Someone's got cabin fever today,' she said, clasping Eva's hand.

'Someone's sick to death of nursing an invalid with no understanding of how lucky he is to be alive,' she grumbled.

Grace tucked her head to Eva's shoulder as they walked, feeling safe for some reason with her friend by her side. She'd been jumpy and tearful ever since that night, and she hadn't been able to stop thinking about Teddy. What he'd done for her, the way he'd saved her and tended to her, was the kindest thing anyone had ever done for her.

'You're usually desperate to get out and about,' April said, catching up to them. 'Why are you so reluctant, Grace?'

She shrugged, not looking at her sister. She'd never been able to lie to her and get away with it before. 'I don't know. Maybe it's not so exciting being here as I first thought.'

She felt Eva stiffen a little and knew that it was unfair making her keep her secret, but with everything April had going on right now, she didn't want to give her something else to worry about. She could see that her sister was trying to put on a brave face despite her knock in confidence, and she wasn't going to add to that.

'You never did tell us about Peter,' April suddenly said, and Grace knew that if she turned, her sister would be frowning, her entire face pulled down into a question. 'I can't believe it was weeks ago! Are you seeing him again the next time he's on leave?'

'Ah, no, I'm not,' she said, trying not to stammer. 'Turned out he, ah, wasn't such great company after all.'

'Turns out I was wrong to worry about you, I guess,' April said. 'Although I bet you took one look at Teddy and you talked his ear off all night instead of Peter's—am I right? The poor man probably never got a word in.'

Grace forced a smile, knowing her sister was watching her now. 'You know me too well.'

They walked awhile longer, past huts with roofs that looked too old and patched up to ever keep water out, and past people relieving themselves within plain sight of those around them. Grace averted her eyes, no longer as interested in their surroundings as she had been. To start with, she'd felt so alive, so energized at how different everything was and how free she felt, but right now she was craving the familiarity of home.

'What's that?' Eva asked, pointing down the road. 'What are they carrying?'

There were navy men up ahead, carrying boxes, and as they got closer, they called out.

'Ladies!' one of the men shouted. 'You hungry?'

Grace held both Eva's and April's hands, one on each side of her, and they ran toward the navy boys.

'What have you got?' April yelled.

'Fresh food! We've got fruit!'

'Navy ship just came in!' another shouted back.

Grace's lips tingled, and her mouth watered just thinking about fruit. Aside from the one orange they received once a month as part of their rations, she hadn't eaten fruit since they'd left home.

They each took apples and oranges from the boys, thanking them as they went on their way, but Grace didn't even wait to say goodbye before she went straight ahead and crunched into her apple.

'This is heaven,' she whispered. 'Pure heaven.'

They all sighed and munched, walking side by side without saying a word. Soon they were at their destination, and Grace stared out at the ocean and wished it didn't remind her so much of Hawaii. She shut her eyes as she thought about Teddy; she could almost feel his arms around her again, the steady, effortless way he'd carried her and brought her to safety, the warmth of his cheek when he'd leaned in to say goodbye.

He won't ever touch you again, Grace. You don't want to tell anyone, that's your business, not mine.

His words washed over her, echoing in her head as she remembered the way he'd looked at her that night.

Don't let one guy ruin your time here, Grace. You have every right to go out and have fun on your nights off.

But it was all very well Teddy saying that to her. Finding the courage to go out again and face the world was a different matter altogether. She touched her hip, her fingers resting gently there. The physical pain was gone, but the ugly purple bruises were a reminder of what she'd almost lost that night.

'Are you thinking about home?' April asked, coming up to stand beside her.

'Yes.' It wasn't a complete lie; she had been wishing she were home less than an hour earlier.

'Me too. Only I'm praying I don't have to go back, not yet.'

'They'll never send a nurse like you home, April. There's no way they'd be that stupid.'

'The only stupid thing here is me, for ever trusting Dr. Grey in the first place.' She made a noise in her throat that Grace guessed was the sound of disgust. 'I can't believe he led me on like that, complimenting me and kissing my cheek. It makes me feel dirty that he behaved like that when he has a wife at home.'

They all sat down, and Grace started to slowly peel her orange. 'It's him who should feel dirty about that, not you.' Just like Peter should be the one feeling awful about that night, not her. But she *did* feel awful, and she knew she'd always blame herself for ending up in a position for him to almost rape her.

'So what are we going to do about your Dr. Grey situation?' Eva asked.

April stood and started to peel her clothes off to reveal her undergarments beneath. 'I have no idea. I keep trying to remember that afternoon, that particular surgery, but there were so many, and I can't seem to get my thoughts straight.' She sighed. 'The only thing I'm certain about today is that we're getting in that water and swimming until we can't catch our breaths. Deal?'

Grace shrugged and glanced at Eva. 'Deal,' she said. 'Just as soon as I finish this orange, because it's the best thing that's happened to me all week.'

They'd swum in the Mediterranean Sea for hours, floating, faces turned skyward. Grace hadn't thought about it at the time, but they'd hardly spoken until they'd all slowly made their way back to their clothes and sat in the sun to dry off.

'It's hard to believe it'll be cold here soon,' Eva said as they dressed. 'This heat has been unbearable.'

They'd all been warned how cold it could get over winter, but until she felt it for herself, Grace couldn't believe it.

'Grace, what's that?'

She froze as April's fingers closed around her wrist, forcing her arm up. She'd forgotten about her bruises as she'd slid from the water. Fortunately her sister couldn't see the ones on her waist, but the inside of one of her arms was still a muddy brown color from the fading mark.

'It's nothing.'

'It's not nothing. How did you get a bruise like that there? Was it a patient?'

Grace glanced at Eva, but Eva wasn't making eye contact. She knew it was unfair to involve her; it wasn't Eva's fault she knew her secret.

'If it was a patient, you should have reported him. They're not allowed to hurt us.'

'It wasn't a patient,' she said, removing her sister's fingers from her skin. She finished putting her clothes on. 'I'm fine.'

'You're not fine. Someone hurt you.' April was like a dog with a bone; there was no way she was going to give up.

'April, there are some things I don't want to share with you, and this is one of them.'

Horror passed over April's face. '*Oh my God*, was it *Teddy*?' she whispered.

'No!' Grace yelped. 'No, it wasn't Teddy. He would never hurt me.'

'You've been strange ever since that night you saw him. Tell me what's going on.'

She stood there, like an animal who knew she'd been cornered.

'April,' Eva said gently. 'Sometimes there are things we need to keep to ourselves. Come on; let's go.'

'You know what's going on, don't you? Am I the only one who's being kept in the dark?'

'Stop it!' Grace said. 'You promised me I could make my own decisions and that you'd stop looking over my shoulder, and this is me making a decision, April. Just let it go.'

'I can't let it go!' April looked furious now. 'I don't care what I said; I'm your—'

'Sister,' Grace said, her voice low, hating how cruel the words sounded. 'You're my sister, April, not my mother.'

They stood, all staring at one another, and Grace watched the heavy rise and fall of April's chest.

'Tell me one thing,' April said. 'Are you wishing you'd listened to me about not going out that night—is that what this is about?'

Grace bit down on the skin inside her mouth for a moment, trying not to cry. 'Yes,' she said. 'But I don't want to talk about it.'

April nodded. 'It's okay. Just know that I'm here for you, if you need me. Promise?'

Grace sucked in a breath. 'Promise,' she whispered.

She was torn; part of her desperately wanted to open up to her sister, but if she did that, then she'd be doing exactly what she'd always done before. She'd asked to stand on her own two feet without April behaving like her mother, and she needed to do it.

They gathered up their things and slowly walked back toward the camp, skirting around the edge of the town. The sun was still hot even though it was late afternoon, and Grace had that same strange feeling she'd had the night of her attack—as if she were looking down on her body and watching from above.

She was starting to wonder about her taste in men; at Pearl Harbor, Eva had stepped in when the soldier had been frisky with her, and then Teddy had come to her rescue here. And then there was Teddy. She was lying to herself if she didn't admit to still being hopelessly in love with her best friend's boyfriend, the man who'd so fondly told her she was like a little sister to him. What must he think of her now? That she was so juvenile she hadn't even realized what trouble she was getting into, leaving a crowded place with a man she didn't even know?

'What's going on down there?' April asked, pointing. 'Everyone's watching something.'

Grace stood on tiptoe as they all stopped and stared, hands raised against the sun. 'We need to go look,' she said. 'Quickly.'

They ran down the incline toward the town, wondering what on earth was happening that would bring everyone out of their homes, lining the streets to watch. Then she saw it—two open-top cars traveling slowly down the narrow streets.

'Is that . . . ,' she started, squinting and wondering if she was imagining the scene in front of her.

'General Eisenhower and Winston Churchill,' April finished for her. 'Oh my lord, they're so close we could touch them.'

They stood and watched the procession, the men riding in the cars as if there were no danger, as if they weren't in the middle of a world war.

'That third man, who's he?' Grace asked.

'General Charles de Gaulle,' Eva whispered. 'It's unbelievable. I wonder what they're all doing here?'

They kept watching, laughing as the men smiled and gave a wave. But it was the much younger man standing on the roadside among the locals that caught her eye. He was laughing and talking with the villagers, but she could see that he was looking in their direction, and he wasn't looking at her.

She nudged April with her elbow. 'I think someone's trying to get your attention.'

April gave her a funny look.

'Straight ahead,' she said. 'A very handsome doctor.'

She saw the smile on April's face as she spotted him. Her sister raised her hand, and the warmth on the doctor's face was unmistakable. He was tall, his legs eating up the ground as he strode toward them, and much younger than the other doctors. His hair reminded her of Teddy's, pushed off his forehead and to the side, and when he smiled, she could see why her sister liked him so much.

'*Annnnd* he's coming this way,' Grace whispered.

'I wonder what he's doing here with the locals?' Eva said. 'Looks like he knows them well, the way they're all talking with him.'

'He's the one who helps them, the doctor that family talked about,' Grace told her. 'And he's the one who's sticking up for April over this whole suspension.'

They waited as the crowd dispersed and Dr. Evans made his way over, his smile as bright as the sun.

'Ladies,' he said. 'Can you believe what you just saw?'

They all laughed, but it was Grace who spoke. It was usually April who took the lead on everything they did, but for once her sister was quiet. 'I would have thought they'd be more safety conscious.'

'It seems not.' Dr. Evans shrugged. 'Maybe it's a sign; the Allies might be turning this war around after all.'

'Dr. Evans,' April suddenly said, her cheeks flushed.

'Harry,' he said with a laugh. 'Dr. Evans is my father's title; it never sounds right when I hear it. Please, call me Harry.'

Grace chewed on her bottom lip to stop from laughing. There was something amusing about seeing her usually unflusterable sister looking so thoroughly flustered.

'Harry, then,' April finally said. 'I wanted to apologize for my involvement in the death of—'

'Stop right there,' he said, his smile replaced with a frown. 'You're a nurse, April, and that means that you had nothing to do with that soldier's death. The surgeon is the only person at fault in this case.'

April looked away, and it was Eva who spoke for her.

'It's nice to hear you say that, but Dr. Grey is still practicing, and April is the one on suspension. She could be sent home any day.'

Harry's eyebrows shot up. 'Suspended? Since when? I wondered why I hadn't seen you.'

'Since last week,' April muttered. 'I've been told not to return. I thought you knew?'

'If I'd known, I'd have done something about it,' he said, his voice an octave lower. 'You leave this to me, okay? There is no way a confident, capable nurse is being sent home over this.'

April seemed surprised. 'You'd do that for me? You'd actually question my suspension?'

He grinned. 'Will you work with me in the burns unit as my nurse? The skills I teach you might come in handy when you go to medical school one day.'

Grace laughed. 'You told him? You actually told someone you want to be a doctor?'

'Hold on; *April* wants to be a doctor?' Eva spluttered.

April groaned. 'So much for my secret.'

'You'll be a great doctor one day,' Grace said, liking the fact that Harry didn't seem outwardly fazed by the idea at all.

'Thanks for the vote of confidence,' April said. 'But there's this little issue of Dr. Grey and my suspension, not to mention that the last time I worked closely with a doctor, it didn't work out so well.'

Grace's heart broke for her sister. It wasn't something she was used to, seeing anything get her down like that, but the suspension had almost broken her.

'Can I walk you ladies back?' Harry asked. 'Perhaps I can convince you that I'm trustworthy on the way?'

Grace grinned and watched as April sighed and then nodded.

'Of course,' April said.

Grace stood back and let April and Harry walk off together, taking up the rear with Eva. They both smiled, and she wondered what Eva was thinking. She'd never really talked about losing her fiancé, seeming to prefer keeping it to herself, and Grace wished she'd been a better friend. Had she been so caught up in herself, in her own grief over Poppy and then the excitement of traveling halfway around the world, that she'd somehow forgotten how to be a good friend?

'Eva, you seem more like your old self,' she said, cringing as she heard the way her words sounded. 'Sorry—that came out wrong. I just mean that after Charlie . . .' Her voice trailed off.

'I actually feel more like the old me, so it's okay—you don't have to apologize for noticing,' Eva said. 'I don't know why, because I still miss him and think about what I'll do when the war is over, but I don't feel so dark anymore.'

She slung her arm around Eva's shoulders as they walked. 'I'm so happy to hear that, and if there's anything you ever need to talk to me about, I'm here. You've been so good to me when I've needed you.'

Eva leaned into her, and Grace wondered how long it would be before her friend actually confided in her what she was so scared of, what it was about home that terrified her so much. She could almost feel Eva's words trapped inside of her, waiting to spill out, but Eva never said a thing, and Grace wasn't going to ask her again. When she was ready, she'd tell her.

'Thank you for not telling April—about that night, I mean.'

Eva's whisper was barely audible. 'We all have secrets, Grace. Sometimes we share them, and sometimes we just learn to live life without ever telling a soul.'

CHAPTER NINETEEN

Eva

'Good morning, Arthur,' Eva said, forcing a smile as she came past his bed, calling out brightly as she always did, as if he were a regular patient pleased to see his nurse. She hadn't told anyone, but today would have been Charlie's birthday, and all she wanted was to get on with her day and keep busy so she didn't have to think about it.

As usual, Arthur didn't even bother to grunt a reply, but she was used to it by now. So long as he let her do her job, she was happy to just do her best with him.

'I see you haven't eaten your breakfast again today,' she said, deciding not to ignore the untouched plate. 'I bet there's a lot of soldiers who'd love to be served that on the front line.'

That at least got a reaction; he glared at her as if he were trying to murder her with his stare alone.

'The doctors have reprimanded me for not getting you mobile yet, so today we're going to get you out of this bed and outside for some fresh air.'

He stared at the wall. Heat traveled the length of Eva's body; it didn't come naturally to her to boss him around, but she had to do it.

Instead of letting him ignore her this time, she walked around to the foot of the bed, folding her arms and giving him a tight smile.

'Ah, there you are. So nice to actually make eye contact for once,' she said. 'If you'd prefer another nurse, please let me know; otherwise you and I are—'

'I don't want *any* damn nurse,' he muttered. 'Unless there's one better equipped at listening to me when I say to get the hell away from my bed!'

She recoiled, his anger so raw she could feel it radiating from him.

'You don't want anyone to help you?' She seethed, digging her nails deep into her palms as she balled them even tighter. 'You want to sit here all on your own? You want your skin to fester as sores spread across your body from being stuck in here? Your stomach to scream out in hunger when no one brings you food? To suffer here, alone?'

Tears were silently dripping down her cheeks, some of them curling into her mouth, tasting like salt as she caught them with her tongue. All these months she'd been desperate to cry, to just feel something instead of being numb, and it had taken the worst patient in history to finally push her over the edge. She'd thought she was okay with Arthur, that he at least respected her enough to let her do his work, but he was just bullying her all over again, and she wasn't going to accept it, especially not on Charlie's birthday!

'Leave me,' Arthur said, but his voice lacked weight this time. 'Just leave me.'

'No!' she snapped, marching over to the wheelchair she'd had sitting there waiting for him, the chair that he'd refused to use. 'You're getting in here today whether you like it or not.'

He stared at her, and she stared straight back at him. All her anger and all her frustrations were pouring from her as if from a cloud finally bursting with rain.

'I saved you. I sat beside you. I cared for you,' she huffed, yanking back his sheets as she ranted. 'I refused to let you die, and I didn't do that to let you sit here and rot!'

For the first time, he didn't snap back at her. He just stared, wide eyed, as she gestured at the wheelchair. She probably looked like a madwoman, flinging her arms around and verbally assaulting him, but she didn't care. She was not going to see a capable, strong, handsome man wither away and die just because he wouldn't try.

'Get in,' she ordered, holding his arm and preparing to drag him out of his bed if she had to. 'Or I can get a corpsman to come and help.'

'I'll do it,' he said, his words low as he pushed himself up into a straight sitting position. 'I don't need your help.'

She hesitated, her anger slipping away as he lifted up, grunting with the effort and shuffling over to the side of the bed. He was using his leg, which was almost completely healed now, doing what he should have been trying to do weeks ago. She quickly reached out, grabbing his arm as he slipped.

'Let go of me!' he snapped. 'I said I'll do it.'

Eva recoiled, breathing a sigh of relief as he lowered himself, almost in the chair, almost safe.

No!

Eva lunged forward just as Arthur tipped forward, grabbing at him and tripping over the tilted chair as he crashed toward the ground. She half broke his fall, but even without one leg he was a big man, much too heavy for her to catch on her own.

They landed with a thump, her breath punching out of her lungs, winded as she lay in a tangled mess with Arthur.

'Get the hell away from me!' he yelled. 'This is all your fault!'

'My fault?' she gasped, shoving at him, her hands to his chest as she pushed him back, all sympathy she'd felt for him disappearing. 'My fault?' she repeated, louder this time.

He glared at her.

'This is all *your* fault,' she screamed. 'It's your fault that you've been stuck in that bed for months, acting like a spoiled, petulant child!' Hysteria took over, rising inside of her, and she wished she could clasp her fingers around his neck and strangle him. 'You think losing a leg is the worst thing in the world? My Charlie would have done *anything* to live, but he's dead, Arthur. Dead!' she yelled. 'As in *never* coming back!'

Arthur didn't move. His eyes fixed on hers, staring at her as if he were seeing her for the first time.

'*I* would have done anything to keep him alive,' she whispered, her voice cracking. '*I* wouldn't have cared if he didn't have either of his legs; I just wish he'd lived. Do you hear me? I wish he'd *lived*.'

She choked on a wave of tears, her eyes blurred as hands tucked beneath her arms and pulled her up, her throat hot as she sobbed.

'I hate you!' she whispered, looking at Arthur on the floor, barely able to make out his face through her tears. 'I *hate* you.'

'Shhh,' the person holding her said, drawing her closer. 'Shhh, come on; let's go.'

Eva turned and saw Grace, her smile kind as she led her out of the hospital, holding her tight to her side as they walked down rows of beds until they were out in the fresh air. Emotion shattered her body like glass breaking into shards, tears engulfing her as she leaned into Grace, sinking to the ground outside their tent when they finally reached it.

'What's going on?' she heard April say.

But she couldn't even see her. Her eyes were too clouded, her heart too broken.

'I need to go back,' Grace said. 'Can you look after her?'

A fresh set of arms embraced Eva, and she clung to April's familiar shoulders as her body heaved, the tears still a flood that she hadn't a hope of stopping.

'This has been a long time coming,' April whispered. 'Let it all out. Tomorrow's a new day, but today you need to grieve.'

She stumbled to her feet with April's help and let her tuck her into bed, keeping hold of her friend's hand, fingers locked around hers, as she finally accepted what had happened.

Charlie's dead. And no amount of denying it is ever going to bring him back.

——— ❧ ———

It had been three days since she'd seen Arthur. Three days since she'd cracked into a million pieces and wondered how she'd ever manage to put herself back together. But somehow she had, and now she needed to apologize to Arthur for the way she'd treated him.

She saw his familiar silhouette propped up in bed, but she balked at the sight of the wheelchair beside it; it was a reminder of what had happened, which she'd rather not be reminded of.

'Arthur,' she said hesitantly as she approached his bed. 'Arthur, I was hoping to have a word.'

Arthur slowly turned, his eyes flickering over hers and staying there. She could hardly remember what she'd planned to say; since when did Arthur ever turn when she addressed him?

She opened her mouth, but nothing came out. Why was he looking at her? He never looked at her. His eyes were bright, the blue reminding her of that day she'd helped to carry him, staring into them, his gaze pleading with her. She'd thought then that he wanted to live, that there was a reason she'd found him, but ever since then all he'd done was resent her for saving his life.

'I want to say sorry for my behavior the other day,' she finally said. 'I understand if you'd like to make a formal complaint about me. I should have shown you patience, care, and understanding, and instead I treated you terribly. I hope you can forgive me.'

'You were right.' His voice was husky, as if the words were hard to find.

She startled, taking a step closer. 'I was?'

'I deserved everything you said to me. You had the patience of a saint being nice to me for so long.'

Eva had no idea what to say, so she just kept her mouth shut.

Arthur let out a big sigh and slowly raised his hand. 'I'm not great at apologies, so can we just start over?'

Eva wished she had the nerve to say no and make him apologize, but this was the man who'd refused to communicate with her, except to shout, scream, or throw things at her, so she wasn't about to look a gift horse in the mouth.

She followed his lead and lifted her hand, too, shuffling closer so he could clasp her palm.

'My friends all call me Art, and I'd like you to do the same,' he said slowly.

'Well,' she said, taken aback at the change in him. 'I'm Eva. You might have missed my name with all the yelling at me.'

He cringed. 'I'm sorry.'

'Oh, so you *can* apologize!' She didn't bother suppressing her laugh, and to her surprise Art joined in. 'You know, that's the first time I've ever seen you smile,' she said quietly.

He nodded. 'I'd almost forgotten how to do it.'

They stayed silent for a moment, both staring, as if they were seeing each other for the first time. Eva studied every inch of his face, noticing how pale he looked. But despite everything, he was still one of the most handsome men she'd ever seen, even with a scruffy beard that had grown over the weeks he'd been in the hospital; she was almost too scared to see how hollow his cheekbones had become beneath the hair.

'Can I get you something to eat?' Eva asked. 'Since you've taken up smiling again, maybe you'd like to take up eating too?'

Art laughed, and this time it was a deep belly laugh, the kind of laugh her Charlie had had.

'Thank you, Eva, that'd be nice.'

She stepped closer and hesitantly lifted her fingers to touch his cheek, fingers quivering as she gently brushed against his skin. 'Then I'd like to shave you, if you'd let me,' she murmured. 'Or if you don't want me to do it, I can get one of the men . . .'

His eyes shut, and she hoped he wasn't in pain. But then they opened, and a faint smile spread across his lips again. 'Thank you; that'd be nice.'

'Promise you won't throw the water and soap at me when I come back, though?' she teased, hoping she wasn't pushing too far. But his chuckle told her that she'd been right to joke.

'I promise,' he said solemnly. 'And maybe I'll even let you help me into that god-ugly wheelchair so I can feel the sun on my face too.'

She froze. 'You will?'

'Yeah, if you promise not to drop me this time.'

They both grinned, and she shook her head as she walked away. Either Arthur had hit his head on the floor the other day or someone had switched patients with her, because there was no way that was the same man who'd made her life hell for so long.

She passed Dr. Evans on her way to get supplies, and he winked as he strode by. 'You look mighty happy today, Eva.'

'I am. It's a good day today, Dr. Evans.'

He stopped, turned, and walked slowly backward. 'This happen to have something to do with Arthur?'

'What do you know about Arthur?' she asked.

'I know that he's a man who should be thanking his lucky stars that some brave nurses saved him, instead of acting like his life is over.'

'You said that to him, didn't you? I thought it was the bump to his head that had changed him, but now I'm thinking I was wrong.'

He shrugged. 'Perhaps I did.'

Eva stepped toward him and kissed his cheek. 'Thank you, Dr. Evans. Thank you, thank you, thank you.'

He laughed and kept on walking, and she hurried to get all the things she needed, terrified that Arthur might lose his good humor if she took too long.

When she returned, she approached the bed quietly, pleased she hadn't been called away to tend to any new traumas. He was staring at the wall again, and it took all her courage to say his name.

'Arthur?'

He didn't turn right away, and she held her breath, waiting for the explosion, waiting to find out that she'd imagined their little exchange earlier. But he slowly turned, and she let her breath go as he looked at her.

'Would you like me to sit up or lie back?' he asked.

She shrugged. 'I'm not exactly used to shaving men, but maybe sitting?'

He groaned. 'Maybe you should hold the mirror, and I'll do it myself, then.'

Eva ignored him and placed the dish of warm water and soap on the table by his bed, then moved a stool closer to sit on before gently soaping his face and picking up the blade. She wasn't fazed about shaving him, as she had a steady hand with all her nursing duties, but it was being close to him that scared her the most. As she leaned into him, staring at his face and slowly dragging the razor across his skin, she smiled. Or perhaps she wasn't scared at all; perhaps she'd been craving the contact. It was starting to feel like a long time since she'd truly touched someone or been touched in return.

'Tell me about your fiancé,' he said quietly when she paused to wipe part of his face with a towel. 'You said you'd lost him?'

'Yes,' she said. 'I lost my Charlie in Pearl Harbor. He was a pilot.'

Art stayed quiet as she worked the blade across his chin.

'He was desperate to go to Europe and fight before America even joined the war, but I made him stay. I refused to let him go, and then he died before we'd even declared we were at war.'

She stopped and looked at Art, feeling his eyes on hers.

'He wanted to join the Eagles?' he asked.

She nodded. 'He did. Desperately, in fact.'

Art closed his mouth, waiting for her to start again, but she didn't.

'One of your friends, they mentioned you'd been an Eagle. Is it true?'

He shut his eyes. 'I was one of the pilots who left home and joined them when we'd been forbidden to,' he said. 'I defied orders and went to England, and then when we joined the war, I regrouped with my old squadron again.'

Eva's chin wobbled as she fought the emotion bubbling inside of her. Tears escaped from her eyes, and she couldn't stop them. One fell to Art's face, and she quickly tried to wipe it away, but his fingers around her wrist stopped her. She saw tears in his gaze, too, knew instinctively that he'd been fighting his own battles all this time, that he'd refused to cry just like she had. Had been unable to let it all out, no matter how much he might have wanted to.

'I'm sorry, Eva,' he whispered. 'I'm truly sorry for your loss.'

Her tears kept spilling, but she didn't try to hide them this time. 'Me too,' she whispered back. 'Me too.'

Art's hand fell away then, and she finished shaving him, not brave enough to try to talk again. But when she finished and set the razor down, giving his face one final wipe down with the towel, she finally cleared her throat.

'You ready to try out that wheelchair yet? Because I need to get out of here, and I'd rather be with you than on my own.'

Art pushed himself up properly and wiped at his own eyes, his smile warming her in a way she hadn't warmed in a very long time.

'I thought you were never going to ask.'

'Take me back,' he barked less than an hour later, his voice croaky as he gripped the sides of the chair with both hands and pressed back into the seat. 'Eva, take me back now!'

She took a deep breath, hearing the familiar angry tone in Arthur's voice.

'Art, listen to me,' she said, trying to keep her voice as low and soft as she could. 'You're going to be fine. Just trust me.'

'Trusting you got me into this mess!'

He spun around in the seat, and her heart almost broke when she saw the terror in his gaze.

'I thought I could do this, but I can't,' he said. 'Take me back.'

Eva gritted her teeth and pushed hard on the wheelchair, propelling it forward with a grunt, his weight heavier than she'd anticipated. 'Sit still and just breathe,' she ordered.

He started to complain again, but she refused to listen, pushing him through the last part of the ward and nodding her thanks when one of the corpsmen opened and held the door for her.

'It's going to feel a little bumpy here until we get onto the grass,' she said, huffing as she kept the wheelchair moving.

'Eva, *please*,' he begged, reminding her of a little boy trying to convince his mother to listen to him. 'I can't do this—I can't balance. I just can't.'

'You can,' she said, exhaling when the chair finally became easier to move, 'and you are.'

She pushed a bit farther, stopping only when they were far enough away from the hospital that he wouldn't ask to be pushed straight back.

'How does that feel?' she asked, leaning against the chair and watching as he lifted his face, eyes shut, basking like a cat in the sun.

He didn't answer right away, but when he finally opened his mouth, a slow smile spread across his lips. 'It feels good.'

She sat on the ground in front of him, looking at the stump above where his knee would have been, since he had his eyes closed. It was different seeing it outside, because in the hospital he was always beneath a sheet or blanket, and when she was checking it, she was so focused on what she was doing that she didn't actually take the time to think about it. But here, out in the open, in the real world, she could see what had been taken from him. His remaining leg was almost fully healed now, and it was a big leg, hairy and strong, as masculine as could be as it protruded from the blanket, but with scars slicing across it where before she imagined there were no marks. But the space on the other side, where his other leg should have been, told her that nothing about his life could ever be the same again.

'Don't go feeling sorry for me.'

Eva looked up, embarrassed that she'd been caught looking at him so openly. 'I'm sorry; I was just . . .' She swallowed. 'I haven't really seen you like this. Up until now, you've just been my patient lying in a bed.'

'And now you've realized I'm a useless cripple?'

She shook her head. 'No, Art, that's not what I was thinking.'

'What was it, then?'

Eva met his gaze, not wanting him to think she wasn't telling the truth. 'I was thinking how your life will change, that there are things you won't be able to do anymore.' She swallowed as her voice cracked. 'But as hard as things are going to be in the beginning, I know that one day you'll be happy that you lived, one leg or not. That's what I wanted to tell you, right from the beginning; it's why I waited beside your bed until you woke up.'

He opened his palms as if to soak up the sun, his head angled upward still. 'I'll never fly again,' he said quietly. 'I'll never sit behind the controls of a plane; I'll never have that feeling of soaring through the sky again.'

She listened. There was nothing she could say, because he was right.

'I'll never hold a woman in my arms and dance again.' He laughed. 'I was crap at dancing anyway, but I'd literally be all left feet now.'

She smiled, liking that he was joking about it, but his face became somber almost instantly.

'I'll never get married and have a family of my own,' he croaked. 'I'll watch my friends live their lives, and I'll be watching it all from the sidelines.'

Eva blinked away tears, wishing she knew how to tell the handsome, strong man in front of her how wrong he was. 'I wouldn't have cared if my Charlie had come home with no legs, Art. I still would have loved him with all my heart.'

His tear-filled eyes met hers. 'But I wasn't someone's Charlie before the war, Eva,' he said sadly. 'You loved him already for the man he was. No one is ever going to look at me now and want to love me, are they?'

'You're wrong. You can't think like that, Art,' she said, quickly wiping at her eyes when he looked away. 'After everything we've all been through, everything we've seen, I think everyone will be more, I don't know, open minded when we return home.'

He shook his head. 'Flying is all I've ever known, but I'll be useless when I get back.'

They sat in silence for a while, Eva lost in her own thoughts as she sat on the ground in front of Art. He seemed happy soaking in the sun's rays, and although she was hot, with sweat slowly spreading across the back of her neck, she never complained. The nights were already getting cooler now, and she had no idea how warm the days would stay, and she wanted him to enjoy it for as long as he could.

'When will I be sent home?' he suddenly asked.

'I'm not sure. Soon, I suspect.'

'You'll help me get used to this chair before then?' he asked. 'I'm still terrified I'm going to fall out of it.'

She smiled. 'Of course I will. And you'll get used to using it on your own soon enough, once you've built up your strength again and figured out your balance.'

Art looked at her for a long moment. 'Thank you. For sticking with me even though I was so rude to you.'

Eva went to reply, but his softly spoken words stopped her.

'I remember that day, Eva. I remember looking into your eyes as you carried me; the pain was so bad, but I stared into your eyes and listened to your words, and I wondered if I'd died already. I knew it was you.'

Eva moved closer to him and reached for his hand, holding it as he spoke, knowing how hard the words must be for him.

'I remember waking, slipping in and out of sleep, and seeing you sitting by my bed. I was even going to ask you out—I kept thinking that there was no way I'd let a pretty girl like you get away without asking you out—but then when I found out my leg was gone, I realized you'd only been sitting with me because you felt sorry for me.'

'That wasn't why!' she gasped. 'Art, I wasn't sitting with you because I felt sorry for you.'

'Why, then?' he rasped. 'For what other reason would you be sitting with a cripple?'

She shut her eyes, not wanting to look at him as she admitted why. 'Because you reminded me of Charlie, and all I could think was that if he'd survived, I'd have wanted someone to care for him,' she whispered. 'For him to wake up and have someone with him so he didn't have to face it all alone.'

'You honestly think you'd have loved him if he'd ended up like this?' Art's voice was gruff now, his eyes searching hers.

'I'd have loved Charlie no matter what happened to him,' she said. 'He was everything to me. I've got nothing left now.'

He frowned. 'You're the one telling me to feel grateful for being alive, and now you're saying *you've* got nothing left?'

She smiled. 'I've said too much.' Something about him made her want to open up, to share with him when she was usually so good at being guarded.

'Tell me why you've got nothing to live for?' he asked.

Eva shook her head. 'The last thing you want is to hear about my troubles. I'm the one supposed to be fixing you.'

Art planted his hands on the armrests and leaned forward. 'I think maybe you spend too much time trying to fix other people. But if I'm going to trust you, you need to trust me,' he said. 'I'll make you a deal. You tell me why you're so sure you've got nothing to live for, and I'll promise to do all the physical therapy you've been trying to get me to do.'

She raised her eyes. She never talked about her life, about what she was going home to, why she was afraid, not with anyone. She hadn't even opened up to April and Grace, not entirely.

'Charlie protected me,' she finally said, deciding to put the same trust in Art as he was willing to put into her. 'He looked after me, and his family opened their arms to me. I was finally going to be safe.'

Art frowned. 'Safe from who? Who did Charlie need to protect you from?'

A big breath shuddered from her. In her mind's eye, hands choked her throat; his breath was bitter, but his boot was the worst part. The thud of the steel cap connected with her thigh, making her leg buckle, but his grip around her neck, her back against the wall, kept her from slipping to the floor. 'My father,' she said, pushing the memories away. 'He has a special way of showing his love for me.' She looked up and saw that Art was staring at her still.

'When you say "special—"'

'I mean that I know what it feels like to have his fingers so tightly laced around my throat that I don't know if I'm going to survive the night,' she said, relief surging through her as the words came out, as she finally admitted to someone what she'd had to live with. 'I mean that his friend is a bottle, and that friend has become his constant companion, so that no day living under his roof is a good one anymore. Sometimes I could be asleep in my bed when he came home, when he wanted someone to take his anger out on; other times I could be standing in the kitchen doing the dishes when he snapped.'

'I see.' Art had a vein bulging on his forehead, and he was tightly clenching and unclenching his fists.

'I'm sorry. I shouldn't have said anything,' she muttered. 'The last thing you need is to know why I'm all broken.'

'You think you're broken?' he asked, his eyebrows shooting up. 'Because what I see is a strong, incredible nurse in front of me. I don't see anything broken.'

'You're just saying that because you need my help to get back to your bed.'

He grunted. 'No. I still couldn't give a damn whether you left me out here to die or not. I just didn't want to keep seeing that hurt look on your face all the time.'

She smiled, not sure what to say to him and not used to the kind expression on his face.

'Will you go home to your Charlie's family after the war?' he asked.

'No.' Eva shrugged. 'Why would they want a reminder of the son they lost? We weren't even married yet. I'll just have to find my own way in the world.'

She thought Art was going to tip out of his chair then, and she scrambled to her feet.

'Your *own* way in the world?' he spluttered. 'What does that mean? What about your mother?'

She laughed, but it was only because if she didn't laugh, she'd cry. 'Well, my mother won't stand up to my father, and my father has cut me off financially. She'd be terrified of the same happening to her. When I accepted Charlie's proposal and then decided to leave home to be a nurse, he made it clear I was never welcome back in his house again.'

Art's hand lifted and hovered, before gently resting over hers. 'Want to hear what my mother wrote to tell me?' he asked. 'Since we're talking about family?'

She was staring at his hand, wishing it would stay there. His palm was so warm, the contact such a relief after feeling alone for so long.

Eva shut her eyes and thought of Charlie, hated that she couldn't make out his face as clearly as she'd once been able to, hoping that he didn't think she was betraying him if he was looking down on them. Art was her patient, but he was also a man—a very handsome man with a much bigger heart than she'd realized.

'Yes.'

'A letter arrived from her last week, and it said she'd been notified that I'd been injured in the line of duty,' Art said. 'And she said that whenever I was feeling sorry for myself, I was to tie my shoelaces as tight as could be and walk around, and then I'd forget all about my sorrows.' He laughed, and she kept her eyes shut, squeezing back tears. 'I haven't the heart to tell her that I'd do anything to have two pairs of laces to tighten.'

They stayed connected, her leaning into his chair and him holding her hand.

'We're a good pair then, aren't we.'

Art looked up at her, and she smiled down at him.

'Yeah, we are,' she whispered.

They stayed like that until Eva noticed the sky swirling darker and realized how long they'd been gone.

'I'm going to get in so much trouble for being out here so long. Come on; let's go.'

'Anyone tells you off, you tell them to come find me,' he said.

Eva resisted a sudden urge to kiss the top of his head as she stood up straight and took hold of the wheelchair. 'You know, I might just do that.'

'Thank you,' he said as she pushed him.

'For what?'

'For saving my life. Twice over.'

She gripped the handles as warmth spread through her body, realizing how long she'd been waiting for him to acknowledge what she'd done. 'You're welcome.'

CHAPTER TWENTY

APRIL

April glanced over at Dr. Evans and wondered if she had rocks in her head. She was still suspended on tenterhooks waiting to see if she was going to be dismissed entirely and sent home, but Dr. Evans had convinced her to come and help him in the village. Part of her wanted to hide away and wallow in her misery, and she certainly didn't want to trust another doctor, but the moment he'd mentioned children needing help, she hadn't been able to say no.

'There's not many nurses who would have said yes to coming with me,' he said, breaking the silence as they trekked across the dirt.

'I think you're wrong. One mention of kids and you'd have nurses flocking to help.'

He laughed. 'Will you turn around and leave me if I confess that you're not the first nurse I've asked?'

April laughed with him, liking his honesty. 'If I'm the first to say yes, then it's still something, right?'

She adjusted the bag on her shoulder, and they walked quickly, the sun beating down so hot that her neck was already slick with sweat and her forehead too.

'It's just up there, not far now,' he said.

'Dr. Evans, how did you start helping them? Did someone ask you?'

'*Harry,*' he said with a grin. 'And no, no one asked me. I just noticed how basic some of the living conditions were and made a few trips around the village on my first day off.'

'So while the rest of us were enjoying extra sleep or socializing, you were volunteering.' She shook her head. 'Great way to make the rest of us feel bad!'

They reached the house then, and she stood back as Harry knocked on the door, taking the time to study him, taking in his easy smile and open expression as the door was answered. In his white coat at the hospital, he seemed no different from the other doctors, but like this, it was obvious that he was a different kind of man.

'This is my nurse,' he said, gesturing toward her. 'April.' She quickly stepped forward and smiled, trying to be as natural and friendly as he was.

'Come in, please, come in.'

April went to follow, but she paused when Harry's hand fell over her arm. 'I hope you don't mind me using first names; I think it's easier for them.'

'Not at all.'

As soon as they entered, she could smell the telltale aroma of sickness, and she wished she'd brought a mask. But Harry didn't even flinch, following the mother through the house and into a crude bedroom with mats on the floor. There were three children, two of them lying, another sitting against the wall.

'Tell me, what's wrong?' Harry asked, and April bent to check them, reaching out and then waiting for their mother to nod before touching them. Their skin was clammy, and she could tell from the way they were holding their stomachs that they were in pain.

'You need to make sure you all wash your hands well,' he said, holding up his hands and showing the mother. 'This spreads by touching. And keep them cool—cold cloths on their foreheads and a lot of water to drink.'

April did her best to make them comfortable. She took out some food from her bag as well and left it for the mother as Harry felt their stomachs. And when they were finally ready to go, she was surprised to see a short line of villagers at the door, waiting in the hot sun for them.

'They're here for us?' she asked, unable to believe what she was seeing.

'We feed you,' the woman said. 'And you help them.'

April swapped glances with Harry, but it was clear that neither of them would leave until they'd helped those waiting.

'One at a time,' Harry said, waving toward the door. 'But no food. You don't have enough to share, and we are very full.' He patted at his stomach as if to make his point, and April hoped no one heard hers rumble. But of course he was right; she didn't want them to share what little they had either.

The first villager to walk through the door was a boy cradling his arm, and April prayed that Harry had something in his bag to set a break with. Although from seeing him work, she was starting to realize that even if he didn't, he'd probably find a way to improvise.

—— ⌒⌒⌒ ——

'Come with me,' Dr. Evans said, beckoning to April.

She shook her head. 'I can't. I was told to meet Matron Johnson here this morning.'

He frowned. 'To discuss being cleared to work again?'

'I think I'm more likely to be sent home than ever be allowed to work here again,' she replied. 'Honestly, even some of the nurses are being hostile toward me now. I don't know what he's been saying, but it's awful. Maybe they think I was having an affair with him or something. I don't know, but whatever it is, it's ghastly.'

'Come on—let's go and see her, then. I'm not having you face that old battle-ax alone.'

April laughed as he gestured toward the office door she was waiting outside of. 'Dr. Evans, I . . .'

'*Harry*,' he said. 'How many times do I have to tell you to call me by my first name? I thought we'd moved past that on Sunday.'

'I'm certain that's only the second time, *Harry*,' she said, wondering how he'd made her laugh when she was so anxious over her fate.

'I owe you after you spent your day off helping me,' he announced. 'You're the best nurse I've ever taken with me.'

She tried not to laugh; he'd already told her she was the only one ever to go with him, and it had hardly been her day off. She hadn't been allowed to work for almost two weeks now.

Before she could stop him, he knocked on the door, beaming when the older nurse opened it. Clearly she wasn't expecting to see a doctor waiting for her.

'Can I help you?' the matron asked, smiling at the doctor and frowning at April.

'It's come to my attention that Nurse Bellamy is still suspended, despite my insisting days ago that it was unwarranted,' he said. 'Have you launched an investigation into Dr. Grey yet?'

'Dr. Evans, I'm sorry, but we can't take an allegation from a nurse against a doctor, especially when it's unfounded. We simply don't have enough doctors as it is.'

'Well, you'll lose *this* doctor if you don't reinstate Nurse Bellamy immediately,' he said. 'I want her on my service in the burns unit, and I insist she has full privileges in the hospital. I'm not having a good nurse take the blame for an incompetent doctor, especially when we've had hundreds of men to care for this past week.' His smile made the matron blush. 'I will personally vouch for her—I'm so confident in her abilities—and if you took the time to investigate, you'd easily discover that she's innocent. It just so happens she's been spending her spare time aiding villagers, so she's hardly the type of nurse you want to send home, is she?'

April swallowed, her palms sweaty as Matron Johnson looked from her to Harry.

'Very well, then. But there will still be a formal investigation.'

'Thank you,' he said before she could continue. 'Come along, Nurse Bellamy.'

April nodded and hurried after him, not daring to look back in case she was called into the office without him.

'Why did you do that for me?' she asked.

He glanced at her as they walked. 'Because I refuse to see a good nurse take the fall.' He lowered his voice. 'Especially one who wants to become a doctor one day. You'd hardly get into medical school if you were fired from nursing, would you? And like I said, I owed you.'

She stopped walking and stared at him. 'Are you making fun of me?'

He shook his head. 'No, I'm not.'

'So you don't think it's amusing that I want to be a doctor?'

'Amusing, no,' he said, starting to walk again. 'Ambitious? Yes.'

'What if I don't want to be on your service?' she asked. 'It didn't exactly work out for me the first time, being on the service of one doctor. I never said I'd join you.'

'It's up to you if you want to join me or not, but I'm nothing like Dr. Grey, April. Nothing at all.' He paused. 'I thought working side by side the other day would have shown you that.'

She hesitated, looking at him as he strode through the ward, his long legs moving him quickly away from her. *Go after him.* Her head screamed at her and her heart tugged, and she knew she had to go instead of hiding herself away just to stop from being hurt again.

April ran after him, slowing only when she was at his side again.

'You're certain you have a strong stomach?' he asked as he pushed open the door to the burns unit and held it for her.

She gulped. 'Yes, I'm certain.'

'Good, because I need someone who can stand beside me without retching, and trust me when I say that at times it's not easy, even for me.'

They walked into the ward, and the first thing that struck April was the smell. The burnt-flesh aroma was unmistakable, and she tried to keep her face impassive when Harry turned to her.

'It takes some getting used to.'

She wasn't going to lie to him. 'Yes, it does.' The smell was one thing on a single patient, but on so many in a small space, it was beyond overwhelming, especially with such poor ventilation.

'I'd like you to become familiar with the patients, gain their trust and talk to them, and then I'll walk you through changing their dressings correctly.'

April surveyed the room. 'I've completed many dressing changes, so I—'

'This is different, April,' he said, keeping his voice low. 'These men, they might not live through their burns, they're so severe. It's why I won't let them be released into a general ward.'

She nodded.

'Infection is our enemy,' he said with a grimace, 'among a hundred other things, and we don't exactly have the best working conditions.'

She looked around the room again and decided to start with the closest patient. But as Harry started to walk away, she stopped him.

'Why me?' she asked. 'Why did you ask me to work with you?'

His smile spread slowly across his face, and she saw a kindness reflected in his eyes that she was now realizing had been missing from Dr. Grey's gaze. She'd just been too awed by the other doctor to notice what he was lacking.

'Because I don't want to see a dedicated, ambitious nurse sent home. I already told you that.'

'It's honestly as simple as that, then?' she asked, finding it hard to trust anyone after what had happened to her.

'Yes, it is.' He laughed as he turned. 'And maybe, just maybe, I'd like to spend more time with you.'

April spun around and headed to her first patient before Harry could see how flushed her cheeks were. Part of her was mortified that he'd said that out loud, but another part of her was tingling with excitement that a doctor like Harry would even want to give her the time of day.

——— ⁓⁓⁓ ———

After hours of walking the ward and assisting Harry with his checkups, April was struggling to stop her hands from shaking. And he'd been right; even the strongest of stomachs would be capable of balking in the burn ward. They were full, too, with not a bed vacant as she looked up and down the rows.

Dr. Evans had left to perform surgeries, and she'd been left in charge of getting lunch out to all the men, but she was starting to see why no other nurses were quick to put their hands up to transfer into the ward. She touched the shoulder of a patient, a young man who'd openly cried as his dressings had been changed. She held out his food.

'No,' he croaked. 'I can't eat.'

She sat beside him and forked some of the potato for him. 'I'll feed you,' she said. 'All you have to do is open your mouth.'

Tears slid down his cheeks, and she had to fight her own tears just looking at him. This poor boy, maybe eighteen or nineteen, had burns to most of his body—he'd have red, scarred skin for life if he even managed to heal before an infection set in, and she bet all he wanted was to go home to his mother. It was like reliving Pearl Harbor all over again, except on land they hadn't seen the extent of burn injuries like the nurses on the USS *Solace* had. Yet another reason, she knew, why Eva had suffered worse than they had through those first few days after the bombing.

'It's okay,' she whispered.

'I'm so hungry,' he choked out. 'But I can't eat with the smell.'

She set the fork down. Why hadn't she thought of that? The smell must have been so much worse for the men living in their freshly charred bodies than for her walking through the ward.

'That's why no one is eating here?' she asked. 'It's not the pain; it's the smell?'

He slowly nodded. 'Most of us can deal with the pain.'

April stood and looked at all the men, seeing that only one of them was picking at food. The rest were either refusing or waiting for her to help.

In a split second that she knew could result in suspension again, she left the ward and hurried through the hallways to get outside and race all the way back to her tent. She should have told someone where she was going, although she knew she'd be reprimanded and told to return to her ward, and there was no point if the poor men she was trying to nurse couldn't stomach any food or water.

'Nurse! Slow down!' an older nurse ordered. 'Where are you going?'

'Sorry—doctor's orders,' she lied as she slowed to a fast walk, running again only when she was outside.

She hurried across the field and then up the hill toward their campsite, not stopping until she reached their tent. She dashed inside and went straight to her toiletries, then grabbed the little glass bottle of perfume she'd brought with her.

'Why are you panting like that? Aren't you supposed to be in the middle of a shift?'

'Grace!' she gasped. 'You scared the life from me!'

'I was sound asleep and woke to heavy panting, and you're the one who got a fright?'

April held out the bottle, trying to catch her breath. 'I needed this. I'm trying to get the burns patients to eat.'

Grace yawned and tucked lower under her blanket. 'And you're going to spray the air with perfume?'

She laughed. 'No, even better, I'm going to dab perfume on a handkerchief so they can hold it to their noses while they eat.'

Grace laughed. 'You've always been the smart one.'

April blew her a kiss and picked up her cream handkerchief on the way past, not hesitating even though it was one of the last things her mother had embroidered for her.

If I can save them, Mama, it's worth sacrificing, she thought as she ran back the same way she'd come only minutes earlier.

April made her way back through the hospital, her body protesting from the unexpected run, knowing the food would be cold by now but hoping it was better cold than nothing at all. She went back to her first patient, the young man who was now lying staring at the ceiling, almost his entire body covered in dressings, and touched his shoulder.

'I think this might work,' she said softly, taking out her handkerchief and dabbing perfume to it before placing it over his nose.

The smile on his face and the twinkle of tears in his eyes made her heart melt, and she quickly forked some food again and held it to his mouth. This time he opened it, and she sat beside him and spoon-fed him until there wasn't a morsel left. Then she reached for his water, holding the straw to his mouth so he could sip it.

'Better?' she asked.

His eyes said it all. 'Can I keep this?' he asked.

She shook her head. 'I need it to get around to everyone else,' she said, gesturing to the others in the ward. 'But I promise I'll try to find some squares of towel or muslin and dab perfume for each and every one of you before my shift ends.'

He shut his eyes, and she left his plate, hurrying to the next man. The smiles and quick consumption of food and water made it all worthwhile, and by the time she'd made her way to the last bed in the room, she realized that every single patient had eaten a meal. It might have taken her half of her shift, but she'd done it.

'I would ask how everything's going, but from those empty plates I think I know the answer,' Harry said as he appeared in the doorway.

She shrugged. 'Sometimes it's about thinking creatively to solve a problem.'

He reached for the handkerchief in her hand, and she passed it to him.

'What's this?'

'A way to stop them from smelling their burns so they can eat,' she said. 'Hardly scientific, but it seemed to work.'

Harry laughed. 'I knew there was something about you from the moment I met you.'

She stretched, rolling her shoulders and trying to ease the tension from sitting and bending forward for so long.

'Do you think I can get permission to take a piece of muslin for each patient in here?'

'I'll steal them for you myself if I have to.'

Harry disappeared, and April laughed as she turned around and then collected all the empty plates to take back to the kitchen. It had been a gamble, but one tiny thing had made a difference to every man in her ward, and it was enough to give her the courage to do whatever she needed to help her patients.

'I thought I might find you in here.'

April clutched the plates she was holding as the deep voice seemed to curl around her. Most of the men were sleeping, and the ones who weren't were hardly in any kind of fit state to protect her.

She turned and found Dr. Grey standing in the middle of the room. His baritone voice had once been so appealing to her, but as she stood before him, all she could think was that he was married. *You have a wife at home, and you acted like you were interested in me.* And that he had a cruel streak that she could never have imagined.

'Hello, Dr. Grey. Can I help you?' she said, trying to be brave as he glowered at her.

'I thought you'd been sent packing, so imagine my surprise to hear your privileges had been reinstated today.'

She stood, not reacting, not wanting to antagonize him.

'Nurses don't get to call the shots in a hospital, April. You don't get away with killing a man.' He stared at her, as if daring her to defy him.

'I did nothing of the sort, and you know it,' she hissed, moving closer to him, not wanting the patients to hear.

'You won't get away with this,' he said, chuckling as he looked down at her. 'You killed that man, April; you just don't remember. I stepped out of the theater for a bathroom break, and you pretended you were a real little doctor and tried to finish my work for me. You think you can open your legs for a doctor and . . .'

Thwack.

Out of nowhere Harry appeared, swinging his fist so fast at Dr. Grey's nose that none of them saw it coming. Blood spurted instantly as Grey staggered back, and April clamped her hand over her mouth as she watched the scene unfold. Harry stood in front of her and waited for Grey to leave the room.

No one said a word, not even Grey.

'You all right?' Harry asked, turning once they were alone and studying her face, his eyes searching hers.

'Yes, I think so.' *Other than the fact my entire body is convulsing from fear.*

'No one gets to speak to you or any other nurse like that—you hear me? It's unacceptable.'

April stood immobile as his hands rubbed her shoulders and trailed down her arms before falling away.

'You did great here today. Are you staying on my service?'

April nodded. 'Yes.'

'Good. Now dab your perfume on those muslins I dropped on my way in, and go take a well-deserved rest.'

'But Harry, I just . . .' She tried to process her thoughts, Dr. Grey's words repeating over and over through her mind.

'What is it? Did he hurt you before I got here?'

'No.' She stared at Harry and then laughed. 'It just came back to me, that day—I remember! He said before about leaving to go on a bathroom break, that he left me with the patient alone, but it wasn't him! He left me alone with a different patient, one we were doing a cast on. And the man had already stirred, so he heard Dr. Grey say he needed to relieve himself; he wasn't unconscious. I remember!'

'That's your proof, then,' Harry said. 'Good work. I knew it would come back to you.'

April walked on shaky legs, wishing she could thank Harry but struggling to make even a squeak in reply as she tried to process what she'd remembered.

'April?'

She looked back at him, seeing a flicker across his face, something about the way he was looking at her telling her that there was something he was uncomfortable about.

'Some of us surgeons, we're going to the front line. The boys at the battalion aid station can't handle the casualties, and we need to help. It's taking the wounded too long to receive medical care, and it's the only thing they can think of to try.'

April swallowed a stone in her throat as she listened to him.

'We need three nurses to come with us,' he said. 'Others will be coming ashore with soldiers as they land, but we need a few from here to join them.'

'I'll go,' she said, without even thinking. 'I'll go with you.'

He stepped forward, his eyes almost sorrowful. 'You'll have nothing more than a helmet to protect you and a pack on your back. We'll have to crawl low across the sand and—'

'I'm here to save lives, Harry. Tell me when you need me, and I'll go with you.'

His smile was reserved, and she wondered what it all meant, if there was something more developing between them.

Harry's hand closed over her shoulder, and he smiled down at her. 'You're the bravest nurse I know,' he whispered.

She laughed. 'Or maybe the stupidest.'

'How about you be the cleverest then?'

April stared back at him. 'What do you mean?'

'Find a way to get Grey to confess,' he said. 'The man has a big ego, and if you ask to see him and pretend like you want to take the fall for it, maybe he'll admit his error. You know what happened—now you just need to make the truth work for you.'

'What use is that if only I hear it? I already know what happened that day.'

'You leave that to me. Just tell me where you're meeting him, and I'll make sure it's overheard by the right person.'

April's heart picked up a beat. 'You really think this is a good idea?'

Harry's smile told her everything she needed to know.

April was starting to have second thoughts. She tried to steady her breathing, knowing that at any moment Grey would arrive, and she'd only have a short window to execute her plan.

Her heart started to race, and just as she was about to run from the room, he entered.

'Your message said you were ready to apologize?' Grey said, stalking closer to her in that predatory way he had the day before in the burns unit.

April glanced down and then slowly back up again. 'I am.' She hoped he couldn't tell how nervous she was.

'So go on, then; I'm waiting,' he said impatiently.

'I'm sorry if it was my fault,' she said, trying to project her voice loud enough so Harry could hear her from wherever he was hiding. 'I should have told Dr. Evans that it was another doctor instead of agreeing that Private Hunt was your patient.'

'So you do remember it was your fault?' Grey chuckled. 'I knew it'd come back to you.'

April blinked and forced herself forward, moving closer, going against her every instinct. Was this even going to work? 'I'll say whatever you want me to say, Dr. Grey. I just miss being with you.'

She stopped a foot from him, eyes on his mouth, trying to be seductive even though she had no practice at what it entailed.

'Ha, you miss me, do you?' He moistened his lips, and she tried not to recoil.

'That day, I remember you leaving the room, but it wasn't with the same patient. It wasn't with Private Hunt,' she said. 'I don't care, though—I'll take the fall. I'm only a nurse. I'll do it for you.'

His smile made her stomach turn.

'You're doing the right thing, April,' he said, reaching for her. 'I'm sorry I had to blame you, but I'm not risking my career for one stupid mistake on a half-dead soldier.'

'So it wasn't my fault?' she asked, her voice louder this time.

'Don't be thick—of course it wasn't.' He grunted. 'Come here and let me make it up to you. You'll be sent home by the end of the week, and—'

'The only person going home will be you, Grey,' came Harry's strong, commanding voice.

April quickly backed away, seeing the betrayal cross Grey's face as he took in Harry and her matron in the doorway. His scowl was directed at her as he launched forward.

'You bitch! You tricked me!' he yelled. 'You absolute little bitch!'

She squeezed her eyes shut and turned her face as Harry grabbed Grey from behind, holding his hands together while he called for help. Matron Johnson's arms shielded her, holding her away from the commotion as she whispered in her ear.

'I'm so sorry, April. Please forgive me.'

All April could do was nod. Harry's plan had worked, and just like that he'd managed to save her job. If she hadn't owed him before, she certainly did now.

CHAPTER TWENTY-ONE

GRACE

'You're doing what?' Grace felt all the color drain from her face.

'You don't have to volunteer; I'm just telling you what I've decided to do.'

Grace gripped the chair beside her and slowly lowered herself into it. They'd had a long day, and they'd both missed lunch, having only a foul-tasting cup of coffee each, and she wasn't sure if it was the lack of food or the shock at what her sister had just told her that was making her feel light headed. She'd thought she'd be relieved when April got her job reinstated, but she hadn't been expecting this.

'The fighting has intensified, Operation Torch has begun, and too many men are dying waiting for help,' April continued. 'Look how many have arrived today, and we've lost so many of them.'

Grace shut her eyes, letting her face fall into her palms for a second as she tried to comprehend what was going on. 'So you'll be on the front line? I thought women weren't allowed to be anywhere near the fighting?'

April's voice dropped an octave. 'We'll be in the thick of it anyway if we don't win, Grace. Have you thought about that?'

She shuddered and opened her eyes again, seeing the pain etched on April's face. 'No,' she admitted. 'I haven't.'

April stood quietly, and Grace sat. Would Teddy be fighting right now, or had he moved on to somewhere else? She thought about him a lot; every night as she lay in bed, she wondered what might have happened to her if he hadn't been there, if he hadn't saved her.

And it was the same reason, what had happened to her that night, that made her terrified of volunteering to go with April. But if her sister was going, how could she not go with her?

'Do you have any other nurses yet?' she asked.

April shook her head. 'Not that I know of.'

Grace took a big shuddering breath. 'I'll go too, then.'

April looked like she was about to burst into tears. 'You will?'

'I'm not letting you go alone, so yes, I'll go. What about Eva?'

Grace didn't think Eva was up to it—she'd barely recovered from what they'd been through in Pearl Harbor—but she didn't want to presume.

'Let's go ask her,' April said. 'She's been more like her old self lately, don't you think?'

'What I think is that Arthur's finally realized how lucky he is to have a nurse as pretty and smart as Eva fussing over him all day.'

They both laughed, and Grace clasped April's hand when she held it out, pulling her to her feet.

'I feel like I hardly see you anymore,' Grace said, dropping her head to April's shoulder as they walked, leaning into her. 'We seem to either be working or sleeping and nothing else.'

'It's only going to get worse too. Harry, I mean Dr. Evans, thinks we could end up treating hundreds if not a thousand patients between this week and next.'

'Harry, huh?' Grace teased. 'You two are on a first-name basis now?'

April just grinned in reply, and they stopped beside Arthur's bed. Grace was surprised to see him sitting upright, his cheeks freshly razored and his eyes bright, with one hand touching Eva's. Eva had fallen asleep, her head tilted to the side where she sat on the stool beside Arthur's bed, and his fingers had inched close to hers, the tips just touching.

'Can't you let her sleep a little longer?' he asked, his voice low.

Grace saw the tender way he glanced down at Eva and wondered how on earth such a sullen, uninterested-in-life man could suddenly seem so human. Eva had obviously worked her magic on him.

She swapped glances with April and hoped her sister was thinking the same thing she was.

'It's fine. We've both finished our shift, and we were coming to collect her,' Grace said.

'You look after her, Arthur,' April told him before she turned. 'She's looked after you from the second we found you, and she needs someone to take care of her.'

He gave them a little salute. 'Yes, ma'am.'

Grace linked arms with her sister as they walked away. 'You're not going to ask her to join us, are you?'

'No,' April whispered. 'Not now. Not when she's finally getting back on her feet again. I don't think it would be fair.'

'Nurse!'

They both jumped back as more men were brought in, a wave of patients being run through the doors on stretchers. *So much for getting something to eat and finally going to sleep.*

'Oh my God, these men . . .' Grace's voice trailed off as she leaped into action, still feeling the urge to run and hide whenever she was faced with blood and gore, the smell alone making her stomach heave. But these soldiers needed her, and that was all that mattered.

'How long have they been like this?' Grace asked.

The two men closest to her were both wrapped in dirty blankets, their faces and bodies caked in mud and sweat and dried blood. Their faces were thickly stubbled with at least a few days' worth of hair, and she could barely see what she needed to work on first.

Her sister took one soldier, and she turned to the other, checking his eyes first and his breathing before taking his hands to move them, wondering why they were so tightly clamped over his stomach.

'If you could just move—' she started, before screaming. 'Help!' Blood spurted from him, his hands soaked red. She could make out loose stitches that were no longer holding, and she clamped her hands over the gaping hole in his abdomen, trying not to cry as she talked to him.

'Stay with me,' she choked out. 'You're going to be fine; we're going to look after you now.'

'Doctor!' April screamed beside her. 'We need a doctor here!'

Grace was trembling, unable to look at her hands, to see what she was holding, to put a name to the slippery part of the man she was connected to, trying to stop him from bleeding to death in front of her.

'We're going to be fine here.' Dr. Evans appeared beside her, his voice deep and commanding. 'Keep your hands there, and walk with us,' he said. 'We're going to save this man's life—you hear me?'

Grace nodded, ignoring the lurch of her stomach as she hurried with them, her hands the only thing stopping the poor man's insides from slipping straight out and onto the floor.

Eva's eyes met hers from across Arthur's bed as they raced past into the operating theater, where Dr. Evans's calm voice guided her when to let go, his practiced hands reaching straight in, frantically starting to sew as more blood pumped out, as another surgeon dashed in to help him and more patients were rushed past in conditions easily as bad.

Grace walked on wobbly legs until she was away from the noise, out of sight, and leaned her back against the wall as she slowly slid down until her bottom hit the floor. She stared at her red hands, at the blood dripping down her arms, opening her mouth and letting out a silent scream that was anything but silent in her head.

Get up.

The voice in her head was insistent, but she refused to listen to it.

'Grace?'

She took a deep breath and raised her eyes, finding Eva kneeling beside her. She hadn't even known anyone was near her.

'Grace, we need you. Get up.'

Grace pushed herself up the same way she'd gone down, her back against the wall, knees shuddering as they tried to collapse on her.

Eva's warm palms were against her cheeks, and Grace slowly focused on her friend's eyes.

'You're going to be fine, Grace,' Eva whispered. 'Come on—there's more men coming through those doors than we can handle. They're talking about closing the hospital if we don't start moving through them faster.'

'I'm going to the front,' she whispered. 'Me and April, both of us. They need nurses there.'

'You can't, Grace. You can't deal with all the blood here, let alone—'

'I'm going,' she said, surprised by the strength in her own voice. 'I have to.'

Eva took her hand, not seeming to care that it was bloodstained.

'Well, if you're going, I'm going too.'

Grace wanted to tell her no, that they weren't letting her now that she was finally starting to find her way again, but Eva's voice was full of authority, and her friend was the same Eva who'd so impressed Grace all those months ago in Hawaii.

'Fine, but be careful. I can't lose another friend,' Grace muttered as they reentered the emergency ward.

'Right back at you, Gracie,' Eva said. 'We're all coming back from the front alive, no matter what.'

'We need morphine and more morphine over here!' someone yelled.

'Bleeding out! Get him to surgery!'

'I need a doctor, now!'

Shouts erupted throughout the ward as it turned to mayhem, with men everywhere they could fit them and nurses who'd already worked twelve hours straight standing alongside surgeons who were on call twenty-four hours a day. If she could survive being in this ward, then she could survive anything. Or at least that's what she was going to keep telling herself.

———— ❧ ❧ ————

A few days later, Grace gave Eva a quick kiss and a long hug goodbye, not sure whether to be relieved or sad that she wasn't coming with them. They'd been overrun with patients, the beds full and their surgeons working around the clock to save the lives of so many young men, and Eva had been grounded.

She hurried after April and Dr. Evans, her pack thumping against her shoulders, helmet clutched to her chest with one hand. She saw the doctor pause after helping April up into the army truck, and she gratefully took his hand and climbed up after her. There were only grim faces to greet her when she stepped into the canvas-roofed deck, taking her position beside her sister.

'It's just us?' she asked. 'No other nurses to help these doctors?'

April shook her head and shuffled over for Dr. Evans to sit beside her. 'They couldn't spare any more, but nurses have landed with soldiers directly onto the beach today.'

'Did anyone see if the mail came today?' she asked. 'I meant to go back and check.'

April nodded. 'It came, but there was nothing for you. I'm sorry.'

Grace nodded and rubbed her hands together, still not used to the change in weather. It had been so wet her boot had disappeared into a mud puddle and her foot had come up without it on her way to the hospital this morning, and she hated to think how cold they'd get if they were forced to sleep out in the open. They'd all been told to start wrapping in newspaper now beneath their blankets, to stop the cold bite of nighttime from freezing them half to death. All she'd wanted was a letter from Teddy to keep her going, something to tell her that he was all right, but she hadn't heard a word from him since he'd left that night, posted to God only knew where. And she'd been too mortified to write to him first, unsure what to say after what had happened.

She held hands with April as the truck rumbled on and as children ran after them when they passed through town, calling out for chocolate and cigarettes, their little hands extended on skinny arms. She would usually have moved farther toward the back of the truck, calling back to them, but today felt solemn. Grace wondered how she, the nurse who was scared of blood, who'd made Eva laugh when they'd first met over her confession, had ended up volunteering to go to the front. She shuddered just thinking about what they might encounter.

She glanced at April, at the strong side profile and tight pull of her mouth, clearly deep in thought. All these years and months she'd slowly started to resent her sister; she'd resented her for telling her to stay at home and not become a nurse, for always being the mother, for making it clear she was the older sister, for telling her not to go on that date that night; and she still hadn't told her she was sorry. That she should have listened to her. That she wanted more than anything for her sister to take over and look after her again. But she couldn't, because April needed to live her own life without having to mother a sister who was barely eighteen months younger than she was. It was her turn to support her sister and show her that she could be there for her too.

'What is that?' April whispered beside her after they'd been bumping along the road for some time.

'The sound of war,' Dr. Evans muttered. 'We're getting close, ladies.'

Grace stared at April, holding her hand tighter as the sound of bullets being fired became louder, as the feeling in the air changed and everyone went deathly still in the truck.

'It's going to be hell out there, isn't it?' Grace whispered.

April had tears in her eyes, and Grace reached forward to brush her sister's cheeks as they started to slide down her face.

'We're going to get through this,' April whispered back. 'We're going to save lives, and we're going to be fine.'

Grace nodded as the truck lurched to a stop and someone yelled at them to get out. She went down right after Dr. Evans, relinquishing April's hand, and soldiers were waiting for them, holding guns. She stared at them, the enormity of what they were doing hitting hard as she eyed their rifles.

A bomb seemed to erupt around them, and Grace instinctively doubled over.

'Stay low!' a soldier yelled. 'It's crawling only on the beach, and get to a beach hut if you can. We need to save as many men as we can here before they're moved!'

The soldiers took the lead, and Grace, her sister, and four doctors followed, with more soldiers bringing up the rear. She ran low, holding her hat with one hand, her pack containing all the supplies she needed.

Ping!

She dropped to the ground as a shell whizzed past her helmet, her body shaking. Soon, earth gave way to sand, and Grace crawled beside her sister, trying to remember to breathe as she saw men on the ground up ahead, her helmet constantly sliding down. Shells were firing from every direction, her head pounding as loud as her heart as she frantically followed the soldiers and doctors.

'Nurse!'

April was beside Dr. Evans, so Grace stopped, hauling her pack off. She kept her head low as she took out morphine, fingers fumbling at the sight of the young man lying beside them, his body convulsing, covered in sand that made it almost impossible to know what was even wrong with him.

And then she saw a doctor bent low, his face covered in splatters of blood as he looked up, glasses foggy.

'We need to tourniquet it before he bleeds out!'

Grace's stomach heaved at the sight of the man's leg, in tatters below the knee, his foot gone completely. She scrambled to help the doctor, both fighting to tie it off tightly enough, forgetting the shells firing over their heads.

'Stop!' she screamed at the sky. 'Just stop!'

'Let's go.'

She looked down at the soldier writhing in agony, seeing the terror in his eyes.

'Leave him; come on!'

'Someone will come for you soon,' she cried, crawling away as he reached for her, breaking her heart as she left him.

The next man was just yards away, cradling his head, and she bent over and vomited almost instantly as she saw his eye socket, part of his face completely blown away. She reached for more morphine, wondering how it was ever going to be enough.

Grace had no idea of the time, no concept of minutes or hours, as they systematically crawled across the beach, finally making their way to one of the beach houses. She lay low, on her stomach, head to the side as she frantically tried to breathe. The beach smelled like death; the metallic taste of blood lingered in the back of her throat, her hands stained with it, the bodies strewed everywhere telling her their work would never be done.

She covered her head with her hands as more shells whizzed past, her heart still pounding. Then she saw a soldier, his hand moving, like a person in the ocean trying to get the attention of someone on land. Only he was on the sand, not in the water. He rolled over and then fell.

'We need to get to that soldier,' she said, blinking the dust from her eyes as she strained to see him.

'He's too far; we won't make it,' the doctor said, his glasses at an angle now. Another doctor crawled in, looking as exhausted as she felt.

Grace looked again, saw the man writhing, and made the decision to save him. She had enough morphine still, and she was going to make sure he at least got that.

She checked her pack and started to crawl, so low her face was covered in sand, praying the entire time she wasn't about to get hit herself.

'I'm coming!' she yelled, not sure if her voice could even be heard.

She crawled past a dead soldier, refusing to look at him, and after what felt like forever, she was finally there.

'I can't sit up; we need to stay low,' she said, rolling over to get her pack off. She kept her head tucked down as she reached inside it. She jabbed him with morphine and hauled at his shoulder to roll him over. 'What's happened to—'

Grace's voice died in her throat. Her heart seemed to stop for a second, the sound of the ocean roaring in her ears.

'*Teddy?*'

He cried out, not seeming to know who she was or what had happened.

'Can you see?' she gasped. 'What's happened to your eyes?'

He was pawing at them, frantically rubbing them now. 'I can't see anything!' he hollered. 'Why can't I see?'

Grace grabbed his hands and looked at him, could see shards of something in his eyes among all the blood. Then she moved to her hands and knees and shuffled down farther, inspecting the rest of his body. *Dammit.* His arm was bleeding badly, and there was a wound to his side that she was certain was a bullet entrance.

'Help!' she yelled, frantically looking for any of the doctors or a soldier or *someone*.

'Leave him! We need you over here!' someone called back from the hut.

'I can't see,' Teddy cried. 'Why can't I see?'

Grace wrapped her arms around him and held tight, cradling him, looking after him just like he'd looked after her the night he'd saved her.

'I'm not leaving you,' she whispered. 'I'm never, ever leaving you.'

She'd tried so hard to stop loving him, to not fall for him, to stop thinking about him—to honor her best friend's memory by never thinking about Teddy that way again. But the man she loved might die on a beach in the middle of nowhere, and she wasn't leaving his side, not even for a second.

She'd loved Poppy with all her heart, but she loved Teddy too.

'I'm here. You're going to be okay.'

Teddy's screams turned to tears, sobs that shook his entire body, and she doubled over him, holding him through every inch of his pain.

'Help!' she screamed. 'Please, *somebody* help!'

CHAPTER TWENTY-TWO

APRIL

'Here, use this on your eyes.'

April took the canteen from Harry and dropped a small amount of water onto her face, wiping with her fingertips. Every inch of skin on her body was gritty—even her mouth was filled with sand—and she took a grateful gulp of water before passing it back to him.

She looked out, still trying to catch her breath, finding it hard to believe what she'd just witnessed. Men in pieces, men shooting, men dying. *Men dead.* She hadn't seen Grace since a few minutes after they'd started down the beach, but she was trying not to think about her. Grace was smart, and she'd grown so much since Pearl Harbor; she was a grown woman in her own right, and she didn't need an overbearing sister watching over her any longer. She'd made that clear, and April knew in her heart it was right.

'They're going to try to bring men to us, but—'

April looked up as a whistling noise shot overhead, catching her attention, followed by a boom that sent her flying across the small room, slamming her into the wall.

Oh my God.

Her spine contracted like it had been snapped in half, her head flying back at the same time and cracking against the wall before she slipped to the floor. April tried to stand but couldn't, and she braced on all fours, stumbling forward. The roof had fallen in; she could see the blue sky above, and the room was filled with dust billowing around her.

'Harry!' she choked, coughing violently and clearing her throat. 'Harry!' she screamed this time, lurching forward. She stumbled and hit the ground before scrambling back up again.

She spun around, disorientated as she looked for him, greeted with nothing but debris and the screams and noises of war outside.

'Harry!' she screamed again, falling on the pile of roofing and other materials on the other side of the room. She dropped down low and started to scratch, clawing with her fingers, screaming his name over and over again.

'Harry!'

Nothing. There was no sound. No muffled cry. Nothing.

And then she heard a gasp. Or a *something* that sounded human.

Her head was spinning, eyes blinking furiously as she tried to see, coughing to clear her dust-clogged throat, her lungs feeling suffocated as she gasped for air.

'Harry! Harry!'

Then she saw his dark-brown hair, and she dug more furiously, throwing pieces of roof out of the way, digging violently to free him.

'Harry, speak to me! Harry, please,' she begged, clearing the space around his face and frantically parting the rest of the debris.

He opened his eyes, regaining consciousness, and she clawed until his entire body was exposed, her shoulders aching, fingers bleeding, head pounding.

When he was free, she fell back down, ear to his chest, listening to his heart and his lungs filling with air. But there was something sticking out of his leg.

'Harry, I need to . . . I . . .' Her voice trailed off. She needed to what?

He groaned and sat up, crying out as he tried to move his leg.

She touched his leg, looking at the wood sticking out of it, sucking back big breaths.

'We need to leave that there,' she said, nodding as if to accept her own decision. 'It's too dangerous to take out—you could bleed out—so I'm going to give you morphine and a tetanus shot to be safe, and then, and then we're, ah, we're going to find a way to get you out of here.'

Harry groaned. 'Are you'—he hissed out a breath—'hurt?'

She shook her head. 'No. I'm fine.'

She wasn't fine—her clothes were torn, she had grazes all over her skin, and her fingernails were bloody stumps—but she could still work, and she could breathe.

'Go and see,' he grunted, 'if there's anyone out there who needs you.'

April glanced at him, not wanting to leave him, but she knew he was right. She grabbed her pack but couldn't find Harry's, so she slung it over her shoulder and stepped out onto the sand again.

'Oh my God,' she gasped.

There was a soldier less than a few steps away, holding his stomach, writhing in pain, and as she got closer, she could see he was trying to stop his insides from falling out.

'Stay still—keep applying pressure,' she ordered, her own hands hovering, not sure what to do. She ducked when the incessant shelling sounded out again, holding her breath for a second before leaping into action the moment there was a pause in shooting. She knew better than to move a critical patient, but there was nothing else she could do; it was the only way to save him.

'I'm sorry,' she muttered. Hands tight under his armpits, she hauled him backward, gritting her teeth as she fought for each step, dragging a man so heavy she could barely move him an inch. When she finally got him to what was left of the hut, she set him down, her arms burning, hands cramping up as she collapsed for a moment, catching her breath.

'What's happened to him? What does he need—'

'His insides are falling out,' she cried. 'When he moves his hands, there'll be blood everywhere—I won't be able to see, I won't . . .'

'You can do this, April. I believe in you, and I can talk you through it. Come on.'

She took a deep breath and hauled the soldier back farther, toward where Harry was lying, propped up on his side now so he could see.

'Get your padding ready, anything you have left to wad inside of him, and your needle threaded.'

She scrambled through her pack, found the last of her surgical thread, and checked it was ready to use.

'Listen to me, and move fast, April. I'll be your eyes; you just need to follow my instructions,' Harry said, his voice raspy and telling her he was in pain, that each sentence was a struggle to get out.

'Oh God!'

The soldier's hands fell from his stomach, and she dropped beside him, watching as the blood spurted out and he went still, his parted lips no longer moaning in pain.

'Check the organs; tell me what you see.'

'It's his bowel,' she said, using the only piece of towel she had left to slow the blood loss. 'I can see it's torn . . . it's . . .'

'Sew it up quickly, as best you can,' Harry said. 'It'll be a mess, but it'll give him a chance to live. The surgeons can fix him up when he gets to a hospital—just do what you can.'

She didn't look up, just listened to Harry's words and let his calmness wash over her.

'Stitch fast, and then you need to sew his side up. Splash some alcohol over him.'

April's hands were steady now, her focus absolute as she finished the bowel, splashed the alcohol, removed the toweling, and then sewed up the side of the poor man. She was only grateful he hadn't regained consciousness.

'Leave some more morphine beside him, in case he wakes up, and go check if you're needed out there,' Harry said.

April checked her work and said a quick prayer for the soldier before jumping to her feet, dizzy as the room spun around her.

'You're going to make a fine doctor one day, April,' Harry rasped.

Panic mixed with pride as she glanced back at Harry and saw the look on his face, knew that he was speaking from the heart.

'I'll be back soon,' she said, and she grabbed her pack and dropped low to crawl back down the beach. 'I promise.'

She low-crawled her way around fallen men, some who'd already been treated and others who were already dead. There was movement in the other beach huts—she presumed the other doctors and possibly the battalion doctors had joined them—but it was screaming that caught her attention.

Is that Grace?

'Help me! Please, somebody help me!'

April lifted her head for a second and saw her sister, on her knees and calling frantically for help. It was only now there was a short lull in shelling that she'd been able to hear her.

She moved fast, crawling like a highly trained soldier, covering the ground quickly until she reached Grace's side. She grabbed her hand. 'What are you doing here? Why haven't you left him and moved on?'

'It's Teddy,' Grace sobbed. 'We can't leave him, April—I won't leave him.'

'Teddy?' She peered down at the dirty face, at frantic wide eyes that appeared not to see anything, filled with blood and shards of something. 'You're sure?' She couldn't even tell.

'You need to help me; we need to move him.'

She did a quick assessment, seeing the bullet wound. 'Come on—we need to get him back there,' she said, gesturing to what was left of the beach hut. 'Harry—I mean Dr. Evans—he'll know what to do.'

'I owe him, April. He saved my life, and now I need to save his,' Grace cried.

'What?'

'I should have listened to you, I should have let you take care of me, I should have . . .'

She had no idea what her sister was rambling about, but she did know they were going to lose Teddy if they didn't do something fast.

'Enough! Pull yourself together, would you?' April got hold of his upper half, fingers under his armpits, willing Grace to compose herself. 'Get his legs. We're going to have to make a run for it, or we'll never get him back there.'

Grace did as she was told, and April started to count.

'Three, two, *one*!' she shouted, and they hauled him up, tripping and stumbling as they tried to run. Bullets whooshed past, but April breathed a sigh of relief as she stepped backward into the house and—

'Grace!' she screamed.

Her sister's body jerked backward, her arm flying back as she dropped Teddy and fell.

'Grace!' she screamed again. She dropped Teddy's shoulders and jumped over him to get to her sister, then grabbed her by the other arm, hauling with all her might to drag her to safety.

Grace moaned but started to move, her feet stumbling as she fell into the open doorway.

'What happened? Who's in worse shape?' Harry yelled. 'Make the call, fast!'

April grabbed Grace and saw the hole from the bullet in her upper bicep, but it had gone straight through, which meant she wasn't in as much danger.

'Morphine,' she muttered, quickly getting out the syringe and administering it to her sister.

Then she left her and crouched over Teddy, ignoring his eyes for a moment to inspect his wound. 'There's no exit,' she said as she examined him. 'Bullet must be lodged there, and I can't tell what damage it's done.'

'Douse your hand in whatever alcohol you have left, and reach in. You need to get it out.'

She sucked back a breath and did what Harry said, plunging her fingers into his flesh as Teddy hollered, then went silent.

'I can't find it, I can't—'

'Breathe, April. Just breathe and concentrate. You'll feel the metal soon.'

She pushed farther, fingers deep inside him now, and then finally she felt it. 'What if I can't get it?'

'You will,' he said. 'There's no other way.'

Her fingers closed more tightly over the slippery bullet, and she tried three times to slide it out, finally succeeding on the fourth attempt. She threw the bloody bullet to the ground and started to panic.

'I can't do the stitches—I don't have anything left,' she cried, after searching her sister and seeing her pack wasn't with her. 'I can't let him die—I know this man—I have to save him.'

Harry was silent for a moment before yelling out, 'Your hair! Quickly—it's thick; it'll work. Pull out a strand and thread it.'

She knew it was insane, that it might not work, that it was stupidly unhygienic, but one look at Grace's face and she knew she had to try.

April yanked at her hair and quickly threaded the needle, surprised how easily it worked and how steady her hands still were. Teddy was crying out again now, his hands over his eyes, but she blocked everything else out and slowly stitched, then used another strand of hair to make sure it would hold.

'He's going to live,' she said, crawling over to her sister. She ripped at her skirt to tie around her bleeding arm. 'Teddy's going to live, Grace.'

April's body started to shake then, and she lowered herself down beside Grace and wrapped her arms around her as shock set in, as bullets continued to fire around them.

'He saved me twice, April,' Grace whispered. 'And you saved me too.'

'He saved you twice?' she asked. 'What else did Teddy save you from?'

But Grace only held her tighter, curling up against her like a baby to her mother.

'You need help in here?' someone yelled out.

April burst into tears as battalion doctors appeared.

'We're going to make it, Grace,' April whispered. 'We're going to make it out of here, and Teddy is too.'

CHAPTER TWENTY-THREE
EVA

'I'm here, girls. You're both here with me,' Eva said, sitting in between Grace and April's beds as they finally stirred.

'Eva?' April croaked.

'Hello, sleepyhead,' Eva joked, leaning over and stroking her friend's hand. 'I was starting to worry I'd lost you both there for a bit.'

'What happened? How did we get back?' April asked, and Eva helped her to sit up and held a glass of water for her to sip.

'You were lucky,' Eva said, holding her as she coughed and tried to sip more water. 'We were so full that the hospital had closed to more patients, and then the ambulance arrived with you and Grace inside.'

'Grace? She's—'

'Alive,' Eva interrupted. 'Right here, on the other side of me. I hear you did a good job stitching her up.'

'And Harry? What happened to Harry?' April gasped. 'And Teddy, did he make it? Where's Teddy?'

Eva placed a hand on April's chest and looked into her eyes. 'Listen to me, April. Teddy is alive, but his injuries are serious. What you did for him on the beach, you saved his life, and I only know that because Dr. Evans—I mean your Harry—told me.'

She saw the change in April, the way she relaxed into the bed the moment she heard everyone had survived.

'And the other soldier—there should have been another with us—he was hurt pretty bad, and I had to—'

'Sew him up yourself without a doctor helping you,' Eva said, laughing. 'We all know what you did, April. You've been out of it for almost a day, and someone has been telling everyone how incredible his favorite little nurse was.'

April's cheeks flushed a deep pink. 'He told everyone?'

'He did,' she said. 'Before they even managed to knock him out and pull that stake of wood from his leg. His other injuries ended up being minor, so he'll be back on his feet in no time.'

'Thank you for looking after us,' April said, and Eva had to hold back her own tears as she saw them glisten in April's. 'If I'd lost Grace, if anything had happened to her . . .'

'But it didn't,' Eva said firmly. 'We've all lost enough, don't you think? And I'm sure Poppy is up there looking down on us, trying her best to keep us all safe.'

They sat for a moment, and Grace started to stir. Eva took it as her cue to leave; she had less than six hours until her shift started again, and she still wanted to check on Art before she hurried back to her tent to sleep.

She bent and pressed a kiss to April's forehead. 'I'll be back to check up on you soon.'

'Eva?' April said, her fingers catching Eva's arm to stop her from moving.

'What is it?'

'Grace said something when I was working on Teddy—that he'd saved her twice and now she had to save him. Do you know what she was talking about?'

Eva took a deep breath and glanced over at Grace, still asleep, her blonde hair fanned out across the pillow.

'It's not my story to tell, April. You'll have to ask her yourself.'

Soraya M. Lane

She squeezed her hand and left the Bellamy sisters to recover, relieved that she hadn't had to say goodbye to another friend. She'd only just emerged from the dark cloud of Charlie's death, and Poppy's, and she didn't ever want to be sucked back under.

Eva hurried into the other ward to check on Art, knowing he'd be awake still, waiting for her to say goodbye before she left for the night. Sure enough, the moment she tiptoed down the row of beds, his twinkling eyes met hers.

'Sorry it's so late,' she whispered, not wanting to wake the other men.

Art's hand found hers, and he pulled her closer. 'Your friends are okay?' he asked.

'Yes,' she whispered. 'They're going to make it. April, Grace, and Teddy, they're all alive.'

She started to cry then, the exhaustion from so many hours on her feet working, fighting to save lives, and the desperation of nursing her friends and praying they'd survive sending a huge wave of emotion through her.

'Hey, don't cry,' Art murmured. 'You've just told me everything's going to be fine.'

'I can't, I can't lose anyone else again,' she sobbed. 'I don't even know how I lived through what happened before, what—'

'You're the strongest person I know, Eva. You just need a good cry.'

The tears flowed as Art pulled her closer, his hand on her back now, drawing her in against him until she was curled to his body, her leg against his, her cheek to his chest.

All those months she'd never given in to her pain, but in Art's arms, she cried like a baby.

'Shhh,' he murmured, cradling her and kissing her hair. 'You're not going to lose anyone else; everything's going to be fine.'

'It's not,' she whispered, raising her head and looking into his eyes. 'Art, I've seen the papers. You're to be sent home soon.' She tucked her head back to his chest, whispering, 'I'm about to lose you.'

308

He went quiet then, his fingers still circling her back, stroking her, his mouth still against her hair, but as she slowly drifted to sleep, he never said another word.

―――― ◦৩৴~৶৹ ――――

'I'll bet your mother will be happy to have you home for Christmas,' Eva said as she pushed Art's wheelchair out of the hospital building and into the cool air outside. A shiver ran through her body, but she ignored it, not about to let a spot of cold weather dampen her spirits. It had been a week since her friends had arrived back, and they were both recovering well, but she needed to get away for the afternoon. Away from the stench of death in the hospital, the echoes of young men whose lives had been snatched away, and the reality that soon she was going to have to face nursing without Art to brighten up her day.

'It's going to be hard leaving here.'

'Hardly.'

'I'm serious.' The gruff tone of his voice made her slow.

'You're not looking forward to going home? To getting away from this godforsaken place?' She laughed. 'Where it's possible to fry like an egg in summer and freeze to death in winter?'

'Stop this damn chair!' he swore.

Eva froze. 'Art? What's wrong?'

She could see his shoulders rising and falling, could tell how angry he was even though she had no idea what she'd said to make him so mad. Eva slowly moved around the chair.

'Art?'

'You think I want to leave you?' he asked, shaking his head. 'You made me want to live again, Eva. Without you, I can't see the goddamn point of it all.'

She opened her mouth and shut it again. 'You don't want to go because of me?'

He glared at her. 'For an intelligent woman you can be as stupid as a donkey sometimes.'

Eva laughed when she saw a smile spread across Art's mouth, finding it impossible not to giggle. Soon they were laughing together, and she went back to pushing him, wanting to get farther away from the hospital.

'You know,' she teased, 'donkeys can be highly intelligent.'

'Don't pretend you know anything about donkeys,' he muttered. 'But I am sorry I compared you to one.'

'For the record, I'm going to miss you too,' she said, pleased that he couldn't see her. She doubted the words would have come so easily if he could have. 'I don't have a lot to look forward to when I get home, and being here is, well, it is what it is.'

'I need you to take me down there.' He pointed. 'To the village. I want to go into the Arab quarter.'

She shrugged, not fazed about having to walk so far. Until she realized how much mud they were going to encounter. 'Ah, I'm not so sure I can get you all the way there. I think we'd end up with the wheelchair stuck and—'

'Fine, just take us somewhere we can stop, then.'

Eva didn't bother telling him off for being so short with her; she just started to push, liking the feel of her arms burning as she propelled his chair forward. He could work it himself now, and he did through the ward and inside, but she liked to push him outside. It gave her something to do, and it was easier on him.

'Here's fine,' he ordered.

Eva stopped pushing and walked around the chair, her arms folded. 'What's put you in such a grumpy mood today? You're almost like the Art I met all those months ago. Do you remember him?'

He grunted. 'Oh, I remember.'

'Well?'

He sighed. 'Tell me what your plan is when you eventually get sent home. Are you going back to your father?'

She stared at the ground, not wanting to think about it. Everything had changed for her when Charlie had died. *Everything*. Tears clung to her lashes as she gulped down the ugly truth, hating how scared she was, hating the shell of a person she'd become after losing everything. She wanted to be that girl on the USS *Solace*, the girl with a future, the girl with a fiancé, the girl who didn't have to be scared of her monster of a father ever again.

'Eva?'

She let out her breath and swallowed, blinking away her tears. 'I honestly don't know. I've written to my mother, but she'll only say that my father is the head of the household and whatever he says goes.' She cleared her throat and raised her eyes. 'I wouldn't go back to a house with him in it for anything.'

'Just because your father earns the money in your household doesn't give him the right to lay his hands on you or your mother,' Art fumed. 'He doesn't deserve to ever see you again, and neither does she for allowing it to happen!'

'Please don't worry—I should never have told you in the first place,' she said, trying to disguise the wobble in her voice with a small smile. 'I can stay with the Bellamys in Oregon for a bit; they've been so kind to me, and I'm sure I'll be able to scrape together enough money to—'

'I wanted to go into town for a reason today,' Art said, folding his arms across his chest. 'Go and pick me some of that grass, would you? A few decent bits.'

Eva laughed and studied his face. 'Grass? We go from me opening up to you about my family to *grass*?'

'Goddammit—just do it for me, would you, Eva?'

She saluted him and went off to pick the grass, bemused. At least it gave her a moment to collect her thoughts.

She had no idea what was going on with Art, and she wasn't about to ask. She tried to remember Charlie then, but she couldn't see his face clearly, as if a whole lot of memories were blurring together and stopping her from seeing his features.

Eva bent to pick some grass and returned to Art, holding it out. 'Here you go,' she said.

'Turn around, and walk a few steps away,' he said.

Eva obliged, turning her back and wandering, staring up at the sky, which looked gray and swirling, like it was about to unleash another torrent of rain on them.

'Can I look now?' she asked.

There was no reply, so she kept waiting.

'Art?'

'Turn around,' he said in a low voice, and she slowly did as he said.

'What's going on? What are you up to?' she asked. 'You're not about to play a trick on me, are you?'

Art laughed, but it sounded like more of a grunt. 'No tricks. Just come closer, and sit on my knee.'

Eva's face was on fire as she slowly moved closer, carefully lowering herself to his knee, nervous all of a sudden. 'Are you sure about this? I don't want to hurt you . . . I . . .' Her words disappeared as she saw the look in his eyes, the change in him. 'Art?'

'I'm scared,' he said, and she could see the tears in his eyes, the hint that he wasn't as strong as he looked sometimes. 'I'm so scared about my life and what it'll be like going home, the look on everyone's faces when they see me like this. Half a man instead of the great pilot that left home.' He sucked in a sharp breath and cleared his throat. 'I'm scared of what kind of life I can even have.'

'The people who care about you, they won't see you as anything other than yourself,' she told him. 'They will only care that you've come home alive.'

'Eva, you saved my life, and somewhere in between being a complete idiot to you and now, I fell in love with you.'

Eva froze. *He's in love with me?*

'You don't have to worry about what to do after the war, Eva, because I want to look after you.' He chuckled and gestured at where his leg should be. 'I'm not a whole man—I know that—but I can still look after you. I can make sure you never have to see your father again. It's time for me to look after you, for you to come home to Oregon with *me*.'

She blinked back her tears, but it was no use, and they fell anyway as Art raised a hand to her cheek, his palm warm against her skin.

'I'll be fine, Art. You don't need to say that,' she whispered, trying to be brave.

'I've never wanted to look after someone so badly in my entire life, Eva,' he whispered. 'You've made me realize that I'm not completely useless. I might not be able to walk or fly again, but protecting you, *caring* for you, that's one thing I can still do.'

She laughed softly. 'You have no idea how much it means to hear you say that, to see you finally understand how capable you are still.'

Art smiled back at her, his voice low when he finally spoke. 'Eva, I want you to be my wife.'

She exhaled. 'Your wife?'

'Eva, will you marry me?' he asked, taking her hand and holding out a crude ring made from grass tied together, which made her burst out laughing.

'Art! You can't. I mean—'

'I can,' he said firmly. 'Eva, don't leave me hanging—will you marry me?'

'It's not because you feel sorry for me? Or because you think you owe me?' she asked, needing to know as she studied his face, searching for answers.

'No,' Art murmured. He lifted his face and tucked his fingers beneath her chin now, slowly bringing her mouth closer to his. She breathed in just as his lips touched hers, whispering against her as he kissed her again, then again, her skin tingling as his hand slid across and stroked her hair, so gentle that she could only just feel it.

'I think I fell in love with you the day you saved me, Eva.'

'You sure had a funny way of showing it,' she muttered, laughing as she kissed him again, lost in the feeling of his lips against hers.

'I'm only going to ask you one last time, Eva. Will you marry me?'

She smiled against his mouth as he slipped the ring on her finger. 'Yes, Arthur. I will marry you.'

They both laughed, and the wheelchair tipped as she leaned too heavily into him. Eva leaped to her feet and corrected it before it fell, smiling down at the pretend ring on her finger and then at Art.

'I want to make you happy, Eva. You deserve so much.' He smiled. 'You never, ever have to be frightened about seeing your father, ever again. I promise I'll always look after you.'

She dropped carefully to his lap again, tucking her arms around his neck.

'Thank you, Art,' she whispered.

He chuckled as he claimed her mouth again. 'You're welcome.'

She pushed gently at his chest, stopping him. 'Art, I need to tell you something.'

He frowned. 'Don't say you can't marry me.' Art laughed, but his face turned solemn again when she didn't laugh back. 'How bad is it?'

'I just . . . well, I've told you how hard it was for me losing Charlie, how much I loved him, and even though he's not here anymore, I've never stopped loving him, and I don't think I ever will. I need you to know that.'

Art's hand was warm against her cheek as he smiled up at her. 'You don't have to forget your Charlie to marry me, Eva.'

'Thank you,' she whispered, her voice breaking as she stared into his eyes. 'Thank you a hundred times over for understanding.'

'I'm the one who needs to be saying thank you,' he whispered back. 'You saved me, Eva. You managed to make me feel like a man again, and I'll be thanking you for that for the rest of my life.'

CHAPTER TWENTY-FOUR

APRIL

'Grace?' April whispered, gently shaking her sister's shoulder. 'Grace, wake up.'

She watched as Grace stirred, eventually moving and opening her eyes, her slow blink making it obvious just how tired she was.

'Is it Teddy?' Grace mumbled. 'What's happened?'

April placed her hand on Grace's shoulder again. 'Nothing's happened to Teddy, Grace. Everything's fine.'

Well, as fine as it could be in the middle of a war zone. April couldn't imagine everything being *actually* fine ever again after everything they'd been through.

'I'm worried about you, Grace. You've hardly left Teddy's side, and I know you feel as if it's your duty to—'

'It *is* my duty,' Grace said, shrugging April's hand away and moving closer to Teddy's bed.

'Grace, you've barely left his bedside since we were brought back, and there's only so long you're going to be allowed to keep behaving like this.' April lowered her voice. 'He's not your husband, and some of the nurses have already been asking questions.'

Grace looked up, and her glare was fierce. 'Let them ask questions. I don't care.'

'Look,' April said, finding a stool and dragging it closer to sit beside her sister. 'We all love Teddy, we went through so much with him when he lost Poppy, and he's always been so good to us, but there's nothing more you can do for him.'

'He can't see, April,' Grace said. 'I want to be here for him, to help him.'

'Like he helped you?' she asked, pausing before adding, 'I keep remembering your words, you telling me that he saved you not once but twice.'

Grace was quiet, her gaze still fixed on Teddy's sleeping form.

'Grace?'

When Grace turned this time, there were tears sparkling in her eyes. 'Eva told you, didn't she?'

April shook her head. 'Eva hasn't told me anything. But I know something happened.'

Grace's shoulders heaved up and then fell. 'That night, when I went out with the British soldier, Teddy was there.'

'I know. I remember how funny you were after seeing him.'

'Eva found him in the tent with me; she walked in on us together.'

'Oh, Grace, oh no, I—'

'No! It wasn't like that. He'd carried me home and put me to bed. He was so kind, so gentle with me, but the soldier, Peter, he, he . . .' Grace's breath shuddered from her. 'He tried to rape me, April, and all I could think was that you were right. If I'd only listened to you, if I'd only been more sensible like you, I would never have ended up in that situation.'

April's heart was thudding as she listened and tried not to over-react. How dare he! How dare any man treat her sister that way, or any woman for that matter!

'Grace, I'm so sorry. I wish I'd known,' she said softly. 'I wish there was something I could have done.' How could Grace not have told her?

'I didn't want your help. I didn't even want you to know. It was bad enough that Teddy had been witness to it.'

'You've always loved him, haven't you?' April asked. 'I mean, I always knew you had a crush on him, but it's something more, isn't it?'

Grace had shuffled even closer to Teddy, her fingers closing over his hand as he slept. 'I tried so hard, after Poppy died, not to think about him like that. And when he told me that he thought of me like a little sister, I knew it was never going to happen, but that night he saved me, the way he treated me . . .'

Grace never finished her sentence, and April bent to hug her, circling her arms around her from behind. 'We're in a war, Grace. Nothing is for certain anymore, but it's been long enough. If you and Teddy love each other, then you have my blessing.'

April kissed the top of her sister's head as Grace held her hands, holding her back.

'But Grace, I need you to know they're moving us. We don't have much longer here, so you have to be prepared. If your arm's healed enough, you might have to move with us and leave him behind.'

She backed away then and went to do her rounds, anxious to finish her work for the day so she could go and find Harry. He was on the mend and wanting to get back to work, but he still had to be cleared for duty again, and she suspected he'd be asked to rest at least a few more days before returning to any doctor duties.

Three hours later she was completely perplexed when she went to Harry's bed and found it made up with no one in it. And none of his belongings or any other evidence of him ever being there seemed to exist either.

'Are you looking for me?'

She turned and found the man in question standing in the doorway.

'Well, yes, I was, but it seems you've discharged yourself.'

He shrugged. 'They're far too conservative here. It's only my leg that's damaged.'

She looked down at the leg in question, pleased to see that he was at least using a stick to help him walk.

'When are you cleared to work again?' she asked.

'Officially, not for another week. But I decided to go into the village and see if any of the locals needed treatment.'

He smiled, and it made her laugh, the look on his face almost comical.

'And how did that go?'

'I've been run off my feet all day! I'm exhausted.' They both laughed together, and Harry surprised her by offering her his arm. 'Would you join me for dinner?'

'Tonight?'

He nodded. 'Tonight. I've been asked to join a local family for dinner so they can thank me, and they asked if there was anyone I'd like to bring.'

'I'd love to join you.'

She took his arm, happy to spend time in his company. 'You're sure they won't mind you bringing me? They might have preferred another doctor.'

He laughed as they walked side by side. 'I told them about a fearless nurse who saved soldiers on the beach,' Harry said, leaning in as he spoke, as if his words were just for her. 'They wanted to meet this incredible woman, especially when I told them she was going to be a doctor one day.'

Now it was April laughing. 'You're just saying that.'

He shook his head, and his laughter died away. 'I'm not, April. What you did that day, the way you worked under conditions that would have tested the most competent of doctors, was incredible.' He pushed the door to the hospital open, and they both walked out, the cool blast sending goose bumps rippling across her skin almost instantly.

'I promise I'll do everything I can to teach you, April. Because one day, if it's what you want, you'll be an amazing doctor.'

They walked in silence the rest of the way, but April's head was far from silent. What had happened with Dr. Grey had made her feel silly for ever believing she could be a doctor, but hearing Harry tell her she could do it was making her believe all over again.

'Welcome! Welcome!'

The family was waiting to greet them outside their hut when they arrived, and April smiled and waved back, wishing she'd brought gifts with her. But they flocked around Harry as if he were the gift, the children eager to walk beside him, grabbing hold of him and escorting him until the man of the house shooed them away and they scattered in different directions.

'They seem to love you,' April whispered.

'I was kind to them; that's all,' he replied with a wink. 'Things that have bothered them for so long can be so simple for someone like me to treat, but they're so grateful that I can ease their suffering. You saw it firsthand the day you helped me, just what a difference we can make.'

'Come!' the woman said, opening her arms and showing off a smile that was missing two teeth at the side, clearly a result of Harry pulling them out to relieve an abscess, judging by how raw and red her gums looked. She pointed to the table, and they obliged as children peeked out from the tiny kitchen area to watch them.

April smiled as Harry waved them over, blowing a kiss to a young girl and giving two of the boys pretend punches as they dodged around him and laughed.

'Do you have nieces or nephews at home?' April asked, realizing how little she knew about Harry.

'Yes,' he said. 'All three of my sisters are older than me, and they have six children between them.'

'Explains why you're so good with these little ones.'

Everyone in the house was smiling at them, and before she knew it, as the smell of vegetables and spices filled the air, she was being shown all the things Harry had done during the day. More villagers came inside and showed her their mouths or feet, one of the children with an arm bandaged, all wanting to pay their respects to him.

'You're a good man, Harry,' April said, when the house was almost empty again and they were being served yet more food.

'We grew up very privileged, but my father was determined that we would understand the concept of giving back,' he said. 'He was a doctor, too, and we used to help him run a free clinic every month. Mothers would line up for hours on end to see him, and his doctor friends would laugh at what a waste of time it was to give up his time for the poor, but he didn't care. He did it every year until he retired.'

'I think I'd like your father very much.'

Harry met her gaze. 'I have a feeling he'd like you too.'

They thanked their host for their meals, but as April went to take her first mouthful, not sure what she was eating but loving the smell of it, Harry caught her eye again.

'When all this is over, when things settle down, I'd like you to meet my family, April.'

She couldn't help the grin that took over her lips, and she nodded as she brought her fingers to her mouth, scooping up the food as she'd been shown the first time she'd eaten with a local family.

April ate and listened to Harry laugh and attempt to learn local words, loving the sound of his hearty laugh and the way he seemed to fit so easily into any situation. He'd been a good friend to her—she would never forget that—and maybe, just maybe when the war was over, it might turn into something more.

When it was finally time to go, they said their goodbyes, and April happily took Harry's arm when he offered it, walking in the dark with only the moon to guide them back to camp.

'Harry?' she asked.

He met her gaze, looking down at her, and she could make out his smile even in the half light.

She stopped walking and touched her hand to his shoulder as he stopped beside her, then swallowed her fears and stood on tiptoe to bravely press a kiss to his lips. He was still for a moment before his arms circled gently around her, his mouth moving against hers.

'Thank you,' she whispered, before lowering herself back to her heels again.

'For what?'

'For tonight, for believing in me, for showing me what makes a great doctor.' She caught his hand and leaned into him. 'For everything.'

Harry tucked her against his side as they started to walk again, pressing a kiss to the top of her head as they moved in silence. They'd spent the evening sharing a meal with strangers, and yet it had been one of the best nights of her life.

———— ⚬⚮⚬ ————

Only hours after dinner, April lay curled up in her bed with newspapers stuffed around her as insulation as she shivered to stay warm. At one point during summer, they'd had to stop taking the patients' temperatures during the day because the thermometers always ran too high due to the scorching weather, and yet now they were so cold she was convinced she'd wake up with part of her body frozen like an icicle.

'I thought I was going to lose you both,' Eva said, her voice barely a whisper in the dark. 'That day, when you never came back and we were inundated with casualties, I honestly thought I was never going to see you again.'

April was grateful for the blanket of darkness as tears welled in her eyes. She wasn't sure if Grace was asleep already, but it had been her greatest fear that day too.

'When we were waiting on the beach, I thought it was the end too,' she admitted. 'I was frozen there with Grace and Teddy on one side and Harry on the other, and I didn't think any of us were going to make it back.'

'I remember holding Teddy's hand, before I passed out, and wondering what I was going to tell Poppy when we arrived in heaven,' Grace said, her voice washing over April as she lay there, listening. 'I felt so guilty holding his hand, but I just didn't want to let go.'

'We've all lost too much,' Eva said. 'Why can't someone see what we're losing and just stop all this bloodshed? I'm so sick of it, of the loss, of all those men dying and blown to pieces every day.'

April listened, feeling the same but not sure what to say. She wondered the same thing, sometimes thought that if only the powers that be could see what it was like at the front line, what these men were actually going through, they'd see how fruitless it all seemed.

'How's Teddy?' Eva asked.

There was a long pause before Grace answered. 'He's broken. There's no other word for him.'

'Arthur was broken, too—don't forget that,' Eva said, her voice cutting through the otherwise silent night air. 'He was so badly broken I never thought anyone could put him back together again.'

'And now?' April asked.

Eva's laugh was warm. 'He actually asked me to marry him the other day.'

'He what?' April gasped. 'How many days ago? I can't believe you've kept it a secret!'

'Three days ago,' Eva whispered.

April shut her eyes, smiling to herself as she thought about Eva and Arthur. He'd been such an ass in the beginning, but she'd seen for herself the way he looked at her friend now, the way he cared about her.

'Congratulations,' she finally said. 'I'm so happy for you. Will you marry before he leaves?'

Silence greeted her for a moment before Eva answered. 'I think so. He knows about my father, about how complicated it is for me.'

April nodded despite the dark, wondering if she would be the only one of the three of them to move on to the new hospital. It would be strange without her sister and Eva, but she wasn't going to dwell on it. Since they'd plunged headfirst into the war, she'd come to realize that nothing ever turned out as she expected.

As she shut her eyes and tried to sleep, she heard Grace sniffling quietly to herself and recognized the sound of her crying. After their mother had passed, Grace had cried every night, and April had always done her best to comfort her, preferring to look after someone else rather than give in to her own emotion. For so long she'd blamed Grace for the burden of having to mother her, but she knew the truth was that she'd taken on the role as much for herself as her sister.

April pushed her covers back and rose, then slipped into bed beside Grace, ready to resume that role again, and scooted her body tight against her sister's warm frame, wrapping her arms around her as her slender body shook.

She didn't know if Grace's tears were for Teddy or what they'd been through or who they'd lost, but it didn't matter. Her sister needed her, and she would hold her all night if she had to.

CHAPTER TWENTY-FIVE

GRACE

'Grace, is that you?'

Grace leaped to her feet and leaned over Teddy, grabbing his hand as he spoke.

'Yes! Teddy, can you see me?'

He blinked, and she watched as he turned his head, frowning slightly. 'I can see you, but you're very blurry. It's like I'm looking through thick glass or peering through rain or something.'

She let out a breath she hadn't even known she was holding. 'You've been in and out of consciousness for over a week, Teddy,' she said, still standing close and squeezing his hand. 'Your eyes were so filled with debris, but I sat and removed every piece myself.'

He grunted. 'I know. I kept waking and hearing you, but I couldn't see you.'

'The doctor was worried you'd never regain your sight.'

He pushed himself up, and she quickly rearranged his pillows, trying to make him comfortable; then she reached for his water and helped him with the straw. She'd surprised even herself with how strong she'd been, determined to tend to Teddy herself no matter how gory the procedure.

'Do you want food? You must be so hungry, and I'll get the doctor to come and check you to—'

Teddy's hand closed around her wrist, and she stopped talking, her heart racing at his touch.

'Thank you, Grace,' he said, his unsteady eyes searching hers. 'Thank you for saving me. I'd have died that day without you.'

Grace opened her mouth, wanting to tell him he was wrong, to pretend like it wasn't a big deal, but the second she did, her throat clogged and she could only sob, tears falling down her cheeks in big ugly plops as she collapsed over him, crying as he held her, his arms warm and firm around her shoulders.

'I couldn't lose you, Teddy. It was like being back there; all I could think of was Poppy and that day, that day . . .' Her voice trailed off, and she tried to catch her breath.

'Shhh,' he whispered. 'You were so brave. You saved me, Grace. No one else would have come for me.'

She knew she'd saved him, because she'd been determined not to leave that beach without him no matter what happened, but hearing the words, knowing how grateful he was, only amplified her emotion.

'You're not just little Grace Bellamy anymore, are you?' He chuckled. 'You've become quite a fine nurse.'

She laughed and finally raised her head. 'Only it wasn't me; it was my sister who stitched you back together that day on the beach.'

His smile melted something inside of her. 'But it wasn't your sister who held me and stopped me from bleeding out while shells whizzed past our heads, was it?'

Grace stared down at him, wiping the tears from her cheeks as she studied Teddy's face.

'When you told me, that night in your tent, that I didn't need to protect you from what I was going through, you were right.'

'I couldn't lose you too, Teddy,' she whispered.

'I know,' he whispered as she fell back down, shoulders heaving again as his arms circled her once more. 'I know.'

———— ❧ ❧ ————

Hours later, she woke to the sensation of someone stroking her hair. Grace slowly lifted her head and licked her dry lips, surprised to find that the firm pillow beneath her head hadn't been her bed but Teddy.

'How long have I been asleep?' she asked.

He chuckled and shrugged. 'I didn't have the heart to wake you, but when I started to lose feeling in my arm, I thought it was time.'

She quickly touched her hair and wiped her cheeks, old tears leaving her skin feeling dry.

'I'm sorry—I don't know what came over me.'

'Perhaps the fact you've been sitting with me for over a week and you're exhausted?' he asked. 'Because that's what your sister told me.'

Grace groaned. 'April saw me like that?'

He smiled. 'Honey, everyone saw you like that, but no one had the heart to move you.'

'What else did they say?' she asked as Teddy's fingers started to stroke against her arm.

'That everyone's moving on to a new hospital, and that I'll be heading home soon to recover.'

Grace gulped. That was what she'd been afraid of.

'I don't want you to go,' she whispered.

Teddy's hand lifted, and she sighed when his palm touched her face, pushing her cheek against him as his eyes met hers. 'I don't want to leave you either.'

She smiled as she saw the way he was looking at her, truly looking at her, and knew from his gaze that his sight had improved yet again.

'Teddy, I know you said you thought of me like a little sister; I know you were Poppy's sweetheart, and that it's inappropriate, but . . .' She frowned at the look on his face. 'What?' she asked. 'What's so funny?'

He leaned forward, his palm still against her cheek, his mouth warm as it closed over hers in a long, slow kiss that left every part of her tingling.

'You're as far from a little sister to me as remotely possible,' he muttered.

She opened her mouth and laughed. 'But you said . . . in Hawaii, you said—'

'That was before I'd had time to grieve the woman I loved, before I saw you like this,' he said. 'You've changed, Grace. You're not the girl I used to know.'

She swallowed. 'I'm not?'

'No,' he whispered as he cupped her head and gently pulled her down, his lips finding hers again and tracing back and forth against them. 'No, you're not.'

She sat up, hand to her mouth as she glanced over her shoulder and saw other soldiers watching them, some whistling at the kiss they'd just witnessed, and her cheeks burned.

'What would you say if I told you we needed to pretend we were married? So I can come home and nurse you?'

He raised a brow at her. 'Married?'

She nodded. 'I'll find rings, and we need to pretend like, ah, that I thought you were dead, but that we've just been reunited.'

He laughed. 'Fine, I'll pretend to be married to you, but you might find it easier to use your recovery as an excuse. April told me you were shot trying to drag me to safety? Is that what happened to your arm?'

Grace shrugged as if it were no big deal, even though the sound of the bullet whirring toward her and driving into her flesh was something she'd never forget for as long as she lived. And she still had her arm heavily bandaged, and it hurt to so much as wiggle her fingers. He was probably right; she'd most likely not be cleared to keep serving anyway.

'Are you sure Poppy wouldn't hate us?' she asked, needing to see his face when she asked him the question. 'I've felt so guilty ever since the day she died, that it was me you saved, that it was me in your arms instead of her.'

Teddy found her hand and linked her fingers with his. 'Poppy was your best friend, Grace. She would have wanted you to live, and I know she would have wanted you to be happy.'

Grace bent low, her forehead to Teddy's as she breathed deep and let his words wash over her.

'Can you see me properly?' she asked.

'Almost,' he whispered. 'But you could be any pretty nurse, for all I know.'

Grace swatted at him, but even half-blind he still managed to catch her hand and pull her down for another kiss as the beds around them erupted into laughter and clapping.

'Grace!' she heard, recognizing her sister's sharp scold. 'Get off that bed right now!'

She slowly turned, red faced as she found her sister standing with her arms full of equipment and a horrified look on her face.

But then she looked down at Teddy, and they both burst out laughing, not caring who saw them. And instead of obeying her sister, she just shrugged and dropped a final kiss to Teddy's lips before slowly extracting herself from his bed. She didn't care who told her off or what kind of trouble she got into; she'd almost sacrificed her life that day on the beach, on the front line, and whoever decided to scold her would be reminded of exactly how dedicated to the cause she'd been.

She glanced at Teddy, seeing the full-of-life man he usually was, not the man in a hospital bed who'd had his eyes bandaged for a week, whose eyes had been so full of debris that the doctors had told her not to bother trying to remove it all.

She'd saved him, and right now, that was all she cared about. She'd always loved Teddy, from the moment she'd first laid eyes on him, and she wasn't going to feel guilty about it for a day longer, not after everything they'd been through.

Not bad for a girl who was reduced to tears at the sight of blood on her first week on the job.

CHAPTER TWENTY-SIX

Eva

'Look what Harry managed to find for us,' April said as she passed out Hershey's chocolate, then winked as she slid Eva an extra piece. 'It's his wedding present to you both, but I've just given you Art's piece too!'

Eva took the chocolate and opened it, grinning at April. 'What he doesn't know won't hurt him. I love the man, but I'm not sharing this with him!'

She popped the chocolate onto her tongue and savored the taste, even though it wasn't quite as delicious as she'd expected. Eva sighed. Since the war, nothing had tasted the same, but still it was nice.

'I can't believe it's your wedding day,' Grace said, opening her own chocolate and sitting down beside Eva.

They were gathered near the hospital, in a clearing that had been deemed safe enough for them to meet for the ceremony. Art had insisted he make his own way despite her protests, so she'd walked with the girls, trying to quell her nerves.

'I can't believe it either,' she whispered. 'All I keep thinking is that he'll change his mind. That he'll realize what a mistake he's making.'

'Mistake?' Grace laughed and pushed Eva's hand toward her. 'Eat the rest of the chocolate, and stop thinking silly thoughts.'

'She's right,' April said. 'He'd be a fool not to marry you.'

Eva unwrapped the second piece of chocolate and took it out. 'There's another reason I think he might not want to marry me,' she said, taking a deep breath before bravely looking up at her friends.

They both sat silently and looked back at her.

'I'm not going home with him.'

Grace spluttered on her chocolate. 'You're not *what*?'

April nodded as if she understood, and Eva cleared her throat, raising her voice this time. 'I'm not going home with Art,' she repeated. 'I lost my way after Charlie—it was like I forgot who I was and what was important to me—but I can't go back with him.'

'Why not?' Grace asked.

'Because I'm a nurse, and I'm a damn good one,' Eva said, wadding up the chocolate wrapper. 'I don't want to go home when there are so many men on the front line who need me. It's just not right.'

Grace's face changed, her smile fading. 'So you think I'm a coward for choosing to go home, then?'

Eva shook her head and reached for Grace's hand, hating how stiff it felt. 'No,' she said softly. 'I think you're wonderful, Grace. You've been a great friend to me, and you're so brave, but you've never loved nursing like I have. It's all I wanted to do, and it still is. I need to do this.'

Grace's hand softened, and her friend's fingers slowly clasped hers back. 'I know I said I would pretend to be married to Teddy to go home, but—'

'Grace, you took a bullet that day on the beach. You're injured, and you have every right to go home to recover,' April said, and Eva had to laugh at the way they'd fallen back into their old ways. Only this time she was almost certain that Grace liked it. 'I saw that bullet hit you. In fact, I see it every time I close my eyes. You're one of the bravest nurses I know.'

'Even if she is still scared of blood?' Eva teased, receiving a swat from Grace that had her ducking out of reach.

'Eva,' April said, her tone suddenly an octave lower. 'Here he comes.'

Eva slowly turned, her pulse quickening as she saw Art, pushing his own wheels with Harry walking beside him. She gave him a little wave as his eyes caught hers.

'Promise me, Grace, that you'll look after him on the way home,' she said, not taking her eyes from Art as she spoke. 'I need to know you'll care for him just like you'll be caring for Teddy.'

Grace's hand fell over her shoulder. 'I promise, with all my heart.'

'Thank you.'

Eva stood with April on one side and Grace on the other, smiling as Art reached her, clearly out of breath from the exertion but no doubt proud he'd made the journey without help.

He reached for her, and she dropped to his knee, nestling in his lap and scooping her arms around his neck. She wasn't going to stand beside him when she could sit with him.

'Huh-hmm,' Harry grunted. 'You're supposed to wait until *after* the vows to kiss the bride.'

'And a man is supposed to have two legs, so how about we forget about rules, huh?' Art sniped back, claiming Eva's mouth as everyone around them erupted into laughter that she knew she'd never forget the sound of, for as long as she lived.

———— ⁌⁍ ————

'I can't believe it's goodbye.'

Eva dropped to her knee, clasping Art's hands, her head falling to his lap as she tried desperately not to cry. For so many months, tears had refused to fall when she'd wanted more than anything to grieve, and instead she'd felt nothing. Now, she felt everything, every stab of pain as she thought of Art sailing home without her, every jab of fear, every burst of nerves.

'This war will be over in no time, and you'll be coming home to me,' he said, his fingers in her hair, stroking her as she lay collapsed against his knee. 'Look at me, Eva.'

She slowly looked up, wishing they'd had just one day together as husband and wife before he'd had to leave. Instead, they'd had hours.

Art's fingers curled beneath her chin, and he smiled down at her, his gaze filled with unshed tears, his smile so sweet it took her breath away.

'I'm so proud to have you as my wife. My family are going to think you had rocks in your head to marry a grumpy idiot like me, but they're going to fall in love with you just like I have.'

She rose and pressed her mouth to his, inhaling the scent of him, drowning in the feel of his lips moving slowly against hers in one final kiss. Eva shuddered as she wondered for the hundredth time if she'd made the right decision or not; as the wife of a disabled serviceman, she could have returned home with him in a heartbeat, but it had felt so wrong to leave when there was still so much help she could give so many men.

'I love you,' Art whispered.

Eva bent her forehead to his. 'I love you too.'

The corpsman assisting Art cleared his throat, and she knew it was time. Eva rose and stood straight, bravely smiling at Art as he gave her one last wave before he was wheeled away from her. Then she turned to say her goodbyes to Grace.

April and Grace had their arms wrapped tightly around one another, and she smiled as she watched them. They'd become like sisters to her, and she knew she'd never, ever forget their friendship for as long as she lived.

When they finally parted, she watched as April gently wiped away Grace's tears before her own, then ran her hands down her sister's arms and gripped her hands before turning away.

'Come here,' Eva said, opening her arms and holding Grace tight. 'I'm going to miss you so much.'

'Me too,' Grace whispered. 'I can't believe I'm going home.'

'You look after yourself, *and* that man of mine, won't you?' she said as she finally stepped back, holding her at arm's length. 'Don't let him fall into his dark thoughts; keep reminding him how badly I need him to be waiting for me.'

Grace smiled. 'I sure will.'

Teddy was also in a wheelchair, but Grace was pushing him, with his leg raised and in a cast, his stomach heavily bandaged, and one of his eyes covered with a large patch. But Eva didn't miss his smile as Grace touched his shoulder, and she glanced over at April and saw that she was watching too.

She quickly went to stand beside her, slipping her arm around April's waist as the people they loved moved farther and farther away. They stood until there was nothing left to see, and Eva eventually squeezed April's arm and gestured for them to go.

'Do you ever wonder if we made the right decision in staying?' Eva asked April.

April shook her head. 'No. We made the right decision, I know that. I just wasn't prepared for how much it was going to hurt.'

'I know.'

They both turned and linked arms, walking back to their campsite. It was almost Christmas, and everything about this year was different from the one before. Last year she'd been grieving so much, numb to everything around her, and this year she was full of anticipation—anxious about what was going to happen but able to feel everything.

When they finally reached their tent, Eva held open the flap in the doorway for them both to enter, then gasped when she walked inside.

'Oh my God, look what she's done!'

They both burst out laughing as they went to their beds, and Eva reached out to touch the homemade decorations Grace had left for them hanging on strings running from one side of the tent to the other.

There was even a sheet fashioned into a stocking hanging above each of their beds.

'Your sister sure is something else,' Eva said as she reached for it and pulled it down. She peeked inside to find chocolate and chewing gum, as well as a little note in Grace's handwriting.

'It was always me, every year, finding presents for everyone and putting out a stocking for Grace,' April said. 'I can't believe she did this for me.'

Eva could hear April's little sob, and she went to her, holding her as she cried, looking in amazement around their tent.

'Let's just keep our fingers crossed that the turkey makes it in time for Christmas,' she whispered, letting go of April and collapsing onto her bed, then staring at the paper decorations hanging above.

'Turkey? Are you kidding me? I'll put money on it: we'll be having Spam for Christmas lunch.'

They both laughed, and Eva unwrapped her chocolate, closing her eyes as she slid it onto her tongue, imagining Art boarding the ship with Grace and Teddy.

'So you really want to be a doctor one day, huh?' she asked April.

'Yes,' April said, and Eva turned onto her side to find her friend smiling at her, eyes glistening with determination. 'Once this war is over, I'm not going to take no for an answer.'

'Well, good for you,' Eva said. 'We need more women like you in the world. Look what women have already done for this war.'

'You think I can do it?' April whispered.

Eva grinned at her. 'April, I think you can do anything you set your mind to.' And she meant it.

A week later, Eva stretched and stared at the changing landscape around her as they arrived by army trucks in Algiers, Tunisia. Despite the chill in the air, the sun was shining, and she smiled at the feel of sunshine on her skin, raising her cheeks skyward for a moment before children chasing their truck brought her back to the present.

Like the children in their last village, barefoot girls and boys ran alongside, hands outstretched and calling out, thinking the Americans were like Santa Claus and waiting for items to be thrown to them.

Eva looked away and toward the peddlers on the roadside with their oranges, eggs, and dates, and she could almost taste the sweet orange flesh as they passed. She knew she'd be making a trip to one of their stalls on her first day off. The houses she passed had bright flowers outside, welcoming and colorful, and they could see down to the Mediterranean, the beautiful blue ocean seeming to wink at them as it rolled back and forth. They'd been told to expect a bitter, cold winter, but so far it had been bearable.

'What do you think the others will be doing right now?' April asked from beside her.

'I'd say they'll be almost home,' Eva replied with a smile. 'You know, we might be eating oranges and fresh eggs before they do.'

April leaned into her as a shout went up from the truck up ahead.

'What is it? Are we under attack?' someone yelled.

A call came straight back as they waited in silence. 'We've just found out the turkey's finally arrived! It's here waiting for us!'

The entire truck erupted in laughter and cheers, and Eva dropped her head to April's shoulder, closing her eyes as she thought of Art coming off the ship, his family swarming him in love as they saw the reality of what had happened to him; of Grace and Teddy taking their tentative first steps toward being a couple; and of the war stretching out ahead of her and April, an unknown they still had to encounter.

It seemed like such a long time ago that she'd left home to join Charlie in Pearl Harbor, to prepare for the onset of war even though everyone had believed it would never happen. And now she was a married woman, on the other side of the world to the man she'd now vowed to spend the rest of her life with.

'You okay?' April asked, squeezing her hand.

Eva took a big, shuddering breath and smiled over at her friend. 'I will be.'

They didn't need words; just one look and they both knew. Some things didn't need to be said; because of the pain and trauma of what they'd lived since they'd been catapulted into the war, no words could ever convey what they'd been through. Or what they'd left behind.

I'll never forget you, Charlie, she thought, looking skyward again. *I hope you've met Poppy up there in heaven, because you two would have one hell of a time together.*

The truck lurched, and suddenly everyone was piling out, ready to set up camp again, ready to save more lives, and she followed the others down the crude steps, taking a soldier's hand to jump the final distance to the dirt below. She had no idea how long they'd be away, whether it would be months or even years, but she was no longer scared of going home, of what the future might hold, and for that she had Art to thank.

She grinned to herself as she remembered the man he'd been; there was no way she'd ever have imagined the grumpy, insolent amputee could ever have captured her heart, but he had. And for that, she would always, *always* be grateful.

EPILOGUE

1945

GRACE

'I don't think they're going to make it.'

Teddy's hand was firm over her shoulder. 'They're going to make it. You know they are.'

'But the weather has been so bad and—'

'Stop,' he said, forcibly turning her around, 'and look who's here.'

'April!' she squealed, running and throwing her arms around her sister. 'I can't believe it! You're here!'

April hugged her back, and they stayed like that until Grace finally pulled back, looking her sister up and down, frowning at how thin she was.

'You're as skinny as a rail,' she said. 'I've never seen your cheeks look so gaunt.'

April laughed. 'Unlike you, who looks very well fed.'

Grace grinned and placed her hand on her ballooning stomach. 'Hey, I'm eating for two here, and Teddy likes a little meat on my bones, apparently.'

'Teddy what?' he asked, coming over to stand with them and then opening his arms to April. Grace watched as they hugged, overwhelmed at finally having the two people she loved most in the world back in the same place.

'She was telling me you like her figure a little fuller,' April teased. 'And supposedly I'm too bony.'

Grace finally let go of her sister to greet Harry as he walked in, his smile wide as he bent to kiss both her cheeks.

'Hello, Grace,' he said.

'Harry, it's so good to see you,' she said, enveloping him in a warm hug. 'Now tell me, have you made an honest woman of my sister yet?' she teased.

'Grace! We're only friends!' April looked horrified, but Grace just laughed.

'You two haven't been just friends since I left North Africa, so stop pretending,' she said, then shrugged as April glared at her. But her sister didn't have time to reprimand her because a wheelchair suddenly appeared around the corner, and there was Eva walking slowly beside Art, her hand on his chair and the biggest smile Grace had ever seen on her face.

'Well, if it isn't the gorgeous couple.' She beamed back at them, winking at Art as he caught her eye. She'd seen Art almost every day until Eva had finally returned, and she'd become fast friends with the quick-witted former pilot. He had a wicked sense of humor, and she smiled whenever she thought of her gorgeous friend marrying a man like him. One legged or not, he was a fine man, and no one deserved him more than Eva did.

They all kissed and hugged until Grace hushed everyone and gestured for them to follow her. It was only a short walk from the park where they'd all met, and she'd wanted them all to make the journey together, to see what she'd managed to do since she'd been home.

They walked in silence until Grace held up her hand, and she almost heard everyone collectively hold their breaths.

'This is it,' she said, staring up at the words on the sign above the freshly painted building. Grace turned to her sister and friends, holding Teddy's hand as she watched the reactions on their faces.

'The Poppy Baker Home for Returned Soldiers,' April read out, dabbing at her eyes with a handkerchief. 'It's beautiful, Grace. I'm sure she would have loved it.'

Teddy cleared his throat beside her. 'I'd like to say a few words,' he said, stepping away from Grace and then facing them all.

She smiled at him, letting her tears freely fall as she watched the man she loved grieve for the woman he'd lost. The woman they'd all lost.

'Poppy was the girl with the biggest smile, who saw the fun in everything and lived every day like it was her last. We lost her too early, but I know she would be so proud of what her best friends have done, the men they saved, including myself.' He laughed. 'And you, Art, if we're perfectly honest. You needed a lot of saving—am I right?'

They all laughed, and Art grunted, which made them laugh all the more.

'I want us all to remember the love Poppy had for us and the love we had for her. She's gone but never forgotten.'

Grace met April's stare, nodding as she saw tears in her sister's eyes, and when Eva cleared her throat beside her, she knew that the emotion was still running deep inside all of them. She didn't dare look at Teddy for fear she'd start crying and not be able to stop.

She took a deep breath and then fixed her smile. 'Shall we go inside and take a look?' Grace asked.

Eva took her hand on one side and April on the other, and they all stood in front of the building before taking a first step forward together. Teddy was right: Poppy might be gone, but for as long as they all lived, she'd never, ever be forgotten.

ACKNOWLEDGMENTS

Soon after finishing this novel, I received the tragic news that my research assistant, Jared Hatten, had passed away. He was a young man full of enthusiasm for the projects we worked on together and so talented at finding much of the information I needed for many of my historical novels. I will certainly miss working with him on future projects, and I'm deeply saddened by his passing. Linda, your son was wonderful to work with, and I hope you enjoy reading this story that he helped bring to life. Jared was particularly helpful when it came to researching all the North African aspects of the setting for this book.

As always, I have a small yet loyal team to thank. To Sammia Hamer and Sophie Wilson, my extraordinary editors, thank you so much once again for all your hard work. You forced me to change my process for this novel, and I think you've converted me from a write-as-I-go girl to a serious plotter! Your belief in my writing and constant support and encouragement will always be appreciated. To all my readers: Sammia and Sophie are the people behind the scenes who always ask me to go deeper with my characters, and they're always pushing me to make sure the next novel is better than the last! I also want to make special mention of my copyeditor Susan Stokes and proofreader Riam Griswold for the care they take in working on my manuscripts.

To the entire team at Amazon Publishing, especially Bekah Graham and Nicole Wagner, thank you. It's an amazing feeling knowing that my publishing team is celebrating all my successes with me, and I thank you for marketing my books, creating incredible covers, answering all my questions, and putting my book out there in the world!

Thanks also to my agent, Laura Bradford, and my team of author friends. Yvonne Lindsay, how would I ever get a book written without you? Thank you for being there for me every single day. And Natalie Anderson and Nicola Marsh, thank you for your ongoing support; your friendship means so much to me.

My family also deserves thanks for all their support. It helps to have an amazing mother (who also doubles as chief babysitter and/or chef as needed!) when trying to balance work and motherhood, as well as a dad cheering on my every success. I'm also fortunate to have a great husband and two awesome little boys, and I think they're finally impressed that Mum writes books! Although they don't believe that I could have written *every* word because there are way too many words, according to them . . .

This book, as with my other historical novels, is a work of fiction, but of course everything is based on real-life events. The real women who served as nurses in Pearl Harbor had no idea that their idyllic time on the island would come to such an abrupt, and horrific, end. The months leading up to the attack were picture perfect, and they felt so safe in Hawaii, but their lives were truly turned upside down. While most of those nurses went on to serve in the Pacific, some went to North Africa, and that's where I chose to set the second half of my story.

North Africa was the one place no one wanted to be sent, and there were many derogatory nicknames for being placed there. It was known for being too hot and full of insects, with terrible conditions for nurses and soldiers alike. But it was the perfect place to explore for this novel, to show how women coped with being sent there. Once again, I tried to show ordinary women doing extraordinary things, and I hope I did the real nurses who served there justice. I am full of admiration for every single woman who served in any capacity during the war; I honestly can't believe what they did and what they endured. This is especially incredible because in the 1940s, women were expected to do little more than be homemakers, and yet women stepped up to do anything and everything during the war!

If you haven't already, I'd love for you to read my other historical fiction novels, which are all about strong, inspirational women—true feminists before their time. I love to hear from readers—it's the best part of my job—so please do send me a message or post a review (yes, I read them all!). You can find out more about me, and my writing, at sorayalane.com.

ABOUT THE AUTHOR

Photo © 2019 Martin Hunter

Soraya M. Lane earned a law degree before realizing that law wasn't the career for her and that her future was in writing. She is now the author of historical and contemporary women's fiction, and her novel *Wives of War* is an Amazon Charts bestseller. Lane lives on a small farm in her native New Zealand with her husband, their two young sons, and a collection of four-legged friends. When she's not writing, she loves to be outside playing make-believe with her children or snuggled up inside reading. For more information about Soraya and her books, visit www.sorayalane.com or www.facebook.com/SorayaLaneAuthor, or follow her on Twitter @Soraya_Lane.